Julian Solo

ORIGIN AND CAUSE

SHELLY REUBEN

Charles Scribner's Sons
NEW YORK

MAXWELL MACMILLAN CANADA
TORONTO

MAXWELL MACMILLAN INTERNATIONAL
NEW YORK   OXFORD   SINGAPORE   SYDNEY

Copyright © 1994 by Shelly Reuben

Charles Scribner's Sons
Macmillan Publishing Company
866 Third Avenue
New York, NY 10022

Maxwell Macmillan Canada, Inc.
1200 Eglinton Avenue East
Suite 200
Don Mills, Ontario M3C 3N1

Macmillan Publishing Company is part of
the Maxwell Communication Group of Companies.

LIBRARY OF CONGRESS CATALOGING-IN-PUBLICATION DATA
Reuben, Shelly
Origin and Cause/Shelly Reuben
p.   cm.
ISBN 0-684-19702-2
1. Lawyers—New York (N.Y.)—Fiction.
2. Arson—New York (N.Y.)—Fiction. I. Title.
PS3568.E77707 1994
813'.54—dc20   94-716

Macmillan books are available at special discounts for bulk purchases for sales promotions, premiums, fund-raising, or educational use. For details, contact:

Special Sales Director
Macmillan Publishing Company
866 Third Avenue
New York, NY 10022

10   9   8   7   6   5   4   3   2   1
Printed in the United States of America

DEDICATION

If you scraped a not-too-thick layer of char and debris off Wylie Nolan's soul, you might get a glimpse of the really shiny stuff that makes up Charlie King.

This book is for Charlie.

ACKNOWLEDGMENTS

Like Wylie Nolan, I am blessed with a talented band of experts, some of whom I've been lucky enough to investigate fires with, others of whom I'm just lucky to know.

Robert J. Gassaway, Lloyd Warren and his family, and Ken Vose helped me to get a feel for and facts about classic cars. Noreen Eaton, Sarah Dodge, Anne Lee, Todd Phillips, and Phyllis Pittinsky gave me valuable advice in matters of law, firearms, and common sense. Dr. James I. Ebert is not only a friend and Certified Photogrammetrist, he also has a longer résumé than Eli Timmerman, *and* he makes noise when he walks. Dr. Dominick J. DiMaio, long a colleague, coauthored *Forensic Pathology* with his son Vincent; and he and their book are a great help to me. My uncle, Jack Reuben, gave me the real *Letters to a Young Lawyer* and by his example showed me how kind and gentle a lawyer can be.

I relied and continue to rely on my mother, Ghita Reuben Olit, for just about everything—wisdom not excluded. And I relied on Antoinette Codispoti's eagle eye to catch errors in my first draft.

My literary agent, Chris Tomasino, continues to favor me with her intellect, her talent, and her sense of honor. My editor at Charles Scribner's Sons, Susanne Kirk, is a staunch ally and valiant advocate of the Written Word.

The most important name, though, on this list of those to whom I am indebted is my husband, Charles G. King, who taught me everything *I* know about fires . . . if not everything *he* knows.

ORIGIN AND CAUSE

CHAPTER

1

Bang. You're dead. When I was a boy, a homicide was a homicide. Call the cops. Get forensic to the scene. Take photographs. Get fingerprints. Do plaster casts of tire treads. Analyze cigarette ash. Send semen or blood samples to the lab. Arrest. Don't arrest. Prosecute. Don't prosecute. Jury trial. Convict. Set free.

I watched cops and robbers on television and wanted to grow up and be a policeman. Max Bramble: Homicide Detective. That's how I saw myself. The way other boys felt about the World Series . . . that's how I felt about justice. Good. Bad. Right. Wrong. It was better than baseball cards. Justice was a high-contrast morality play. A black-and-white movie. No fuzzy lines. No smears. No obfuscations. No obliterations of boundaries.

Then the Supreme Court got busy. It threw away its fine-line black ink pens, took out its pastel chalks, and proceeded to draw an impressionistic clown's mask on the face of justice.

So I didn't grow up to be a cop; instead I became a lawyer. I defend individuals or corporations who are being sued in a civil court of law. And the Supreme Court ruling that affected me and my old friend Justice the most involved a case called *Dole* versus *Dow*.

Before that landmark ruling, a plaintiff (the person doing the suing) had to prove *total* negligence on the part of the defendant (the person being sued). Even one percent negligence on the plaintiff's part meant that he couldn't recover any damages.

After *Dole* v. *Dow*, though, the plaintiff only had to prove *comparative negligence*. This meant that if the jury found in his favor, a percentage of his own negligence would be factored in when awarding damages, and the financial award would be reduced accordingly.

Or, to translate that into English, when Timmy was growing up, if he climbed a cyclone fence, broke into a schoolyard, shimmied up a drainpipe, scampered along the roof, and then crashed through the skylight over the gym and broke his back, he would have been arrested in the hospital, injury or not, for criminal trespassing.

Now, with comparative negligence as a criterion, Timmy can flick the glass off his broken bones and tell Mom to call his attorney. Then he can sue the school for six million dollars (factoring in his pain and suffering and loss of future earnings), claiming that the school's Risk Managers should have planned for the possibility of trespassers and put security bars over the skylight to protect Timmy (and them) from his actions.

If the jury finds in his favor (they usually do), Timmy's six million dollar award might be reduced by one or two million because of his comparative negligence in having been up on the roof in the first place.

So, he'd get only four million dollars for violating the law and destroying school property, instead of six.

Woe is Timmy.

I'm getting rich on *Dole* v. *Dow*.

And, no, not because I represent the trespassers of the world. And I don't practice criminal law, either. My idea of justice isn't getting a thug off on a technicality. What I do, though, and what I'm pretty good at, is defending my clients in civil-liability lawsuits. Meaning that if I had been the defense attorney for the school with the sky-lights, by the time I was through with Timmy, his parents would not only have *lost* the case, they'd even have had to pay the school's court costs—*after* we'd won.

I switched to product-liability law after the Catholic Church got involved in a homicide in the little town of Burgess, New York—a homicide that, because of the church's intervention, rapidly became a "celebrated case." Don't ask me why they got involved. It was a big mistake in terms of public relations. Crazy. Seems Hugh James was an altar boy (they all are), and his mother, devout, decent, long-suffering (they all are), was inextricably involved in the church's Good Works. So when Hugh raped, killed, and carved his initials on the breast of a schoolteacher he abducted on Eversham Road, the Catholic Church, at the request of Hugh's parish priest, undertook his defense after his arrest.

They hired Golan, Hipkiss, Ferrara, Stern & McGee; and Mr. Golan himself assigned me to be Hugh James' attorney. I was supposed to meet Hugh and Mrs. James in the booking room at the County Sheriff's Office on the third floor. I had just gotten off the elevator and pushed open the door, so I *saw* what Hugh did. I didn't read about it later in a law journal or see it watered down, spiked up, or reenacted on the six o'clock news.

What happened was the little psychopath elbowed Deputy Ringwall in the gut, slammed a knee into Dianne Singer, who had the bad fortune to be walking between the water cooler and Ringwall's desk at the time, and knocked over the assistant district attorney, whose name I forget but who fell down and busted his nose. Then Hugh (the altar boy) leaped over a shoulder-high barrier, dashed past a row of file cabinets, and crashed through the half-moon window that ran along the south wall of the Sheriff's office.

Hugh fell three stories, landed on his ankle, which broke, scampered to his feet, limped into the street, and got sideswiped by a fire department Battalion Chief's car as it was racing out of the fire-house to respond to a five-alarm fire.

After Hugh James was reapprehended, my law office instructed me to sue the Morton County Sheriff's Office for negligence (the window should have been barred so that Hugh couldn't jump out); to sue Deputy Sheriff Ringwall (he should have prevented the es-cape); the fire department (it ought to have been prepared for per-petrators plummeting from the sky); the Battalion Chief's driver; and of course the Battalion Chief himself for good measure.

I had already worked at Golan, Hipkiss, Ferrara, Stern & McGee for five years and had been promised a full partnership by the end of that July. I was making good money and was in line to make even better than an attorney who never went to an Ivy League college had any right to expect. But money isn't a pat on your back from the part of yourself that wants to polish its own ego; and let's face it, there are certain things a man can't do if he ever wants to have a son that will dress up as a lawyer on Halloween.

Or, to rephrase all that, I don't sue heroes.

So, I said thanks but no thanks to Golan and Hipkiss (Ferrara, Stern & McGee were dead), and I opened my own office on Wall Street, a short walk from the South Street Seaport in lower Manhat-tan. Since a few of my best accounts came along with me, I never ex-pected to be gnawing on my fingernails for lunch. I also didn't expect to have to hire twelve more associate attorneys within eleven months, or to have to expand to two floors, or to have to open up a branch office in Albany. And I didn't expect the Courtland Motors Corporation account to follow me to my new firm, or to be doing all of the East Coast product-liability work for Davis Consolidated In-dustries.

The name on my letterhead reads: Bramble, Harris & Associates. I'm Bramble. The "Harris," after the comma and before the am-persand, doesn't exist. He did a long time ago, when he published the booklet *Letters to a Young Lawyer*, in 1912.

This booklet consists of a series of letters written by Arthur M. Harris, a lawyer, to his son (Dear Boy) upon the latter's graduation from law school. They offered advice and encouraged the fledgling attorney to be *"wise without guilt"* and *"with fine inward calm to look unshrinkingly into the searching eye of To-morrow."*

My father, who is also an attorney, used to include admirable bits of wisdom from Arthur M. Harris's book in the letters he wrote me in college. Such as, *"Don't try to carry on a strenuous love affair and build up a law practice at the same time. It would kill Hercules."* And my personal favorite, *"In your dress be moderate and modest. Do not dress like a race track tout."*

I was also adjured to *"Demonstrate to the world that an honest lawyer is a possibility even if it puts you on a cracker-and-cheese diet for ten years."*

Fortunately, I've escaped a diet of crackers and cheese, even if I have not managed to escape a steady diet of Arthur M. Harris. As he said in his booklet, *"A good law partner is like a good wife—pretty hard to find, but a great help."* So I made Arthur M. Harris my good and very silent partner; he never argues with me, never interferes, is a big help when I read and reread his "Letters," and has been dead for over sixty years.

Our partnership is doing very well, thank you. Arthur M. Harris and me. We've become successful enough to turn down cases; my calendar has trial dates set five years into the future; and even though I never became a cop, that's okay, because I love product-liability law. And after all these years, I still think that justice is more fun than baseball.

Of course, a lot of that has to do with Wylie Nolan.

Until he came along, I was making the same mistakes on fire cases that most lawyers still make. If I had a fire that was supposed to have started in a microwave oven, I would have hired a mechanical engineer, an electrical engineer, a metallurgist, and a chemist to analyze what was left of the product. (Usually, the plaintiff keeps only the mechanical part with the alleged defect and throws out everything that would be of use to the defense.) Then I'd have prepared our case based on product integrity alone: i.e., that the fire couldn't have started the way plaintiff said it did because this type of oven can't overheat in this way, never has, is electronically and mechanically incapable of doing so . . . and so on.

That was before Wylie Nolan.

Wylie taught me to treat every product-liability fire case as if it's a potential arson. He taught me about burn patterns. He convinced me that fire investigation is a legitimate forensic science and that the "arson consultant" is as necessary in determining where and how a fire started as a Medical Examiner is in finding out how and why a human being died.

My first exposure to Wylie Nolan wasn't in person, though. It was between the covers of a magazine I was reading on a flight from Boston to LaGuardia. The article was about a high-rise fire in mid-town Manhattan that caused damage to the building in excess of fifty-five million dollars. Before the flames were even put out, insurance companies representing everyone from the building owners to the architectural designers to the sprinkler installers to the security guards had called their independent experts to the scene.

Rumor had it that the fire was electrical in origin, a cause that guaranteed thousands of billable hours in attorney fees spent on lawsuits and subrogation. (Subrogation is the domino theory as it applies to liability. I sue you because I tripped on your carpet. You sue the carpet installer. He sues the carpet manufacturer. They sue the fabric weaver. The fabric weaver goes home and slaps his wife. She kicks the dog.)

According to this article, everybody who had any interest in the fire building—claims representatives, insurance adjusters, lawyers, engineers, tenants—were all impatiently waiting outside the smoldering shell of the high-rise for the fire marshals to relinquish the scene.

The fire department was slow to give it up, though, because one stubborn New York City fire marshal wasn't satisfied with a nonspecific call of "electrical" as the cause of the fire. He sloshed through the waterlogged debris, scraped off char to examine light switches, unscrewed electrical outlets, pried open conduits, and examined circuit-breaker boxes. But no matter where he looked, he couldn't find any tripped circuits, any blown fuses, or any beaded wires.

What he did find were some interesting flammable-liquid burn patterns on the floor outside the elevators, though. And a similar burn pattern in the men's room. And a third pour pattern at the back of a utility closet. Three separate and distinct points of origin, unconnected by a path of fire in between. Three places where an accelerant had been used and three places where a fire had been ignited.

According to this article, fires don't spontaneously originate in three places.

Fires don't even start at two points of origin at once.

Not unless someone sets them.

So, the fire department retained possession of the scene, and that bull-headed fire marshal in charge of the case pulled up a chair to have a chat with the man of the moment, a Mr. Hector Emilio Alvaraz.

Hector was a guard employed by Vector Security Systems to patrol the high-rise in question. His job was to go up fifteen flights of stairs. And down fifteen flights of stairs. Up. Down. Up. Down. No variation in the routine. Day in. Day out. Up. Down.

Until eventually, Hector got bored.

And to alleviate his boredom, Hector decided to be a hero.

In fire-marshal lingo, Hector is what's called a Vanity Fire Setter. Their modus operandi is to set a fire, turn in the alarm, and then be conspicuously and courageously attempting to extinguish the flames just as the fire apparatus arrives.

After the fire marshal who found the flammable-liquid burn patterns also learned that Hector Alvaraz both discovered the fire and turned in the alarm, he took Hector aside to "have a little talk." This same fire marshal is reputed to have a hypnotic style of interrogation, and I've heard other fire marshals say half-jokingly that perpetrators stand in line to confess when Wylie Nolan is investigating a fire.

Because that's obviously who we are talking about. Wylie Nolan. And according to the article I was reading on the plane, that's what happened as a result of Wylie's investigation. All of the billable hours projected by lawyers in lawsuits against the building, the electrical contractors, architects, the owners—all disappeared after Hector confessed and Wylie Nolan discovered the corroborating multiple points of origin of the fire.

7

When my airplane landed, I took the article about Fire Marshal Nolan with me, telephoned the New York City Fire Department, and asked to speak to him.

I was told that Wylie Nolan had retired and gone into business for himself. He was a private investigator, specializing in arson investigation. His office was in Chinatown, on Lispenard Street. Just off Broadway.

CHAPTER

2

"One of the attractions of the practice of law is the pleasurable feeling that some day you may find a good windfall that will make you rich overnight. In this respect the practice of law has all the zest and excitement of prospecting for gold."

Arthur M. Harris (my silent partner) wrote that to his son. It started to apply to me four years and eleven months after cable-television mogul Stanfield Standish died.

"You never know but that over the next hill, or in the next gulch, a fortune may be lurking, just waiting for you to stumble upon it."

Stanfield Standish had owned Stanfield Standish News—SSN—

and his heirs were suing Courtland Motors for product liability because of a fire that occurred in a 1930 Duesenberg restored by their
Classic Cars Division. At the time of the fire, the car had been on a
lonely stretch of road in an upstate New York community, and Stanfield Standish had been in the car. The way I heard it, and nobody
was anxious to talk, counsel in charge of the *Standish* v. *Courtland*
lawsuit had come to Courtland Motors with a lot of hype practically
as a child prodigy.

*"Your door may open any day, and somebody creep in with a cause
of action that will be worth thousands of dollars to you."*

By age twenty-five, this budding barrister had a caseload of over
a hundred files. By age thirty-two, he was second in command; and
by age thirty-five, he was the head of the entire legal department. By
age thirty-six, though, he was getting a reputation for misquoting
long passages from T. S. Eliot during five-martini lunches, and the
liquor bottles in his briefcase had begun to clink like castanets.
There was also scuttlebutt about a foreclosed mortgage, a DWI arrest, and a computer that ate a seventy-two-page report on which he
had forgotten to press the SAVE button.

*"From the life of an anchorite and the diet of an ascetic, you may sud-
denly find yourself arrayed in purple and fine linen."*

For the past three years, Courtland had hired me to defend them
against small-potatoes stuff with claims of less than ten thousand
dollars—but they'd never used me on a case involving a big money
demand or on one in which a death had occurred.

*"This is just the reason that keeps many a good man plodding hope-
fully along through the dusty years of near-poverty."*

Head of Legal, so the story goes, had assigned himself the *Standish* versus *Courtland Motors Corporation* case, which would have
made sense except for the stacks of depositions he never took, the
motions he never filed, the witnesses he never interviewed, the evidence he never examined, and the D.T.'s he didn't know he was having.

*"Your luck may come to you in strange ways, in ways you will not at
first recognize, and you may even shut the door in its face."*

Suffice to say, when I got a panicked phone call from the *new* head
of Courtland Motors Legal Department telling me that a trial date

for *Standish* v. *Courtland* had been set for less than a month away, and would I could I please fly to Detroit immediately to discuss taking over the defense of the case, I:

    1) recognized instantly the strange way in which luck had come to me, and

    2) wasn't even remotely tempted to shut the door in its face.

CHAPTER
3

Why would an attorney for Courtland Motors Corporation be looking for a building on Lispenard Street in Chinatown, where he was
scheduled to meet a retired fire marshal who'd just gone into business for himself, when said attorney could have easily hired any of a
number of long-established firms with impressive names like Fire
Engineering Analysis International, or Compu-Chem Techtronics,
Incorporated?

"If a man is truly competent in his particular sphere of work," wrote
my long-deceased partner, *"the world, always anxious to obtain the
best, will beat a pathway to his door."*

An elevator operator directed me to the seventh floor, where the door in question looked out at me like a cliché from a detective novel. A brown wood frame surrounded a panel of bubbled white glass, on which were the words:

WYLIE NOLAN
Arson Consulting
Fire Analysis & Private Investigations

Our appointment was for 2:00 P.M. I tapped a knuckle against the glass and heard a rustle of papers inside. A few seconds later, a woman with the look of a Chinese schoolgirl opened the door and tilted her head to one side. She stared at me that way for half a minute. I stared back. She had straight, dark hair of no particular style with a red plastic barrette plugged into a wad of it that would have otherwise flopped into her right eye. She wore no lipstick and no eye makeup and didn't seem to know that she was pretty. Her dark brown eyes observed me speculatively.

"Are you the guy from Courtland Motors?" She stepped aside to let me in. She was wearing a blue pleated skirt that looked like a holdover from parochial school, and a white nondescript blouse, over which hung a shapeless navy blue cardigan with six generations of knubbies on it. She was clean, but not exactly a fashion statement. And she had great legs.

"Yes. I'm the guy from Courtland Motors. Are you Mr. Nolan's secretary?"

"I'm Miranda Yee. I'm a lawyer. I've got the corner office. Suite 700. Wylie went downstairs to get us coffee, so I'm guarding the fort. I hope you drink coffee."

She pointed to a brown, suede-covered chair. I sat. She sat. The office had a tiny reception area with two chairs separated by a small table and a blue lamp. Another panel of bubbly white glass divided the waiting area from a secretarial station with a desk, a typewriter, a stack of papers, and a red telephone. Beyond the desk was a solid wood door with a brass plaque engraved:

WYLIE NOLAN—ARSON INVESTIGATOR

Miranda Yee observed me as I took my silent inventory. She said,

"Behind that door are another ten offices, staffed by over one hundred highly trained field personnel."

I blinked.

She shrugged and said, "Only joking."

Just then, we heard something kick at the door to the hall. Miranda pulled the door open, and I got my first look at Wylie Nolan.

He was balancing three coffee cups in two hands, along with some napkins, sugar packets, and stir sticks. He kicked the door shut and turned around to grin at me. When I caught that grin, I flashed for a second on some advice my father had once given me. He said that if I ever encountered a mountain lion in the street (not a great likelihood in Bay Ridge, Brooklyn), I shouldn't look it dead in the eye, because a wild animal might misconstrue a friendly greeting as a challenge.

This advice notwithstanding, I looked Wylie dead in the eye and grinned back.

Dutch courage.

He held the miscellany and two cups out to us.

"Careful. Their hot. Are you Max Bramble?"

"Guilty."

"Good. Take these. Did you two introduce yourselves?"

We nodded.

"Then come into my office and we can talk."

Miranda had started to follow us in when we heard another knock on the door, followed by three more; each was loud and aggressive.

Miranda whispered, "Don't answer it. Don't make any noise."

I looked at her questioningly. She said. "It's my secretary. If we're very, very quiet, maybe she'll go away."

We were very quiet. The hot coffee inside the paper cups scalded my palms. I watched the door.

The doorknob began to rotate slowly. Also slowly, the door started to inch open. Then, as though on an assignment to catch an adulterous couple *in flagrante delicto,* the door flew forward, exposing in the opening a tiny Chinese woman with stylish black hair, thin lips, and a mean face. Her hard black eyes locked on Miranda, whose spine and confidence seemed to shrink at the same time.

"Miss Yee," this nerve-jangling creature snapped. "Your client

George Wong, who pays you lots of money, has called four times in the last five minutes. He says the seller's lawyer didn't bring a statement of what's in escrow account and . . ." She spat out the rest in a dissonant combination of syllables I've been told are Mandarin Chinese.

Miranda sighed heavily. She turned, walked towards Wylie Nolan's inner office, opened the door, went inside, dropped the napkins, sugar, and stir sticks on Wylie's desk, and came back.

Then she told her secretary, "Wait for me in my office. Go on. I'll be there in a minute."

The haranguing apparition smirked at me and Wylie Nolan like a reformed drinker who has just succeeded in snatching away a bottle of Night Train from two unregenerate drunks. Then she darted out the door.

"I can't stand that woman," Miranda said wearily.

I could see why.

"Take your coffee with you," Wylie said.

"No. I'll come back for it later. It'll give me another excuse to escape."

Miranda left, and I followed Wylie past what I thought was his secretary's desk.

"Do you have a secretary?" I asked.

"I do," he said evenly. "But he's up in SoHo auditioning for an Off Broadway play."

I didn't want to touch that one, so I looked around Wylie Nolan's office instead. It was about as big as your average mud room. Against the right wall were a row of wood-grain metal file cabinets. On top of them were a postage scale, a paper cutter, and three potted plants. To my left, a photocopy machine and a plastic percolator sat on a waist-high cabinet. Beside that was another cabinet with a fax machine on top, and above them, bookshelves were stacked to the ceiling with titles all concerning fire: *Fire Investigation; Investigating the Fire Scene; Fire Officer's Handbook; Fire Engineering; Investigating the High-Rise Fire; Pathological Fire Setters; Apprehending the Juvenile Fire Setter; Ignition Temperatures of Fabrics and Wall Coverings;* and so on.

Wylie Nolan's desk was in front of me, and behind it was a large window. There were plants hanging from the ceiling and file folders stacked on the shelf under the plants. The desk itself was cleared for action, with only a Rolodex, another red phone, a pencil cup, and an ashtray in evidence. There were no keyboards in the office, no computers, no modems, and no complex telephone systems (his red phone had only two lines).

And I didn't see anything portable anywhere that beeped.

"They do not care to open elaborate offices in New York, with pages, clerks and assistants," Arthur M. Harris had written. *"Their worth, their ability, provides them with all they can reasonably attend to, and as profitably, if not more profitably, than if they followed the ornate office plan some of their less skilled but more unscrupulous brethren resort to."*

Framed diplomas hung on the walls at either side of his desk. They testified that Wylie Nolan was a licensed private investigator, that he had guest-lectured for the New Jersey State Division of Criminal Justice, the Pennsylvania Association of Arson Investigators, and the New York State Academy of Fire Science. Other diplomas indicated his memberships in the International Association of Bomb Technicians and Investigators, the National Fire Protection Association, and the International Police Association. There were also diplomas from the Cornell Institution on Organized Crime, the Drug Enforcement Administration, and the FBI Bomb Investigation School. And over the fax machine, there was a small, gold certificate modestly attesting that Wylie Nolan was an expert marksman.

I put the coffee cups on his desk and indicated the wall of diplomas and certificates.

"Did you really do all that?"

"Blindfolded," Wylie said.

Then he gave me a smile that contained about a million teeth.

CHAPTER

4

Technically, my meeting with Wylie was a job interview. I was supposed to look over his curriculum vitae, check his references, evaluate how I thought he'd go over with a jury, and get a basic feel for what value he would be to my case.

But it didn't work out that way. From the minute I sat down, Wylie Nolan was interviewing *me*. He wanted to see everything I had, read the summons, review the plaintiff's Request for Answers to Interrogatories, and most of all, he wanted to see all of my pictures.

"What pictures?"

"The photographs of the fire scene. Of the road where the car was found. Of the burned vehicle. Of Standish in the vehicle. Of Standish after he had been removed from the car. Of the car after . . ."

"I don't have any photographs."

"*You* might not have photographs, but somebody has them. Somebody took . . ."

I cut Wylie off. I told him that I'd been the attorney of record for only forty-eight hours. I told him about my predecessor, whose itinerary was now hopefully filled with Alcoholics Anonymous meetings. I told him that I'd just gotten back from Detroit the night before, that nothing had been done on the case, and that we had a trial date in less than a month.

Wylie surprised me with a *non sequitur*. "How did you find me?"

I told him about the article I read on the airplane, and that must have been the right answer, because he pulled out a legal pad and shoved it across the desk. I suppose I passed *his* interview.

"Write down 'shopping list' at the top of the page," he told me.

I wrote down "shopping list" at the top of the page.

"This is what we need in order to do even a half-assed investigation. First, get newspaper clips of everything that happened before, during, and after the fire. Write that down."

I wrote that down.

"Check newspaper morgues and ask them to send you proof sheets of the negatives for the photos that were *not* printed in the papers. Call the network and cable television stations. See if you can get videotapes of the news broadcasts after Standish died. Also, of events immediately preceding his death. And get all the video outtakes of the coverage at the fire scene. Call the local fire and police departments. Find out who handled the case. Small upstate counties have no fixed procedures for investigating fires, so it could be anybody or everybody or nobody. There were probably some local cops there and a member of the fire department who took a course in fire investigation. Find out if the State Fire Marshals got involved, and the State Police. Find out who was the first fireman on the scene and who was the responding fire captain. Get all the Police and Fire Incident Reports from all of the departments involved and hope like hell that none of this stuff has been thrown away because it's already been five years. Find out who discovered the fire, and who called it in. Call the Weather Bureau and get a detailed weather report. Snow. Rain. Wind conditions. Everything affects the rate of burning. Contact the Medical Examiner's Office if there is one in Northland County. If it doesn't have one, find out who handles deaths. Get their report. If an autopsy was done, get copies of the autopsy report and copies of the morgue photographs. Call the hospital they brought Standish to. If there are any records on Standish, get them. Contact *all* of the hospitals within a radius of one hundred miles of the fire and find out if anyone else checked into an emergency ward that night with injuries resulting from a fire."

Wylie watched me writing rapidly.

"And we need a prototype of the burned vehicle," he added.

"What for?"

"I have to know what something is supposed to have looked like before a fire to reconstruct what happened to it during the fire." Wylie pulled a pipe out of his jacket pocket and filled it. Loose tobacco overflowed the rim. He struck a match, held it over the bowl, inhaled, and sucked the leaf of flame downward. Bits of tobacco glowed red hot and then drifted down and landed in Wylie's Styrofoam coffee cup, where they hissed once and went out.

Wylie's eyes followed the cinders. His lips bent upward. He looked lean, laconic, and amused. Like a cowboy in an old Western.

Not that Wylie thinks of himself as a cowboy. During trial preparation, when I was trying to decide how to present Wylie to the jury, I asked him to describe himself in three words or less. Without missing a beat, he said, "Former tenement fireman."

Wylie Nolan is about six feet tall. At business meetings, he wears conventional suits and ties; but when he's investigating a fire, he shows up in battered blue jeans and his old Army fatigue jacket, looking exactly like an undercover cop trying not to look like an undercover cop.

He has brown hair and dark, marble-blue eyes. I thought his eyes were friendly until I saw him looking at a plaintiff's attorney once during a deposition. I'll tell you about that later. Wylie's face is narrow and long-jawed. And he has a big nose that he told me a ninety-pound weakling broke in a fight a long time ago.

More about his eyes.

Motorcycle gangs like to park their bikes on the street meridian outside my office building because we're near the bars on the docks. Wylie and I were working late a few weeks into the case and didn't leave my office until after midnight. We'd just left my lobby when two Neanderthals in leather and chains started toward us. They looked menacing. That's because they *were* menacing. I lagged behind, muttering something to myself about discretion being the better part of valor. Wylie kept walking forward, not being the muttering type. We got closer. They got closer. Seconds later, we were hard up against the whites of their eyes. Wylie looked at them. They looked back at him. We stopped. They stopped. For about ten seconds, nothing happened.

And then *they* crossed the street.

That's what Wylie's eyes look like.

He's got two deep lines that go from his nose to the corners of his mouth. His lips are thin and hard. His eyebrows are bushy and he has big ears that stick out.

Another thing about Wylie Nolan is that women like him. All women. Old, young, thin, fat, good, bad, ugly, beautiful. Twice over the course of the Courtland Motors case, I had to fly to Detroit and Chicago with Wylie, and it pains me to admit that the stewardesses always gave him two bags of peanuts to my one. At a deposition he gave a while back in San Francisco, plaintiff's attorney, a dyed-blond job with big boobs, long fingernails, and too much lipstick walked up to Wylie, planted her feet wide right in front of him, and looked him dead in the eye.

Challenging.

She said, "Max Bramble here tells me you're the toughest man he's ever met, but you don't look so tough to me."

Wylie stepped back, narrowed his eyes, and said softly, "You're absolutely right, ma'am. Why don't you just think of me as a big old ineffectual pussycat."

During that trial, this same plaintiff's attorney did everything she could to humiliate and discredit Wylie in front of the jury. It didn't work. We won the case. Afterward, she came over to us outside the courthouse with a big smile on her face, extended her hand to Wylie and said, "Nothing personal, Wylie. I was just doing my job."

Wylie peered at her through those two blue marble eyes, cleared his throat noisily, directed a projectile of spit to a bull's-eye midway between her feet, and then said softly, "Nothing personal, Sweetheart. I was just clearing my throat."

Wylie Nolan is the kind of man that men want sitting next to them if their plane is hijacked by a guy wearing a turban and carrying an AK-47, and that women just want.

I thought the article I read on the plane had prepared me for what to expect from Wylie Nolan, but I still had much to learn.

He saw me staring at him.

"How hard is it going to be to get a prototype of the car that burned?" he asked.

"Only four hundred and seventy Duesenbergs were ever built. That was sixty years ago. For all I know, there are only four left."

"How much do they cost?"

"About two million dollars."

"Each? Or for all four hundred and seventy."

"Each."

"Get me four," Wylie said. "I have to do some burn tests. You won't mind it if I set fire to them, will you?"

I dropped my pencil.

"Only joking," he said. Then he grinned again.

Between him and Miranda Yee, I was either going to have to stock up on antacids or fine-tune my sense of humor.

He went on, "If we can locate one Duesenberg, though, I'd like to take a look at it. Drive it. Kick the tires. Poke under the hood. Nothing beats a hands-on examination. Get an idea of its specifications. What's flammable in the interior? What's not? What does the engine compartment look like when it's clean? How thick is the fire wall? What's the composition of the upholstery in the driver's and passenger seats? What kind of fabric covers the car's roof? Things like that."

Wylie pointed at my pad. "And write down that you have to put an ad in the local paper offering to pay for photographs of anything related to Stanfield Standish taken on the night of the fire."

I wrote that down, too.

"When can I examine the car?"

21

"Tomorrow."

Wylie said. "You can put away your list."

I put my list in my briefcase.

"All right," Wylie said. "Now, tell me everything you know about the case."

I didn't know anything about the case. So instead, I asked him what he knew about Stanfield Standish.

"Just that he was a big-deal television executive, and that he's dead."

I popped open the lid on my cup of coffee and dumped in a few sugars. "Okay," I said. "Then I'll tell you what *I* know."

CHAPTER

5

I had dinner with Stanfield Standish once, about twenty years ago, when he was just a movie script writer and before he'd put together the largest broadcast and information-gathering network in the world. I didn't like him then, I didn't like him after he became a big television mucka mucka, and I didn't like the son-of-a-bitch on the day that he died.

He was a genius, I suppose. If that's what we call a guy with an infallible instinct for ferreting out the lowest and commonest components of human behavior. Or, to condense "essence of Stanfield Standish journalism" into just one quick concept: If a man were stranded on the ledge of a skyscraper and all of the other media people were trying to convey to the world the drama of the *rescue* operations, Stanfield Standish News would just as clearly be conveying, through camera angle, commentator sarcasm, script, editing, and so on, that what it really wanted the poor sucker on the ledge to do (and what *we* all wanted by association), was for him to jump.

Jump. Jump. Jump.

You could almost hear the crowd shouting in the overheated eyes and flared nostrils of the SSN reporter.

Jump. Jump. Jump.

Stanfield Standish's politics were an extension of his personal philosophy. He called it "neo-internationalism" and professed to scorn all national boundaries, all patriotism, and all attitudes or terminologies that encouraged divisiveness. The SSN reporter, so a press release had stated, was an impartial, nonpartisan "citizen of the world." His "beat" was earth, and when he was on a story (i.e., under contract to Stanfield Standish), he *had* no native land.

Or so they said.

But Stanfield Standish did have a native land.

The United States of America.

And despite their protestations to the contrary, his reporters did express a national point of view.

It just became increasingly obvious over the years that the point of view was never ours.

It was almost as if Stanfield Standish saw America the same way that he saw the man balanced on that narrow ledge. And from down below on the pavement, he sent up the "voice" of the SSN reporter, malicious, nonverbal, and authoritative, urging his country and his countrymen to:

Jump. Jump. Jump.

Jump—in the name of world harmony (of course).

Jump—In the name of world peace (also of course).

On a universal scale, Standish disseminated his philosophy without subtlety. If a U.S. marine were injured by a terrorist bomb in a Paris bistro, SSN would not include an interview with the injured serviceman. He wouldn't be given a chance to signal thumbs-up to the people back home or to croak out a feeble Semper Fi. Nor would we see footage of indignant Frenchmen inflamed by the terrorist attack.

Instead, SSN would film the carnage, the torn bodies, and the screaming police sirens and couple those visuals with a retrospective of alleged atrocities committed by U.S. troops in North Vietnam, Korea, or Kuwait.

And after fifteen minutes of this kind of innuendo, it was a rare viewer who felt anything but that the marine who'd been mangled by the terrorist blast (and all of the rest of us) got just what he (we) deserved.

When Croatian killed Serb . . . When African starved African . . .When Chinese shot Chinese . . . When Hindu and Moslem rioted . . . No matter where . . . No matter when . . . Stated or implied in every Stanfield Standish News broadcast was the premise that *whatever* happened, it was somehow and always the fault of the United States.

And as this policy was instituted by Stanfield Standish, so did it prevail.

With but one exception, and I'll tell you about him in a minute, all of SSN's reporters toed the neo-international line. This included the elimination of proscribed words from their vocabularies, words that included "alien," "foreign," "oriental," and "occidental."

Bad words, so sayeth Stanfield Standish. Bad. Bad. Bad.

The exception I just mentioned was a writer named Mark Greenberg. Mark's background may have had something to do with his iconoclasm. His mother and father had escaped from Nazi Germany in 1939 and fled to Cuba. Mark was born in Havana in 1950; Castro overthrew Batista in 1959. Mark's parents, who were outspoken anticommunists, disappeared. Their property was confiscated, and Mark was smuggled out of Cuba and sent to live with a great-uncle in Miami. He never returned to Cuba; he never saw his mother or his father again.

Mark's response to being uprooted, exiled, orphaned, and transplanted was to express gratitude to the country that took him in. He did so in a torrent of words.

Mark believed that America, as a nation, worked. That the hodgepodge of immigrants who'd come here (of which he was one), defined us as a nation. But that the strength of the immigrant contribution was being weakened by a trend to romanticize the politics, customs, and languages of the lands they'd either been kicked out of or fled, and to view assimilation into American life as a betrayal of their "roots."

Mark started writing for small, regional newspapers when he was still in high school. Before going to work for Stanfield Standish News, he'd already written two books. One, called *Re-heating the Melting Pot*, contrasted the way America had historically absorbed her immigrants with the way she was doing so now.

The second book was a tribute to his great-uncle Emil, who had taken him in when Mark was smuggled out of Cuba. Uncle Emil was Emil Bergman, the same Emil Bergman famous for composing the soundtracks of Cinema Select Artists' greatest motion pictures of the 1930s, 1940s and 1950s.

SSN's hiring of Mark Greenberg was a miscalculation on their part and misbegotten idealism on the part of Mark. Whoever hired him should have taken the precaution of reading his books first.

Mark applied for the SSN job because, even though he knew that he couldn't change the world, he'd suckered himself into believing that he could affect one network's editorial point of view.

Mark lasted at SSN for exactly one week. His first assignment was to produce a half-hour TV script called *Dissident Factions—the New America on Parade*. Featured in the story were pissed-off Puerto Ricans in Chicago, indignant Haitians on Fifth Avenue, boiling-mad Cubans in Miami, outraged Mexicans, Latvians, Serbs, Hungarians, Albanians . . . all proudly waving the flags of the countries that, for one reason or another, they'd fled. And all angry, angry, angry at the United States.

Mark threw out the script.

He went to SSN's video library. He made a few quick phone calls. He exchanged a few favors. He sent out camera crews, did interviews, sat down at his desk and wrote. He sat down at the video console and edited. And Friday night, just seconds before his broadcast, he slipped the video of his show to the SSN engineer.

Suffice it to say, Mark's production was not what Stanfield Standish had in mind. It opened on the president of the Ladies' Lions Club in Chinatown leading the membership in a stirring if curiously pronounced recitation of the Pledge of Allegiance. It highlighted people from different racial, ethnic, religious, and national backgrounds at bicycle races, lined up at voting booths, at football games, rock concerts, museums, beaches, and barbecues.

And all of them were getting along with each other just fine.

Mark ended his story with a montage of American Olympic medal winners: The boxer whose parents had emigrated from Jamaica, the figure skater whose great-great-grandmother had come here from Thailand, the high-diver who'd just moved here from Israel, the discus thrower whose ancestors had fought against the colonists in our War of Independence. All had hand on heart as they stood on the podium under the American flag. And all had tears in their eyes as, over the brassy orchestration of the national anthem, a narrator's voice said the words, "These are her people, and *this* is the U.S. of A."

Thirty-five seconds later, Stanfield Standish telephoned Mark Greenberg personally and added two more words to the assemblage.

He said, "You're fired."

Mark became relevant to our lawsuit later on in the investigation, when he fell into a category Wylie Nolan labeled "disgruntled employees."

CHAPTER

6

The relic of the Duesenberg sedan that was the subject of the lawsuit I was defending was stored in a barnlike structure owned by the plaintiff's attorney, about thirty miles north of Stilton-on-Hudson. Clyde Prouty, who'd been hired by the Standish clan to sue Courtland Motors, was a senior partner in the law firm of Prouty, Pankovich, Nestor & Lum. Prouty was said to be the first attorney ever to initiate a client's slip-and-fall lawsuit against himself.

The way it came about was that a man named Dillard Smith went out in the dead of winter after an ice storm to throw around some salt. On the way down his own steps, he slipped, fell, and broke his leg. Since he didn't have medical coverage, but he did have home-owner's liability insurance, Prouty told Smith to sue *himself* for negligence under his household insurance policy. He did. The insurance company denied the claim, and Prouty took them to court for "bad faith." By the time Prouty got through with the jury, they were so confused about who insured what and which policy covered whom that they awarded Smith one million dollars for tripping over his own two feet.

Clyde Prouty took fifty percent out of those damages for his contingency fee, and an additional one hundred and fifty thousand dollars for expenses (now tell me that you still wonder why your insurance premiums keep going up).

If Prouty didn't single-handedly invent the "deep pockets" theory of civil litigation, he can at least be credited for giving it new depth. "Deep pockets" means that at any accident or incident or crime scene, if an attorney stands in the middle of a room or street or building and does a three-hundred-and-sixty-degree rotation, his eyes will fall on at least five companies that have enough money to pay large sums in either settlement costs or damages if he brings them to court and accuses their product of having caused the accident or incident or crime.

Let's say your husband came home late one night after a drinking binge, got hungry at two o'clock in the morning, went to the gas range, threw some bacon into an aluminum pan, turned on all four burners, and then passed out on the living room sofa. Did the bacon then start to sizzle, a flame ensue, and the grease in the pan begin to spatter and burn? Did a potholder and some cotton toweling next to the stove ignite? And did the flames spread to the walls of the kitchen, the ceiling, the curtains, and the cabinets before a neighbor smelled smoke and called the fire department?

And is your husband now dead from smoke inhalation?

If Wylie Nolan had been a fire marshal at the time and investigated that scene, under "Cause and Origin of Fire" on his Fire Incident Report he would have written: Cooking carelessness, alcohol contributory.

By the time Clyde Prouty had gotten through talking to the wife of the deceased, though, the scenario for the event would have changed. The heartbroken widow would be telling one and all that her husband fell asleep on the sofa, cold sober, after an exhausting evening spent writing out checks to the Sisters of Christian Charity; and the fault for the fire would have become everybody's but the drunk's.

Plaintiff would sue the landlord for installing a defective stove, the stove installer for careless installation, the manufacturer of the stove for faulty product design, the manufacturer of the wallpaper in the kitchen for chemical components in the paper or adhesive that gave off toxic fumes if inhaled, the fire department for delayed response to the alarm, the building superintendent for failure to maintain the smoke detector with a fresh battery, and so on.

The Prouty philosophy of liability includes everybody *but* the individual who caused the calamity.

Clyde Prouty portrays himself as the "little guy's David" whom the Big Bad Corporate Goliaths are out to slay. His justification for initiating so many product-liability lawsuits is that "consumers will benefit in the end because the products (he says) will be made safer."

Since the actual products have nothing to do with most of his lawsuits, except that they were in the same room or in the same building or on the same street at the time Prouty was doing his three-hundred-and-sixty-degree rotation looking for Deep Pockets to plunder, there are at least four major consequences to these lawsuits, none of which is beneficial to the consumer:

One. A lot of manufacturers will go out of business, cut back on research and development, cut back on production, and/or decide not to go into production on a new product;

Two. The consumer's prices go up;

Three. An irresponsible or culpable plaintiff will walk away with a lot of money he obtained by defrauding a manufacturer;

Four. Clyde Prouty, the noble defender of the soft-tissue injury, will make millions of dollars in contingency fees.

"The contingent fee has become a habit with the litigating public, and they claim it as if it were almost a right," wrote my old friend Arthur M. Harris over eighty years ago. *"It has this in its favor, however, that when you do win such a case, you usually get a whole lot more money than your services were actually worth."*

I don't work on a contingency basis. I charge an hourly rate. The money I can earn on any given case is pennies compared to what Prouty gets after he's had a big win. But win or lose, *I* get paid.

Prouty *has* to win, or he doesn't make a penny, *and* he's out-of-pocket on all his expenses—court costs, salaries, expert-witness fees, etc.

Which sets up a situation where he and others like him will do anything to win. This includes coaching their witnesses to lie, falsifying tests, destroying and/or altering evidence, and refusing a reasonable cash settlement when it's offered if he doesn't think that his own cut will be high enough.

It was this type of lawyer who met us at the door to the building where the Duesenberg was being stored.

Clyde Prouty's "team" consisted of a Stilton-on-Hudson attorney, hired to give the town grocers and druggists someone they could relate to, whose job was just to keep his mouth shut during the trial and look morally indignant every time any of my witnesses took the stand. Prouty also brought along two junior attorneys from his New York office, a paralegal, and a photographer with bad skin and a video camera. Prouty led this team himself.

Clyde has a hawk face, a pronounced Adam's apple, and shirt collars that always seem to be in free float around his neck. He usually wears London-tailored tweeds accessorized with a lot of gold. He has a beak nose, two red patches on skeletal cheeks, bluish purple slits where his lips should be, and perfect teeth. His eyes look like birdshot, and his eyebrows look like black caterpillars inching across his forehead.

And he is charming. Not to me and not to Wylie Nolan. But to the many, many people who've been seduced by the deep, flattering interest he apparently takes in their cases. His pellet eyes lock onto yours and bore in. The message he sends to you is: You are the most interesting person I have ever met; your cause is a just one; I sympathize with you greatly; together we will accomplish miracles. Give me your hand; give me your moral code; put me in charge of your value system and code of ethics. You think that you were only slightly injured when you pried the cap off the bottle and it flipped up and struck your cheek. I'll show you how the injury crippled you for life, ruined your career, made you sexually impotent, affected your earning power, and destroyed your whole life. Together, we will get you compensated for the deep, searing injustices you have suffered. All you have to do is to trust me. Trust me. Trust me.

Clyde brought five people along to watch Wylie inspect the Duesenberg, and I knew that there were at least three more experts on his team. None of them would be candidates for a Nobel Prize in ethics. One was a fire-and-explosion man who worked only for plaintiffs and had never turned down a case; another was a mechanical engineer with a heavy Indian accent, whose name was Namoor Paiamee, but whose reputation inspired Wylie to call him Dr. Pay Me; and the third was a medical woman who had been a physician and lost her board certification when she took out a gallbladder that was supposed to have been a gallstone. What she did now was testify for plaintiffs on the monetary value of the pain and suffering experienced by the deceased prior to his death.

That was plaintiff's team. When our car pulled up to the storage barn, six of them were standing at the window, looking out at us.

As of then, *our* team consisted only of Wylie Nolan, a forklift operator who was also our mechanic, and me. We'd driven up from Manhattan in Wylie's car and during the two-hour drive had exchanged war stories. Or . . . Wylie had told war stories. Mine probably rated as only skirmishes (a fire marshal's past is inherently more colorful than that of a lawyer).

By the time we got to the inspection site, I'd forgotten that I didn't know anything about doing a cause and origin investigation. I knew I'd have to learn, though, so when Wylie pulled open the trunk of his car to take out his gear, I watched him as intently as did the members of plaintiff's team.

The temperature that day was about thirty-seven degrees; adding in the wind chill factor, it felt more like fifteen. The temperature inside the unheated barn where the Duesenberg was stored was about twenty-five degrees. The trench coat I was wearing would have kept me warm only if I'd been going to work in a *heated* building. I felt like I was having an out-of-body experience in a Siberian wind tunnel.

Wylie was wearing his uniform for investigating a fire: blue jeans and a sweater under his army fatigue jacket. He pulled a small, bruised black leather suitcase out of the trunk of his car, slung a large camera bag over his shoulder, handed me a rolled-up screen with holes a little bit larger than the mesh on a screen door, and walked into the barn.

CHAPTER
7

If you'd asked me a day earlier, I'd probably have told you that every arson investigator has to bring to a fire scene an expensive device that gives digital readouts. The purpose of this gizmo is to "smell out" areas where flammable liquids like gasoline, kerosene, or turpentine have been poured in order to determine whether or not an arson has occurred.

So, when Wylie flopped down his suitcase and flipped up its lid, I said coolly, "I assume you brought along a hydrocarbon detector?"

I was smugly pleased with myself for knowing that such an instrument exists.

"Sure," Wylie answered.

He pulled a crowbar out of his battered bag.

I looked around.

"Where it it?"

"It's the smallest and best hydrocarbon detector in the business," Wylie said.

This time he pulled out a fat, thickly bristled paintbrush, followed by a rusty screwdriver and an old hammer with a wood handle. Across the base of the hammer were the words, Property of the New York City Housing Authority.

"Smallest and best," Wylie repeated. He was still unpacking. This time a roll of yellow measuring tape.

I looked around again. "I don't see any hydrocarbon detectors."

Wylie took a box of self-sealing plastic bags out of the suitcase. Then he turned to me and pointed to his nose. He sniffed twice. "Hydrocarbon detector," he said, and flashed me one of his let's-jump-out-of-the-airplane-together grins.

I had to laugh.

Wylie continued to take things out of his battered suitcase: A tin of bandages. A flashlight. A smaller paintbrush. Two garden spades.

"That's all?" I asked. "There's no burlap sack or pickaxe in there with the rest of your sophisticated equipment?"

I was being facetious when I asked about the pickaxe, but he answered me seriously.

"I don't have a pickaxe, but I usually bring along a shovel.

"Why?"

"Because essentially, a fire investigation is just like an archeological dig."

Wylie turned his attention to unloading his camera bag. He took out two thirty-five-millimeter cameras, two flash attachments, and a macro lens. He hung both cameras around his neck and then tucked one under each side of the down liner of his Army fatigue jacket.

Just about then, Clyde Prouty and his people walked across the barn and pushed themselves between us and the Duesenberg.

Wylie and I looked at each other.

We looked back at plaintiff's team.

Prouty stood in front of the others, crossed his arms over his chest, and began in the tight, angry tones he never uses when addressing his clients or a jury, "Okay, these are the rules." He spread his legs apart like a pissy genie protecting the entrance to his cave. "You will be permitted to do no destructive testing. You are not permitted to remove any of the car parts without prior permission. You cannot remove any parts at all from this facility. If you do receive permission to remove a part, said part must be videotaped prior to, during, and after removal by our videotape cameraman, who has set up his camera to run throughout your entire investigation. If testing is to be done, it will be done at a laboratory of our choosing. And, of course, we will be observing your entire examination today. Do you have any questions?"

Wylie took a step back from his suitcase and raised his hand.

"Yes?" Clyde Prouty acknowledged sternly.

"Where's the bathroom?"

I thought I heard a half-repressed laugh coming from one of the two junior attorneys, a small man with a chipmunk face and intelligent eyes. Clyde swung around to locate the snicker, but the attorney had rearranged his face in time.

We'd been inside the barn for about fifteen minutes by then. I was freezing. The pimply faced cameraman was hopping from foot to foot and pounding the sides of his arms with his fists to stay warm. I was also happy to see that Dr. Pay Me's teeth were chattering.

"Oh, yeah. And another thing," Wylie added. "It's a little warm in here, Clyde. Could you get someone to turn down the heat?"

The chipmunk snickered a second time. There was definitely insubordination in the ranks. I didn't foresee a brilliant future for that young attorney unless he changed his attitude. Fast.

Wylie motioned our mechanic to bring over an empty steel drum. When he got it, he unrolled the screen he'd brought from the car over the top of the drum. Then he asked me if plaintiff's video camera had sound.

Before I could answer, Clyde Prouty said, "It is an audio-video recorder." His voice was aggressive. "It can pick up anything you say."

Wylie nodded. He turned to the camera lens, smiled broadly, waved and said, "Hi, Mom. Hi, Dad."

And those were just about the last four words he said during the rest of our inspection.

How do you investigate a car fire? I didn't have a clue. To me, fire was the great equalizer. I thought that finding out where or how a fire had started in a vehicle would be like trying to figure out which end of a chuck roast had burned first.

The reason I'd hired Wylie Nolan was to find out where the fire started in my client's car. As a matter of practical reality, though, I didn't think he could do it. I didn't think anyone could.

I was wrong. Wylie could. And did. And he was even able to explain it to me.

The Duesenberg that had belonged to Stanfield Standish was sitting in the middle of Prouty's storage facility. A few more wrecks and some rusty refrigerators and stoves from other lawsuits in which he was involved were off to the side, but we had enough room to take good pictures of the Duesenberg from all angles, including above. There was also enough floor space to maneuver the forklift so that we could see what it looked like underneath.

In preparing my defense for this case, I had to learn as much as I could, not only about Courtland Motors, their Classic Cars Division, and how they got into the business of restoring cars, but also about the Duesenberg itself. I didn't have enough time to become a Duesenberg expert, but I did pick up one or two interesting facts.

Like when it was introduced in 1928, the J series Duesenberg Arlington sedan was advertised as "the world's finest motor car." It sold for sixteen thousand dollars new when the model A Ford was selling for only about four hundred dollars. Over sixty years later, Standish's car, before the fire, would have brought in more than two million dollars at auction.

Other specifications of the J series Duesenberg were a mighty 420 straight-eight engine with 350 horsepower and twin overhead camshafts. It had an aluminum body and could go ninety miles an hour in second gear and 116 miles an hour in high. When I first saw these mph specifications, I wasn't sure I was reading them right. That seemed altogether too fast for a 1928 car. But I *was* reading them right. And racing Duesenbergs went even faster.

The instrument panel was made of turned oxidized nickel; it contained a brake-pressure gauge, ammeter, oil-pressure gauge, tachometer, split-second stop clock, 150-mph speedometer, gas gauge, water-temperature gauge, ignition lock, carburetor control, and altimeter barometer.

And it was a giant of a vehicle. The Duesenberg was big. It was beautiful. It was powerful.

Once I drove from Laramie to Casper during one of the worst winters in Wyoming's history. As the winds howled around my rented Jeep, I realized that I was the only car left on the road. The vehicles on the *side* of the road, though, told a different story. Every few miles, I saw another overturned tractor-trailer, victims of the deadly winds of the night before. The truck cabs were twisted away from their bodies at crazy angles like heads on broken necks. They looked solemn and prehistoric underneath the snow drifts, and as I drove I felt as if I had traveled through time into a dinosaur graveyard.

When I looked at the rusted shell of the Duesenberg in that cold barn, I felt very much the same as I had when I'd driven past the overturned trucks. Here was what had once been a perfectly designed, mighty hero of a machine, one that had attained almost mythological proportions. And now it was gone.

Wylie Nolan began his examination of the Duesenberg at ten A.M. For forty-five minutes, he did nothing but circle it, peering through the broken windows, kneeling to inspect the tires, lying flat on his back to look at the undercarriage, standing thoughtfully in front of the front fenders, quietly contemplating the trunk. And not touching anything. Not a door handle. Not a headlight. Not a hood lock.

During the first fifteen or twenty minutes of this inspection, Prouty, his two junior associates, the paralegal, and the videotape cameraman followed Wylie around like paranoid Marx Brothers afraid that if they dropped their guard for even a second he would march off with the sterling silver.

The video footage on Prouty's camera during that three-quarters of an hour would have put an insomniac to sleep: Wylie Nolan standing with his hands in his pockets; Wylie Nolan staring through the window of the driver's seat; Wylie Nolan staring at the dashboard; Wylie Nolan staring at the trunk; Wylie Nolan staring at the license plate; Wylie Nolan kneeling beside the right rear tire and staring at what was left of the rim.

Wylie Nolan staring.

If Wylie was doing this just to aggravate Plaintiff's attorney, I wouldn't have been unhappy. But he wasn't. Before and during any cause and origin investigation, Wylie Nolan stares a lot. And he thinks. He observes burn patterns. He notices a patch of unburned gray leather here. He sees a deep scar in the fabric there.

Staring. Thinking. Staring. Thinking.

For twenty minutes the paranoid Marx Brothers followed Wylie around. Then they started to dart out of the barn for five minutes at a stretch. They'd climb into their cars with the engines running and the heaters turned on full blast. After we'd been in the barn for forty minutes they didn't even bother to check up on what we were doing. They just cowered in the warmth of their cars.

A few minutes before noon, though, the attorney with the chipmunk face popped back to tell us they were going to town for lunch. He'd started to ask if he could bring us back anything when Clyde Prouty appeared in the barn door.

"Lindsey," he snapped, as though issuing a command to a dog. "Now."

And he glared at us.

The chipmunk grinned apologetically, shrugged, and followed Prouty.

Meanwhile, the video cameraman had set his camera up on a tripod and also scampered away for warmth. Which was starting to look like a good idea.

I stamped my feet to get my circulation going. Wylie said, "Why don't you sit in my car for a few minutes to warm up?"

But I wasn't about to do that. There is something about Wylie Nolan that makes a normal go-to-work kind of guy want to slap the flank of his horse and shout, "Who was that masked man?" or exclaim, "It's a bird, it's a plane, it's . . ."

I know. I know. It's only Wylie Nolan. But still, when we work together, I get the urge to survive what he survives, go where he goes, and keep up with his long strides on the weary march to Bataan.

He brings out the Gunga Din in me.

So I refused to return to the car, and Wylie conspired with the mechanic to build a fire in a spare steel drum next to the entrance to the barn. It probably saved my life. I *know* it saved my circulation. Wylie took one of his cameras out from under his fatigue jacket and gave it to me.

"Tuck it close to your body," he said. "Cameras have to be kept warm or the shutters will freeze".

He put film in the camera that he'd kept, adjusted the flash and f-stops, and began to shoot the exterior of the car. He photographed the Duesenberg from all sides, climbed a stepladder, and took pictures of its distended roof.

When he finished photographing the car's exterior, he handed me his camera, took back the one I'd kept under my coat, and started the whole process again.

"Why two cameras?" I asked.

"If I only use one and it malfunctions, I won't know about it until it's too late. The scene might have been altered, or the plaintiff won't let us come back to take more pictures. The second camera is my backup system."

After he was finished with his exterior photographs, Wylie told the forklift operator to raise the Duesenberg so that he could shoot the undercarriage.

Wylie didn't get around to photographing the interior of the Duesenberg until it was back at ground level. We alternated cameras again. I fed scrap wood into the fire in our steel drum, and I sent the forklift operator to Stilton-on-Hudson to bring back lunch.

Wylie and I kept our conversation to a minimum. We acted on the principle that the plaintiff could see and hear everything we did and said as long as his audio-video camera worked.

The camera had been left on a tripod with the lens pointed at an area which included the steel drum, the heavy mesh screen on top of the drum, and the entire passenger side of the car. Prouty had accurately assumed that Wylie was going to sift the debris inside the car through the metal screen and look for evidence of how the fire had started, where it had started, and why.

Wylie looked at me. He pointed to my side of the steel drum. I looked at him, nodded, and pointed at his. Without saying a word, we lifted and carried it outside the camera's viewing range, to the driver's side of the Duesenberg. Then Wylie grabbed one of his garden spades, opened the car door, got down on his knees, and began his "archaeological dig." He was concentrating on the area around the driver's seat and on the flooring under the steering wheel.

Wylie picked up jagged pieces of metal and shards of glass with his bare hands. He put some of them aside and tossed others out of his way. Using his spade, he scooped up shallow helpings of debris, and then gently sifted them through the screen. A fine dusting of char fell into the barrel. Other, larger pieces didn't fall through. Wylie examined them, held them up to the light. He dusted off some with one of his paintbrushes. And he photodocumented what he did. This procedure of observing, digging, scooping, screening, examining, photographing, and discarding went on for most of the day.

When it was possible, I helped Wylie. When it wasn't, I watched. I learned.

Our mechanic came back with lunch before Clyde and his people returned. I scarfed up my sandwich and gulped down my coffee while I was standing next to the burn barrel, still trying to get warm. Wylie wouldn't stop working, so I ate his sandwich, too.

As the day went on, I sensed an almost animal electricity coming from Wylie Nolan. He was the hunting dog who'd suddenly smelled the fox. Wylie was on point, all senses alert. Completely in focus.

His camera was out. I knelt down next to him. He snapped one shot. Then another. And another. He handed me the camera and lifted a paintbrush. Delicately. Delicately. He dusted away the powdery ash. I saw a flicker of gold. Two more gentle strokes of the brush. More gold. A sparkle. Wylie reached down and probed deeply with his fingers. Three stones sparkled. He told me to take a picture. Then, out from under the accelerator pedal of the car, he lifted a thick, gold ring mounted with four diamonds.

Wylie held the ring in the palm of his hand. I snapped more pictures. He flipped it over. I photographed the ring from different angles. He gave it to me to hold. While he was putting a macro lens on his camera, I did something unconsciously. Like when you're asked to hold someone else's coffee cup, and after a few seconds, you inadvertently take a sip. I slipped the ring on my finger.

And that's how I knew it was a big ring. For a big man. For a big man's hand. I'm five eleven and weigh a hundred and eighty-five pounds, but it fell right off my finger. Wylie indicated that I should hold up the ring so he could take closeups. First at this angle. Then at that. As he was shooting, I thought I saw an inscription running along the inside, but I couldn't make out any of the letters. We took the same photographs with the second camera.

Then Wylie raised his head above the dashboard and looked toward the barn doors. We heard car motors. Wylie lowered his head and grinned at me. He took the ring out of my hand and put it back under the accelerator pedal of the Duesenberg. With his paintbrush, he gently dusted the powdered ash over the pedal until the picture it presented was exactly as it had been before Wylie found the ring.

We got up and brushed ourselves off. Wylie jutted his head toward the steel drum. I nodded and picked up my side of the barrel. We carried it around the car and put it back where we'd found it, by the front passenger door in full view of Prouty's video camera.

It was a little after three P.M., and I wasn't cold anymore. Wylie's enthusiasm had been contagious. He walked over to the two hoods that folded over the center of the Duesenberg's engine compartment. I propped them open and held his flashlight while he focused his camera. I loaded and unloaded film.

I toted that barge. I lifted that bale.

After inspecting the engine compartment, we moved behind the Duesenberg to examine the trunk. Wylie tried to open it. It wouldn't budge. He studied the lock and photographed it. He pulled out his crowbar, did a fast check of the barn door, and made sure he was out of the video camera's range. Then, with a quick application of leverage, he popped open the trunk's lid. We looked inside.

There were a few articles of clothing, a leather golf bag, some golf clubs, and a plastic bottle. The bottle was melted.

Wylie sniffed a few times. The hound dog at it again. Alert for a telltale scent. He leaned into the trunk and inhaled deeply. He sifted through the debris, took some more photographs, and then lowered the lid of the trunk.

After he had put his cameras away and repacked his sophisticated fire investigation equipment (flashlight, measuring tape, paintbrushes, garden spades, plastic bags, crowbar, hammer, and screwdriver), he slipped the mechanic a ten-dollar bill. And that's when I saw his hands. They weren't just black with char, they were also crusted with dry blood.

"Why don't you wear gloves?" I asked, thinking about lockjaw and tetanus shots and what I'd learned in Boy Scouts about dying after stepping on a rusty nail.

Wylie shrugged. "No big deal. I always cut myself. That's what bandages are for."

"But . . ."

"Max, I have to be able to feel things. When I touch it, I find it." We were beyond the range of the audio-video camera now, on our way out of the barn. "That's how I found the keys."

"What keys?"

"The ignition key, and the key for the doors, hood, and trunk."

I thought back for a second. I didn't remember him finding any keys.

"When did you find them?"

"When you were off with the girls having lunch."

So much for Gunga Din.

"Where did you find them?"

"How about instead of me telling you where I found them, I'll tell you where I didn't find them."

"Go on."

"I didn't find either one of them in the ignition switch."

CHAPTER
8

I alluded earlier to my dinner with Stanfield Standish about twenty years ago. But I didn't tell you much. I met him through his father, an interesting man with a powerful personality. Standish's father's name was Hugo Scheidler. I don't know how Stanley Scheidler became Stanfield Standish, but he had already evolved into "Stanfield" by the time I met him. And he was *called* Stanfield. Not Stanley. Not Stan.

I sat next to old man Scheidler on the return half of a flight to Chicago. Scheidler was going to Manhattan, and in a talkative mood. He said he was on his way to a classic-car auction in New York

City with his "girl friend" and planned to buy her a 1940 Packard Darrin Victoria convertible and himself a 1930 J series Duesenberg Arlington sedan. The auction, the Russian Tea Room, and a hit show on Broadway, he said, would be a nice diversion from the norm—which I took to mean his wife.

Hugo's conversation on the plane led me to believe that his wife knew about his mistress, that at least one of Hugo's four children, Stanfield Standish (A.K.A. Stanley Scheidler) knew about her, and that his mistress' son knew about the affair, too.

Hugo Scheidler was an interesting man. He'd been a Horatio Alger hero, scraping through the Depression doing two, three jobs at a time, scrimping on necessities, accumulating capital, and when he was seventeen years old, buying a gas station, even though when he started, he didn't know the difference between a snowshoe and a brake shoe or a crankcase from a camshaft. Hugo's business philosophy was to "say yes" no matter what a customer asked for, and then to beg, borrow, or steal the mechanical knowhow to get the job done.

Hugo Scheidler's prices were competitive; his warranties were above average; his employees had been trained to do it right the first time. And they did. Over a period of time, both his reputation and his business grew.

One garage became two, two became three, and so on.

With his gas-station profits, Hugo bought a moderately successful department store, renamed it Harriet O'Brien's after his mother, expanded it, and started to branch out. In the early 1960s, Harriet O'Brien's became one of the first major retailers to locate in shopping malls, a move proving so successful that Hugo Scheidler started to design and package malls as outlets for his own stores.

Within ten years of opening his first store, the business of building malls became even more profitable than the O'Brien chain, and by the time Hugo Scheidler was ready to retire, he was a very, very, very wealthy man. He stayed on as chairman of the board of six of the companies he still owned, and as a hobby, he collected limited-edition, luxury American cars.

Hugo Scheidler was over six feet tall, big-boned and erect, with a confident backward thrust to his shoulders and a handshake like tape gripping a boxer's palm. He had a large, straight nose in a face so angular his features seemed to be jumping from one ledge to another. His eyes alternately conveyed charm, magnetism, and raw power.

His mistress's name was Marguerite, as in the Dumas novel *La Dame aux Camélias*, and I liked her. She was in her mid thirties and was memorable mostly because of a streak of white hair that ran back from her widow's peak. The rest of her hair was glossy and black. Her eyes were black, her mink coat was black, and her earrings were diamond.

Marguerite was pretty, in a sensuous, porcelain doll kind of way. She had beautiful, dark ivory skin and sexy, pouty lips.

She and Hugo made a nice-looking couple. He held doors open for her, and she looked up at him with tolerant affection.

During my conversation with Hugo on the plane, he told me that he and Marguerite planned to have Thanksgiving dinner alone in a restaurant. This went contrary to my upbringing, so after we landed I told him to give me a second on the phone because I wanted to call my parents.

At the time, I was twenty-three years old. I had a studio apartment on East 84th Street, I had just passed the bar, and I was working at my first job as an assistant district attorney. My parents lived in Bay Ridge, Brooklyn, and I was still going home every Friday night, with or without a date, for a home-cooked meal.

My mother said, "Sure. Bring your friend and his wife for Thanksgiving dinner." (Okay, so I wasn't exactly explicit about their relationship.)

Hugo accepted my invitation with a degree of gratitude that was almost embarrassing (F. Scott Fitzgerald was right. The rich *are* different). And then he sandbagged me into including his son, Stanley (yes, Hugo still called him that), in the invitation. Stanley, Hugo told me proudly, was in town to negotiate a three-movie deal with the Myron Asher Management Talent Agency.

That Thanksgiving dinner was the first and only time I ever sat face to face with a living, breathing Stanfield Standish.

We spent about six hours together.

I didn't dislike him from the minute he walked through the door of my parents' house. It took me about fifteen minutes. We were the same age, Stanfield Standish and I. But we bore only a chronological resemblance. And back then, Standish didn't look anything like the silvery slick entertainment magnate he eventually became. He was posturing and arrogant; he played at being world-weary and reeked of tailored tweeds and designer cologne. I, on the other hand, was fresh out of law school, drunk on the high principles of law, and marching to the tune of Arthur M. Harris's words syncopating in my mind, to wit: ***"The true lawyer is a pacifier, not a provoker. His efforts are more than commercial, higher and nobler than merely mercenary."***

I sat down opposite Standish at dinner and tried to act the genial host. What I learned was that Stanfield Standish was as new to Hollywood as I was to the law. He'd just written his first film and was almost giddy from the effort of trying to be nonchalant.

The movie was about a secretary who falls in love with a professional bowler. Her boss makes a nasty pass at the girl. The bowler tries to defend her. The boss kills him. (It doesn't matter how.) Then the bowler comes back from the dead to avenge his own death, after which he guides his girlfriend safely through a series of life-threatening events. His time on earth is limited, though. So, to tie up loose ends, he finds his girlfriend a new lover (but is it really a new lover, or just a new incarnation of old, dead him?) and then goes back to heaven, where he belongs.

Sound familiar?

There were thirteen movies with the same plot made the year I was twenty-three. The one written by Stanfield Standish was called *Love To Spare* (groan), and it hit top-grossing movie of the week the day before that Thanksgiving dinner when Stanfield Standish came to call.

Twenty-odd years ago, Stanfield Standish was about five feet ten inches tall (in recent photos he seems much taller). His hair (then) was reddish brown. His eyebrows were dark and thick over light green eyes, and his five o'clock shadow looked like a fine powdering of graphite on his jaw.

Standish smoked a pipe, and when I saw him fumbling with his tobacco pouch and pipe lighter, I wondered if the long sleeves on his tweed jacket weren't a failed attempt to hide his hands. Because Stanfield Standish had girl's hands. There were no hairs between his knuckles and his wrists. His fingers were long, thin, dead-white and came to points like dinner candles. Over the points were manicured fingernails.

When Standish caught me staring at his hands, he stamped out his pipe and began to shoot hostile questions at me on matters of the law, almost as if to deflect my attention from some vaguely perceived act of moral turpitude.

I shot back monosyllabic answers and studied his face.

Let's start with his eyes. I already told you that they were light green. What I didn't tell you was that their only attribute was their color. They had no depth. No passion. No involuntary movement. They were like Crayola eyes drawn on a blank sheet of paper.

In contrast, Standish's mouth was so soft it was almost sensual. He had full lips. Like on a Greek statue. But the sensual effect was spoiled because he never smiled. Nor did his face seem to have any range of expressions. Toward the end of dinner, I thought I saw his top lip angle into a sneer. But then I realized that it wasn't Stanfield Standish's face that sneered, it was his attitude.

Everything about the guy annoyed me. You know the kind of people who go into a store, hold a piece of fabric up to the light, and then get a look on their faces like they're smelling shit? That was twenty-three-year-old Stanfield Standish in what must have been the incubation period of his neo-international point of view. Me. My family. The turkey. His father. His father's mistress. Hollywood. The movie-going public. The universe at large. He held us all up to the light, and he saw shit.

I said it before and I'll say it again. I never liked the son-of-a-bitch.

After dinner, Standish became conversational. He decided, over a glass of Dewar's—his father brought the bottle; my parents' speed is Mogen David diluted with an ice cube—to expostulate about the movies.

By then, he and I had moved to the blue silk arm chairs in the corner of the living room. Standish with his pipe and me with my cigarettes. Looking back, I suppose we were both a little bit full of ourselves. The young lawyer, careful not to drop any ashes on his mother's carpet. The young filmmaker, tapping the tobacco down in the bowl of his pipe with awkward hand movements and no expression at all on his face.

"What I learned in Hollywood" (puff, puff) "is that the way to get a successful film produced" (puff) "is to carefully position the subject matter you're dealing with" (heavy exhalation of long draw of smoke). "The important thing to remember is who your audience is." (puff, puff) "What we're dealing with in a country of this size is an enormous, untapped well of mediocrity." (puff) "People who watch half-hour situation comedies on TV and think that's culture. People who have never read a classic, whose opinions are based on what cause their favorite rock singer last supported at a benefit concert. People who think American domestic policy means to hire cleaning ladies and nannies who were born in the United States." (puff, puff) "Keep that in mind, and you'll never lose a big case." (puff, puff, deft sleight of hand to reignite pipe with minimum finger action) "That's why I'm so successful at selling scripts." (puff, puff) "Never aim too high. Never aim too low." (puff) "Observe the human equation. Calculate what people want to hear. Factor in what you're willing to tell them. Put all of that data into your computer" (tap of the pipe bowl against forehead, which, presumably, is the Standish computer) "and what you come up with is your operating principle. I call that operating principle the lowest common denominator. That's my target area. That's what I aim for." (puff, puff)

Stanfield Standish stopped talking, and I couldn't help but stare at him. Here, sitting before me, was an articulate, intelligent, conniving, implacable merchant of mediocrity. And worse than that, he was proud of it. I shook my head at him as though he were pathetic, crushed out my cigarette, got out of my chair, and crossed the room to join my parents. My mother, as usual, was interrogating instead of talking to her guests, while my father was listening in lawyerly silence.

How many children did Hugo have? My mother asked. What were their careers? Which colleges did they go to? How many grandchildren were there? And so forth. Then my mother came out with her zinger.

"So," she said. "Why haven't you married this beautiful lady yet?"

Fool that I am, I'd thought my mother had assumed Hugo and Marguerite were married.

My mother liked Marguerite. You could tell that by the way she looked at her. I liked Marguerite, too. Or, at least I didn't dislike her. And Hugo seemed to love her. I wasn't sure how Stanfield felt about her, but how would any man feel about his father's mistress?

"So," my mother repeated. "Why haven't you married this beautiful lady yet?"

This was followed by one or two audible gasps and some conspicuous seconds of silence during which I, and possibly the others, asked myself the same question: Why *hadn't* Hugo married Marguerite?

I looked at Marguerite. The expression on her face was so lacking in expectation, so tolerant, so enduring, so nonaccusing and accepting. It's an expression I've seen fairly often over the years in Manhattan. I call it "the mistress look." You can usually—no, change that to *always*—see it on the faces of women who are in love with the men whose beds they only occasionally share.

My mother's question permeated the silence.

We all turned to look at Hugo Scheidler.

His answer came out, fast, slick, without appreciable hesitation.

"We live our own lives. My wife and I. She goes her way and I go mine. We have an understanding."

"So why don't you marry Marguerite?"

"We're happy the way we are."

"Marguerite, would you marry this man if he asked you?"

No answer. Passive, accepting shrug.

Back to Hugo.

My mother, the pile driver, persisted.

"Where do you spend Christmas?"

"With my daughters. My children don't know about Marguerite. Except for Stanley. Stanley's a man. He understands."

If any expression at all could be said to have fluttered across Stanfield Standish's face at that moment, it came closest to being a wince.

"If my daughters found out about Marguerite, though, or if I left their mother . . . I couldn't hurt them like that. I couldn't do that to my girls."

My mother looked Hugo dead in the eye and stood up.

"For a rich, charming, intelligent man who worries so much about so many people, you forgot to worry about one very important person, didn't you, Mr. Scheidler?"

Hugo also stood up. "And who is that?"

Without saying another word, my mother turned her head and looked directly at Marguerite.

For about sixty seconds, Hugo Scheidler didn't move. He stared at my mother. Just stared. Then he broke it off. He took a step forward, inexplicably reached out for my mother's hand, raised it to his lips, and kissed it.

My mother's right. He was a charming man.

We heard from Hugo three times after that.

He sent my mother a huge bouquet of roses the day after Thanksgiving.

He wrote me a long, friendly letter offering to contact the senior partners of three prestigious Manhattan law firms on my behalf.

And six years later (I never answered his letter; my mother never responded to the flowers), I got this short note in the mail.

> Dear Max:
>
> I thought you would want to know that Stanley has relocated to Wilmington, Delaware, and purchased the old Wilmington Cable TV News station. Since he is creating a legal department, and since I have been following your career, I have written to him recommending that he hire you as Chief Corporate Counsel.
>
> I strongly advise you to contact him.

I never answered that letter of fourteen years ago, either. Of course, I never called Stanfield Standish. And other than the occasional scatter-burst of resentment I felt for him every time I read that he purchased another television station or bought another radio station or took over another newspaper and another and another and another, I didn't give him a whole lot of thought.

Stanfield Standish wasn't usually *in* the news. He was more a force *behind* the news. Making sure that his broadcasters didn't aim too high. Didn't aim too low. And thereby reducing both ends of the spectrum to a great, burbling mass of inconsequentiality.

Jerk.

Five years ago, though, Standish made headlines. This gave me the opportunity to observe him long and hard for the first time in fifteen years.

The change in him was both cosmetic and dramatic. Instead of the tweedy, intellectual look he'd affected earlier, he was now movie-star handsome. I don't know how he did it, but he was taller. And his hair had metamorphosed into a wavy, perfect metallic bronze. His hairline had changed. There was more forehead. And his five o'clock shadow was gone. You could ice-skate across his jaw. He'd done something to his nose, too. It was fuller and straighter. More like his father's had been. Or like Hugo Scheidler must have looked when he was the same age.

But Stanfield Standish's fingers were still long, tapered, fluttery things. And his eyes were still flat Crayola O's. And his lips still held a latent sneer.

Five years ago, Stanfield Standish became headlines when he bought the complete library of films produced and distributed by Cinema Select Artists, Incorporated. I don't remember what he paid for them, but it was such a high dollar amount that Wall Street was buzzing with rumors of his financial doom.

Wall Street should have saved its breath.

No risk.

Standish bought Cinema Select's library for the *entertainment* branch of his television network, called Stanfield Standish Presents. Standish owned the films, owned the network, leased the films to himself, and then paid himself for the television rights to broadcast the films. An impressive system wherein his right hand knew exactly what his left hand was doing.

But that was just the beginning.

Standish didn't think that the potential television viewing audience was big enough for these old movies. There were (his statisticians advised) more than thirty-three million Americans under thirty years of age with purchasing power measured annually in billions of dollars who spent most of their spare time lip-synching to electronic music and buying torn designer blue jeans at shopping malls. This audience would not, Standish asserted, be willing to watch an "old movie" on television unless it could recognize and identify with a *contemporary* cast of stars.

The "Mall Generation," Stanfield Standish said, neither knew nor cared about Arlene de Grasse, with her liquid sapphire eyes and that little glint of wet you could see on her lip just before she took a puff on her cigarette. Nor did they give a damn about the cleft in Roy Douglass's chin deep enough to hide a two-by-four, or his offhand way of delivering dialogue as though it were a worn-out saddle he'd just flung up easy on the back of his horse. I used to practice Roy Douglass looks in my mirror when I was ten years old. If I remember right, this consisted of squaring my jaw, lowering my brows, peering ruggedly at my own reflection, and saying, "As long as I'm around this valley, the settlers here will be able to live in peace."

Arlene de Grasse, Roy Douglass, Louise Eastman. Their images . . . their mystique. They were larger-than-life movie stars who belong to a rapidly diminishing group of people who justifiably transcended the era in which they lived.

Or, at least, they had until Stanfield Standish bought the rights to the Cinema Select Artists library of film.

CHAPTER
9

During the Golden Age of moviemaking, each of the major studios was famous for a different type of film. For MGM, it was musicals. Warner Brothers presented social themes. Columbia made nothing but "A" movies. David O. Selznick maintained high production standards. And Paramount had the light touch.

But what Cinema Select Artists had was its stars. Every schoolkid growing up knew its motto:

The Faces
The Names
The Talent to Enthrall

Cinema Select was started in 1913 by three brothers-in-law in Fort Lee, New Jersey. Samuel Rosner was in charge of production; Jacob Pollock was in charge of film distribution; and Ira Bushman stayed back in New York to raise cash.

Of the three brothers-in-law, however, only Samuel Rosner had the powerful personality and artistic vision to bully his talent until they had no choice *but* to enthrall.

And he made great movies.

He was the one who discovered the stars that made Cinema Select famous. *He* hired the writers, bought the screen rights for obscure books, tyrannized over his talent and drew great performances out of them, calling them "artists" or sometimes "players," but never just "stars."

There is a famous photograph taken on a Cinema Select sound stage over fifty years ago. And luck, chance, or planning had it that all of the studio's top contract players were in the same place at the same time. Looking at the picture now, it's hard to believe that one barely literate Russian immigrant had the genius, let alone the energy and wherewithal, to accumulate so much talent in such a short, but monumentally creative, period in time.

Why am I telling you all this?

What has it got to do with Wylie Nolan, Stanfield Standish, and the fire?

First, I have to tell you about everybody's (and my) favorite romantic movie, *Idlewild*.

Sometimes a story comes along that's good enough to work a cynic's tear ducts into a wet lather. That's what happened with *Idlewild*.

Howard Ingram played Noah, the scientist sent by the War Department to the desert to work on America's secret weapon. There was no A-bomb when *Idlewild* was made; but as with so much good fiction, art anticipated the event. Ingram had world-weary eyes, two deep lines of rugged determination carved into either side of his mouth, and the hawkish face of a man who would rather be a wounded hero than a dead saint. Howard Ingram gave the role of Noah much more than just an interpretation. He *became* Noah.

And Louise Eastman became Pearl.

Pearl was the original self-made man. Except that she was a

woman. She was born in a depressed Pennsylvania mining town. Her mother died or disappeared.

Her father abused her.

She ran away.

She survived.

But how had she survived? What compromises had she made along the way? With whom? At what cost?

And how far was she willing to go to keep Noah from finding out the truth?

Noah was a physicist teaching in an ivy-covered college town when the War Department came to him for help. Noah's parents had escaped to the United States from France just days before Hitler invaded Poland. Noah went to graduate school in New York, got his Ph.D. at Columbia University, loved America, hated Nazis.

Myrtle and Clement McCallum played Noah's parents. Myrtle immortalized Ma with a gesture I still remember. She reached up to Noah's chin with the edge of her dishtowel, gruffly wiped away an imaginary crumb, and said, "There. You think I should allow my son, the physicist, to go out into the world looking like that?"

The plot of the movie went like this:

On his way to the government's lab in the desert, Noah changes planes at Idlewild Airport. It is there, when the city is hit by a freak snowstorm, that he meets Pearl.

Pearl, by now, has become a sophisticated businesswoman. She'd recognized early that there would be a wartime need for qualified, temporary office personnel; and in response to that need, Pearl opens up her own employment agency.

When someone in a position of power has an unexpected opening for a secretary or a typist, it is to Pearl's Girls that they go because Pearl interviews, tests, trains, and places all of her people herself.

How do the scientist and businesswoman meet?

The airport is snowed in for seventeen hours. Noah and Pearl are jammed together on a crowded bench. They talk. They fall in love.

But Nazi Germany is on the move, and Noah has to get to the desert to work on America's atomic weapon.

The blizzard stops. The runways are cleared.

Noah and Pearl promise that they will meet again at Idlewild six months later.

Six months go by. They meet at Idlewild again, and they are still in love. Pearl tentatively hints that she has a past with which Noah might not be thrilled. Noah says that he doesn't care. But the Nazis are still advancing, and he has to be on the next plane back to the lab in the desert.

One slow, long, silent kiss. Noah boards.

The plane stops over in Chicago.

At Midway Airport, Noah is kidnapped by Nazi spies who want the plans for America's atomic-weapon system. If Noah refuses, his parents will die.

The camera moves into a closeup of Noah. There's a look in his eye—a fleeting, calculating glint we can't interpret.

Noah agrees to the Nazis' demands. He will write out the formula for the secret weapon. In return, his parents will go free.

Noah's mother and father are brought to Chicago. An exchange is made.

Then the plot speeds up the way it does in old movies when everything seems to happen at once.

First Rolf, the Nazi with whom Noah made the exchange, disappears. Rolf is the only one who can prove that Noah turned over bogus information. Instead of an atomic weapon, the formula Noah delivered was a complicated set of equations that would have resulted in an internal combustion engine with the consistency of angel food cake.

Meanwhile, Rolf approaches Pearl and tells her that if she doesn't allow him to infiltrate Fifth Columnists into strategic companies where her girls work, certain unpleasant facts about her past will be given to a certain scientist with whom she is in love.

About Pearl. She was small, awkward, and feminine all at the same time. She had the graceless agility of a young girl peeking over the bannister at a party she's too shy to enter. But her eyes were a woman's eyes. Large, fringed with clustered triangles of long lashes, wide open, and unafraid.

Everything about Pearl was like that. Sunny. Clean. Open. And she did this one thing when she was afraid or unsure of herself that

I've never seen another actress do. She would bite the inside of her upper lip, as if trying to force back tears. And that look was so child-like and unsuccessful in its attempt to be brave that the audience's heart went out to her.

Back to the plot.

Lots of chases ensue.

Pearl contacts the State Department. They tell her to pretend to go along with the Nazis. Meanwhile, a journalist finds out about Rolf's spy ring and exposes it in the press. Pearl makes headlines. She is accused of being a spy.

Will the State Department come to her rescue?

Will the phony formula Noah gave Rolf be discovered so that Noah can prove he isn't a traitor?

The lovers are back at Idlewild Airport. American agents find out that the same spy ring tried to blackmail both Pearl and Noah. The Nazis had discovered that the two of them were in love and thought that each would be a weak link to the other.

But they were wrong.

Pearl holds up an envelope and tells Noah that it contains facts about her past of which she is not proud and that the Nazis had tried to blackmail her with these facts.

She hands him the envelope.

Noah gives Pearl a hard, penetrating look. Then he walks away from her. The camera follows him through the door at the back of the airport, behind the hangar to an oil drum on fire with sparking cinders.

Pearl silently follows him. There is a look on her face of lost hope.

Then, Noah throws the envelope into the fire.

He turns to Pearl. Her eyes fill with tears. The camera glints off each individual tear. Before they fall, Noah yanks out a handker-chief. He gently wipes away the tears and, imitating his mother's thick, European accent says, "There. You think I'm going to allow my future wife, the businesswoman, to go out in the world looking like that?"

The screen goes to black. The words flash:

THE END

And everybody sobs.

That was the movie so many of us loved. *That* was the movie Stanfield Standish had just bought, along with hundreds of others, from the Cinema Select Artists library.

Now, I'll tell you what he was planning to do with it.

•

He began his career as a rock singer. His stage trademark was gauzy white pants with a string-tie waist. Before each performance, he'd drench himself with water and run on stage soaking wet, an apparition that apparently so inspired adolescent girls and thirteen-year-old boys that they migrated to shopping malls in hordes to buy his records and videos. By the millions.

His act consisted of rubbing those parts of his skinny white body that our mothers told us never to let anyone else touch against the same parts of his back-up singers' anatomies.

Surprisingly, despite the water, strobe lights, electric guitars, and amplifiers, he was never electrocuted. Other than perform, he also wrote his own songs, took many mood-altering chemicals, and made lots of money.

The lyrics to the songs he writes celebrate acts of violence to women, not excluding rape, disfigurement, dismemberment, and death; his music has no melody; and the voice that sings the lyrics is that of a thirteen-year-old boy whose nuts have just gotten caught in the suspension springs of his bicycle seat.

He goes by the name of "Skidder," and as part of his performance he skids around in the puddles of water that accumulate on stage. As a finale to his act, the music and high-tech stage effects stop. One spotlight pierces dramatically down on his bony, wet body. He turns to face the back of the stage and drops his pants. Then he moons the audience (to wild, screeching applause), and the stage goes black.

Remember that image. Remember the name. Skidder. His last name is Freebody.

Skidder decided that it wasn't enough to be a rock star, so he told his agent that he wanted to be a movie star, too.

Skidder Freebody.

That's one.

The second name I want you to remember is Lucrezia. As in Borgia. As in Renaissance poisoner. *Our* Lucrezia, however, is not a poisoner. She is a contemporary performer and the daughter of two obscure *film noir* directors who made movies that they insisted were *not* pornographic, in San Francisco during the mid-1970's.

Lucrezia began her film career in a self-produced movie wherein she played Peter Pan as a man who has become a woman via a sex change. Of course, he/she still called himself/herself "Peter" to avoid apprehension during the process of his/her life-work, which was to collect lost boys. I'll spare you a description of what Dr. Hook was going to do to these "boys," and you definitely don't want to know about Wendy.

After *Peter Pansy*, Lucrezia starred in a film produced by revisionist historians in Germany. Briefly, Lucrezia plays a concentration-camp victim who *wants* to be beaten, starved, and raped by Nazis. She falls in love with the commandant of the same concentration camp where her family has been killed, and she believes she can expiate her own guilt—we are never told of what she is guilty—by making him her lover.

The theme of this movie is that no one is guilty and that we are all guilty. And we are all at one with humanity. Or something. There are lots of scenes with black garter belts and swastikas, and Lucrezia gets to take her clothes off a lot and get chained to things.

Lucrezia co-produced her third movie. It received the Manhattan Film Critics Award and the European Theatrical Achievement Award, and it made her a superstar. In it, she plays an artist whose works are body paintings, meaning that she, herself, paints her own body, which is her canvas. The plot revolves around an art-gallery exhibit, which was paid for with a government grant.

As part of this exhibit, Lucrezia stands naked on a pedestal with a light bulb in her mouth and a pull chain looking something like—and emanating from the same place as—a Tampax string. Visitors to the gallery are invited to pull said chain and witness that the light really does go on and off. The plot thickens when a group of citizens who comes to the gallery to see how its tax dollars are being spent alleges that said light bulb, pull chain, and crotch are something less than what Michaelangelo might have considered "art," and implies that same might be closer to pornography. Blah-blah and so on.

In the movie, Lucrezia gets to paint starbursts around her nipples and decorate her navel (an outie) with acrylics, glitter, and neon paint. The theme of the movie is that the evil, suppressive government should not interfere with an artist's right to self-expression. We know this because Lucrezia pontificates on it over and over and over again. Then, to illustrate her point, she slashes her wrists, which are really her art, since she is her own body canvas.

Remember?

Anyway, Lucrezia doesn't die in the movie. She does bleed a lot, though, which we find out is also part of her art. In fact, prior to her wrist-slashing scene, she had arranged for an artist/friend to photograph her blood dripping over the red-and-white stripes going up and down her anatomy, which, by now, has inevitably evolved into a body canvas of the American flag.

The movie, called *Old Gory* (of course), ends as her artist/friend's photograph of her bleeding wins him a new government grant; and the freedom of artistic self-expression is preserved.

The pissed-off taxpayers still have to pay for all of this, which makes us wonder about *their* freedom of expression, but I'm a lawyer, not a political philosopher, so we won't go into that.

Instead, we'll pause a moment over the image of Lucrezia, red-and-white stripes extending down her stomach and between her thighs, fifty white stars positioned strategically around her upper torso, nipples, ears, and eyes and around her shaved head.

Remember the name: Lucrezia.

Hold onto the image.

And *now*, I'll tell you what all of this has to do with Stanfield Standish, the Cinema Select Artists film library, product-liability law, Wylie Nolan, and me.

CHAPTER
10

Five years ago, on February 14, Stanfield Standish made a televised announcement that was broadcast via satellite and press releases throughout the world. Valentine's Day, he said, was an appropriate date for his message, because "What we are doing today is about love. Lovingly preserving masterpieces of the cinema and lovingly bringing these movies to a new generation of viewers so that young people can relate to the great stories they have to tell."

Standish sat at a desk made of chrome and black marble, with his perfect metallic bronze hair and surgically enhanced neo-international movie-star profile. He looked like the captain of the command center of a technologically advanced beauty salon. When he spoke, the camera captured his lack of facial expression from varying angles, and the strong studio klieg lights did nothing to add warmth or depth to the blank absorption of his eyes.

At strategic places throughout Stanfield Standish's speech, he interjected clips from Cinema Select Artists classics, the most significant of which came from *A Poor Man's Paradise*, made in 1939. The scene Standish showed opens on Roy Douglass's back as he hesitates outside the door to his cabin, believing that the years ahead will hold nothing for him but terrible loneliness. Slowly, he turns to face the camera. As he edges the door open, a warm glow comes from inside. The door continues to open. Roy Douglass enters; the camera cuts to the fireside, where Arlene de Grasse, the woman he'd thought he lost, is sitting on the floor, intent on winding yarn into a ball. Roy makes a noise. Arlene looks up. "Hello," she says. "What took you so long?"

Standish showed four or five more clips along similar lines. All were classic scenes from classic movies familiar to everyone who has ever watched late-night TV.

After showing the last clip, Standish moved toward a rectangular object that had no recognizable purpose. He rested his hands on the top of it and then jerked them back to his side, as if he'd suddenly remembered that his hands weren't his best feature.

"This computer," he explained, "is an I-Quad 400 Series Four Di-Od Enhancer. Here at Stanfield Standish Presents, we refer to it simply as an 'Image Transformer.' " Standish expelled a shallow, fake laugh. "Some of my older viewers may remember the silent screen actress Clara Bow, who was called the It Girl, because she had so much of It, and It was what the audience wanted. Well, we call our Image Transformer the IT Machine, because it's going to give a whole new generation of viewers exactly what *you* want."

Standish looked off camera, and in an exaggerated, theatrical voice, commanded:

"Lights. Cameras. Action!"

Our TV screens went to black.

Seconds later, we were looking at the same scene from *A Poor Man's Paradise*. We saw Roy Douglass's back as he hesitated outside his cabin. We saw his head begin to turn slowly toward the camera. We saw . . .

For some, what happened next was as traumatic as if we'd awakened one morning to find the law of gravity revoked. Because Stanfield Standish tore away the security blanket we comfortably call reality and replaced it with something a whole lot of people were violently committed *not* to accept.

What should have happened during that film sequence from *A Poor Man's Paradise* was that Roy Douglass would turn around and *be* Roy Douglass. That Arlene de Grasse, winding yarn by the fireside, would *be* Arlene de Grasse. That their heads would be the same sizes they'd always been; their faces would still poke in and out in the same places; their eyes, noses, cheeks, and jaws would still fill their skins and bones in the same ways that they always had.

But what we hadn't factored in was Stanfield Standish.

Slowly, dramatically, Roy Douglass edged the door open. Slowly. Dramatically. He turned around to look at the audience. And . . .

The face looking out at us from the cabin door didn't have Roy Douglass's formidable black eyes. It didn't have his hectic, Fuller-brush eyebrows. It didn't have his expression of placid, good-natured strength or his jowly, easy-to-smile mouth. The clip from the movie was the same. And the scene still opened on what was unmistakably Roy Douglass's back.

But the face was all wrong. The nose was bony, with vertical slit nostrils, collagen-enhanced lips, pale eyes, almost translucent eyelashes and a smooth, hairless jaw.

The face was Skidder Freebody's.

Its scrawny neck had been expanded by a computer to fit onto Douglass's heavy shoulders, and the effect was like looking at a snowman with the head of a pea. Skidder's features had been superimposed on, or chemically dissolved into . . . I don't know how it was done but Stanfield Standish's IT Machine took Roy Douglass, took his gestures, his mannerisms, his screen presence, and melded them into a mongrel that had Douglass's brawny, mature body but Skidder Freebody's petulant, adolescent face.

Where did the computerized Skidder start and Roy Douglass end? The flat, psychotic stare belonged to Skidder Freebody. But the eyes blinked when Roy Douglass's eyes had blinked. And when they turned to look at Arlene de Grasse, they filled with tears the way Roy Douglass's eyes had always filled with tears. But those same tears were now puddling in the flat, lashless eyes of a rock superstar whose trademark was dropping his pants and mooning teenaged girls.

Nor should we forget the woman winding yarn by the fire. You're right that it wasn't Arlene de Grasse anymore. The body was still small and graceful, and the clothes were still the same clothes and the fingers still pulled against the same yarn. But instead of being Arlene de Grasse's face, it was the face of the actress who'd just gotten Europe's highest award for portraying a bleeding American flag. Lucrezia's features merged with those of Arlene de Grasse, and the computerized hybrid that resulted was now looking up at the actor who had once been Roy Douglass with an expression on its face that was a cross between a leer and a sneer.

The screen went black.

Stanfield Standish stood beside his Image Transforming IT Machine. He put his hand on top of it and said, "The excerpt you witnessed from *A Poor Man's Paradise* is just a hint of things to come from Stanfield Standish Presents. Our long-range goal is to Image Transform all of the Cinema Select Artists movies we have acquired. The first film to be completely recast in the new Stanfield Standish mold will be the classic *Idlewild*. Playing the part of Noah, the brilliant anti-Nazi scientist, will be Skidder Freebody. And Pearl, the woman whose patriotism is beyond reproach, will be played by our new Stanfield Standish contract player, Lucrezia."

Still standing beside his IT Machine, Stanfield Standish looked proud. Possessive. Terrific. Blue pin-striped suit. European cut. Geometric tie. And a silk handkerchief that looked like it had made a perfect three-point landing into his breast pocket.

Standish projected the confidence and control of a man who had arrived. *He* was the one who set the standards and wrote the rules. It was *he* who issued orders, hired, fired, made decisions, praised, punished, forgave. The world was *his* world, and it would be Stanfield Standish's neo-international view that ultimately prevailed. All borders would crumble, dissolve, including those of excellence. High would become low. Low would become lower. Images would not be the only things transformed. Standards would also be redefined. Lucrezia would become Sarah Bernhardt. Skidder Freebody would stride down Main Street at High Noon.

And smutty hands would leave dirty little fingerprints on all of our old heros' souls.

CHAPTER

11

The party Stanfield Standish announced that he would be throwing after his broadcast stirred up the little town of Stilton-on-Hudson like fluttery bridesmaids waiting for the bride. The local sheriff (a full-time employee of the Department of Highways who drove his patrol car on weekends) had to work overtime to prevent limousine gridlock. And the catering services in Belton-on-Hudson, the nearest town with a good restaurant, had been on red alert for two months with dawn deliveries of Beluga caviar.

Of course, since Standish's announcement took place on Valentine's Day, the theme of the party was hearts. The cakes were shaped like hearts. There were heart-shaped flower arrangements, and the hors d'oeuvres were served on heart-shaped trays.

Five years later, when Chief Lon Bandy and I got together to knock around a few facts, he was still scratching his head over what he called the "whole darned commotion."

I like Chief Bandy. In the four or five times we've sat down to discuss this case, I've always come away admiring his false modesty and down-and-dirty realism. He says he doesn't think much of his own forensic skills; that he can't tell a microscope from a kaleidoscope; and that in hiring him, the town got just what it paid for, which he pretends to think isn't all that much. But he brags about his skill at hauling in the town drunk, getting cats and raccoons out of trees, talking to schoolkids about drugs, directing traffic at Christmas or during Jewish high holidays, picking up returned runaways from the bus station, and protecting Stilton-on-Hudson's only prostitute from what he calls "the wrath of church ladies." ("Heck, she's only obeying what I call the law of supply and demand.")

Chief Bandy's public comment about the entire Standish "commotion" was that other than cordoning off the vehicle after it had become a fire scene, "it didn't have a gol-darned thing to do with me.

"Heck, them big boys from the governor's office came in with those cute little decals on their windbreakers, saying they were the official New York State Fire Investigators. Then they'd whip out their combs so their hair looked Just So for the cameras when they announced their Official Findings to them people who report the news. . . ."

I have heard Chief Bandy testify in court, and it's amazing how his grammar improves when he isn't talking to politicians, attorneys, or members of the press. In fact, by our third meeting, I expected him to be quoting long passages from *Lady Windermere's Fan*.

But five years ago, which was also five years before I got involved in the case, Chief Bandy had a good reason to be annoyed. Bandy said that Standish was treating Stilton-on-Hudson as his personal fiefdom. The townspeople didn't mind. He was bringing in money. He staffed his estate with Jed, Ethel, and the gang, who'd been laid off ever since Henderson Tool & Die closed. His people ate at local restaurants, bought toothpaste at the Stilton Pharmacy, and had their cars fixed at Freddie's local garage.

Standish even occasionally took the Pierce-Arrow or one of his other classic cars to pick up a celebrity at the Stilton-on-Hudson airport or to drive a visiting dignitary up and around the reservoir, past the turnoff to Paddy Lakes, to the Cliff Overlook Restaurant at the end of Snake Hill Road.

And so, Stanfield Standish, whether he was liked or disliked for being there, was incontrovertibly a *presence* in the community.

Standish's primary residence, along with his corporate headquarters, was in Wilmington, Delaware. But—a weekend here, a week there—he came up often enough to make local cash registers flutter, give Chief Bandy heartburn, and cause a "commotion" on Valentine's Day, when he seemed to have invited all of Hollywood into town.

And, based on my analysis of numerous videotapes I later reviewed of the festivities, Hollywood did come. The most visible were aging teenagers with shaved heads or safety pins in their ears, who lip-synch on all-music television channels to choreography that simulates sexual encounters with fire hydrants.

The managers of these video stars had tagged along. As did their producers and directors, their mixed-gender paramours, their attorneys, hair dressers, press agents, and drug dealers. Present, too, were a selection of dapper Japanese gentlemen who acted as though they had just purchased all five of the Great Lakes. And for good measure, there were a radical politician from San Francisco, an obscure mayor, a famous governor, a socialite on voluntary leave from a drug rehab, and a representative sample of security personnel in blazers with walkie-talkies.

And, of course, the press.

Some uninvited guests also made an appearance outside the gate of Standish's estate. They were there to protest his IT Machine and how Standish planned to use IT to alter the Cinema Select films. This group called itself "The Curators" and said they wanted to do only what curators do, that being to take care of a valuable collection. Their methods were lawful, civilized, almost boring. They were few in number, but the word was out that their numbers were growing.

How they had found out about the IT Machine and managed to organize a protest on what seemed to be such short notice was a mystery I didn't solve until just before our case went to court.

It was thought, though, that Stanfield Standish left his party early because he wanted to avoid a confrontation with this group.

His arrival was what I've heard described as a "photo opportunity." He drove up in a sleek 1930 maroon-and-black Duesenberg and stood on the running board waving at the crowd for about five minutes before he turned the car over to his chauffeur. Then he strode up the steps of his columned Greek Revival manor house like a politician after a big win. He welcomed his guests in what he called his ballroom and said a few complimentary words about his two new stars. Lucrezia was there in a gas mask, black mesh stockings, and combat boots. Skidder Freebody made an entrance wearing a white tuxedo but with no shirt, no socks, and bare feet. He also told everyone who would listen that he didn't have on any underwear.

Subsequent interviews with domestic servants and other witnesses gave us an idea of Stanfield Standish's actions from that point on.

Standish told his chauffeur to drive the Duesenberg around back and leave the motor running. Then he passed his butler in the kitchen, who later told investigators that he'd seen Standish go out the back door of the house fifteen minutes after he had arrived.

Rebecca Katz, managing editor of the *Stilton-on-Hudson News*, said she'd sensed a "story" the minute Standish left the ballroom. She slipped away from the crowd and worked her way through the bushes to the rear of Standish's house, where she thought he would reappear.

He did.

She waylaid him just as he was opening the door to his Duesenberg, pushed a tiny microphone at his mouth, and said, "Mr. Standish, not only my paper but the entire world is anxious to know how in God's name you can take a great work of art like *Idlewild* and ruin it by putting an idiot like Lucrezia and an unregenerate cretin like Skidder Freebody in the leads?"

The last words Stanfield Standish were known to have spoken were those picked up by Rebecca Katz's tape recorder. Some have said that they would make a meaningful epitaph for his tomb:

"Bottom line," he said. "They're mine."

The following day, a series of altered masterpieces appeared in the *Stilton-on-Hudson News* under the headline:

BOTTOM LINE, THEY'RE MINE
OR—IF STANFIELD STANDISH
RULED THE WORLD . . .

Among the images portrayed were:

Rodin's massive, muscled sculpture, *The Thinker*, the visage of which had been supplanted by Skidder Freebody's vacuous face.

Botticelli's *Venus* rising out of the foam, with a snaky tongue flicking hungrily out of *Lucrezia*'s mouth, as if to catch a fly;

Similarly transformed were Michelangelo's *David*, Velasquez's *Venus and Cupid*, Titian's *Flora*, and Gainsborough's *Blue Boy*.

The illustrated feature, with a byline by Rebecca Katz, was picked up by the wire services and reprinted in every major newspaper throughout the country.

CHAPTER

12

People want to *possess* their celebrities. We might not actually like any or all of the people in the limelight, but we take pleasure in both their accomplishments and their indiscretions. We may look down on them, feel superior to them, admire them or envy them, but what really matters is that we love to *watch* them.

They have better suntans than we do, their wives are better looking, their cars have more horsepower, and their monthly transatlantic phone bills are higher than the mortgage payments on our houses.

We like to see where and how they live, whom they're sleeping with, and what they wear.

We accord them celebrity status because they're larger and richer than life and because, like the mountains, they're there.

And so, five years ago, when Stanfield Standish died, the gory manner of his death hit us like a jolt, and what we felt was something akin to actual grief. I wasn't the only one who got caught up in the daily, detailed accounts of where his car had been found, who found it, how it was discovered, and so on.

And I hadn't even liked the guy.

After having spent almost two decades practicing law, there's only one conclusion I've been able to come to about justice, and that is that it isn't always served. The wheel isn't consistently round. What we sow we don't always reap. And people who have sinned against us often go through life with radiant complexions, clear eyes, happy marriages, and platinum credit cards.

So, when fate seems to take a right turn for a change and does away with a guy whose highest goal in life was to immortalize mediocrity, I think I can be excused for having indulged in a little good, old-fashioned, Old Testament glee.

STANFIELD STANDISH CREMATED IN VEHICLE BLAZE

At 3:00 this morning, Stanfield Standish, multi-millionaire media magnate of the news and entertainment empirc that bears his name, was found burned to death in a Duesenberg automobile, one of a collection of American vintage vehicles that he owned.

Standish's body was discovered by handyman/painter Ralph Arkus, age 55, who resides in Belton-on-Hudson. Mr. Arkus, employed part-time as a maintenance worker for the Cliff Overlook Restaurant, had been called to the restaurant at 11:30 p.m. to assist with a minor plumbing leak. The restaurant is located at the north end of the Stilton Reservoir. After making his repairs, he returned home at approximately 3 a.m., at which time he encountered the fire.

Mr. Arkus stated that he almost ran into Standish's vehicle, which was parked in the middle of Snake Hill Road, near the turnoff to Old Fishing

Hole Road. He said that thick, black smoke was coming out of the passenger compartment of the car.

Although a positive identification of the driver has not yet been made, the description of the deceased and of the wallet contents, some of which survived the fire, indicate that the driver *was* Stanfield Standish.

No foul play is suspected, stated a representative of the New York State Fire Marshal's Office. Investigators from the Stilton-on-Hudson Volunteer Fire Department are looking into the possibility of mechanical failure as the cause of the fire, which may have originated in the engine compartment of the car.

Representatives from Mr. Standish's family are expected to arrive in Stilton-on-Hudson tomorrow to arrange for the memorial service and funeral.

In response to what has been described as impending Wall Street panic about the future of Standish Communications, a press statement has been issued from SSN corporate headquarters naming Astrid Scheidler, sister of the late Stanfield Standish, as the new president of both Stanfield Standish News and Stanfield Standish Presents.

Miss Scheidler has an MBA from the Harvard Business School, and for the past six years has been Chief Executive Officer of the Harriet O'Brien's department store chain.

Within six hours of Standish's death, his cable network was televising hour-long retrospectives about his life and achievements. This show was broadcast twice daily for a week. I don't subscribe to cable television; but after I was brought into the case, I was able to study a videocassette of the telecast, and one thing about that program held a chilling fascination for me.

Really extraordinary.

The retrospective covered Standish's life from his childhood to the last picture taken of him just before he died. What I noticed in viewing this video, which I hadn't picked up on before, is that over the years, and taking into account the differences in their ages, Stanfield Standish had practically *become* his father.

This struck me as odd, since they hadn't looked all that much alike when I'd met them.

On the second day after Standish's body was discovered, Mrs. Eva Scheidler, Standish's mother, made a brief statement to the press. She was about eighty years old at the time and so ugly that Wylie Nolan said her face looked like the stuff you scrape off the bottom of your shoe.

Eva Scheidler was exceptionally tall. Even with the inevitable geriatric stoop, she was almost six feet. She had a long nose that gravitated down toward a narrow witch's chin that levitated up. She had flat blue eyes, thick black eyebrows, and a turkey neck. She had the same hands that her son had, with the same tapered fingers and the same look of dead-white ineffectuality.

And when Mrs. Scheidler made her televised announcement, her voice was as expressionless as her eyes.

> My family and I are deeply saddened by the loss of my beloved son, and we express gratitude to both the State Police and the Governor's special fire investigation unit for the sensitivity and concern they have shown to us in our time of grief. We have full confidence that all of the Standish holdings will be managed in the same professional and highly profitable manner that has always been the hallmark of Standish Enterprises.

By the third day after Standish's death, Courtland Motors' legal department had received notification from her attorneys that Eva Scheidler, et al., had filed papers listing Courtland Motors Corporation as defendant in a wrongful-death lawsuit. The suit claimed that defective workmanship and parts from the Classic Cars Division of Courtland Motors, Incorporated, had caused overheating to the engine compartment of the Duesenberg, which resulted in the fire that killed Stanfield Standish.

The dollar amounts in the *Standish* versus *Courtland Motors* lawsuit were high. Fifty million for "conscious pain and suffering," which derived from the allegation that at the time of the fire Standish was alive, conscious, and aware that he was going to die. Standish's people also wanted three million dollars for the Duesenberg, and by the time I was brought into the case, we still weren't sure that all of the numbers were in.

CHAPTER
13

There are two professions I consider almost the same in terms of living a vicarious life. One is the actor. He has to speak someone else's lines, sleep with someone else's wife, and suffer from someone else's mistakes. Which could be fun, unless you're playing a tragic character like Othello, who has to die every night to "O beware, my lord, of jealousy; It is the green-eyed monster which doth mock the meat it feeds on."

Exhausting.

Product liability lawyers are in some ways comparable to actors, but without the emotional pyrotechnics. We have to become proficient at professions in which we have no interest, learn things about dishwasher motors we'd rather not know, and forge emotional bonds to everything from a carburetor to a defrost timer in order to understand and defend a client's product when it's the subject of a lawsuit.

The actor becomes someone he isn't; the lawyer develops expertise in areas about which he doesn't really care.

But an engineer cares. Really cares. He has to. His life is valves, clamps, and pressure gauges. Both his self-esteem and his salary depend on the products that he builds. *He* has to build them right, and *I* have to find out what right is so that I can defend the product's integrity in the event that he is sued. Pretty dry stuff for the most part.

The emotional payoff for the attorney, if he likes to try his own cases, is in court. That's when he gets to pull out all the stops and go for the gold.

First, though, both the attorney and the actor have to learn their lines. For me, that means reviewing the complaint, which means finding out what my client is accused of having done or not done, provided or not provided, performed or not performed, warned or not warned—as in Failure-to-Warn lawsuits in which, for example, a pillow manufacturer might be sued because he hadn't printed in twelve languages and fourteen-foot-high letters on the plastic bag in which the pillow came:

THIS IS NOT A TOY.
DO NOT WRAP YOUR CHILDREN'S HEADS IN IT.

I admit I'm being facetious, but that's because I would expect normal parents not to wrap their children's heads in plastic bags, even without instructions to the contrary.

Of course, there are always going to be those embarrassing cases where a client is so obviously at fault the only honest thing we can do is pull him aside and whisper those nine words no defendant in a civil suit ever wants to hear, i.e.: "I think we should settle this out of court."

Or, as Arthur M. Harris wrote to his son, *"Many and many a dispute have I settled without the trouble or expense of going to court. . . .*

The true lawyer is a pacifier, not a provoker. His efforts are more than commercial, higher and nobler than merely mercenary. On his integrity and good sense depend the well-being of the community, which prospers when time is saved by a peaceable settlement of disputes, and money goes into the land, instead of into the pockets of ravenous lawyers for fees."

Ah . . . love that man.

Settlement, however, was the farthest thing from my mind when I reviewed the material given to me in the *Standish* versus *Courtland Motors Corporation* case.

First, I want to introduce you to a few things you may not know about Courtland Motors. Such as that the firm has never competed for the market in midsize or midpriced automobiles; it manufactures only luxury cars and top-of-the-line recreational vehicles. Nothing about Courtland Motors Corporation has ever been "mid" anything, because a Courtland car is *not* what the average American family man buys to cart around the groceries or pick up the kids from hockey practice.

It's the kind of car you dream of owning after the kids are out of college, when you've sold the house in Levittown and have moved to the circa 1776 Federal-style farmhouse in Pennsylvania with your second wife (the one who really likes you).

Courtland's all-terrain vehicle is the stuff of a man's dreams; it's an eight-cylinder, hard-driven, no-nonsense, elemental tool. It's the car that wildcat oilmen use to get to remote fields off rocky back roads, or that construction engineers drive over mud when half of California has slid into the Pacific Ocean. It is sturdy, it is reliable, it gets good mileage, and it costs a lot of money.

Why? Because almost *everything* in a Courtland is made out of metal, wood, leather, or glass. There is virtually no plastic. No polyester. No vinyl. And there's never been a contemporary Courtland car under six cylinders or that you could buy for under forty thousand dollars. An early advertising slogan claimed that "all Courtland cars are luxury cars."

They weren't exaggerating.

Add to all of that my favorite option in a car. Every vehicle that

Courtland makes has window vents. For those too young to remember, these are the small wings that cars used to have on their front or back windows.

Manufacturers stopped making them when air conditioning became a standard feature. Except for Courtland, and except that Courtland didn't just keep making side vents; they made and improved them. Now, you can crank them open or pull them open, or just press a digitalized computer whatnot and direct as little or as much fresh air as you like on your face.

There are two bottom lines in the manufacture, marketing, servicing, and selling of a Courtland Motors product: luxury and control. For example, each Courtland car has a heavy I-beam frame and a sturdy steel chassis. If you snap your fingers into any other car, its body is so tinny you can hear it "ping." Hit a Courtland with anything short of a crowbar, and you're the one that's likely to go "ping."

And then, there's the matter of control. The windows open and shut automatically *and* manually. The doors lock and unlock automatically *and* manually. The mirrors, lights, sound system, gas, hood, and trunk locks can all be adjusted by just pressing a button or turning a knob or a key. For every computerized system in the car, there's a mechanical backup so that if I ever drive my Courtland off a bridge into Lake Erie, I don't have to sit in my airtight coffin and wait to die. I can just roll down the windows like people used to be able to do and save my own life.

But none of that has anything to do with my lawsuit because it wasn't a Courtland car that burned; it was a 1930 J series Duesenberg Arlington sedan.

So why, if Courtland Motors Corporation manufactured only new, technologically sophisticated machines, were they being named in a lawsuit involving a car made by a company that went out of business over sixty years ago?

The answer lies in the history of the company.

Courtland Motors was conceived as a family business and is still owned and operated by people with the Courtland name. Since its inception in 1927, only two chief executives have led the concern. The second is the son of the first. Both are alive and active at the plant.

Oscar Courtland, the first president of Courtland Motors, came with his three brothers from England to America in 1914. The brothers learned about cars by building bicycle engines, and about racing cars by building airplanes.

Their Courtland Model A came in second at the 1920 Daytona Race with a land speed of 150 miles per hour. The car that came in first had an engine crafted by Fred and August Duesenberg, and made a new land-speed record of 156.04 miles per hour.

In 1920.

Hard to believe.

Each of the four Courtland brothers contributed something different to the manufacture of their cars. My favorite is Charlie, the one with the daredevil eyes. In the testing lab at Courtland, there's a framed picture of Charlie wearing a leather helmet at a crazy angle on his head. He has one foot up on the fender of a battered speedster and a leather jacket flung cavalierly over his shoulder. And the look of exhilaration in his eyes makes you think that if life had been hovering around the planet for a few million years searching for the perfect place to land, it had found it . . . in Charlie.

Last time I visited corporate headquarters at Courtland Motors, Charlie Courtland was ninety-one years old and still going into the office every day. I won't vouch for his labor output, but the staff love him; and I can state unequivocally that he's indispensable to office morale. When I passed him in the corridor on my way to the legal department, I heard him propose to two secretaries and offer to run away to the Cayman Islands with a third.

Charlie test-drove and raced the new cars and also made suggestions about what had to be fixed and how to fix it. Designing new automobile engines and chassis was the responsibility of Charlie's older brothers, Russell and Leo Courtland. Russell not only designed the Courtland chassis, he also got rid of running boards two years ahead of the competition; and Leo almost single-handedly created the early Courtland "look."

Russell and Leo are still on the board of directors. But unlike Oscar and Charlie, they come in only three times a week.

The youngest brother, Oscar, is the heart and soul of the operation. He is the chief who passes around the peace pipe and makes his brothers smoke it whether they want to or not. And it is Oscar who passes judgment on second- and third-generation Courtlands to see who will be allowed in the family business and who will not.

Diverse opinions are encouraged within the family structure of the Courtland Motors Corporation. Dissension is not.

Which is why, sixty-four years after Courtland was founded, it is still both family-owned and very profitable.

Now, to get back to why Courtland Motors was being sued for a product defect in a J series Duesenberg Arlington motor car.

One day, when all four brothers were at the office, a 1932 Cord L-29 two-door sedan sputtered and wheezed into the executive parking lot of Courtland Motors Corporation. After its cacophonous arrival, the driver of this vintage vehicle started and continued to honk his horn nonstop, creating such discord and commotion that one by one, Charlie, Leo, Russell, and Oscar Courtland were all drawn to the window and looked out.

"Can it possibly be . . . ?" Charlie said to Oscar.

"He looks a good deal like . . ." Leo began.

"But I thought he died during . . ." Russell contributed.

"My, my." Oscar shook his head, thereby putting the whole question to rest. "Izzy certainly does look old."

The man who was the subject of this speculation was something of an apparition. He was as grizzly as an old-time prospector and as manic as a jack-in-the-box. His thin face, although deeply lined, was still recognizable to the Courtland brothers as the high-voltage mechanic who'd worked in their engineering department over forty years before. He sprang out of his car (he was only seventy-two years old at the time), strode to the front left tire of the Cord, and kicked it.

Oscar, Charlie, Leo, and Russell got down to the parking lot just in time to hear Izzy yell, "There. Take that, you son-of-a-bitch!" He moved rapidly over to the other side of the car and started to kick the right front tire.

Then several things happened almost simultaneously. First, the Courtland brothers yanked Izzy away from the Cord. Next, all five men started talking at once.

"What happened to . . . ?"

"When did you . . . ?"

"Where are the . . . ?"

"How did they . . . ?"

"Did he ever . . . ?"

And so on.

What they found out about Izzy was that after he left Courtland Motors, he bought a piece of Thompson Aircraft and went to work in their engineering department. Twenty years later, he sold his Thompson Aircraft stock, used some of the money to buy land in Florida, invested the rest in triple-tax-free municipal bonds, and then spent the next twenty-five years designing refrigerator motors in Detroit. Three years before this reunion in the parking lot, he had retired. During the intervening forty-five years since the Courtland brothers had last seen him, Izzy had married and buried three wives. Otherwise he had multiplied his fortune, and he'd kept every single car he had ever owned.

Izzy collected and restored them.

Or at least, he tried to.

He'd been having trouble lately because the old craftsmen were dying out, old casting molds were being thrown out, and modern machinists didn't want to bother hand-tooling small quantities of obsolete parts.

Izzy ranted. Izzy raved.

Meanwhile, the Courtland brothers had gathered around Izzy's car.

It was an odd experience for them, because from the day they'd designed their first piston and installed their first air filter, the four men had looked to the future instead of to the past. None of them collected cars, and if it hadn't been for Oscar Courtland's wife—no one knew her name; she was always called Mrs. Oscar—there wouldn't even be a Courtland archives. Luckily, Mrs. Oscar began to document events that concerned her family from the first newspaper that covered the first race that a Courtland car won. Mrs. Oscar is still the company librarian.

But you would never catch her husband there. Or Charlie. Or Leo. Or Russell. Their eyes were always pointed at the future.

It would be fair to say that in all of the years since they'd first driven Izzy's Cord L-29, they hadn't given it a moment's thought. Which makes their reaction in the parking lot all the more interesting.

Charlie slipped into the driver's seat and examined the instrument panel. Russell popped open the hood and poked at the 298.6-cubic-inch, 125-bhp straight-eight engine. Leo ran his hands over the radiator grill, scraping off mud spatters with his fingernails. And Oscar stood to one side, his left hand cupping his right elbow, his right hand cupping his jaw, and his fingers drumming thoughtfully against his cheek.

After a few moments, the three older brothers noticed Oscar's inactivity. They looked at him. He looked back at them. He smiled. They smiled. They were all thinking the same thing. That this was something they could have a lot of fun with.

And that was the frame in time and their frame of mind when the new division of Courtland Motors Company was born.

Courtland Classic Cars never really made money. But it hasn't lost money, either. If you take public relations into account, it's probably done the parent company a lot more good than harm. And people who own vintage American automobiles greeted its formation like the arrival of a serum for a disease about which they'd long given up hope.

Courtland Classic Cars operated a twenty-four-hour hotline with mechanics and salespeople standing by to answer questions about old cars. It published a catalogue, maintained a busy mail-order business, and occupied an area about the size of a DC-10 airplane hangar. Some of the mechanics who restored the cars brought to Courtland Motors were retired Courtland executives who'd gotten tired of playing golf and liked the idea of fiddling around with the same cars that they'd designed or built forty or fifty years before.

The cost to restore an old car is high. But consider this. Five years after spending one hundred and forty thousand dollars to restore the 1940 Packard Darrin that you bought for only sixty thousand dollars, it's going to be worth at least seventy-five percent more than you paid for it.

On my first trip to corporate headquarters, I toured the Courtland plant in Detroit. I felt like I was on another planet. The workshop is spotless and cheerful. Every morning, the mechanics are handed a pair of clean, white overalls, which they return at night stained with grease, paint, and oil. Audiotapes of old radio shows from the 1920s, 1930s, and 1940s are piped in on speakers, because someone got the idea that it would be fun to work in an ambiance of the era when the cars were first built.

Courtland Motors was born out of a love for machines. And in this atmosphere, the business grew, thrived, and survived for over sixty years.

Now, Courtland Classic Cars was being sued for an amount in excess of fifty million dollars. And the brothers were royally pissed off because the division *being* sued existed solely as a labor of love and was never even expected to turn a profit.

The lawsuit had been filed five years before, for work done during the restoration of a 1930 Duesenberg Arlington sedan, owned, at that time, by Hugo Scheidler, father of Stanfield Standish.

Courtland gave me carte blanche to be in a dozen different places at the same time, analyze documents that had never found their way to my desk, read the minds of witnesses we had never deposed, and, in less than a month, go up against Clyde Prouty, the most successful plaintiff's product-liability lawyer in the country. And they expected me to come out with an unequivocal win.

And there would be no settlement negotiations.

I bet you think I was nervous.

Hell. I couldn't wait for the trial to begin.

CHAPTER
14

Wylie Nolan and I met him at the door to the C & J Bake Shop. Newspaper clips and the corner of a Kodak print envelope bulged out of the manila folder he was carrying. He shifted a dead cigar from one side of his mouth to the other with a deft upheaval of teeth and tongue and said, "Yup. Chief Lon Bandy of the Stilton-on-Hudson Police Department. That's who I am. That's what I do." Bandy thrust a callused hand in my direction and we shook. Then he did the same for Wylie Nolan.

He was wearing dirt-kicking boots, a red-and-black hunting jacket, and a baseball cap with the words "Police Chief" stitched across the front. "Smallest police department in the state," he said, motioning to the waitress. "A cup of coffee for me, Muriel. Leaded. How about you gentlemen. Leaded or unleaded?"

I stared at him blankly.

Wylie translated, "Caffeine or no caffeine?"

"Caffeine." I wasn't going to have these guys think I was a wussy.

Wylie grinned at the waitress. "Brewed decaffeinated if you have it, ma'am." Then he grinned at me as though he'd known what I was thinking.

Muriel came right back with three thick crockery mugs, a metal milk dispenser, three spoons, and a pink plastic ashtray. The chief temporarily surrendered his cigar.

"Fine, Muriel. Just fine. And since these two gentlemen here are paying, why don't you also bring me one of them glazed things with all of that creamy custard inside." The chief turned to us. "What about it, boys?"

I ordered a sticky bun.

Wylie said, "Anything chocolate."

Bandy went on, "In this here town, it's my word that's the law." Muriel brought the pastries. Each was sitting on a white doily inside a small dessert dish made of the same thick crockery as the mugs. "But with the County Sheriff looking over my left shoulder, and the State Police looking over my right, it ain't more than a word is just about all I ever get."

He laughed, lifted up his mug, and said, "Cheers, boys!"

We drank coffee for about fifteen minutes and conversed about pretty much nothing: "Yep. Caught me a three-pound bass down by Wilkins Creek." And, "Nope. Deer season's a week shorter this year." That kind of stuff.

Bandy was on his second custard doughnut and Wylie was nursing a chocolate brownie when we'd finally gotten to the point in the conversation where Wylie was casually tossing off credentials while pretending not to do so, and Chief Bandy was circling him, poking his nose in a little here, pawing at the ground a little there.

I was beginning to get a glimmer of what the rules were. Wylie and I come in out of nowhere. We're the visiting team. But it's Bandy's turf. What Wylie was establishing, I assumed, was that we could be trusted (i.e., *he* could be trusted. I was just keeping my mouth shut and trying not to look too much like a lawyer), and that we were all playing on the same team.

Wylie said, ". . . maybe you remember me from the ninety-hour course on arson investigation that I teach for the Attorney General?"

"Well, I'll be—go to hell," Bandy responded. "Now that you mention it, I do remember. You said something that always stuck with me. That looking for a fire's called a cause and origin investigation, but that rightly it should be called origin and cause. You said this was so because first a person's got to figure out where the fire started before he can figure out what it was that caused the blaze. Made sense to me."

"When did you take the course, Chief?"

"Five, six years ago. Before the State Police took over arson. We didn't have anyone to do cause and origin back then. And some barns were burning. Maybe one or two of them fires was caused by spontaneous combustion. Wet hay, like the book says. But two more hunting sheds and a log cabin burned down, and I figured that combustion wasn't all that spontaneous after a while."

"Did you catch the guy?" Wylie asked.

"Sure did. Burned down another eleven sheds though, before we got his trace. Turned out he had a grudge against you city folk. Sheds belonged mostly to people that only come up here during hunting season. Guess he figured they was shooting *his* deer. Don't know what got into him. Always was a little stupid, though."

"Who was he?"

Chief Bandy rolled his cigar between his thumb and forefinger and a sly gleam came into his eye. He looked right at Wylie.

"I'll tell you what, son. Why don't you tell me who *you* think it was setting all of them fires?"

Wylie flashed his daredevil grin.

"Next time give me a hard one, Chief. Your perp was a volunteer fireman."

Slowly, slowly, a gruff smile deepened the heavy creases in Bandy's face, and he nodded his head. His gaze was deliberate. He didn't blink. He pulled a book of matches out of his jacket pocket, flipped up the cover, bent a match and dragged it against the striker, all with one hand. He took a few short pulls on his cigar and addressed me.

"A few years back, I heard your friend here talk for a couple, three hours about how to figure where a fire started, and if you're lucky, how maybe you can find out what started that fire. He showed us a videotape of a fire in an automobile." Bandy paused for a moment and looked at the burning tip of his cigar. "But I never was real comfortable doing a car fire myself. Cars got lots of steel in 'em. Lots of combustibles. Lots of polyvinylchloride in a small, contained space."

Wylie pushed the metal creamer, spoons, and plastic ashtray out of the way. He put our three dessert dishes in the center of the table in a straight line, one behind the other, the edges touching. The paper doilies were still intact, so I could see that Bandy's custard doughnut came first. My sticky bun was second. And Wylie's chocolate brownie was last.

"The way I do a car fire," Wylie said, "is to divide the automobile into three compartments, as if they're three rooms of a house." He pointed to the custard dish. "Engine compartment." Then to the sticky-bun dish. "Passenger compartment." And lastly, to the brownie dish. "Trunk.

"There are no connecting doors between the three rooms in this house, and unless someone or something comes along to breach the structural integrity of the walls, there is no communication between any of the three rooms, either." Wylie looked first at me, and then at Chief Bandy. "Follow?"

"We follow."

"Given what I've just told you, then, if I had a fire in the engine compartment,"—he lit a match and dropped it on the custard-smeared doily in the first dish—"what would you expect to happen? Where would you expect the fire to go? How far would you expect the fire to extend? What would you expect to burn?"

The flame sat quietly for a second or two in the center of the doily. Then the paper beneath and around it ignited, the fire flared into a wide, shapeless flame and slowly consumed the rest of the doily. It sent out a few bits of floating gray ash and extinguished.

Wylie lighted another match and dropped it in the dish that had held the sticky-bun. "Passenger-compartment fire," he said. The same thing happened to the doily in the center dish.

His third match flared into the brownie plate. "And our last fire takes place in the trunk."

Chief Bandy and I watched the third flame consume its small bit of doily and go out.

"The point is," Wylie explained, "that the fire in the custard plate didn't extend to the combustible in the sticky-bun plate, and the fire in the sticky-bun plate didn't extend to the doily in the brownie plate. If a fire had begun accidentally in any one of the three compartments of the car, that compartment and that compartment only would have burned. Other than minor flame-and-smoke impingement, the fire would not have extended to any of the other sections of the car.

"Engine compartment." Wylie slid the custard plate forward on the table. "Between it and the passenger compartment is a piece of metal called a bulkhead or a firewall. The purpose of the firewall is to protect the passengers from contamination by anything that gets into the engine compartment. This would include dust, heat, noise, vibrations, fumes, fluid, and, if the occasion arose, fire. In a contemporary vehicle, which is made of lighter and cheaper synthetic materials than earlier models, the design of the firewall is still sufficient to compartmentalize almost any flames that might initiate in the engine compartment, unless they penetrated the heating and air-conditioning openings. And if a fire in an engine achieved sufficient momentum to spread through these ducts, we can usually still trace a clear burn pattern back to whatever failure in the engine compartment caused the flames.

"In a vehicle as old as the Duesenberg, though, which has a cast-aluminum dashboard that extends from the back of the instrument panel all the way down to a wooden toe-board, there is a solid wall of insulation between the engine and the passenger compartments. Also, if a fire had started in or on the engine block of this old car, there are so few flammables in the engine compartment to sustain combustion that, like the doily in the custard dish, the fire would have just consumed itself and gone out."

Wylie next slid forth the sticky-bun dish. "If there had been an accidental fire in the passenger compartment, let's say a carelessly discarded cigarette on the upholstery or a short circuit in the overhead light, the same compartmentalization would have occurred. The Duesenberg was built before flame-retardant fabrics had been developed, so the broadcloth and cushion materials would have ignited rapidly. But they wouldn't have burned long. And the fire wouldn't have been very hot. It definitely wouldn't have been hot enough to melt cast aluminum and burn through the fire wall to the engine compartment. And it wouldn't have burned in the other direction, either, through the metal sheet separating the back seat of the passenger compartment from the trunk."

Wylie slid the brownie dish forward. "Which brings us to the trunk. We have some small, insignificant burning on the exterior hood. Some radiant heat damage inside the trunk. Some melting. But there are no mechanical parts inside the trunk to overheat and malfunction. There's very little oxygen to sustain fire. And fortunately, there were no flames inside the trunk, which is positioned directly over a twenty-six-gallon gas tank."

Wylie pushed the three dishes back into alignment.

He asked Chief Bandy, "Did you bring along any photographs of the Duesenberg?"

Bandy pulled two Kodak envelopes out of his folder and sorted through the contents. He tossed a four-by-six picture on the table. It was a long shot of the car in which Stanfield Standish had been found dead, taken from the driver's side. The photograph gave a clear view of the entire car, extending from front bumper to rear bumper.

Wylie glanced briefly at the picture and held it out to us.

"Which of the compartments in this vehicle are burned?" he asked.

Bandy and I looked at each other. We both said, "All of them."

"Given what I've explained to you, then, how could that have happened?"

I shrugged.

Chief Bandy executed another upheaval of his cigar.

Wylie jerked a paper napkin from a dispenser on the table behind us and rolled it up lengthwise to form a cylinder. He laid it across all three dishes. Then he lighted a match to the end of the napkin that extended over the custard dish. The napkin ignited. The flame moved slowly across all three dishes, eventually consuming the napkin and leaving behind only a straw-shaped residue of loose, gray ash.

Wylie dropped his finger to the charred napkin, tapped gently, and the ash fell into the three small dessert plates.

"All three compartments of the car are now burned." Wylie looked up at Lon Bandy. "Tell me how it happened, Chief."

Bandy shifted the cigar from one side of his mouth to the other. "Arson," he said.

CHAPTER

15

There are high points in almost every case that a lawyer works on. The more he loves his job, the more high points. *Standish* versus *Courtland Motors Corporation* should have been a problem from day one. We got into it late. We were always playing catch-up, and the stakes were much too high to allow any relaxation of tension. But from the minute I got the call asking me to undertake Courtland's defense until the day the verdict was brought in, I was happy.

I don't mean to imply by this that we won the case, or that the judge was sympathetic to the defense—he almost always ruled in plaintiff's favor—but that I was able to put together a dream team of experts. It was like having Leonardo da Vinci on palette, Caruso doing vocals, and Babe Ruth at home plate. Win or lose, it was a hell of a party.

What were we up against? First, we had a lawsuit alleging a product defect. Since the subject Duesenberg had been manufactured by a long-defunct company, we were obviously not being sued for product design. But since Courtland Classics restored the vehicle, we *were* being sued for just about everything else. The complaint made vague allegations that one or some or all of the parts located, reconditioned, and/or manufactured and subsequently put in the vintage vehicle by Courtland were either defective, improperly installed, or dysfunctional.

This complaint also claimed that there were unspecified flaws in the carburetor and/or fuel-inlet line and/or fuel pump. Affixed to this grab bag of infamy were allegations of improper installation of fuel-line clamps, which permitted the fuel line to come into contact with the exhaust manifold. The only thing left out of the complaint was the accusation that the exhaust pipes had deliberately reached inside the passenger compartment, wrapped themselves around Standish's neck, and strangled him to death.

In a letter to his son, my old friend Arthur M. Harris described this type of a complaint as being **"smothered in verbiage, clogged and cloaked with matters of evidence, conclusions of law, and remarks of perhaps general literary interest, but certainly out of place in pleadings of law."** He added that the person being sued has to **"hunt for the issue, which is known to be lurking somewhere in the depths of that literary foliage . . . hoping that some lucky flash of insight would reveal the real trouble."** Then, according to Arthur M. Harris, the attorney who had written this deliberately incomprehensible complaint would stop work on the case altogether, turn out the lights, and sleep **"the sleep of the just, feeling that he had done his whole duty."**

That's the problem with most plaintiff's attorneys, by the way. They do all their work at the beginning of a case, before the complaint has even been submitted. They wrap up their pleadings in a complicated knot of circumlocution, resist exposing themselves to facts as though they're dangerous ultraviolet rays, and expect to win their cases based on eloquence alone.

94

That had been Clyde Prouty's style in the past, and I expected it to be his plan of action now.

It had done well by him, too. He had a history of winning astronomical damages for his clients. I suppose I should have been impressed. I wasn't. I'd gotten ahold of transcripts from some of his old trials and studied the cases he won. In every one, he won by default. Not because he was good, but because the defense attorneys representing the companies he was suing were so bad. Without exception, they were the high-priced, expressionless corporate types that had no intellectual or emotional investment in their cases, and even less in the way of scruples. They could no more relate to a jury than a mercenary could to the country that paid him to fight. They perfectly fit the description of being "hired guns."

Prouty, on the other hand, gave a jury passion. *I* knew that his passion was for dollars. But he always managed to convince the jurors that it was for justice.

In the defense of Courtland Motors, I planned on challenging Prouty passion for passion. But I also planned on credibly, logically, ethically, and efficiently building up a case based on facts.

If a jury needed a "smoking gun" to come in with a verdict in my client's favor, I'd find the smoking gun. I would, or Wylie Nolan would.

Our team was growing.

Nothing had been explicitly stated, but it was beginning to look as though the police chief of Stilton-on-Hudson was on our side. Bandy made us copies of all his news clippings, police reports, and fire reports; and he loaned us his negatives so that we could make blowups of the pictures he took of Standish's car.

The chief of the Stilton-on-Hudson Police Department had an estimate of himself as a law-enforcement officer that did not correspond with mine. He considered himself nine-tenths aw-shucks and one-tenth cop. I thought it was more the other way around. Bandy was the only one who'd taken photographs of the crime scene. Without them, our case was all tip and no iceberg. With them, we had a foundation of facts. He was the only investigator who took pictures of the car *where* the car had been found and so soon after the fire had extinguished that smoke was still steaming off Stanfield Standish's body.

Bandy shot two rolls of twenty-four frames each, with a point-and-shoot thirty-five millimeter camera that had a small, automatic flash, under less than ideal predawn conditions.

Forty-eight photographs, and every damn one of them had come out. You would have thought Ansel Adams had been the photographer. Chief Bandy was my hero. I wanted to take him into my law firm as a partner. I wanted to marry him off to my oldest daughter, if I'd had a daughter. I wanted to adopt him. He told us an interesting story.

"Like the newspaper said," Bandy expostulated around the end of his cigar, "Ralph Arkus practically drove smack into the Duesenberg. It was near to three o'clock in the morning, and Ralph had half a load on, like he always does. He was just darn lucky he was driving that old Zephyr of his, which can't do more than twenty-five miles an hour with a tailwind.

"Ralph says he saw black smoke coming out of the Duesey, and it scared him. One good thing about Ralph is that he don't like trouble, and he don't poke his nose in where it can get burned off. So he turned right around, drove back to the restaurant, and dialed police emergency.

"I'd just finished responding to a family altercation at the Rendezvous Bar when the call came in on the radio. The reservoir is my jurisdiction, so it didn't take me but five minutes to get there." Bandy indicated the pile of photographs on the table with the tip of his cigar. "About them pictures, I always carry a camera in my car. Always have fresh batteries in the glove compartment. Always have a spare roll of film.

"I got out of my car and started to look around. Three, four years ago, I went to one of them FBI courses down in Quantico. Another cop taking the class with me gave me a pointer I never forgot. He told me his philosophy of investigation was to treat every scene like it was a crime scene. Every one. Don't matter which. Domestic dispute. Collision. Missing person. D.O.A. Fire on a kitchen stove.

"Made sense to me, so I stored away this special technique along with my other ammunition, and I take it out and use it each time I respond to a call.

"Treat every scene like it's a crime scene. That's what I was thinking that night. And it didn't seem far off from the truth. What I had was a burned vehicle in the middle of a deserted road. And a dead body behind the steering wheel. It didn't look to me like no rich guy who died from a real bad sunburn in the front seat of that car.

"I radioed the State Police where I was, and I advised that everything was under control. A State Police duty car can patrol an area up to seven, eight hundred square miles. So I figured I'd have maybe another twenty or thirty minutes alone at the fire scene before the first trooper got to me.

"I started poking around. The Duesenberg was still smoldering; it was that hot. I touched the driver's side of the car, and got a heat blister on my middle finger. The body was real bad, too. No way to tell who he was from the face. Nose had been burned off. No ears. No hair. No skin. Dead as a dog in the road. Later on I found out he was Stanfield Standish. But back then, he was just a dead guy in a car.

"Now, I'll admit I don't know much about fires, but common sense tells us one or two things, and the first of them is that if a car starts on fire, and a guy is alive when he smells smoke, he's gonna get the heck *out* of the car. Think about it. It's just common sense. This guy, though. He never leaves the car. Why not? I'm getting interested now. But like I said, I don't have much time. So, real careful, I stick my head through the window on the passenger side. Pulled my head right back out again, too. Couldn't stand the smell. Don't know what it was. Burned flesh, maybe. Or gasoline. Maybe kerosene. Whipped out my camera, held my breath, and stuck my head back in. Used up a whole roll of film, just on the inside of that car.

"Used up another roll outside. Looked for tire tracks, but couldn't see none in the dark. Took pictures under the car, though. And next to it. Behind it. And in front. Shot film of the road, the intersection, and the burned vehicle at all angles. Tires. Windshield. Trunk. Passenger side. Driver's side. Front bumper. Back. Even stood on the hood of my car so as I could get a shot from the top looking down.

"Treat every scene like it's a crime scene. Still makes sense to me. That, and another thing. That you don't trample evidence. Now, trample isn't a word that the average man uses in everyday speech, and I'm not sure that ordinarily it would even pop into my head, but when them State Police drove up, the first thing they done was say, real polite-like, 'Thanks, Chief, but we'll take over from here,' as if they was dealing with a retarded child, and then they started to try and shuffle me away from the scene.

"But being as this was my jurisdiction, I hung around to watch what they was doing. And damn foolishness it was, too. They drove that patrol car right up to the the Duesenberg. Got out and started to stomp around. Didn't bother to photograph nothing. Two, three minutes later, a fire engine drove up. Then comes the ladder apparatus from the Stilton-on-Hudson Volunteer Fire Department.

"Hell, the darn fire was already out, but them amateurs poured five hundred, maybe a thousand gallons of water into the car. And they still weren't satisfied. When they was done flooding the crime scene, then they figure the time must be right to *alter* it. Ambulance arrives. Lights flashing. Sirens screaming. Like it's the Fourth of July. Attendants jerk open the driver's side door. Head and torso fall out. Two cops pull the corpse from the car, dump it on a stretcher, and push it into the back of their van. Nobody takes pictures of nothing. Not before they move the body. Not after.

"Then come the reporters. The television cameras. The news trucks. And after them, the ambulance chasers. Insurance adjusters. Slick lawyers. And finally, a guy in a Mercedes wearing five hundred dollar Italian shoes. He says he represents the Standish interests, whatever the hell that means.

"I figure that by then somebody must have ID'd the vehicle and called the Standish estate, and this is where Italian Shoes comes from. He flashes his press card and whips out his car phone. He snaps orders into the phone, like 'the governor said this,' 'the attorney general said that' and hangs up. Then he engages in a verbal dispute with one of the state troopers, and I hear him ragging that poor trooper out, and the troopers don't want all of them reporters from Stanfield Standish News mad at them, so when Italian Shoes threatens them again, they back down. And next thing I know, the body's gone.

"It never did get to the Belton Hospital. No autopsy was performed. Wasn't looked at by a forensic pathologist. No postmortem pictures taken. No tests done. Whatever evidence there was was drowned. What wasn't drowned was trampled.

"I could see the State Police was pissed off, what with the body being hijacked out from under them. I tried to give them what I had. Told them about my two rolls of film. Told them what I thought I smelled. Asked them to think why the victim didn't escape from the car. But they didn't want to hear me. One of them, a tall, good-looking fellow, said to me, 'Out of my way, Pop.' I said back to him, 'Don't you give me no Pop or I'll pop you,' and that's the way things went.

"I never did give my pictures to anybody. And until Wylie Nolan here called me the other day, nobody ever asked me about them neither. The State Police report, the Fire Incident report, the State Fire Marshal report, all of the official documents say the same thing. That the cause of the fire was 'accidental' and that the fire started in the engine compartment.

"But that wasn't their original idea. No. None of them was calling it anything until the lawyers and ambulance chasers got to the scene. And, of course, Italian Shoes. It was Italian Shoes who said it first. I was standing right beside him when he said, 'It's a terrible tragedy for Mr. Standish to die as a result of a fire caused by a defect in the engine compartment.'

"He said it, and then all of them state policemen and firemen and reporters and cameramen and even the two cops that hauled away the body, they all got to repeating the words 'engine compartment fire' and 'defect' and 'terrible, terrible tragedy' like they was repeating some sort of a religious mantra.

"But I wasn't fooled. I been around for a long time, and I knew what it meant. Whenever you let them ambulance chasers run the show, what they're looking for ain't the cause of a fire, it's dollar signs, and dollar signs means lawsuits. So I just sat back on my haunches and I waited.

"I still pick up the town drunk when he's had one too many, and I break up a domestic dispute now and again when the Missus finds out that the Mister has been diving into an unauthorized pool. On nice nights, I harass the local prostitute, but not too much, because Betty's a real likeable lady. And every now and again, I read a story about this here lawsuit that the Standish people have brung against your client, and I clip out the story. And because what goes around comes around, I know that someday, someone's going to call me to find out what I know about the fire; and sure enough, that's just what you people sitting right here have went and did."

CHAPTER

16

It was when Wylie Nolan was doing case development that he found out Hugo Scheidler had died a year before Stanfield Standish. He'd remembered my story about Hugo and his mistress coming over for Thanksgiving, and that I'd met Standish the same night.

The more he found out, the angrier he got.

"Max, this was a *solvable* crime. If they'd just let Chief Bandy alone for half a day, he'd have been able to make an arrest. Instead, people tracked all over the crime scene as if it was a garage sale, and then they tracked right out again carrying Standish's body as if they'd paid for it. And no autopsy. State law mandates an autopsy. How could there be no autopsy?"

And more mutterings along the same lines.

The official paperwork on the Duesenberg car fire was flimsy: an incident report from the volunteer fire department and an accident report from the State Police. This gave us the time the alarm came in, who called in the fire, which firemen responded, and so on. No photographs. No interviews. No follow-up investigation. Not even a physical examination of the burned car.

Wylie found out that Standish Enterprises sent a truck to tow the Duesenberg to Clyde Prouty's storage facility the day after the fire. He compared dates on documents and also found out that the *Standish* versus *Courtland Motors* lawsuit was filed two days *before* Prouty's experts had even examined the car. This is about par for the course, the only difference being that most plaintiff's attorneys at least have the good grace to look inside the deep pockets before trying to turn them inside out.

After listening to Wylie grumble for two days about how solvable the case still was, I thought it might make my life easier if I explained, "We weren't hired to solve a crime, Wylie. We were hired to defend a lawsuit. So why don't we just concentrate on where and how the fire started and let the police worry about who started it."

Wylie laughed. I didn't know what the laugh meant, but I had a strong feeling it wasn't compliance.

The night before this discussion, Wylie and I sat down again with Chief Bandy and made up a list of potential witnesses.

We'd gone through back issues of the local newspapers, writing down anything that looked like a lead. Caterers. Landscapers. Delivery services. Bartenders. Postmen. Auto mechanics.

Auto mechanics. That set Chief Bandy to remembering.

"Man by the name of Freddie Eckeles. Kids tease him. You know, like that guy in the horror movies. When he comes down the street, they scream 'Freddddiiieee's commming!' and he snarls at them a little just to get their blood going and make 'em laugh. But a nice guy. I mean, a pussycat. If your car's broke down, Freddie'll pick you up in Albany and tow it back to his garage, and he'll only charge for the repair work. Won't even charge you for the tow. Started his own service station when Standish fired him, but Freddie used to work for old man Scheidler when he owned the place."

"Owned what place?"

"Standish estate. Wasn't called that then, though. Back then it was just the Scheidler place. Always was big, but when Hugo had it, it wasn't so darned stuffy. Mrs. Scheidler weren't no bargain, but neither was she there most of the time. Their daughters always came to visit Hugo during the summer, and the pretty one, Astrid, once she and my son had something going between them."

"Son? I didn't know you had a son."

"My boy's name is Patton. After the general. Pat took to the law. Like me. He's a State Trooper. C Troop. Out of Sidney. Two hours west of here on Route 17. Best investigator in the state. If Pat'd been here when that Duesenberg was torched, we'd of caught the guy that same night. Pat's with the Criminal Investigation Division. Has no authority in this county, though. Darn shame, too."

"What happened between him and Astrid Scheidler?"

Instead of answering directly, he said, "People here always said that the boy took after his ma and the girl took after Hugo."

"What about the other two daughters?"

I knew that there were two more, because they'd been named as principals in the lawsuit.

"As like their mother as claws on a tiger's paw. Hugo and little Astrid, though, they had a nice quality about them. One time, I thought as Astrid was going to be my daughter-in-law. She used to tool around on her bicycle when she was yea-high. Never was a summer day you didn't see her zipping up the road on that bike. And Hugo. Lots of times, you'd see him down at the C & J Bake Shop, just shooting the breeze with the boys. Wouldn't even know he was a millionaire, except for where he lived and all of them cars. He never know'd what broke 'em up, my boy and Astrid. I saw him down at the Bake Shop after Pat already joined the Marines, because that's what boys did back then when their hearts was broke. And it was me that told him."

"Told him what?"

"About Eva. And Stanley. Back before Mr. High and Mighty changed his name, Stanfield Standish was just plain old Stanley Scheidler, and Stanley was a mama's boy. Sneaky little weasel, he was. We saw him grow up, just like we watched the girls. He stayed pretty much to hisself during the summer. And there always was friction between him and Hugo. You'd see 'em together and the feeling you got was Stanley didn't think all that much of his dad. Never nothing out in the open. Just his nose bent out of shape and an all-purpose sort of contempt. My own feeling is Hugo didn't like his son, so he tried double hard to make Stanley feel he did. Took him fishing. Brought him on business trips. But it didn't do no good. Stanley always was sullen. Like one of them kids you want to slap. I'll give this to Hugo, though. Poor man. Never did stop trying."

I thought back to when Hugo Scheidler asked me if he could bring the newly renamed young screenwriter along to Thanksgiving dinner all of those years ago. I remembered the way he'd bragged about Stanfield's accomplishments. Had all of that bragging just been a father's way to disguise disgust? Or disappointment? Or dislike?

Bandy went on, "So, Eva Scheidler didn't like my boy Pat. Don't know what set her off. Could have been any reason or no reason. They was just seventeen and eighteen years old. You know how young kids are when they're in love. Astrid'd say 'I love you, Pat,' and Pat'd say, 'I love you, Aster,' sometimes so much you'd just want to kick the two of them out of the house to shut them up. But still, it was awful cute.

"Hugo was away on business that summer, so Aster'd ride her bicycle over almost every day. Stay for lunch and dinner, and then Pat'd put her bike in the trunk of my Buick and drive her home. One night, Pat and Aster was necking in the car in front of her house. You seen that driveway. Right out in the open. Not a place two kids'd go if they was up to any no good. Nowhere to hide. So, they're going at it hot and heavy, like young kids with all of them hormones will do. Kissing and hugging and no doubt putting their hands into places they technically aren't supposed to be. They're at it no more than five, maybe six minutes when Pat's door jerks open and someone grabs him by the throat and yanks him out of the car. It's Stanley, of course. And Stanley comes with a message from Eva. More or less, the message is that if Pat don't leave Astrid alone, Eva's going to have him arrested for statutory rape, since Aster's only seventeen years old, but my boy is already eighteen.

"Meanwhile, Aster's screaming at Stanley to leave her alone, and yelling that she and Pat didn't do nothing wrong, and how he don't have no right . . . and so. Next thing you know, Stanley has dragged Aster into the house, and Pat's sitting alone in my car, and he don't know what to do. So he comes home, and I give him all sorts of fatherly advice. Next day, the two of us go together to old man Scheidler's place to reason with Stanley. And when we get there Freddie Eckeles tells us they're gone."

"Gone?"

"Don't know if Stanley had to put Astrid into a straitjacket to get her out of there, but Freddie said there was a whole lot of crying and banging going on the night before, and that next morning, they was both gone. Went in Stanley's car. And never did hear from them again.

"My boy Pat, he wrote letters to Astrid, and he telephoned, and one time he even drove to New York, because Hugo thought she might be there. But Hugo couldn't help much, because that was the summer he had the heart attack. So, like I said, my boy joined the Marines. When he got out, he went to college and studied criminology. Always did want to be a state trooper. Always wanted to put the bad guys in jail. Pat's a good boy."

I figured the 'good boy' to be about thirty-eight years old now.

"Did he ever get back in touch with Astrid . . . with Miss Scheidler?" Wylie asked.

"No. It was like she went to the moon. Never heard nothing about her from then on. When Stanley died, Pat drove in from Chenango County for the funeral. Hoped he'd get a chance to see Astrid. Just curiosity, he told me. But I don't know. She never did come to the funeral."

"Did Pat ever get married?"

"Nope. So far as I know, hasn't even come close."

"Hummmmm," I mumbled to myself. Then I met Chief Bandy's eyes. He looked right back at me and nodded.

"Yep. Ought to speak to Freddie Eckeles. That's what you two fellows ought to do."

CHAPTER
17

"Case development," Wylie Nolan said for no apparent reason. Then he pulled his car into Freddie's Service Station and asked, "Did you ship the pictures I selected to Eli Timmerman in Chicago?"

"I sent them out this morning."

"Good. I want to see what's inscribed inside that ring."

"How's sending them to Chicago going to help you do that? The enlargements we made from your negatives are already fuzzy. If we make them bigger they'll just get worse."

"Not worse. Clearer. And not bigger. Better. What Eli Timmerman does is called photo-enhancement. He doesn't just enlarge pictures. Eli uses something called an analog image-analysis system. It brings out things hidden in the film without distorting them and without losing definition. It's the same procedure NASA used with the pictures it got from the moon. Eli will explain how it works when we get to Chicago."

"Oh. Are we going to Chicago?"

"We are if you want exhibits that'll knock the jury's socks off. That's what Eli does. When you see his work, guaranteed, you'll be impressed."

"How much is Eli and this photo-enhancement going to cost my client?"

"A bundle," Wylie said and grinned. "But in my experience, if you pay peanuts, you get monkeys."

I groaned.

"We have to hire someone else, too, Max."

"Who?"

"A forensic pathologist. Dr. Alexander Urda."

"Urda. Urda. I've heard that name before."

"He was Chief Medical Examiner of New York City about ten years ago. Chubby old black guy. Real happy-go-lucky. Looks like he should have big ears and deliver Easter eggs. Deep voice. Talks like God. Best pathologist in the business. Juries love him. I love the guy, too."

"Why?"

"Well. For one thing, he thinks I'm the best arson investigator in the world."

We got out of the car. I had called earlier to tell Freddie Eckeles that we were coming, and I assumed it was he walking towards us now, looking exactly like a tall, boneless, congenial scarecrow too good-natured to scare away the birds.

"Mr. Bramble?" he said.

"Call me Max."

"And you must be Mr. Nolan."

"Just Wylie."

"Come this way, gentlemen."

Freddie led us into the cleanest service station I've ever seen. The plank flooring was thickly covered with polyurethane, and there were two church pews by the window wall that smelled of lemon furniture polish. Framed pictures of covered bridges hung over the pews, and an old-fashioned black dial telephone sat on a wood teacher's desk next to a row of sharpened pencils, a receipt book, and a pink message pad. A gleaming coffee percolator gurgled on a small table next to the door.

"Coffee, gentlemen?" Freddie Eckeles asked, and Wylie answered, "If I ever say no to a cup of coffee, I didn't hear the question."

•

I was still on my first cup and Wylie was on his third when Freddie finally started to talk about his years with Hugo Scheidler.

"Twenty-five years, wasn't it?" I asked.

"Yes, sir. I started working for Mr. Scheidler when I was twenty-eight years old. He died when I was fifty-three and he was eighty-three. He came to my wedding, and he was godfather to my oldest boy. We had the same blood type, he and I, and when he went into the hospital for that second bypass operation, it was my blood that went into his veins. We spent just about every day of our lives together, except when he was out on business or in Europe on vacation. When Felicia, his youngest girl, got rheumatic fever at Marymount, he sent me to the city to pick her up. And when Victoria, the oldest, got married, I took the 1932 Cadillac Sports Phaeton and picked up her and her husband at the Plaza Hotel, and drove them in style to the pier for their cruise on the Queen Elizabeth II. I was always there for Mr. Scheidler, and Mr. Scheidler was always there for me. Weddings and funerals. Good times and bad.

He didn't trust Stanley to keep me on. No. Mr. Scheidler never said anything to me to that effect, but when two people drive around together for twenty-five years, each of them gets to know what the other is thinking. A lot of people around here think that when Stanley inherited his father's estate, he fired me, but he didn't. I'm not saying that he wouldn't have, but I quit before he got the chance. I always saved my money, and I could have started this service station with my own capital, but I didn't have to. Mr. Scheidler knew everything there was to know about cars. Cars and gas stations was how he made his fortune. He tidied up his affairs and made his peace with his maker before he died. I don't generally advertise this publicly, but Mr. Scheidler bought this garage outright and brought me to his lawyers and signed it over to me. This occurred more than one month before he died. He told me that he wasn't leaving me anything in his will, because a will might be contested, and he asked me to stay on with him for the rest of his life until he was buried in the ground; and that's exactly what I did."

Freddie Eckeles made this statement as a narrative, exactly as I've written it, without any prompting from me or Wylie, and without any noticeable display of emotion. When he stopped talking, Wylie and I looked at each other. Neither of us knew what to say next. We'd gone in there hoping to squeeze out a few drops of information, and had been deluged instead. Freddie seemed not to notice our silence. He was cupping a mug of coffee in both hands, staring down into it.

Freddie not only spoke without inflection, but he also struck me as being a man who rarely spoke at all. He reminded me of a speaker at my great-uncle's tenth Alcoholics Anonymous anniversary. Uncle Billy is a sweetheart of a guy who doesn't have any children, so every year as a representative of his family, I have to go to a meeting to help Uncle Billy celebrate the day he put down his last drink and came into AA.

One year, Uncle Billy asked a man to speak for him who'd been sober for only ninety days. I'll call him Adam. Adam had already been to over a hundred meetings, but up until Uncle Billy's anniversary he'd always been too terrified to say a word. In AA, it's supposed to be some sort of a catharsis to get up in front of the group and talk, and even though Adam didn't want to do it, Uncle Billy was just such an all-around nice guy that Adam didn't feel he had the right to say no.

So, he sort of stumbled up to the podium and cleared his throat. He stood there, and then he coughed twice. He stared out at the group. They stared back at him. He cleared his throat again. This went on for a while and the group was starting to get restive. Then, in a scratchy, whispery voice, Adam finally said, "Hi. My name is Adam, and I'm an alcoholic."

And from that sentence on, you couldn't shut him up.

Which is what I think happened to Freddie Eckeles.

"Hi. My name is Freddie. I was Hugo Scheidler's chauffeur, and there's no way in hell that you're going to shut me up."

But for the moment Freddie was still staring into his coffee mug.

Wylie prodded him back into action (in court, it's called "leading the witness").

He leaned forward and said, "Freddie, you didn't like Stanfield Standish very much, did you?"

Freddie placed his coffee mug carefully down on the teacher's desk. His eyes were steady and pensive. They'd be hard eyes to lie to.

"That's true. I didn't like him one bit. As a matter of fact, I didn't like any of Mr. Scheidler's children, except for Miss Astrid."

"How about Mr. Scheidler himself? Do you have an opinion on which one of his children *he* liked best?"

"Well, sir. If you asked him outright, he'd say he liked them all equally, just as parents do. But if you asked me, I'd say Miss Astrid was his favorite. He doted on her. Very often, I heard him refer to her as his legacy."

"Legacy," Wylie repeated thoughtfully. "Explain something to me then, Freddie. If Astrid Scheidler was Hugo's legacy, why did he leave his estate in Stilton-on-Hudson to Stanfield Standish?"

"Well, sir. I see you've put your finger on the problem. But I'm afraid it was even worse that that. Mr. Scheidler didn't leave Stanley only the estate. He left him his collection, too."

"What collection?"

"Of classic American cars."

"You're losing me, Freddie. Where does . . . ?"

"Excuse me for interrupting, Mr. Nolan, but I believe I know what you're going to say, and I have to admit I've wondered considerably about it, too. I think that I may have come up with the answer. Although the one who could tell us if I'm right or wrong is long past asking. The question, I think we will all agree, is this. If Miss Astrid was Mr. Scheidler's favorite child, why, then, did he leave his estate and all of his cherished automobiles to his son, Stanley?"

Freddie turned to look at me for a moment, and I shrugged to let him know that I didn't have the foggiest idea.

"I believe the answer to this question lies in Mr. Stanley's competitive nature and in his desire to take over all of the accoutrements that he associated with his father. I believe Mr. Scheidler perceived this and feared that if he left the estate to Miss Astrid, Stanley would almost certainly contest the will. Therefore, prior to his death, Mr. Scheidler assigned Miss Scheidler all of his extensive business interests, including the Harriet O'Brien's chain, which, you probably know, is a group of successful department stores that he owned. Mr. Scheidler also gave Miss Astrid and her sisters a considerable sum in cash, as well as several million dollars in stocks and bonds. Of course, you also know that Mr. Scheidler only left Stanley a life interest in his estate."

"Of course," Wylie lied.

"And happy I am about that, too. I never had a moment's relaxation when he owned the cars. You can see what happened to the Duesenberg. I was always afraid he was going to drive them around on back roads as if they were motorcycles instead of treating them as you would treat a classic work of art."

Work of art?

Again, Wylie Nolan and I traded a baffled glance.

But this time, Freddie caught us. "I see you two gentlemen doubting what I say. I see you thinking that I'm just an old fool, faithful to the man who employed me for twenty-five years, and completely out of touch with reality. Oh, yes. That's what the two of you are thinking. But I can also see that you are men of discrimination, and I trust that you are also individuals of good taste."

Where was Freddie going with this? For the first time since we'd come into his service station, he seemed vitalized. His voice gained resonance; his eyes took on the same sheen as his polyurethane floors. "Gentlemen," he then said, "I'll make you a wager."

This was a new Freddie.

"If after viewing Mr. Scheidler's antique cars, you two agree with me that the vehicles in the collection are actually works of art, then you will take me to the best steak dinner in Stilton-on-Hudson. If, on the other hand, you disagree and perceive them as merely modes of transportation, the steak dinners will be on me. What do you say, gentlemen? Are we on?"

"We're on," Wylie answered.

"Excellent. The cars are kept on the estate, under lock and key. I have the key. When Stanley died, Miss Astrid inherited the cars. And the estate. And, I might add that I felt I had her father's blessing when I informed her that she had also inherited me."

CHAPTER
18

Stanfield Standish's estate, which was now Astrid Scheidler's estate, was located in farm country slightly north of the town of Stilton-on-Hudson (population 1,045), where land can still be purchased in large parcels comparatively cheaply. The house itself is a clapboard extravaganza with Greek revival columns, wide porches, and tall windows. Wylie counted the chimneys from the outside of the house and estimated that it had four fireplaces, but Freddie Eckeles said there were six.

According to Freddie, the house has a large center hall with an impressive *Gone With the Wind* staircase that branches off into balconies overlooking the foyer. We knew about the ballroom from the press accounts of Standish's Valentine's Day party, but found out from Freddie about the wine cellar and the seven bathrooms and ten bedrooms.

Since this was farm country, there were also several outbuildings originally built to smoke meat, stow farm implements, age tobacco, and store wagons, buggies, and carriages. A few barns and sheds also dotted the two hundred and thirty acres of land surrounding the house. And down a narrow asphalt road, there was what looked like a large stable.

The closer we got to it, though, the more I could see that it wasn't just any ordinary stable. For one thing, it had new windows that seemed to be made of double thermal insulated glass. For another, the road we'd taken to the stable had been paved all the way up a steep incline to two giant sliding doors. These doors were white, as was the trim on the windows and shutters, and they'd clearly been designed to look like conventional stable doors. But they weren't conventional; they were made of steel. And to the right of the door frame, at eye level, there was a small digital burglar-alarm pad.

Freddie pushed a plastic key in a slot, fingered in a few numbers, and we heard three low beeps. Then he told each of us to grab a door, and we pulled them open along a well-oiled metal track. Freddie flicked on the lights.

My first impression was of cherry wood, oiled to a high sheen. Each stall was twice as big as your average Manhattan condominium, and there were twelve stalls in all. Six on each side. The plank wood floors also were varnished until they shined, and light poured in through skylights that never had been in the ceilings when the stable was first built.

Thermostats were strategically placed along the walls, so it wasn't difficult to conclude two things. One, that the temperature in the stable was climate controlled, and two, that this stable didn't hold horses.

Freddie Eckeles left us in the doorway and went to a small side room that looked like a control booth. We heard a click, some static, and then music. Violins and flutes at first. Soft. Subtle. The music filtered through the air and collided with the walls, the floors, us—as if instead of being made out of sound waves and vibrations, it had been made out of sunlight.

When Freddie rejoined us, he looked the way a man does when the smile on his face isn't really there for you. It's just a spillover from something else. He led us toward the stalls.

The oldest cars were displayed on the left side of the stable; the newer models were on the right. On a vertical beam in front of each stall was a framed photograph and data sheet that identified the automobile inside and related pertinent information about the car.

We read the first one.

MODEL A FORD—1930

Like most American schoolchildren, I'd been brought up to believe that Henry Ford put the world on wheels, and that the car he did it with was the Model T Ford.

But Hugo hadn't chosen to start out his collection with a Model T. His first car was a classic Model A. According to the caption, the Model A was historically significant because it bridged the gap between the obsolete Model T and the next generation of cars, which incorporated the 1932 V-8 engine.

My eyes wandered past the data sheet (over five million Model A's were built) to the car itself. It was a two-door sedan with a light olive green body and a darker green roof. Its black fenders and balloon whitewall tires brought to mind split-rail fences, dirt roads, hills, rickety bridges, and an America in the full flush of its youth.

My father had once owned a Model A Ford. He had bought and sold more than ten cars by the time he was twenty-seven years old, and once reverently told me that his Model A had cost four hundred and ninety five dollars new. When he was growing up, he loved cars the way later generations loved girls, and he talked to me about them the way an aging Lothario might describe an old flame.

I moved to the next stall.

CADILLAC SPORTS PHAETON—1932

It was in this car that Freddie told us he had driven Hugo's daughter and son-in-law to the QEII after their wedding. It was impressive. The fact sheet said that only two hundred and ninety-six of them had ever been made. They had sixteen cylinders and could go seventy miles per hour without strain. They'd sold for about five thousand dollars new. Freddie told us that the Cadillac I was looking at was worth over two hundred thousand dollars in today's market.

It was a big car, weighing more than two and a half tons. The die-cast aluminum radiator core screen was handsome, and the chrome heron on the hood would be considered sleek and modern even to-day. Nobody would call it graceful, but it wasn't clumsy looking ei-ther. What it looked like was money, prestige, and power; and what it brought to mind was speakeasies, jazz, Ziegfeld Follies chorus girls with hard nipples in satin dresses and gangsters wearing tuxedoes standing on the running boards of their cars. The music in the back-ground would have to be Gershwin's.

It . . .

That was odd. I stopped and listened. The music hadn't been just in my mind. I really was hearing Gershwin. Ira and George. White tie and tails. Tin Pan Alley.

Hugo Scheidler had programmed the music to accommodate the mood of the times.

I moved on to the next stall.

PIERCE ARROW V-12 LE BARON CONVERTIBLE SEDAN—1933

I looked into the stall. Very big. Very impressive. This one was a tan four-door, with a beige convertible top and leather seats. It had wide running boards, fat whitewall tires, and a side-mounted spare. What I liked most about it, though, was the little naked Indian sitting on top of the radiator with a bow in one hand and an arrow in the other. The arrow was aimed at the tires of one of the newer model cars in the stall across the way.

I walked forward and read the information plaque in the fourth stall.

AUBURN BOATTAIL SUPERCHARGED SPEEDSTER—1935

With its plump pontoon fenders, this was a curious-looking ma-chine. The caption said that the car had sold for $2,245 new, and described it as "heart-stoppingly gorgeous." I wasn't sure how gorgeous it was, but I'll admit it was a sporty two-seater. Just the kind of a car you'd imagine as a background for an F. Scott Fitzgerald type wearing a tennis sweater, carrying a racquet, and saying, "Tennis, anyone?"

I felt a little intimidated by the "clever new cowl-forward styling" and was relieved to move on to the stall on my right. Wylie Nolan was already there studying the next caption. He motioned me forward.

I read:

J SERIES DUESENBERG ARLINGTON SEDAN—1930

"This is it," Wylie said.

I looked into the stall.

It was empty.

Wylie and I simultaneously turned to Freddie Eckeles. His eyes went past us to the empty stall. The smiles we'd seen earlier were gone. He shook his head and mumbled, "It's like he killed her."

Wylie stepped toward Freddie. "Like *who* killed *what*?"

"The most beautiful car in the world," Freddie continued. "We loved her, Mr. Scheidler and I. She was the queen of the collection."

"Like who killed what, Freddie?" Wylie repeated, his voice soft, like the light in the stable. Like the music. Soft and pervasive and confiding. I was beginning to understand why bad guys stood in line to confess to him.

"Mr. Stanley, of course. Like he killed it with his own two hands."

"Freddie, Stanfield Standish is the one who was killed. It was his body that was found *in* the car. He didn't kill anybody or anything."

Again Freddie Eckeles shook his head. "If Mr. Stanley hadn't inherited the car, hadn't owned it . . ."

"Are you talking about the Duesenberg?"

"Yes. The Duesenberg."

"Freddie, if Stanfield Standish hadn't inherited the Duesenberg, do you think that *he* would be alive today?"

Freddie gave Wylie a dismissive look. The honest eyes I had noticed before were blank now. Blank and hard and impenetrable.

He shrugged. "Who cares," he said. And he moved forward.

We followed him. I got goose bumps.

I whispered to Wylie, "Someone just walked over someone's grave."

We stopped in front of the last captioned stall on the left side of the stable. It, too, was empty.

PACKARD DARRIN—1940

The look on Freddie's face was remote. I couldn't tell if he was feeling sadness or bitterness or grief. When he broke the silence he said, "They belonged together. Side by side."

"What belonged together, Freddie?"

"The Packard and the Duesenberg."

"Where's the Packard now?"

"It was a beauty," Freddie responded, but not exactly to Wylie's question. "A super-eight one-eighty Victoria convertible. Every one of those Darrins was handmade. Only one hundred were built. They couldn't compare in quality to the Duesenberg. Nothing could. But still, the Packard Darrin was a sweet machine. It cost forty-six hundred dollars new. Today it's worth about two hundred thousand. It was a movie-star car. Even built in Hollywood. The first one was custom-made for that actor. Can't remember his name but he was in a lot of cowboy movies. Always wore a hat."

Wylie tried to bring him back on course. "Where's the Packard now, Freddie?"

"They bought them at the same time. That's how come they're next to each other in the collection. The Duesenberg was for Mr. Scheidler, and the Packard was for Mrs. Cataliz."

Now we were getting somewhere.

"Who's Mrs. Cataliz?" Wylie asked.

"Marguerite Cataliz." Freddie pronounced the name as though he were reaching for syllables out of a mist. "She was the woman he loved."

Of course. Marguerite.

Wylie looked at me. I looked at him. I wasn't sure if he'd remembered the story I'd told him, so I lip-synched the word "mistress." But, as before, Freddie Eckeles caught me.

"That's right. Marguerite was Mr. Scheidler's mistress. Before that, she was his nurse. Other than Miss Astrid, she was the only good thing that ever happened to my old friend. My old employer. Except for the cars."

"When did . . . ?"

"He met her the summer he had his first heart attack." Freddie glanced back at the empty stall that had once contained the "queen of the collection."

Then, as though a hypnotist had snapped his fingers, Freddie's whole manner changed. In a businesslike voice, he suddenly said, "Nothing more to do here. I've got to get back to my work."

He retraced his steps to the small office at the front of the stable and flicked a switch. Abruptly, the music stopped.

With it seemed to go the magic of the cars. The magic and the illusion—that our world could be or would be or should be as glamorous as the world from which those beautiful machines had come. I turned back for one last look. My eyes drifted to the right side of the stable, toward the cars we hadn't looked at yet. There were a 1957 Ford Thunderbird and a 1967 Corvette Sting Ray.

I sighed.

The illusion had disappeared with the music, but not the allure. Suddenly, I knew why my father had bought ten cars in eight years. It had something to do with machines. And lust. It was primal. It was automotive.

Against my will, I was hooked.

Freddie slid the steel doors shut, cutting off our last look at the collection. I turned to him and said, "You win, Freddie. Wylie and I owe you that steak dinner. Where do you want to—?"

But Wylie came in with a question fast and low, like a one-two punch right below the belt.

"What happened to the Packard, Freddie?" he asked.

At first, Freddie seemed not to have heard Wylie. He didn't turn around; he continued to program the code into the burglar-alarm pad.

Wylie repeated, "What happened to the Packard, Freddie?"

And then, in that faraway voice we had heard before, Hugo Scheidler's former chauffeur said, "I drove it to her house."

"To whose house, Freddie?"

"Marguerite's house."

"Why did you do that, Freddie?"

"Because it was her car. Because it belonged to her."

"When did you drive it there, Freddie?"

"Immediately after the funeral."

"Right after Mr. Scheidler died?"

Freddie turned around to face us. He looked tired. Limp. Depleted. For a man who was not accustomed to speaking, it seemed as though in one afternoon he had used up more than his lifetime allotment of words.

"Gentlemen," he said politely, his voice and manner once again that of the courteous sole proprietor of his own establishment, "I thank you for your invitation, but I must return to my service station now. Perhaps you'll permit me to take a raincheck on that steak."

CHAPTER
19

It took us two and a half hours to drive back to the city. We stopped at a diner on the New York State Thruway because I wanted to call my office.

"Don't you want to call in, too?" I asked Wylie.

"Hell, no."

"But what if your office has more work for you?"

"I've already got too much work."

I dug into my wallet for my telephone calling card. With all of the new rules and companies that had emerged since the not-too-recent breakup of AT&T, it was getting harder and harder to figure out how to make a long-distance call from a public telephone booth.

"I can't find the damn thing."

I continued to rifle through my credit cards, receipts, and little slips of paper. "I don't know why I'm wasting my time. I should just get a car phone. Have you ever thought of getting a car phone?"

"Hell, no," Wylie said again. "I'm thinking of getting the phone in my office taken out."

I laughed.

Finally I found my calling card and punched in the twenty-five digits that connected me to my office.

My paralegal had a few messages for me, some questions about where to send the material we'd accumulated on *Standish* versus *Courtland Motors,* and a bonus question about Astrid Scheidler. Sarah asked if I'd noticed that the complainants in the lawsuit were Eva Scheidler, mother of the deceased, and Victoria and Felicia Scheidler, sisters of the deceased. Astrid was not listed as a party to the lawsuit.

I hadn't noticed.

"What do you think it means?" Sarah asked.

"I'm not sure. But if Astrid Scheidler isn't suing Courtland Motors, there's nothing to keep me from contacting her. Standish Enterprises are in Wilmington, Delaware. Get her address and send her this letter. Type it on plain white bond. Don't use my letterhead. Dear Miss Scheidler. I don't know if your father ever spoke to you about me, but I met him some twenty years ago on a flight from Chicago to New York, and he spent Thanksgiving with my parents and me that same night. Over the years, he had contacted me from time to time to pass along advice and opportunities for my professional advancement. I am hoping that I can presume on my brief acquaintance with him to impose on you for an interview. As you may know, I am representing Courtland Motors as defense counsel in the Misses Scheidler's lawsuit against my client for wrongful death. The purpose of this interview would be to ask you several questions about an object that I uncovered in Mr. Standish's car. Its discovery may have some bearing on the nature of the fire. If you are amicable to this meeting, I could drive down to Wilmington, and your schedule permitting, we could briefly discuss this matter over lunch.

I can be reached at blah, blah, blah and so on. What do you think, Sarah?"

"You uncovered *an object that may have some bearing on the fire* in her brother's car? Very mysterious. I'd bite. And by the way, I found an article on Astrid Scheidler in one of your old business magazines. Do you want me to send that along?"

"Put it on the top of the pile."

Wylie walked over to me. I put my hand over the telephone mouthpiece and said, "The material you asked for is in my office. News clippings on the fire, videotape of Standish's party, videos and outtakes of newscasts, newspaper morgue photos, weather reports, a copy of the complaint. Sarah says it fills a small carton. She wants to know how to get it to you."

"Sarah's your paraplegic?"

"Paralegal."

"Whatever. Have her call Vincent Marchand. That's M-A-R-C, not M-A-R-S. His number's in the phone book, and his office is a few doors down from mine. Have Sarah tell Vincent I want to borrow his videotape player tonight and that if he goes home before six P.M. to leave it with Miranda Yee. Then have Sarah call Miranda. She's—"

"Wylie, why don't you just write down these people's phone numbers and keep them on you? Then you could call them yourself."

"I tried. Trouble is, I lose the numbers. Miranda Yee. That's with two e's. Tell Sarah to send the box to Miranda's office and to ask Miranda to hang around until we get back."

I gave Sarah these instructions. Yee, with two e's, Marchand with a C and not an S, and hung up. Then I turned to Wylie with a question that had been bothering me ever since Freddie Eckeles ran out of words.

"What's the going rate for a private detective these days?" I asked. "Not a fire expert like you. A standard operational gumshoe. Someone with a hook in the police department who can find people, do license-plate checks. That kind of thing."

Wylie raised an eyebrow. "With or without a bottle of Fleischmann's in his desk drawer and a voluptuous brunette to answer his phones?"

I laughed.

Wylie said, "Depending on location, thirty-five to seventy-five dollars an hour, plus expenses. Why?"

"Because I need to hire one."

"Why?"

"Because we have to find Marguerite Cataliz, and your time's too valuable to waste on something like this."

Wylie gave me a pitying look. He took the telephone out of my hand, tapped in the area code for upstate New York, and punched in the numbers for Information.

"Marguerite Cataliz," he said. "It's in Stilton-on-Hudson or one of the surrounding communities. Can you check that for me, please?"

Wylie spelled the first and second names for the operator. When she came up blank, he flirted with her, got her laughing, and cajoled her into looking longer and harder.

This process went on for another five minutes before he pantomimed that he needed a pencil and a pad of paper; then he scribbled two words and a telephone number and hung up.

The two words were: Paddy Lakes. A town. Where? I'd never heard of it.

Wylie picked up the receiver again and called New York City Information. Half a minute later, he wrote down a number with a Yorkville exchange, and an address on East 83rd Street.

So much for hiring a "real" private detective.

I took the telephone from Wylie and dialed each of the numbers. I let the Paddy Lakes number ring thirty times before I gave up. There was an answering machine on the Manhattan number. I left a short message identifying myself to Marguerite, reminding her that twenty years ago we'd met, and asking her to call me back at her earliest convenience.

CHAPTER
20

We found a parking spot at a broken meter on Church Street, one avenue west of Wylie Nolan's office. We walked two blocks east to a Chinese restaurant on Canal and waited for takeout coffee and custard buns. Then we went the block or so back to Wylie's office building on Lispenard Street. When the elevator opened on the seventh floor, instead of turning left, we went right and stopped in front of a solid wood door with a brass plaque on it that said:

VINCENT P. MARCHAND
ATTORNEY AT LAW

Wylie knocked. A few seconds later, a small man elegantly dressed in a double-breasted pinstripe suit opened the door. He had a narrow jaw, a small, bony nose, and skin so dark it was a perfect color-match for a mahogany Steinway concert grand. His face was matinee-idol handsome. But miniaturized. The crown of his head only came up to my chin. He was so dapper and small and trim, I had a wild urge to pick him up and put him on top of a wedding cake. His eyes were light brown with yellow specks and friendly.

"Max Bramble, this is Vincent Marchand. Vincent, Max is the lawyer I was telling you about."

Vincent gave me a strong handshake.

"I'm very pleased to meet you," he said. His voice was deep, as though it had come from the barrel chest of a giant instead of from a diminutive dandy, and he pronounced his words with an Island lilt that I thought might be Jamaican.

"How about the video player, Vincent?"

"At your disposal. I'll bring it over immediately."

Our next stop was at Miranda Yee's office. The closer we got to her door, the louder came the yelling from inside.

Wylie knocked.

The door jerked open. There was a wild, desperate expression on Miranda's face. She looked furtively back into her office once and slipped out the door. The yelling continued. Miranda was even more disheveled than the first time I'd seen her. Half her hair was bunched into a ponytail. The rest of it spread-eagled around her neck. The shirttail of her blouse hung over her waistband, her shoes were scuffed, and she looked like she'd just fallen out of a tree. It would have been hard to find a more extreme contrast to the scrupulously groomed Vincent Marchand.

"Hi, Vince," Miranda expelled a frantic breath to the attorney behind me. "Hi, Max." I was surprised that she'd remembered my name. "Hi, Wylie. Your carton's inside on my desk. I'd get it for you, but I'm not going back in there until Irma leaves. Or dies."

I took it that Irma was the secretary with the voice of a knife grinder that I'd encountered on my last visit.

Wylie said to Miranda, "You know, you really should fire her. Or kill her. I'll get the carton."

Irma was still yelling when he went into and came out of Miranda's office.

"Who's she screaming at?" I asked.

Miranda shuffled towards Wylie's office, looking back once more to see if we were being followed.

"Me. The walls. The carpet. The computers. She doesn't discriminate."

"Why do you put up with it?"

I was already starting to like Miranda. She reminded me of a basset hound I'd once had who thought that if he tucked his head under a blanket, he became completely invisible.

"I have to. She speaks three Chinese dialects, her English is tolerable, and my clients like her."

"How can your clients *like* her?"

Miranda looked at me bleakly. "I've never been able to figure that one out. But I don't like my clients, so maybe they have something in common; they scream a lot, too."

We settled into chairs around the desk in the back room. Wylie asked what we wanted to eat and suggested Chinese food, because the restaurant on the corner delivered. I separated out the videotapes from the rest of the file material in the carton that Sarah had sent over, and Vincent set up the video player on Wylie's desk. We ate. We talked. Miranda locked the door to the outer office, called her own office, and told Irma the Shrew to go home. Seconds later, Irma tried to open Wylie's door.

She rattled the doorknob and wiggled it. She huffed. She puffed. I felt like one of the three little pigs. Outside, the Mandarin Wolf was threatening to blow the house down. Miranda put her finger to her lips.

Then we heard a nasty expostulation of what I was told were Cantonese swearwords.

Irma left.

Sarah, my paralegal, had put the videotapes in chronological order and numbered them. We watched "One" first. It was the Valentine's Day broadcast in which Stanfield Standish described the Image Transformation process and showed what he had done to

Arlene de Grasse and Roy Douglass in the film *A Poor Man's Paradise*.

The second videotape contained SSN coverage of the Valentine's Day party itself, including Standish on the running board of the Duesenberg and his welcoming speech in the ballroom of his estate. There were also some "cast of thousands" shots of the partygoers and the arrival of limousines through the gates at the bottom of Standish's driveway.

The third video was an aggregate of news stories covering the discovery of Standish's dead body in the Duesenberg, his mother's announcement to the media, footage of the funeral, and brief bibliographical obituaries.

The fourth video combined all the SSN retrospectives on Standish, excluding only the one where he walks on water.

And the fifth confirmed the old adage about the best coming last. On it, everybody noticed something that would be of help to me.

Of course, five videotapes were not watched nor dinner consumed without numerous questions being asked and answered, and just as many digressions being indulged in, all of which were revealing not only of the facts of our case, but also of the other occupants of the room.

For example, I found out that Vincent Marchand was a movie buff. His favorites were 1930s musicals, and he liked his male dancers dressed in top hats, tuxedos, and canes. Vincent's favorite studios had been RKO, MGM and, fortunately for me, Cinema Select Artists.

On weekends, Vincent and his two daughters (Ginger Rogers Marchand, age six, and Judy Garland Marchand, age eight) came to Manhattan from Montclair, New Jersey, where they lived, to take tap-dancing lessons in a studio across from Radio City Music Hall. Vincent belonged to half a dozen film-preservation societies and collected black-and-white publicity shots of his favorite old movie stars.

Miranda Yee, on the other hand, never watched old movies. Her secret addiction was to television documentaries, political commentaries, and early-morning editorial talk shows. She watched *Out-*

Speak, Point of View, Decision Format, and *The Sunday Morning Religious Hour.* She also liked to visit obscure houses of worship with names like The Temple of The I Ams or The Church of the Holy Rollers.

I asked her why.

Miranda tilted her head up in the best basset-hound tradition and answered, "I guess because it's cheaper than going to the movies."

It took two hours to get through the fifth videotape, which contained outtakes of the five major network and cable-television news shows. This footage was spliced together in no particular order, but after watching the four previous tapes, it was pretty easy to figure out what had happened when.

All of the material in tape five was unedited, and most of it was without voiceover narration, which made it easier to focus on the visual without any audio distractions.

We were about ten minutes into an outtake showing Standish getting ready to make his announcement about the Image Transformation machine. He was standing behind his desk. A makeup artist was dabbing at his nose with a powder puff. He ignored her and shouted to a klieg-light operator outside the range of the camera to "Get that damn thing out of my eyes." Standish pointed up at the light source with his left hand, while with his right hand, he pushed away the powder puff.

Wylie bolted forward. "Freeze," he said.

I pushed the freeze-frame button on the remote control.

Stanfield Standish loomed large in the middle of the frame.

Wylie said, "Look at his left hand. What do you see?"

"Fingers."

"What else?"

"Nothing else."

"What about on his right hand?"

"Same thing. Creepy fingers. Nothing else."

Wylie stood and started pacing, which in his small office was more like jogging in place.

"I knew I'd missed something before. He'd even had his hand on top of the computer, and . . ."

I turned away from the screen and gave Wylie a questioning look.

"The ring," he said. "Standish isn't wearing the ring. Not on either hand. And if he wasn't wearing it when he died, then . . ."

He didn't have to finish the sentence. We pulled the fifth videotape out of the television and, one by one, reviewed the earlier four. We fast-forwarded, rewound, searched, slow-motioned, and used the freeze frame. We watched Standish graduating from college, Standish accepting an award for the script of one of his movies, Standish signing a contract for the purchase of his first radio station, Standish escorting Lucrezia to the opening of a movie, Standish shaking hands with the governor of New York. In none of those sequences did Stanfield Standish wear a ring.

Yet we'd dug a man's ring out from under the gas pedal of the car in which Standish had been found dead. A man's gold ring, with four evenly spaced, small diamonds, and inside, an inscription that we hadn't been able to read.

I turned to Wylie and said, "It was the killer's ring. That's what you're thinking, isn't it? And when we find out who the ring belonged to, we'll have found out who set the fire."

Instead of answering, Wylie put videotape number five back into the video player and we continued to watch the unedited footage from where we'd left off on the night of the Valentine's Day party.

First, we saw an establishing shot of the little town of Stilton-on-Hudson and the camera panning to a long, empty stretch of road. Next, we saw a medium shot of an old hand-lettered sign that said LOCUST DRIVE. Then the camera panned to the road itself and zoomed up it to an elaborately scrolled wrought-iron gate mounted on two six-foot fieldstone pedestals. The iron gate was shut and the surrounding area was vacant. In the distance, we could see the tall Grecian columns and the spotless white facade of Stanfield Standish's house.

I didn't remember the wrought-iron gates from our visit to the estate.

Before I could ask the question, Wylie answered it.

"Astrid Scheidler probably had them torn down."

The next video sequence brought us back to the gate, which was now surrounded by a group of well-dressed people, several of whom were carrying placard-size signs. At first, they huddled in conversational groups with their backs to the screen. Then one of them noticed the camera and said something to the others. They instantly turned around and adjusted themselves artistically in front of the camera. Their postures were perfect. Their manner was stagey. Two of them—smartly dressed women who looked vaguely familiar—took a position side by side, dead center on the television screen.

They supported a large, cylindrical object between them, and slowly, dramatically, unrolled what turned out to be a narrow rectangular banner.

Embroidered in black calligraphy on a white background were these words:

CURATORS FOR PRESERVATION OF FINE AMERICAN FILMS

Not exactly your basic, rabble-rousing protest slogan.

Vincent P. Marchand started pointing at the screen so frantically he almost fell off his chair.

"Max. Wylie. Look at the woman on the right."

We did. She seemed to be somewhere between sixty and seventy years old. Her hair was a soft, silvery color. Most of it was piled on top of her head, but a few loose strands escaped artfully around her neck. The bones of her face were delicate, and she had tiny wrinkles around deep green eyes. Just as she looked into the camera, I saw her expression change. First there was distress in those still beautiful eyes. And then her mouth moved, and I knew she was biting the inside of her upper lip. That was when I recognized her. It was the actress who'd starred opposite Howard Ingram's Noah in *Idlewild*. The woman who had become the immortal Pearl. It was Louise Eastman, and she was attending a protest rally on the night Stanfield Standish had announced a new film process that would obliterate her classical features and turn them into a truly calamitous thing.

Hell, I'd protest, too.

I turned to Vincent Marchand.

"Who are these people?"

"I never met them."

"But you recognized Louise Eastman."

"Only because I see pictures of her from time to time in our newsletter."

"What newsletter?"

"For The Curators. That's one of the movie clubs I belong to. But I've been a member for over a decade, and I don't remember hearing or reading anything five years ago about a demonstration against Stanfield Standish. And I don't see how The Curators could have put it together so quickly, since Standish only announced he was going to transform the images of his movies that very same day."

I shook my head. "I don't understand, either, Vincent. Tell me about these people, though. This group you belong to."

"We call ourselves The Curators. Exactly as it appears on the banner. We meet once a month, and once a year we have a members' convention. That's when we get together to buy or trade movie posters, publicity shots of the stars, original screen treatments, autographs, and souvenirs. We invite a guest speaker and some minor celebrities, and we organize a few panel discussions. We don't have much of a budget; but every once in a while the gods smile on us, and a famous movie star or a director will appear free. Usually, we have a theme. Last year, it was horror films. This year, it's going to be—"

Vincent Marchand suddenly interrupted himself. He leaned toward the television monitor. "Well, I'll be darned. Will you look at that."

I looked at the screen.

The old people in front of Standish's gate had taken off their overcoats or minks, and there was no mistaking any of them now. The effect they were trying to achieve was staged and deliberate. What was happening was eerie.

The faces.

The names.

The talent to enthrall.

Right there, before our eyes, they were recreating the famous studio portrait of Cinema Select Artists stars. They'd lined up in exactly the same positions they'd been in fifty years before, and they were wearing facsimiles of the exact same clothes. Their makeup was the same. Their jewelry. Their hats. Their hairstyles.

Of course, not all of them were there. Some had died. Some had found or lost religion. Some had found or lost themselves. But eight were left. And recognizable. Funny just how easily recognizable they were. And it wasn't just the 1940s styles of their clothing or their arrangement on the screen that told us who they were. Because they still had those faces. That confidence. That *je ne sais quoi* that had made each of them a star.

Louise Eastman had turned into a beautiful old lady with delicate bones and that telltale nervous habit she'd always had of biting the inside of her lip.

Her former co-star, Howard Ingram, stood next to her. His hair had turned gray, but he hadn't lost that imperious hawk nose; and there was still something majestic emanating from that massive, decrepit frame.

I even recognized Kirby Clark without his cutlass, parrot, and pirate pantaloons. According to an article I'd read a week earlier, he was still swashbuckling and was scheduled to open shortly in a new translation of an old Alexander Dumas play.

Standing to the right of Kirby Clark were the actor and actress whose images already had been transformed by Stanfield Standish's IT Machine: Roy Douglass and Arlene de Grasse. Often, thirty, forty, fifty years after the fact, when we see people who'd once played an important part in our fantasy life, we're horrified by how they look, how they've aged. "Who is that? No. It can't be so-and-so." We can accept aging in ourselves, but not in our heroes. Not in our stars. We feel betrayed and a little bit angry. How *dare* they have grown old like that. How *dare* they rob us of our memories.

But there were no robberies being committed by the movie stars lined up across our small television screen. Louise Eastman. Howard Ingram. Kirby Clark. Roy Douglass. Arlene de Grasse. They were powerful or majestic or handsome or beautiful. They were old. They were alive.

And their eyes glittered with indignation from under the brims of their 1940s hats.

"What kind of funding does this Curator group get?" I asked Vincent Marchand.

"Dues are thirty dollars a year. That barely covers mailing costs on the newsletter."

I gestured towards the screen. "It took a lot more than thirty dollars a year to stage an event like that."

Vincent shrugged. "What can I say? I'm on the board of directors of the New York chapter, such as it is, and I didn't know anything about it. If I'd known, I would have been there and brought along my wife, my daughters, and my autograph book. But we aren't a political group. We'd never sponsored a protest before. I have absolutely no idea how this one came about."

The video camera moved away from the movie stars and finally panned to the elderly men and women milling around the gate. And it was then that I realized they weren't carrying protest signs. What they were carrying was movie lobby posters.

The camera zoomed in tighter, and I could see the face of one nicely dressed old man who reminded me of someone.

"Vincent. Who's that guy?"

"I don't know."

"Wylie?"

"Unless he set a fire, I wouldn't recognize him, either."

"I know him from somewhere. But I don't remember where."

Vincent asked, "Is it important?"

"I'm not sure, but in case it is, would you show this video to some of your film buff friends? Maybe one of them will know who he is."

"I'd be happy to."

The camera zoomed in closer and closer until we could make out the artwork on the poster. Across the top was a stylized streak of letters: *Idlewild*. Beneath the title was a passionate illustration of Noah and Pearl. Pearl's head was tilted back. Her eyes were blazing into Noah's eyes the way women's eyes used to blaze fifty years ago. Noah's head was bent toward her protectively, the way men's heads used to be bent. You get the picture. His jaw was strong. The look in his eyes was fierce. The poster was a microcosm of the movie. Strong man with a purpose. Strong woman in love. For a second, my mind flashed to the same image with Skidder Freebody and Lucrezia as the leads. It was not a pleasant projection.

I looked back at the television monitor in time to catch the video camera panning away from the protesting actors. Then, for a second, the screen went black, followed by blinding lights, followed immediately by a clear, high-contrast image of Stanfield Standish on the running board of his Duesenberg. His face was expressionless, his arms were raised over his head in triumph. I couldn't tell if he looked more like a boxer who'd just won a match or a Baptist preacher collecting souls. Journalists, hangers-on, guests, chauffeurs—all were a tangle of arms, legs, torsos, and faces trying to get close to the media magnate or to get away from Stanfield Standish or to get past him and up the stairs into his house.

There was motion. There was chaos. All participated in the *sturm und drang*. Except for one dark-haired individual off to the right. He was in his mid to late thirties, and he had a pleasant, unspectacular face. What struck me most about him, though, was the quiet, speculative, *thinking* look in his eyes.

Miranda made a noise. I turned to her.

"Do you know who he is?"

"Sure, Max. I watch him all the time. He's a regular on *Point of View*. His name is Mark Greenberg."

"Tell me more."

"He used to work for Stanfield Standish. He lasted only one week. Standish didn't like his political philosophy, so he fired him. Greenberg got the Thomas Jefferson Award for Journalism that same year."

We watched Mark Greenberg. What was he doing at the party of a man who had just publicly and unceremoniously fired him? And what was he thinking? At first, Mark stood quietly to one side, watching Standish play the crowd. Then, when Standish unexpectedly turned his head and his eyes latched onto Mark Greenberg's eyes, something tense and electrical seem to pass between them.

But as soon as it started, it was over, and a tall, slender, fast-moving brunette strode onto the screen. She grabbed Mark Greenberg by the arm and abruptly pulled him out of the camera's range.

Strange.

I only got a glimpse of her. We studied that interaction frame by frame, rewinding, fast-forwarding. Still, I couldn't get a handle on any of her features. Shoulder-length hair with bangs. Short skirt. Long, chorus-girl legs. Very, very high-heeled shoes. And that was all.

She looked brisk. Competent. Efficient. Deadly.

CHAPTER

21

Eli Timmerman's area of expertise is photoanalysis. He is a Certified Photogrammetrist, the meaning of which Wylie unsuccessfully tried to explain to me on our flight to Chicago. He is also an expert in the use of digital and analog image analysis, which I now understand. Sort of.

Our plane landed at O'Hare in the early A.M., and it took us another forty-five minutes by cab to get to Eli Timmerman's office in Highland Park.

Watching Eli and Wylie work together was something like watching perfect doubles partners play tennis. It was the two of them against the obscurities, impurities, and distractions contained in a frame of film. Hidden within the pictures of the Duesenberg fire scene was evidence. It might be buried under debris, hidden by shadows, or lost amidst thick layers of char. But Wylie knew what he was looking for. And if it was there, Eli had the equipment, the experience, and the expertise to find it.

Eli Timmerman & Associates was impressive. We walked through a large, chart-infested room with computer terminals at long desks on which were piled unrolled sheets of schematics, maps, and computer plots.

Wylie was carrying a briefcase stacked with fire scene photographs. He led me to a door at the back of the room and pushed it open.

"Hello, Hump," he said to the large man inside who was tinkering with the knobs on a television monitor.

Eli Timmerman turned around.

Jesus, I thought. This is one big, scary, mean-looking son-of-a-bitch.

Wylie had told me a little about Eli on the plane. He'd been the Navy's star quarterback during his last two years at Annapolis. He'd graduated with an engineering degree and opted to go into Naval Intelligence, where his speciality had been analyzing early reconnaissance photographs of North Vietnam. He retired as a lieutenant colonel after a blank period he doesn't talk about when he was captured and made a prisoner of war by the Viet Cong, escaped, and was returned stateside.

After leaving the Navy, he worked six years for the Cook County District Attorney as a special investigator, got a master's degree in forensic science and a Ph.D. in philosophy, and built the computerized photogrammetric equipment with which we were about to work.

Eli Timmerman is huge. His shoulders look like crossbeams in a log cabin. His hands are baseball mitts. He has an enormous face. Like Frankenstein's monster, except handsome in a frightening way. Each high cheekbone looks like it's been swollen under a boxer's fist. His eyes are black and impenetrable. When he walks, he doesn't make any noise.

Wylie tossed his briefcase down on a swivel chair and introduced me. Once that was accomplished, Eli seemed friendly enough, which I guess meant that he didn't need to be strapped down and fed lightning bolts of electricity in order to function.

We got to work.

Wylie had enlarged all of our photographs into clean, unmarked prints eight inches by twelve inches and separated them into roughly eight categories. These were photographs of the ring, of the interior of the vehicle, of the engine compartment, of the trunk compartment, and all of Wylie's exterior shots of the Duesenberg. All the rest were Chief Lon Bandy's fire scene photographs, including interiors of the back seat and interiors of the front seat that showed Stanfield Standish's dead body.

We started with the pictures of the ring. Eli and Wylie rummaged through the pile and pulled out the ones that showed most of what we'd hypothesized was an inscription. Eli put the first of these on a light box about the size of a picnic table.

My understanding of how the image-enhancement system works is that the illumination from this table shines through a very small, highly magnified portion of an object in the photograph, and a video camera poised over the table records how light or dark the object or component of that object is in the photograph. This camera isn't interested in what the objects *are*, but rather in how light or dark they are, and how the density or intensity of that lightness or darkness changes throughout all the areas of the photograph. These gradients of lightness and darkness are transformed within the camera into voltages. And the change from light to voltage is exactly proportionate. If the camera picks up a lot of light, the light is transformed into a high voltage. If the camera picks up a dark reading from the photograph, then the voltage is low.

This may all seem like gibberish, but the analog image-analysis system can be invaluable in the way it uses the voltages it gets from the video camera to adjust the contrast within the photograph under observation. In doing so, the photograph itself is not altered in any way, but the photogrammetrist can adjust for maximum light to dark contrast and thereby enhance visibility. And he can do this with the entire picture. Or just with the part of the picture under consideration. He can also increase the definition of patterns or of the edges of objects in a photograph, where the most drastic contrasts between light and dark values occur. This aspect of the analog image–analysis system is called "edge enhancement."

It was with edge enhancement that we were primarily concerned during the analysis of the photographs of the ring. Engravings are, essentially, composed of horizontal, vertical, circular, and semicircular lines or edges. In engraving initials, varying combinations of these lines or edges are carved into an object.

When Wylie and I examined the Duesenberg at plaintiff's inspection site, we'd been hampered by bad lighting, icy weather conditions, and our need to return the ring to where we'd found it before Clyde Prouty and his people returned. On the flight from New York to Chicago, Wylie told me that he often discovers things in photographs that he'd missed at the fire scene.

"During a fire investigation," he explained, "your eye is caught up with what your brain tells you is top priority. You have to work fast; you're surrounded by other interested, sometimes hostile, parties—including the police, the property owner, and his insurance adjuster or attorney. All of them can have a vested interest in your not being there. The utility company has turned off the electricity, lighting is bad, visibility is terrible, and your equipment is usually inadequate. So, the best back-up system you've got is your trusty thirty-five millimeter camera with a lot of fast film and a powerful flash."

Wylie stressed that at the fire scene itself, his immediate concern is what he *knows* or *thinks* is important. It's only when he gets back to his office that he has time to analyze the pictures he's taken and look for things in them that may later prove to be significant.

When we'd inspected the Duesenberg in Prouty's barn, Wylie and I had only had time to do a quick study of the ash-covered ring. I'd held it in my hand, slipped it on my finger, and got a fast, hot look at it each time Wylie's camera flashed. But I couldn't make out a single letter, let alone the whole inscription on the ring.

Things were different now, though. With the aid of electronic image enhancement, magic was happening.

Eli put a macro lens on his video camera to get a really big blowup of the markings inside the ring. Data from the images in the photographs were being processed by three different video subsystems positioned around the light table. I didn't understand the images on the color monitor. Nor did I understand the significance of what was appearing on the second monitor, a raster scan, which showed the density, hills, and valleys of the lightness and darkness of the image being analyzed. But I could see and understand what was on the third monitor, the high-resolution black-and-white television screen.

This was the one I could read. This was the one that seemed, literally, to have raised the phoenix out of the ashes. The only thing I can compare it to is looking at a dim aquarium in which all of the contents are obscured by filthy water. Someone—a photogrammetrist with marine water in his veins—flicks one of two hundred switches. The water instantly becomes crystal clear, and you can actually *see* for the first time all of the vivid colors and beautiful shapes of the fish.

Let me try again. Photogrammetry—image enhancement— brings out in a simple black-and-white or color photograph things that are already there, in the picture, recorded in the film negative, but which cannot be made visible by less sophisticated equipment. It finds depths, discovers contrasts, brings out and uncovers the edges of objects. Imagine leaning over a black circle in the road and then discovering that it is not a black circle at all, but a hole. Next, imagine leaning into the hole and discovering a steel ladder descending to the inside. Then, imagine getting down on your hands and knees, looking down the ladder, and discovering that at the bottom of the hole is a man, and he's waving at you.

That man is often there, in the picture, at the bottom of the black dot, in the film negative. It just takes a certain kind of equipment and a special kind of expertise to get him out.

Eli Timmerman says that the two words most commonly expressed by all who see enhanced photographic data for the first time in a previously inarticulate photograph are "Holy shit."

I can vouch for that reaction.

The macro lens enlarged the ring bigger and bigger. Because of the nature of the video equipment used, the enlarged pictures did not become grainy or lose definition. Actually, they gained definition. The edges surrounding the lines and curves of the letters inside the ring became clearer and clearer.

It took us two photographs at different perspectives to read all three hundred and sixty degrees of lettering inside the ring. The inscription read:

TO D. ALL LOVE. A.V.F.S.

Who was D?

Who was A.V.F.S.?

I copied down the inscription. Eli took pictures of the photo-enhanced ring. Then, he and Wylie went on to study the rest of the photographs of the fire scene; and with the aid of photogrammetry, Wylie was finally able to explain the fire to me. Using his terminology, Wylie "walked me through the fire," or we "did the fire."

The next photograph Eli enhanced was of the interior of the Duesenberg. It exposed a series of unusual burn patterns that I'd seen when Wylie did his physical examination of the car, but which he didn't explain to me at the time. These burn patterns snaked across the top of the leather upholstery in the car as wide, one-dimensional black lines.

"Here," Wylie pointed at one of them. "What we're looking for is a deep rut in the leather."

Eli focused his video camera, and we all turned to the black-and-white TV monitor.

"Holy shit," I said.

It was like looking at the Colorado River winding through the Grand Canyon. Not only could we see the edges around either side of the rut, but we could also see that the channel had been deeply gouged into the upholstery.

"What *did* that?"

"A flammable liquid," Wylie said softly. But I could sense his excitement.

"What kind?"

"Wait."

Wylie fed more pictures to Eli. Eli enhanced the areas where Wylie thought that something—a burn pattern, a pour pattern, a suspicious downward burning—might be. Using the video camera and monitor, Wylie and Eli found flammable-liquid burn patterns in the shape of a "puddle" on the floor of the passenger side in the front of the car.

A pour pattern or a "puddle" pattern is an attack of flames into some manner of flooring that leaves a burn pattern in the shape of the poured accelerant in the exact location where that accelerant had been poured. Think of spilling ink onto a carpet. It puddles into a pattern. Think of pouring corrosive acid onto a wood floor. The acid "eats" into the flooring. Think of pouring and then igniting a flammable liquid. It, too, burns downward into the shape of the liquid that has been poured.

Moving upward to the passenger seat, photo enhancement revealed a long ribbon-shaped pour pattern similar to that on the upholstery in the rear. A puddle of burning was also found on the floor in the back seat of the Duesenberg. And yet another one of those ribbon burn patterns seemed somehow to have clung to the vertical upholstery cushion in the back.

"I've never seen anything like it," Eli said.

"How is it different?" I asked.

"It's as if it adhered into the upholstery where it landed. Like . . ."

"Like napalm," Wylie said.

"Right. And it seems to have a viscous quality."

"What can you buy that does that?" I asked.

"You don't buy it," Wylie said. "You make it. If you add a flaky laundry detergent to a container of flammable liquid, what you end up with is a volatile mixture that'll burn like an oil-well fire and stick where it lands like glue."

"What kind of a flammable liquid are we talking about here?"

"It wasn't gasoline. Gasoline is so volatile that if . . ."

"Slow down and tell me what you mean by volatility? I know how *I* used the word, but when *you* use it, I want to know what a fire investigator would mean."

"By volatility, I mean the relative ease of evaporation of a flammable liquid. For example, gasoline is very volatile; comparatively, kerosene and fuel oil are nonvolatile. The volatile ingredients in gasoline have boiling points below room temperature and are converted to vapor or gases as soon as the liquid is exposed to air. When a match or other ignition source is applied to a flammable liquid, it's the fumes that go on fire, not the actual liquid itself. Therefore, the more volatile the liquid, the faster and hotter and more destructive the fire.

"If it had been a gasoline mix that our arsonist applied to the Duesenberg, not only would there be no burn patterns in the upholstery to examine, there wouldn't be any upholstery left at all. The fire would have gotten so hot so fast that it would have burned through the aluminum and wood frame of the chassis and heated up the twenty-six-gallon gas tank; then the gas tank would have exploded, and once that rupture had occurred, the melting point of aluminum, which is 1100 to 1500 degrees, would have been rapidly reached. By the time the fire had burned itself out, instead of the shell of a Duesenberg, all that would have been left of the car would be a melted hunk of burned metal; and instead of a dead body, all that would have been left of Stanfield Standish would be gray ashes and white bone. As if he had been cremated."

"If it wasn't gasoline, then what flammable liquid do you think was used?"

"Kerosene. Fuel oil. Charcoal lighter fluid. Something less volatile but still capable of fueling and sustaining a fire. Personally, I'd opt for kerosene. Add some of that to your soap flakes, and you've got a nice little napalm bomb."

Wylie handed his stack of engine compartment photographs to Eli. One by one, we examined them on the system's screen. We could see that flammable liquid had been thrown or poured onto the eight-cylinder engine block and that thick, globlike burn patterns had been scorched into the metal. But they didn't seem to extend anywhere after that. Nor had the spatter-mark fires that seared into the underside of the engine compartment's hood extended beyond their own tiny perimeters.

All four tires had also been burned to the rim at ground level. We examined the tires carefully in each photo. As the screen flickered, our excitement grew.

"If the fire started in the engine compartment or as a result of any mechanical or electrical failure in the car, it would be impossible for the tires to have burned like this," Wylie said.

I stared at the video screens. The top halves of all four tires were distorted and discolored, but otherwise intact; but the rubber on the bottom halves of the tires had been completely consumed.

"Go on."

"And if the fire started in the engine," Wylie said, "the flames would have to travel from the engine compartment in a downward direction towards the tires. Then in order to burn the bottom halves of the tires, the fire would have had to burn through the tops first. Simple logic. For A to get to C, it has to go through point B first. These tires, though, are burned only at the bottom. The midsections aren't burned. Therefore, this fire burned from the ground level up. What do you think would cause a fire to burn that way, Max?"

"We're eliminating an engine compartment fire?"

"We have to. You can clearly see now that the fire didn't come from that direction."

"And we're eliminating a passenger compartment fire?"

"Yes. Because the tops of the tires aren't burned. So if the fire didn't come from the engine compartment and it didn't communicate from the passenger compartment, then where did the fire come from?"

"Street level."

"All right. Now since there is no natural source of ignition at street level, no fireflies in February, no fireworks because it isn't the Fourth of July, then how did the fire start?"

"An accelerant?" I suggested tentatively.

"Exactly. Somebody poured flammable liquid at the bottom of each tire."

The next photograph we analyzed was of the interior of the Duesenberg's trunk. The trunk contained a golf bag and clubs, some crumpled-up papers that looked as though they'd been baked in an oven, some clothing or rags bunched up in a corner, and what looked like a plastic drinking container. The plastic had melted. There was also a rusty stream of blotches running along the outside of the trunk's hood.

"What happened here, Wylie?"

"Either the arsonist was in too much of a hurry to open the trunk or he was smart enough not to want to get too close to the twenty-six-gallon gas tank. But he threw some of the accelerant against the outside of the trunk. See this flammable-liquid burn pattern here. It was probably ignited by radiant heat when the rest of the car went up in flames."

We systematically viewed the rest of the pictures of the passenger compartment at high magnification. Wylie explained that the low burning on the rocker panels of the car was another indication that a flammable liquid had been used. This was because the flames were coming from below the level where any natural source of ignition might occur, and because fire, without the addition of an accelerant, normally burns up and not down. Eli also showed us vignettes of irregular buckling on the Duesenberg's roof.

"Distortion of the roof doesn't mean much today," Wylie explained, "because there are about six hundred pounds of plastics and other combustible materials in the average American car, two to three hundred pounds of which are in the passenger compartment alone. So, once a fire gets going, whether that fire was the result of a short circuit in the wiring harness or the result of arson, there's enough fuel in the car to create such a hot and fast fire that buckling and distension of the roof will almost inevitably occur.

"This Duesenberg was different, though. Other than upholstery, the passenger compartment contained very few combustibles and no plastics. For the passenger compartment to have gotten hot enough for the Duesenberg roof to distend, which it did, a flammable liquid had to have been introduced."

Wylie had taken eight rolls of film during our inspection of the Duesenberg, which amounted to one hundred and ninety-two pieces of developed film. We brought half of those pictures with us to Chicago. Of that half, we photo-enhanced only about a dozen. Wylie had brought along the other pictures so that he could visually reconstruct and explain the fire to us. He laid them out on all of the available tables in Eli's lab, and "walked" us through the fire.

Fire analysis, I was beginning to understand, is a strange but coherent kind of detective work. It's subtle and it's cerebral. It's almost all inductive reasoning. Or do I mean deductive reasoning? Or both? For one thing, in the course of almost any other criminal investigation, you know beforehand if a crime has been committed. Otherwise, you wouldn't waste your time poking around where you don't belong.

But when you're dealing with a fire, you can't possibly have even the remotest idea as to whether or not a crime has occurred until after you've already investigated the fire scene. When people die, it can be from any number of causes that are noncriminal, nonsuspicious. These are what are called "natural causes." Old age. Shock. Disease. Heart attack. Whatever.

But fire is different. There is no such thing as a "natural" fire. Death, at the end of a long life, is supposed to happen. Fire is *never* supposed to occur. All fires are aberrations. A house doesn't get sick and ignite. A car doesn't feel a pain in its chest and spontaneously combust. A hotel doesn't go to the doctor to be treated for a little bit of flame. There is no acceptable amount of burning. Therefore, all fires must be viewed as incidents where something went wrong. All fires must be viewed as potential crime scenes.

Whether it was the result of an accident or if the fire had been deliberately set, you always have a corpse to deal with. The corpse of a building, or the corpse of a house, or, as in the case of Stanfield Standish, the corpse of a car. And in our case, our corpse of the automobile contained the corpse of a man inside.

Fire is emphatic business. It doesn't fool around. I was beginning to realize that Wylie Nolan didn't fool around, either. Until Wylie came into this investigation, not one single investigator, not one single individual, not one single law-enforcement officer (despite the brief flurry of activity from Chief Bandy), had breathed a word that the fire in the Duesenberg might have been arson. Nor, until Wylie explained the meaning of the distended metal on the roof of the car, had I myself fully and completely understood that the lawsuit and death we were dealing with was the consequence of the commission of a felony crime.

The last set of Wylie Nolan's pictures were of the keys to the Duesenberg. There were two keys, held together on a small metal ring. In the first photograph, they were still where Wylie had found them.

Encased in the floor mat on the front passenger side of the car. There was a clear pour pattern where the flammable liquid had savagely attacked the floor mat, almost obliterating it and burning through it down to the wood floor. A small section of that mat remained relatively intact, though, and had sculpted itself in melted rubber around the keys.

Looking at that photograph of the keys lent itself to speculation. How had they come to be discarded there on the floor? Had they been thrown there by Stanfield Standish? Or by the arsonist? Or had they fallen there during a struggle? Maybe th keys had been in Standish's pocket, the pocket had burned off during the fire, and they'd slid to the floor. Or maybe someone had deliberately hidden them there with the intent to retrieve them at a later date. Regardless of *how* they'd gotten there, there was no mistaking that they were on the floor at the time when the fire started, and that, therefore, the car's motor cannot have been on.

One of Wylie's pictures gave us a panorama of both the ignition switch in the OFF position, and the ignition key outlined on the floor in melted rubber; both were in the same photo frame at the same time. It was this picture that I wanted to blow up to poster size as an exhibit for the trial: "Ladies and gentlemen of the jury, how often have *you* been able to drive your car without a key and when the ignition switch was in the OFF position?"

We looked up on the video screen at that picture for a moment. Its significance was horribly obvious.

During his investigation, Wylie had removed this same ignition key from the floor mat and photographed it in a variety of positions. One of which, to prove that it was indeed the key to the Duesenberg, was in the ignition switch, with that switch turned on.

Then, he'd replaced both keys where he'd found them under the burned floor mat, where Clyde Prouty and his crew had never bothered to look.

•

We were almost finished. Wylie saved the most dramatic photographs for last. By which I don't mean the pictures that he'd taken, but the ones taken by my all-time-favorite law-enforcement officer, Chief Lon Bandy of the Stilton-on-Hudson police.

Now might be a good time to tell you something you probably don't know about burn victims. Or, rather, about photographs of burn victims. If an individual died in a fire, not as a result of smoke inhalation or fumes, but as a result of flame impingement, emergency service personnel such as ambulance drivers, policemen, and forensic pathologists sometimes deal with the horror by engaging in a characteristic black humor or "gallows humor" that gets them over the rough spots of dealing with death.

A lot of firemen are guilty of this kind of glibness at a fire scene. When they see a dead body that has been burned beyond recognition, they might call it a "crispy critter" or a "roast." Granted, they would never do this in front of the victims' families, but such unapologetic bantering has gone on in Wylie Nolan's presence and in mine.

Why do they engage in such uncharacteristically insensitive behavior?

Because anyone who dies in a fire represents a failure to a fireman. Someone they couldn't save. And saving lives is their job.

Joking about a D.O.A. at a fire scene is a way of distancing themselves from the terrible consequences of fire. A "crispy critter" doesn't have to be viewed as a horribly burned human being whom they weren't able to save from the worst possible death. Unfortunately, "crispy critter" and "roast" are also relatively valid descriptions of what a body looks like if it has been subjected to intense flame.

I've looked at hundreds of pictures of burn victims since I've been practicing product-liability law, and the only generalization I can make about all of them is that they no longer look like people. Granted, they aren't pleasant to look at; and, in fact, some of the pictures are downright sickening. But what's depicted within the frame of the photograph looks more like something that came out of the makeup department during a horror movie than like anything that was ever a human being.

Stanfield Standish dead did not look like a dead Stanfield Standish. He looked like the Creature from the Black Lagoon.

Callous I may sound and callous I may perhaps be, but you look at five hundred photographs of people burned way beyond recognition, and I challenge you to tell me what *you* see.

There is little left to remind us that what we are looking at was once human. It doesn't take a lot of courage or strength or even a strong stomach to look at or analyze the pictures of a badly burned D.O.A.

It's like looking at a thing.

I know. I know. I still sound like a heartless S.O.B.

Be that as it may, Wylie spent hours studying the pictures Chief Bandy had taken of Stanfield Standish's dead body in the front seat of the Duesenberg. He'd stare at one photograph for twenty minutes at a stretch and then move on to do the same thing with another. When I looked at the same pictures, all I'd ever see was the Creature from the Black Lagoon. It was hard for me to believe that within the dark, ugly, impenetrable husk of what had once been Stanfield Standish, Wylie could see anything, learn anything, or come to anything resembling a conclusion.

I was wrong.

Arson homicide.

Those were the two words that, by the end of our session with Eli Timmerman, had been hammered inextricably into my brain. Arson homicide. How had it happened? Where had all of that violence come from? I was a corporate attorney. I was supposed to be working on a nice, clean, white-collar, nonviolent product-liability case. A civil matter. Not criminal.

Wylie threw a picture on the light box. He and Eli bent over it. I shouldered them apart.

"What are we looking at?"

"This hole over here on the right side of Standish's head."

"Where's the head? I don't even see a head."

"All right. Relax. Don't panic. We'll go slower."

Wylie took that picture off the light box and replaced it with one taken from farther away. A medium shot that showed the full interior of the front seat of the car.

"Do you see the body?"

"Yes."

"How would you describe it?"

I stared at the picture for about thirty seconds.

"It's leaning back against the driver's seat."

"How would you describe the arms and hands?"

"Wait a second. Let me see if I can find them."

Almost everything inside a car that has been set on fire is black. The seats are black. The interior shell of the car is black. The clothing on the body, if any are left, is black. And the body is black.

"I think I found it. Is that one of the arms?"

"No. That's part of the upholstery. Keep looking."

I squinted down at the photograph. Eli turned the contrast down so that we could see more of the detail inherent in the photograph.

"Here." Wylie put a second picture on the light table. "I'll make it easy for you. Look at this. Over here. To the right of the steering wheel. What is it?"

"Okay. I can see it now." I could trace the length of—it must have been what was left of an arm—back to what I thought might be a shoulder. My eyes went back and forth between both photographs for about fifteen more seconds, orienting myself, trying to pick shapes out of the varying degrees of blackness. And then—

"Now I've got it."

"You're sure you found the arms?"

"Yes."

"How would you describe them?"

"Relaxed. The right arm is lying loosely on the right side of the body, and the hand is open, palm up. The fingers, if those are fingers—"

Eli turned the contrast down even more, and the brightness up, and the details leapt into view. I pointed to a distorted, crabbed-up collection of bones.

Wylie said, "You're right. Those are fingers. What do they look like to you?"

"They're curled up, like a claw."

"How about the neck?"

"I see it. It's leaning back against the cushion."

"And his head?"

"The head. Okay. I can find the head now. That's flopped back too. Against the driver's side door."

"You're sure you found the head?"

"Yes."

"Okay. Now, look at this."

Wylie whisked away the two medium shots at which we'd been looking and replaced them with the first picture he'd had up on the light box.

Eli turned a knob or two and focused down on the photograph.

"Now can you see the head?" He asked.

Yes. Now I could see the head. In fact, now it was so obvious to me where and what it was, that it was hard to conceive of my visual illiteracy of just a few seconds before.

"I see the head, Wylie."

"Good. Now look at this little hole over here."

Since almost everything that has been burned is visible to us in varying shades of gray or black, photogrammetry—enhancing the contrasts between values of light and dark—can be of inestimable value in analyzing the evidence of a fire. The difficulties I had in trying to locate Standish's head in the debris may also give you some insight about why Wylie Nolan stares so much when he investigates a fire. What he's doing is trying to make distinctions. Clarify observations. Adjust his mind to compensate for the minimum visual input. Black on black. Black on gray. Gray on black. Not easy to figure out what's what.

It took me over a minute to find the hole.

"Okay. I found it. Now what?"

Wylie and Eli Timmerman looked at each other. For the first time, Eli smiled. I mean, really smiled. Then he focused his video camera on the photograph of Stanfield Standish's head and zoomed into a closeup of the black dot that Wylie Nolan had called a hole.

I turned to the monitor.

We all turned to the monitor.

Unbelievable.

Was there anything that Eli and his machine couldn't do? Was there anything that Eli and his machine couldn't find? What we were

152

looking at wasn't just a black dot in the area of Stanfield Standish's temple, magnified, with the light and dark values enhanced and the edges defined.

It was a crater.

It was barely puckered at the edges. I could see the slight eruptions.

It had depth. I could see down into it.

It was a hole. A hole in a dead man's head.

I looked at Wylie.

"Arson-homicide," he said softly. And I could almost smell that bird—dog intensity again. He was on red alert. The hunter who had picked up the scent.

He put all three pictures back on the light box at once, and said, almost as if to himself, "If somebody dies in a fire, Max, one of the first questions you have to ask yourself is why he didn't get out."

Wylie pointed to the photograph that showed Standish's arm resting against the upholstery of the front seat, palm up.

"Look at this picture over here. Look at Standish's body. It's open to the fire. People don't open their bodies to heat and flame. If they can't escape, they try to protect themselves. Children in a fire curl up and hide under beds. Grownups who can't flee are found huddled up against what they think is an escape route, bodies tucked in the fetal position. Now, look at Standish."

Again, I studied the photograph.

"He looks like he's sunbathing," Wylie said.

"So?" I asked my fire investigator.

"So," he said. "Stanfield Standish was already dead before the fire started. If he hadn't been, he would have escaped from the car."

"Go on."

"And this," he pointed to the small, tight, neat crater on the right side of Standish's head. "This is a bullet entry wound."

CHAPTER

22

Alexander Urda would not have been my—or I think anybody's—idea of what a retired chief medical examiner should look like. Maybe he could be conceived of as the president of a company that makes those little Valentine hearts that say "Be Mine." Or possibly he'd make a great Ho Ho Ho bald black Santa Claus. I could even see him as the back half of a successful vaudeville team. The half that wears the drooping horse's feet and tail. But as far as looking like a man who's spent his entire life carving up dead bodies. No. No way.

Because Alexander Urda is effervescent, good-natured, and by all accounts, a very jolly man. He was about seventy-three years old when I met him. He's seventy-five or thereabouts now. I use him on every case I have where a death is involved. And as Wylie Nolan once said, juries love him.

He has a fringe of stone-gray hair that squirrels around the back of his head, the pate of which is bald and shiny brown, like chocolate pudding. He also has large, laughing brown eyes and large, laughing brown jowls. He's short and rotund, with something of the happy hippopotamus about him. Back during the Depression, he worked his way through medical school as the only black stand-up comedian on the Borscht Belt circuit of Jewish resort hotels. He's married to a woman who writes what he calls high-cholesterol cookbooks; has five children, every single one of whom has become a forensic pathologist; and smokes rancid Persian cigars. His specialty, for which he is known worldwide, is gunshot wounds.

Since his retirement from the city, Dr. Alexander Urda has written a textbook on forensic pathology, built up a successful private consulting practice, and joined the staff of the forensic-science department at Rosedale College. Rosedale is a small, private school two blocks from the best view of Manhattan in the city, on the Brooklyn Heights promenade.

We agreed to meet him at the Old Budapest Restaurant, his favorite place for eating lunch. A sour-faced man in his late seventies met Urda and Wylie and me at the top of a narrow flight of stairs and grunted when we opened the restaurant door.

Urda returned the grunt with a grin, turned to us, and said, "My friend Franz. He treats the whole world as if we are communist conspirators."

Franz said something that sounded like "Ptuouy," which I assumed was an expression of contempt.

"Franz, Hungary is free. The Soviet Union has crumpled. The KGB isn't hiding under your bed any longer. You can relax. These are my friends, Max Bramble, an attorney, and Wylie Nolan, a man who locates the cause and origin of suspicious fires. Do you think you can take time away from your brooding philosophic meanderings to find us a seat in your fine and overcrowded establishment?"

Franz grunted again and led us past three empty tables to a small table by a large window overlooking Montague Street.

We sat down. We were the only customers in the place. I kept my voice low and asked, "Does he really think that we're communists?"

Urda shrugged. "Who knows what he thinks?" He looked up at our host. "What *do* you think, Franz?"

"I think that the Wiener schnitzel is good today. Order that."

"Does anybody here like Wiener schnitzel?" Urda asked.

"Not me."

"Not me, either."

Franz grumbled, "So stop whining and order the goulash instead."

We took the path of least resistance and ordered the goulash, and Franz stalked away.

There were rustic paintings of Alpine villages done in bright primary colors on the walls of the Old Budapest Restaurant. The spaces between the paintings were dotted with plates displaying colorful primitive European designs, and at the back of the room sat an old upright piano.

I looked at it. Then I looked at Dr. Urda and asked, "Who plays?"

"Franz, of course. When God handed out pleasant dispositions, my friend Franz wasn't standing in line. But when he handed out musical ability, Franz pushed everybody else out of his way. You know, of course, that Franz Liszt was Hungarian. Our Franz was named after him."

When "our" Franz came back to the table and gruffly placed three small bowls of pickled cucumbers on our plates, Dr. Urda asked, "Will you play for us today, Franz? If I asked you nicely?"

"Nice! Humph. Can nice buy bread for my starving people? Can nice bring back the heroic fools who died in the revolution of 1956? Nice. What is nice? Nice is an old shoe." Franz snorted and stalked back toward his kitchen.

"Franz has a long memory," I commented.

"Franz is old," Dr. Urda said. "Old people are allowed to have anything they want. Especially if they can prepare goulash and play rhapsodies on the piano."

We ate the pickled cucumbers. Seconds later, Franz returned with a basket of hot pumpernickel rolls and a loaf of pumpernickel bread.

"So!" Franz exclaimed. And once more, he disappeared.

Before I took a bite out of my pumpernickel roll, I looked at it speculatively and said, "The food must be pretty good here if you're willing to put up with Franz."

"Put up with him?" Urda repeated. "I don't put up with Franz. I seek him out. I choose to be in the glowering circle of his miserable disposition. He's so cranky and unpleasant, he's so disagreeable that I feel completely at home here. Here I am safe. Here I am at ease. Here it is impossible to distrust. For what is there to mistrust about a man who never has a single nice thing to say?"

I didn't know how to respond to Dr. Urda's convoluted logic, and Wylie distracted me when he took a handful of photographs out of his briefcase and stacked them beside his plate. Franz brought us bowls of borscht. I hate borscht. I looked at Franz. He glared down at me. I ate the borscht.

I still hate borscht.

And I think I hate Franz.

Over their bowls of goulash, Wylie Nolan and Dr. Alexander Urda flipped through pictures of exposed tendons, heat fractures on skulls, and flame-discolored tissue. They had one of those you-start-a-sentence-and-I'll-finish-it types of relationships.

After they'd gone through the photographs once, they went through the whole pack again, this time much slower, and focusing on specific body parts to which damage had been done and from which evidence could be extracted that would give us more information about the fire.

Franz brought us three cups of espresso.

I'd asked for American coffee, but there's no way I was going to engage in a battle of wills with a dispossessed anti-Bolshevik in Brooklyn. Not only did I not know *where* I was in Brooklyn, I had no idea how to get back to Manhattan.

"Good goulash," I said to Franz.

Franz snorted.

I returned my attention to the photographs on the table. We went through a few more; and just as Wylie was pulling out a print of Standish's body, I heard a soft sound emerge from the back of the room. It continued as a light fluttering of piano keys in the high octave range. I raised my head.

Dr. Urda whispered, "Don't look at him or he'll stop."

"What's happening?" I hissed between my teeth.

I felt as though I'd suddenly become a member of a political underground, conspiring over borscht and black bread to overthrow Stalin.

Urda leaned forward and said in hushed reverence, "Franz is playing the piano."

And so he was. Not that the dichotomy of Chopin and dead bodies seemed to bother anybody but me.

Wylie pointed to a savage attack of fire in the shin area of Standish's leg on the right side of the steering wheel.

"What do you make of this, Alexander?"

"Hot." Dr. Urda said. "Very hot. Victims of burns fall into five categories. The first are those who actually come into contact with flames. The second are people who are exposed to radiant heat. The third group are people who get scalded. The fourth are victims of chemical burns, like from acids and alkalis. And the last category of burn victims are people who get burned by microwaves, which is almost nobody, so you can forget them."

Dr. Urda shuffled again through the photographs on the table. The piano action at the back of the room was now passionate. Romantic. High notes. Low notes. Heavy pounding on the chords. Fingers flying up and down the keyboard. I recognized the music. *The Desert Song* by Sigmund Romberg. Desert? Fire? Heat? I guess it was appropriate.

"Of the five types of burning, it is obvious here that this guy came into contact with flames. And look at this. And this. And this. And this." Urda happily pointed to various parts on Standish's body where deep blotch marks could be observed. "When you have isolated burning of a limited area like that, burning in unrelated patches, it probably means that someone threw gasoline on him." Urda looked up at Wylie. "What do you think?"

Wylie described how the combination of soapy detergent flakes with an accelerant such as fuel oil or kerosene would create exactly that effect.

"Sounds right to me," Urda said. "But do you think he was dead first? Where are your autopsy photos? What about your lab reports?

How do I find out if there was any carbon monoxide in the blood? How about inside his nose and down his trachea? What color were they? Were they covered with soot? What color were his lungs? Were they cherry red? What kind of a case is this? Is this all that you got?"

I told Dr. Urda about the Standish family's power-heavy tactics at the fire scene and their political influence, about the State Police's mishandling of evidence, and the release of the body to the funeral parlor before an autopsy could be performed. Meanwhile, Wylie was still thumbing through the photographs; he pulled out the one he'd spent so much time on at Eli's office. The one with the small black dot on the right side of Standish's temple, and laid it down between the pumpernickel basket and the butter dish. Then he put his finger on that barely visible dot, looked across the table to Alexander Urda, and gave Urda one of his kill-or-be-killed grins.

Urda didn't react.

Wylie placed the second photograph, the one that Eli had enhanced of the same area, on top of the first. Urda looked down again. An enlightened smile started to separate the lips over his happy hippopotamus teeth.

"Good," he said merrily. "A gunshot entrance wound from a small caliber pistol."

I leaned forward eagerly. "Are you sure?"

"Of course I'm sure."

"Fired at close range?"

"Naturally. Look at the puckered skin."

"Does that mean you think Standish was already dead before the fire started?"

"Look at how the guy's lying. Most people, if they're dead or alive when the fire reaches them, assume what's called a 'pugilistic' pose. The muscles coagulate because the heat causes their fibers to contract. When this happens, the arms curl up like a boxer holding his hands up in front of him."

"Go on."

"When you don't find a burn victim in a pugilistic pose, when the guy looks like this guy looks . . ." Urda's finger indicated Standish's neck relaxed against the driver's seat, his head resting against the door, as if it had flopped there after having absorbed the impact from a bullet. "When a guy looks like this guy looks. Bang. One shot to the temple and he's dead. Then, a little flammable liquid here. A little flammable liquid there. Strike a match. And whoosh! Right, Wylie?"

"Right, Alexander."

Wylie and Dr. Urda continued to flip through photograph after photograph of the body, unrecognizable as Stanfield Standish and barely recognizable as a corpse. They talked about household fires rarely exceeding 1600 degrees Fahrenheit.

"Since human beings are composed ninety-seven percent of water," Urda told me, "we are virtually fireproof. It would be hard to achieve such intense levels of burning on a body without the application of an extremely flammable substance."

I was shown a photograph of Standish's leg in which something gray protruded through blackened, split skin.

"For the fire to have burned through muscle and tissue all the way down to the bone like this, the temperature inside Standish's car had to reach between 1800 and 2000 degrees Fahrenheit."

Franz, our grumpy restaurateur, was playing a Hungarian rhapsody by Liszt. Wylie started to gather up his photographs, and Dr. Urda smiled benignly, his head swaying back and forth to the music. Then his eyes drifted over to meet mine, and he said, "So?"

So what? Had I missed something in the conversation?

"So, have you decided yet if I'll make a good impression on your jury?"

Great. Alexander Urda looked like a dancing hippopotamus, cut up dead people for a living, and read minds.

He went on evenly. "Some attorneys think I'm too old."

Not me, buster. I wouldn't dare think *anything* around you.

"But I always say a good expert is like fine wine. The older he gets, the better he gets."

The music stopped.

I reached for my wallet and took out a credit card. Franz appeared at my elbow, snapped the card out of my hand, and stalked away.

Urda said, "He likes you. He played Liszt."

He had also played Sigmund Romberg. What did that mean?

Seconds later, Franz reappeared with our bill. He hadn't charged us for the borscht, for the pickled cucumbers, or for the coffee. I pointed this out to him.

He snarled at me.

On the way out the door, Urda made a point of going over to Franz and thanking him effusively for the concerto. Franz shouted, "Music! Music! So! Who needs music! What is music anyway! Don't bother me. Who needs you!"

Urda walked back to us, still smiling, but now shaking his head gently.

He said in a low, amused voice, "I can't help it. I absolutely love that man."

CHAPTER

23

"Of course, I was aware of my family's lawsuit against your client, but I haven't really been apprised of any of the details."

Astrid Scheidler, much to my surprise, had responded positively to my letter. I'd told Sarah that if I was out of town when such a miracle occurred, to set up lunch with her in Wilmington's Hotel du Pont. Time and date to be at Miss Scheidler's convenience.

Before driving down to Delaware to meet her, though, I wanted to bone up a little on what Astrid Scheidler had done since she'd stopped riding bicycles in Stilton-on-Hudson, other than successfully managing the Harriet O'Brien's chain of department stores left to her by her father.

Apparently, according to the article Sarah gave me, Miss Scheidler had been busy. Very busy. In fact, before her brother had even cooled off in his grave, she'd sold off his holdings in Stanfield Standish News. All of them. Every single one.

The most popular theory as to *why* she did that had to do with Standish's very public firing of Mark Greenberg after his *These Are Her People* broadcast. And when Greenberg got the Thomas Jefferson Award for Journalism *for* that show, it seemed to a few skeptics that the award had been given less to honor Mark Greenberg than to spite Stanfield Standish.

Standish's sacred cow of neo-internationalism had also come under attack. Jokes were being made about his neo-inter/this and neo-inter/that, with one newscaster going so far as to suggest that Stanfield Standish's real neo-inter/motive was to use his vast telecommunications network to accumulate enough power to take over the whole blasted neo-inter/world.

Be that as it may, the business community was already abuzz with the whys and wherefores of Astrid Scheidler's sale of SSN when she knocked them right off their seats again by taking the proceeds from the sale of SSN and pouring it back into Stanfield Standish Presents.

SSP, if you remember, was that arm of Standish Enterprises that had bought up the Cinema Select classics targeted to be "image transformed" by the god-awful IT Machine.

Astrid Scheidler, the article said, was not a fan of IT. She was too smart to come out against it directly, because she didn't want to risk a breach of contract lawsuit from either Lucrezia or Skidder Freebody. So, rather than firing them, she convinced them to abandon the "remake" of *Idlewild* and make new theatrically released music videos instead.

The first of these cinemavideos, as they were called, was a spectacular success. It was terrible, of course. And therefore, the pre-teens loved it, and therefore it made a lot of money.

After producing a few more cinemavideos, Astrid Scheidler toppled her critics off their tuffets again by bringing together a group of talented unknowns to write, produce, and direct a low-budget black-and-white movie called *Star Bright*.

I saw *Star Bright* in the theatre when it first came out, and I loved it. Partly, I admit, because it brought back a few of the old movie greats, like Arlene de Grasse and Howard Ingram. And partly because Emil Bergman had been taken off the mantle and dusted off to compose the movie's score. The same Emil Bergman who wrote the soundtrack for *Idlewild* all of those years ago.

Star Bright was quite a Cinema Select reunion, which was all the more meaningful because, instead of transforming the images of the legendary stars, as her brother had planned to do, Astrid Scheidler immortalized them.

Sarah's article ended aptly with a line written by a drama critic who'd loved *Star Bright* and hated the dreaded IT Machine.

He said (and I quote): "that the success of this brilliant little movie is the *epitome* of spitting on Stanfield Standish's grave."

CHAPTER
24

The ride down to Delaware is only a hair over two hours. Easier to get to from my office than New Rochelle or Scarsdale. And it's against traffic all the way. A breeze.

The Hotel du Pont is very European, both in its outlook and its atmosphere. It's got marble and mosaic floors, hand-carved and gilt ceilings, vast carpeted corridors, and large rooms that look as though they'd been personally decorated by Queen Victoria. The hotel also displays its art collection of some of the best work done by N. C. Wyeth. And it has my favorite restaurant on the East Coast, the Green Room, where I met Astrid Scheidler for lunch.

The Green Room is *the* place in Wilmington to meet. It's where deals are consummated, love affairs start or end, champagne glasses clink at anniversaries, in-laws are introduced, corporate mergers are made, and psychological fences are knocked down or mended. There are carved oak panels on the walls, the windows are intimidating arches surrounded by velvet drapes, and the ceiling—a neck-craning two and a half stories above sea level—is a grid of solid oak beams crisscrossing this way and that and decorated with carved botanical doodads. The ceilings are hung with massive chandeliers, the walls with oil paintings in heavy gilt frames. And on a balcony above the diners, a harpist plays études and minuets. All together, it was a perfect backdrop for Astrid Scheidler.

I'd gotten there early and was sitting at a secluded window table when Miss Scheidler arrived. I watched the maître d' point me out to her; and as she walked across the room, I felt myself being drawn into another dimension of standards by some magnetic aspect of her personality that seemed to exist outside of space and time.

Much to my surprise, I stood up. The way men used to do when a lady walked into the room. It was a purely automatic response. Like your hand swinging up to your heart when the national anthem is being played. I stood, and before I could pull out the chair for her (another automatic response), I watched three waiters fall over themselves and each other in eagerness to beat me to the punch. She laughed at their confusion, calling each waiter by his first name, putting them at ease, and turning what could have been a disaster into an Entrance with a capital E.

How to describe her . . .

My first instinct would be to say that she was a creature out of somebody else's dream, because I wouldn't have had the imagination to dream her up. Her eyes were a clear, direct lavender blue; her hair was so pale and soft, I had to control an urge to blow against it and make a wish. Her skin? Her delicate bones? Like a Renaissance drawing of a perfect woman sketched with a sepia pen.

She held out her hand and directed her smile at me. "Astrid Scheidler," she said. "I never accept luncheon appointments. I never talk to attorneys. And I don't particularly care to meet strangers, as there are already too many people in my life. But you get the award for Most Intriguing Letter of the Year, so here I am."

First, we shook hands. Hers, I noticed, were unlike her brother's. They were beautiful. I released her hand reluctantly when she reached for her purse. She took out the letter Sarah had typed and glanced at it. Then she looked up at me. "A meeting twenty years ago with my father?" Her manner was relaxed, tinged with humor. Her eyes dropped again to the folded white page and she continued, "Sporadic contact with him about your professional advancement? A mysterious object found in my dead brother's car?" She dropped the letter onto the table. "All this scenario lacks is a one-eyed blackmailer in a trench coat and a woman with a gold tooth knitting messages into a woollen shroud." She paused for a second. "Mr. Bramble . . ." I could still hear the humor in her voice.

"Max," I interjected automatically. "Call me Max." (Call me 'darling' is what I was thinking).

Instead of responding, she folded up my letter and motioned for the waiter. "William, please get Mr. Bramble a cup of strong coffee."

I guess she thought I'd need it.

"And I'll start with a pot of tea."

She looked at me expectantly. I supposed it was getting to be the time when I contributed something to the conversation instead of just ogling her, so without thinking, I blurted out, "I met a man last week who said he'd almost become your father-in-law."

I know. I know. It was a stupid thing to say. And the minute I did, I regretted it. But if I had planned on saying something that would have a cataclysmic effect on Astrid Scheidler, I couldn't have picked a better combination of words.

She stopped moving and stopped talking. For a long lapse of seconds, she just sat there, looking exactly like a pre-Raphaelite painting of herself. The expression on her face was that of suspension in time. As though she'd been caught between a tick and a tock. Then, she took a slim silver cigarette case out of her purse, tapped a filter tip that didn't need tapping, and raised it to her lips. William and two other waiters leaped forward with matches.

"Thank you," she said absently. She tilted her head to one side.

"Lon Bandy," she said. And a smile softened something in her eyes that hadn't been all that hard in the first place. "Mr. Bandy's wife, my almost-future-mother-in-law, used to make this incredible fudge. It was so heavy with sugar you could literally grind the granules with your teeth. But you could never really *chew* Mrs. Bandy's fudge since it wouldn't stay solid. Not even when she tried to freeze it. Pat and I called it 'magic fudge' because it seemed to defy chemistry." She laughed.

William hovered over the table with my coffee and her tea.

She shooed him away and then asked, "How *is* Mr. Bandy? If you see him again, please tell him that I have fond, fond memories of him, and much, much affection." She was still smiling, but not particularly at me, when she added in a dreamy way, "Did Mr. Bandy tell you about me? About me and Pat?"

"He told me that you and his son had once been in love."

"Puppy love. And exceedingly young puppies, at that. But before I get lost in this sudden flurry of reminiscences, you did tell me to call you Max, didn't you?"

"That's right."

"Good. And you call me Aster."

"Chief Bandy calls you that."

"Nobody has called me Aster for a long, long time. Tell me, Max Bramble, and I want you to give this serious thought before you answer. Do you think that anybody in the whole world was ever really seventeen?"

I thought about it for a moment.

"No," I finally answered. "I think seventeen is a mythological period that exists after puberty and before your first mortgage payment."

Astrid Scheidler laughed. "But I was seventeen once, Max Bramble. And mythical or not, it was the happiest time in my life. And the saddest. That was the year I fell in love with my future, and the year my future fell out of love with me. For a long, long time afterward, I was terribly, terribly angry at my family. I hated my brother very much. But, as *I* said, that was when I was seventeen, and as *you* said, nobody was ever really seventeen. What else did . . . Chief Bandy tell you about me? And why are you calling him that? What's he chief of?"

"The Stilton-on-Hudson Police Department."

Astrid made a small gesture in the air like a victory punch. "Good for Stilton-on-Hudson. And good for 'Chief' Bandy. What else can you tell me about the goings-on in what used to be my hometown?"

"Probably nothing that you don't already know."

"But I don't live in Stilton-on Hudson. I rarely go there, and when I do, nobody tells me what's happening. Not even the man who waters the lawn. So that's your job, Max Bramble. You lured me to this lunch table. Now, do what you're supposed to do."

So I gave Astrid Scheidler an update with what I knew. I told her that Pat Bandy had joined the Marines to get over his broken heart; that he eventually went into law enforcement; that he was now a New York State Trooper working in the Criminal Investigations Division. I even told her that he had gone to her brother's funeral hoping, according to Chief Bandy, that he would see her there. And I mentioned that Pat had never married, because there's a little bit of matchmaker even in the worst of us, and I was thinking what the hell, maybe it's never too late.

Astrid sipped at her tea, looking very pensive and very beautiful. A swan with a brain. She said, "Pat's parents were kind to me—to us—during all those summers I spent in Stilton-on-Hudson. They were sweet, good-hearted people. They didn't treat us like idiot children with some sort of an adolescent disease. They—"

She put down her tea cup, shook her head abruptly and said. "Enough of that, Max Bramble, Attorney at Law. What does *my* childhood have to do with the contents of your letter and our reason for being here? But before you explain, first tell me if you liked my father. He was a really nice man, you know."

Had Hugo Scheidler been a nice man? Would I have noticed if he had? I wasn't sure.

"He tried to help me on more than one occasion," I said diplomatically.

That was true. I just hadn't wanted his help.

"I found your name in his date book. Exactly where you said it would be. You had Thanksgiving at your parents' house in Bay Ridge, Brooklyn. Afterwards, he sent your mother a bouquet of flowers. No carnations. He made a notation about that, too. My father hated carnations. But what about the other contacts you mentioned over the years?

I told Astrid about the letters her father had written me. About his offers to recommend me to attorneys he knew. About his suggestion that I contact Standish for a job.

"But you didn't."

"No. I didn't."

"Why not?"

I shrugged, not wanting to say anything derogatory about her brother, but not wanting to say anything nice, either.

Astrid laughed. "I know. My brother had that effect on a lot of people. My father's calendar said that Stanley was there, too. At your Thanksgiving dinner. And so was Marguerite. What did you think of Stanley, Max? Did you like him?"

This was tricky. I was sitting across from the sister of a man whose heirs were suing my client for allegedly causing his death. She'd implied that Standish hadn't been her favorite person, but he was also her brother. It's one thing to hate your own family and another to tolerate in others that same degree of hate.

I thought about equivocating around the edges of the question instead of answering, because I knew that if I said the wrong thing, the interview would be over. Then my gut said to hell with it, and I blurted out the truth.

"As a matter of fact, I didn't like him at all."

Astrid looked me in the eyes and flipped open her cigarette case. She raised a cigarette to her lips. I struck a match and held it out to her. She said, "You can relax, Max, that was the right answer. Now, what is it that you wanted to know?"

•

Over lunch I told Astrid about the case. I waited until after dessert to ask, "Why aren't you party to the lawsuit initiated by your mother and sisters?"

"Because I don't like my mother and sisters. Do you like your mother, Max?"

"She's terrific."

"How about your father?"

"A pussycat."

"Sisters? Brothers?"

"A dog named Bruiser. He's blind in one eye, his hair is falling out, and he has no personality. But for some reason I don't understand, my whole family is crazy about him."

"You too?"

"Me too."

"Well, I wasn't as lucky as you are, Max. Other than my father, I didn't have anyone to love. No terrific mother. No dog named Bruiser."

"That wouldn't have stopped most people from suing my client."

"I'm not most people."

"Do you believe that your brother's death was the result of a defect in the Duesenberg?"

"I don't care what my brother's death was the result of."

"Do you think that the litigation in which your family is engaged is legitimate? Do you think they have a just cause?"

"I would doubt very much if justice ever entered into their consideration."

"Miss Scheidler—"

"Aster."

"All right then, Aster. Why are you talking to me?"

"Sheer perversity, I suspect. I think it's like playing hooky, whispering four-letter words in church, or showing up barefoot at the senior prom. It's something I can do to spite my mother even though I'm far too old to engage in such adolescent behavior now. Twenty-one years ago, Stanfield Standish, my beloved brother, dragged me into my house and out of my life. He and my mother packed me off to Europe and together stamped a no-forwarding address on my past. That's behind me now. But your letter has given me permission to pay a long-overdue debt to the seventeen-year-old girl I used to be. So, in answer to your question, I'm not sitting here talking to you out of kindness. And my motive isn't malice, either. I couldn't care less about cars, carburetors, justice, or your client. What I'm

171

here for is purely and simply myself. You mentioned my father in your letter as a hook to get my attention. Fine. You got my attention. Now, let's get down to business."

I opened my briefcase and brought out the enhanced photographs of the ring.

TO D. ALL LOVE. A.V.F.S.

Astrid gave me a curiously attentive look and took the pictures from me.

"Where did you get these?"

"My fire expert took them. He found the ring under the gas pedal of your brother's car."

Astrid gave the pictures back to me and asked, "Where is it now?"

"You mean the ring?"

"Yes. The ring."

"I assume it's where we found it. Back in your brother's car."

"Why didn't you take it?"

"Because I'm not permitted to do so by law. It doesn't belong to me. It's evidence."

"Does my mother's lawyer know about this?"

"I hope not. I didn't tell him that we'd found it."

"Why not?"

"Because I don't trust Clyde Prouty, nor do I intend to do his work for him or to give him the opportunity to destroy evidence, which I firmly believe he would have done if he had found the ring first. It is also my belief that this ring belonged to someone other than your brother. And that if we can figure out who it belonged to, that would be proof positive that there was someone else in the car at the time of his death."

Astrid Scheidler shook her head. "No, Max."

"'No, Max' what?" When she didn't answer, I added. "I tried the ring on my finger when we found it, and it slid right off. It couldn't have belonged to your brother. His hands were small. Like a woman's hands. As small as yours. Much smaller than mine."

Astrid was still shaking her head and for some reason not talking.

I prodded her. "Do you recognize the ring?"

"Yes. I recognize it."

"Do you know who it belonged to?"

"Yes. I know who it belonged to."

I was beginning to feel like a computer teller on a bank cash machine.

"Well, who—"

"Order us another pot of coffee, Max. And I'll tell you a children's story about a ring."

I made the appropriate hand signals to the waiter.

"Once upon a time," Astrid began, "there was a family with a mother, a father, and four children. No Goldilocks. No porridge. And no three bears. It wasn't a particularly happy family, because the mother is a superficial human being with a rigid belief system of what was and was not the 'right thing' to do. For example, it was 'right' to go to an Eastern college and 'wrong' to go to a state school; it was 'right' to marry a member of the country club and 'wrong' to marry the son of a man who repaired potholes in the road; it was 'right' to have had four children with a man you didn't love and 'wrong' to fall in love with someone whose mother wasn't on the board of directors of the North Shore Ballet League. It was also 'right' to live six months a year in Europe spending Daddy's money and to threaten him that if he tried to divorce her, she would take away his children and make sure that he'd never see them again.

"When I grew up, Max, men in marital disputes had no domestic rights. Unless a woman was an out-and-out drunk or a nymphomaniac, she got custody of the kids. Regardless of what kind of mother she was. Women knew how to cultivate and nurture their status as victims and how to use it effectively as a weapon against a man.

"As a rule, I don't like women, Max. And I dislike my mother intensely. She married my father for his money; she had his children to consolidate her position; and when she said 'until death do us part,' what she was marrying was not him but his assets. She called all the shots in that marriage, bar none. The bullets in her arsenal were her children, and she never missed her aim.

"As long as he didn't make waves, though, my mother left my father pretty much alone. She had a small apartment in Paris and condominiums in Palm Springs and Chicago. She hated New York. My father loved New York. She hated the house in Stilton-on-Hudson.

My father loved the house in Stilton-on-Hudson. She hated her children, although she can make quite a show of loving us. My father loved his children. Even when we weren't all that worthy of his love. He was a wonderful, wonderful father. I was an adoring daughter. I've been accused before of having a father complex. If that means having minimum standards of behavior that are consistent with what you know a man is capable of being, based on your own personal experience, then so be it. I have a father complex. I expect a man to be as much of a man as my father was. He was powerful. He was massive. There was something of the redwood forest about him. You met him, Max. What did you think of Hugo Scheidler?"

Astrid's elbows were leaning against the table, her arms forming a triangle with her chin balanced on her cupped hands. She looked at me solemnly, as though she expected a truthful answer.

Like father, like daughter, I thought.

I said, "He seemed like he had a big appetite for life."

"He did."

"He struck me as being a man who would set goals and, regardless of the difficulties, find a way to achieve them."

"He was very, very strong."

"He seemed loyal to his children."

"He was."

I remembered back to the night I had met him, and added, "But he seemed to be afraid of his children, too."

Astrid raised her head. Her chin pulled away from her hands, and she demanded, "What do you mean by that?"

Again, I had said something that I immediately wished I hadn't said.

"Answer me, Max."

So I answered her. "The night I met your father, I also met Marguerite—"

"Ah, yes. The eternal Marguerite. What is it the Bible says? 'The poor and Marguerite always ye have with you.'"

"—and towards the end of the evening, my mother asked your father why he didn't marry Marguerite if he was in love with her. Hugo answered that he would never leave his wife because he couldn't bear to hurt his kids."

Astrid nodded.

"Yes. That's exactly what my father would have said. Max, you certainly do deliver the goods in terms of earthly reminiscences. And what did you think of my father when he made this astonishing revelation?"

I didn't want to answer that.

"Tell me, Max. And tell me the truth, or I won't tell you about the ring."

Damn it.

"I thought that Hugo Scheidler was a man who had given his children too much power over his personal life. And—"

"And." Astrid finished the sentence for me. "He was a king everywhere except in his own castle. You're right. He was a coward at home. My mother could manipulate Hugo with emotional blackmail and tirades. Victoria and Felicia could manipulate him with threats to withdraw their love. And Stanfield could manipulate him with contempt. My brother always treated my father as though he were a newspaper delivery boy instead of one of the most successful men in America."

Astrid shook her head sadly. "We're an odd species, Max. The strongest of us sometimes seem so apologetic about our strength. Over the years, I've watched the men and women around me—myself included—with an eye to understanding why they—we—do what we do. And do you know what I've found out?"

I didn't say anything.

"I have concluded that men—really, really strong men like my father—are terrified of their own strength. Hugo Scheidler was strong, and when the need arose, he could be ruthless. Single-minded and unstoppable. But he had no subtlety. He didn't know how to manipulate. He didn't know how to deal with sly, clever weaklings like my mother. In the business world, he would never have spent two minutes in her presence. He would have avoided her or destroyed her. But in the domestic arena, she triumphed over us all. She was Queen Greed, and her coin of the realm was Hugo's children. He did not know how to negotiate with her. So he surrendered to her completely. To my mother. To Victoria. To Felicia. To Stanfield. To all of them."

"And to you?"

"No. I would have done anything for him. I was my father's ally. We had an implied conspiracy of sorts, he and I. He could talk to me and I could talk to him. He was never afraid of losing my love. He trusted me. Poor, lonely guy. He called me his legacy."

"His legacy," I repeated. Freddie Eckeles had already told me that but I wondered, anyway. "What do you think he meant by that?"

"I'm not sure; whatever it was I *think* that he would be proud of what I've done. But that's neither here nor there as far as you're concerned. What you want to know about isn't my family history, but the ring."

William came up to the table with fresh pots of coffee and tea. He refilled our cups and left the carafes.

"When I was fifteen years old, way back before his first heart attack and before Marguerite, I knew how lonely my father was. Neither Stanfield nor my sisters were ever very kind to him. I used to call them the Gimme Kids, because all they ever did was take, take, take. In return, he'd occasionally get a perfunctory kiss, but whenever he tried to reach out to them, and he tried so often and so hard, they'd treat him as though he were a servant too stupid not to have tracked mud on a priceless oriental rug. It broke my heart to see him so dependent on us for love and approval. I was desperate to make him feel that he really *was* the father he wanted to be, and that he really had the children he should have had."

Astrid lifted up the two photographs. One by one, she pointed at the letters inscribed on the ring. TO D. ALL LOVE. A.V.F.S.

"'D' stood for Daddy. 'A' was for Astrid. That's me. 'V' was for Victoria. Victoria was sixteen years old at the time. 'F' was for Felicia. She was only twelve, but from the day she was born, Felicia was a miniature of my mother. And 'S' was for Stanley. You know, of course, that Stanfield changed his name when he went to Hollywood."

I nodded.

"I got quite a big allowance back then. Ten dollars a week. So I saved up all my money and supplemented it with what I'd earned on weekends and Christmas when I worked at one of the Harriet

O'Brien's stores. Then, I ordered the ring custom-designed by Mr. Olskey. Olskey Jewelers was in Stilton-on-Hudson. Mr. Olskey is still there, across the street from the C & J Bake Shop. It had one diamond for each of his children, because I wanted my father to have a perfect Father's Day from all four of his perfect children. I literally begged them, Victoria, Felicia, and Stanfield, to give me something towards the price of the ring. A dollar. Twenty dollars. Fifty dollars. Anything. Just so that it would truly be from them too."

Astrid tilted up the edge of the photograph and stared for a moment at the ring.

"The diamonds were tiny. All four of them didn't even make half a carat, and it cost me two hundred dollars. That was a gold mine when I was fifteen years old. But I didn't get a penny for it from the other three."

She dropped the edge of the photograph and looked up.

"Do you wonder, Max, why I'm not party to a lawsuit involving my mother and two sisters that disputes the cause of my brother's death?"

I shook my head. "That wasn't a very nice children's story."

"No. It wasn't."

"But it still doesn't explain how your father's ring got under the gas pedal of your brother's car. Do you think he gave the ring to Stanfield and maybe your brother was carrying it on him when he died?"

"Absolutely not. My father cherished that ring. To his dying day, he believed that it came from all of us. And that's what I wanted him to believe. He never took it off. Never. Because it symbolized his success as a father. No matter how remote or aloof his children seemed to be, the ring proved to him that deep down, all four of us really loved him and really cared."

"But if he never took the ring off, how—"

"About seven years ago, it disappeared. He didn't know where it went or exactly when, but one day, he looked down at his hand and it was gone. It had been so much a part of him that he never checked to see if it was there or not. Just like you never look down to count your own toes. His theory was that he lost it in Japan. A client had taken him to one of those public baths. He'd gotten thinner by then. Thinner and smaller as old people do. I suppose the ring could have just slipped off his finger and—"

Astrid's voice drifted off, and she spread her hands, palms up. "He never did find out where the ring went, but I'm absolutely certain that he didn't give it to Stanfield."

"How about Marguerite?"

"You mean did he give it to her? No. He was distraught when he lost it. He called everywhere. Even his client in Tokyo to see if they had found it. But, no. I'm sure he didn't give it to Marguerite."

"Do you know if Marguerite had any theories about what might have happened to the ring?"

Astrid shrugged. "I have absolutely no idea."

"Didn't the two of you discuss it?"

"Max. I've never met my father's mistress. I've never seen her. I've never spoken to her. If she walked up to our table this minute, I wouldn't be able to identify her if my life depended on it."

CHAPTER
25

Wylie Nolan was sitting at his desk, sorting through photographs, taking one from pile A and moving it over to pile B.

"We need a graphic artist," he said, and he pulled out a picture of the engine compartment.

"What for?"

"Overlays. I'm going to have to explain burn patterns to a jury, and that's an unfamiliar concept. I want to make it easy to understand. How many burn patterns had you seen in your life before you met me, Max?"

I thought for a moment. "Well, I grew up in a house with a fireplace, and hot cinders were always spitting out and landing on the rug in front of the screen. By the time the cinders went out, there were about ten new black marks on the rug. I don't suppose you could call that a burn pattern."

Wylie said, "Sure you could. The sequence and position of the singe marks on the rug are just as much a burn pattern as the blotches on an engine block. What I want to do with our trial exhibits is make it as easy for the jury to understand the burn patterns in the engine compartment as it was for you to understand the burn marks on your rug."

Wylie held up a picture. "Courtland Motors will have to get me a graphic artist to paint overlays on clear plastic sheets. I'll do a preliminary sketch of what I need. The photographs I choose will be of the Duesenberg after the fire. On the overlay, the artist will isolate where the flammable liquid was poured and then paint in small flames around the burn patterns to make it easier for the jury to see them and for me to explain what they mean. When I lift the plastic sheet, they'll be able to see the actual photograph. When I drop it down, they can see exactly where the fires were set. It'll be like looking at lift-off freckles on a sunburned face."

"How many of these overlays will you need?"

"At least five. Maybe seven or eight. One for each of the three compartments of the car and a few exteriors." Wylie continued to sort through the pictures. He looked up again only to ask, "What did Astrid Scheidler tell you about the ring?"

I gave Wylie an abbreviated version of our lunch, after which he asked, "And where was she on the night Standish was killed?"

I stared at Wylie.

He didn't move. I didn't move.

Then he said, in a low, subtly sarcastic voice, "You *did* ask her where she was. Didn't you?"

I was tempted to clear my throat, but thought it might be a little too obvious as a delaying tactic. Instead, I just shook my head and mumbled, "No."

"No? Meaning 'no' as in she refused to tell you where she was, or 'no' as in you didn't ask."

"I didn't ask."

"Why didn't you ask, Max?"

Because she has eyes like wet sapphires, I thought.

What I said was, "Because it was obvious that she couldn't have killed her brother."

"What exactly is obvious? Am I missing something here?"

"Well, from the evidence of the ring, it's obvious that someone else was in the car with Standish before he was killed."

"That's right," Wylie said. "And that somebody else may have been his sister."

I didn't like the way this conversation was going. "Do you mean Victoria or Felicia?"

"I mean Victoria or Felicia or Astrid."

"It wasn't Astrid."

"Why wasn't it Astrid?"

"Because she didn't have a motive."

"How does a seven million dollar car collection, an estate worth over three million dollars, and control of Standish Enterprises strike you as a motive?"

"Inadequate," I said peevishly. "But to satisfy your curiosity, I'll call Astrid up and ask her what she was doing that night."

"While you're at it, find out if her brother owned any guns. Preferably a .22 caliber handgun."

I dialed the number for Standish Enterprises. I was annoyed with myself for having forgotten to establish something as elementary as an alibi, and annoyed at Wylie for making such a big deal about it.

The ringing stopped, and a voice on the opposite end said, "Standish Enterprises."

I asked to be put through to Astrid Scheidler.

"She's unavailable at the moment. May I take a message?"

I left my telephone numbers, office and home, and told the secretary to make certain that Miss Scheidler returned my call immediately.

And who knows. Maybe Astrid really did get my message. Maybe she didn't. Either way, she never returned my call.

I was still in Wylie's office, though, when Sarah called.

Wylie picked up the phone. "It's your paraplegic."

"Paralegal." I took the phone.

Sarah told me that Marguerite Cataliz had called. The message was that she remembered me, and she would be home from four o'clock on if I wanted to stop by that afternoon and see her.

CHAPTER
26

Marguerite Cataliz lived in one of those new, narrow Manhattan condominiums that stand on a brownstone-size lot and shoot up to the sky like a long stick of Wrigley's spearmint chewing gum. Other than its disconcerting length, it was a nice enough building to look at. The outside was made of a slick polished gray stone, and every apartment had its own balcony. Until someone bulldozed the surrounding brownstones to put up more skyscrapers, most of the tenants would probably have a spectacular view.

The doorman in Marguerite's building was a fat, friendly Irishman with attentive eyes and a heavy brogue.

"Ah, and you two gentlemen will be visiting our Mrs. Cataliz. A fine figure of a woman she is at that. And aren't we proud to have her here in our beautiful establishment for all these past five years. If you'll just be holding onto your horses for a moment, I'll advise the lady that you're present and accounted for."

He pressed a button on his intercom, announced our arrival into a speaker, and pointed us through a stylish Art Deco lobby to a bank of elevators enclosed in a narrow corridor of sepia mirrors. The elevator door slid open, a mechanism inside went 'ding,' and Wylie pressed the button for the thirty-fifth floor.

•

When Marguerite Cataliz opened the door, something happened that I hadn't been prepared for. Wylie was standing a little bit behind me and to my left. Marguerite's eyes had barely glanced past mine, and then they immediately locked onto those of Wylie Nolan. Neither she nor he moved. If Marguerite hadn't been standing absolutely still, I would have thought by the look on her face that Wylie had slapped her.

But Wylie hadn't moved. Nor had Marguerite.

During that frozen few seconds, I was able to observe her and answer some of the questions I'd been asking myself about what time had done to the woman who had once been Hugo Scheidler's mistress.

Time, I decided, hadn't done a damn thing *to* her; but it had done a whole lot *for* her. She was barely recognizable as the sensuously attractive but almost meek creature I'd met some twenty years before.

It wouldn't be accurate to describe this older Marguerite Cataliz as just attractive, though. She was streamlined. Sleek. Her beauty had a forbidding, drop-dead edge to it, as if touching her would make something sizzle.

Probably me.

She abruptly broke eye contact with Wylie; gave me a cool, welcoming smile; and pulled her door open all the way.

We followed her inside.

Based on my calculations backward, Marguerite had to be somewhere between fifty and fifty-five years old. She seemed taller than she'd been when I'd first met her, but self-esteem can do wonders towards adding inches to the illusion of height. And there was no mistaking the proud angle at which Marguerite now held her head. This was no longer a self-effacing mistress anxious to please and appease an unavailable married man. This was a creature of poise. This was the self-assured older woman that is the stuff of a younger man's fantasies.

Marguerite was slim, like an Erté bronze. She wore tailored black slacks with a man-cut white silk blouse. The color outlining her lips was scarlet, and the polish on her long nails was Chinese lacquer red.

Her skin was the same rich ivory I remembered from all those years ago, and her hair was glossy black, pulled severely away from her face and piled on top of her head like that of a Spanish dancer. The white streak she'd had before was wider now and had turned silver.

But none of that was what set Marguerite apart. What lifted her over and above the normal parameters of beauty was her bone structure. She had the high-cheekboned, haughty look of a marquess. Her slimness extended to her face, with its narrow, arrogant nose and perfectly shaped, unforthcoming lips.

Her neck was long, like Astrid's, but not swanlike. More stylized. Like something Modigliani would have painted. It rose from two prominent collarbones.

All together, her look was dramatic. Very eighteenth century. Very Madrid. And when she moved, she absolutely reeked of sexuality.

Wylie Nolan and I followed her into the living room. She consciously avoided meeting his eyes. He stared openly at her.

Her apartment externalized her quiet sensuality. Two walls of windows with plush window seats looked out on the East River, Roosevelt Island, and the FDR Drive. Huge sofas with loose-backed, thick velvet pillows sat in the middle of the room. There was a white marble coffee table in front of the sofas. Placed here and there were chrome pedestals, globe lamps, and dark green plants with shiny leaves. There were no pictures on the walls. No bookshelves. No television set. But in that section of the living room where it turned right to form an "L," instead of a dining room table, Marguerite had put an ebony Steinway grand.

On top of the piano there were two framed photographs and a tall cylinder of silver containing a spiky red flower. I think it's called a Bird of Paradise. I walked over to the piano.

The first picture I looked at was of a man about thirty years old. He had the same high cheekbones, narrow face, and dark eyes as Marguerite. I turned to her. "Your son?"

"Yes. My son. Dennis Cataliz."

Marguerite's voice was low and expressionless. She didn't smile.

The other framed photograph was of Hugo Scheidler, standing on the running board of his Duesenberg. His eyes gazed into the camera with masculine, cocky pride; and what shone out of his face wasn't just Hugo Scheidler. It was Essence-of-Self-Made-Man. He looked big. Confident. Happy. Successful. Like the man I'd met on the airplane and invited to dinner all those years ago.

I walked back to Marguerite and Wylie Nolan.

When I tried to introduce him formally to her, she looked, not at Wylie, but at me. And her eyes never left mine during my long explanation of why we were there. I told her about Stanfield Standish's heirs, the Scheidler family's lawsuit against my client, the fire, and Wylie's findings; I gave her a quick rundown on what losing the lawsuit would mean to Courtland Motors.

Marguerite immediately grasped the essentials. "You are telling me that somebody deliberately set fire to Hugo's car."

"Standish's car. But, yes."

"And that Stanfield Standish was murdered."

"We believe that somebody was inside the car with Stanfield Standish just before he died. The reason I'm here is that we found something in the debris of the car that might help us to identify the killer."

I took out the two image-enhanced photographs of Hugo Scheidler's ring. "This is what we found."

Marguerite studied the photographs. I studied Marguerite. I waited for her to say something or do something that would give me an indication of what she was feeling.

"After Hugo turned over control of his business to Astrid," she said, "he had the Duesenberg completely restored. It cost over one hundred thousand dollars. I believe the restoration work was done by your client."

"It was."

"We took it all around the country. It won 'Best in Show' three times in Duesenberg competitions. Hugo loved that car. It was a great joy to him."

Marguerite looked down again at the photographs. I thought—but maybe I was imagining it—that her eyes got a little bit misty.

"The ring belonged to Hugo, of course. But he lost it long before Stanfield Standish died." She paused and seemed to be thinking. "It disappeared at least a year prior to his death. Possibly two years or three."

I pretended not to know where the ring had come from.

Had she given it to Hugo, I asked? Did she know who had? Had she seen the initials on the inside?

"'No' to all of your questions. I always assumed that the ring was an heirloom, since Hugo never took it off. As to the inscription, I didn't know there was one. And I have no idea what the letters might mean."

Marguerite handed me back the photographs. "I'm not going to be of much help to you in apprehending your killer."

I shook my head. "I'm not here to catch a killer, Marguerite. I don't care who killed Stanfield Standish or why. My client doesn't care, either. Our problem doesn't fall within the province of criminal law. It's a matter of civil litigation. We're being sued because Standish's heirs say that he died as a result of a defect my client caused in his car. The only way I can prove to a jury that there was no defect is to show them that the fire was deliberately set. Which is why I keep harping on the ring. Where did it go after Hugo realized that it was missing? Who held onto it for over seven years? And how did it finally get into Stanfield Standish's car?"

Marguerite got up and walked across the room to a small lady's desk. She came back immediately with a long, skinny cigarette. One of the brands that wasn't around twenty years ago when I still smoked. She took an expensive-looking gold lighter out of her slacks pocket, flicked it once, and leaned the cigarette into the flame. On her, the gesture was provocative.

She barely breathed in the smoke from her cigarette, and it seemed to play around the edges of her slightly parted lips for an instant before it disappeared.

"I have always believed that Hugo's ring was stolen," she said.

This was a new one.

"Who do you think stole it?"

Marguerite shrugged. A small shifting of bare skin over smooth, ivory collarbones.

"Perhaps the person in whose possession you found it is a clue. Perhaps the inscription is a clue." Again, she lowered her head to examine the photographs. "Who is 'D'? Who is 'A.V.F.S.'?"

Of course, I already knew the answers to those questions. But I wasn't about to tell Marguerite. I did have more questions to ask her, though, and wasn't ready to leave. So Wylie took me by surprise when he stood up and said, "I have to go."

He walked very deliberately over to Marguerite.

"Goodbye, Mrs. Cataliz," he said, his face less than twelve inches away from her face.

The same wordless exchange that had happened between them when we walked into her apartment was happening again now, and I still didn't know what it meant.

Marguerite again broke eye contact first, and inclined her head slightly.

Wylie nodded his head in response. Then he walked alone to the door and let himself out.

•

What do you talk about with somebody that you never knew very well in the first place, after a hiatus of twenty years? I decided I couldn't go too far wrong by beginning with what's familiar. So I told Marguerite how my parents were. I described an incident that involved my mother during her brief foray back in the work force. She'd brushed up on her typing, gotten a job through an employment service, and for her first assignment was sent to work at a collection agency. Given my mother's temperament, that can hardly have been considered a good idea.

Her boss at the collection agency was just about what you'd expect. He smoked an eight-inch Turkish cigar, wore green-and-yellow-checkered sports jackets and green snap-on bow ties. He was obese. He had ink marks from his blue ballpoint pens coming out of the bottom of his shirt pocket, and a wart on the left side of his nose.

My mother managed to get through the morning of her first day without incident. But when Mr. Wartnose came back from lunch and said, "If anyone calls, tell them I'm not in," he had preordained a disaster.

At first my mother just sat quietly at her desk. Thinking. She was only a little bit angry. Nothing to hide your pets and children about. But the more she thought about it, the angrier she got. Until finally, she rose to her feet, stalked into her boss's office, and said, "Mr. Wartnose, when I was sent here by the temporary agency, I agreed to do your typing and your filing. I did not agree to do your typing, filing, and lying. If you personally want to tell the people who call that you are out, I have no objection. But I only type for a living. I don't lie for it."

Marguerite smiled.

"After her little outburst, Mr. Wartnose was so terrified of my mother, he just hid in his office until the end of the day."

Marguerite's coffee was hot and strong. Good lubricant for the tongue. But it still took me three cups and a few more Max Bramble stories to get her relaxed enough to talk about herself. If listening skills are a criterion for being a good mistress, talking must be something that they rarely, if ever, get the chance to do.

She went to work for Hugo Scheidler, Marguerite finally told me, only a year before the trip to New York when we'd met. At the time, she was working as a general nurse practitioner in Northland County. Her name was listed with a reputable nurses' registry when Hugo Scheidler had his first "coronary episode." Hugo's doctor installed Marguerite in the millionaire's house in Stilton-on-Hudson with instructions to revamp Hugo's lifestyle and teach him basic cardiac survival skills.

"Hugo ate three fried eggs and a rasher of bacon every day for breakfast," Marguerite explained. "He drank eleven cups of coffee, a thick, strong Colombian brew, with heavy cream. Lunch was a corned beef or pastrami sandwich, potato salad, rolls, butter. Salt on everything. He never exercised. He didn't know what a vegetable was. Nobody took care of him, and he hadn't the faintest notion of how to take care of himself. I devised an exercise program for him. I fired his cook and took over the kitchen. He lost fifty pounds and never gained them back. I taught him how to take his own pulse. I took him on long walks. And I fell in love with him."

I remembered, as she spoke, the bleak portrait of Hugo Scheidler that Astrid had painted for me at that time of his life, and said to Marguerite, "Under the circumstances, falling in love may have been inevitable."

Marguerite appraised me with those motionless, careful eyes. "Perhaps. Perhaps not. In any event, it happened. My husband died the year that Dennis was born. I had been alone for a long time. I was lonely. It had been difficult. Hugo was lonely, too. He had been ill. We were both vulnerable when it happened."

Marguerite stopped talking. She said nothing for a long moment, and then added. "Hugo was very good to my son." She made an involuntary turn toward the photograph on the piano. I turned to look at the photograph, too.

"He's a handsome boy," I said.

"Yes. He is. Hugo sent Dennis to private schools; he paid for his university education. Through him, Dennis got his first job in telecommunications, and eventually, he became a producer at Stanfield Standish News."

"How's he doing now?"

"I don't know. He isn't part of my life. He dislikes me intensely."

I wasn't sure how to respond to that, so I said, inanely, "That's too bad."

Marguerite didn't say anything.

"But it isn't uncommon," I hurried to add. "When I met Hugo's daughter Astrid, she told me that other than her, all of Hugo's children were—" I poked around in my mind for the right word, "—distant."

Marguerite lifted her large black eyes. For the first time, I noticed that her eyelashes were so long, they made triangular shadows on her cheeks.

She stood up, "Neither Hugo nor I were very successful as parents," she said. And she walked across the room to the piano. I got up and followed her. She slid the photograph of Hugo Scheidler over the piano's smooth ebony surface and spoke to it as though Hugo had suddenly become a participant in the room.

"Do you want to know how he died?"

"Yes. I do."

"Hugo owned a condominium on East Seventy-Ninth Street. It was quite a beautiful place. I lived with him there whenever we were in the city. I had my own room. My own closet. It was the only place we occupied together as a couple. It was where I took care of him. He was quite old when he died, you know."

"How old was he?"

"Eighty-three. But he was still a strong man. A determined man. And his mind was still fast. He was sharp, decisive, and witty."

"He was good company? Even at that age?"

"Hugo was always good company. The night he died, we had gone to the ballet. It was a lovely performance of *Giselle* by the Dance Theater of Harlem. Poignant. Superbly danced. Very romantic. Hugo was quiet afterwards. I asked him if he was feeling unwell, and he took my hand and said, 'No, my dear. Perhaps a slight case of mortality.' And that was all he said until we arrived home. He went to bed almost immediately. When I went into his bedroom later to kiss him goodnight, he was dead. Very quickly. Very dignified. Very like Hugo."

She held onto the frame of the picture while she talked, as though addressing her comments to a Hugo of long ago. Then she turned to me. "All of those years we were together, Max, we had never spoken of what I was to do if I was with him when he died. All of those years to have had such an important subject looming over our heads, and yet still to have managed to avoid talking about it. Hugo hadn't wanted to face the possibility, and I had allowed him to ignore it. He was a coward, and I was a coward's mistress."

Marguerite set the photograph back on the piano and led me to the sofa.

"Did he leave anything to you in his will?"

"I was like oxygen to Hugo. Necessary for his metabolism, but not something that you have to put a name on or put in a box or quantify or justify. You don't do anything about the air that you breathe. You just assume it will always be there. And I was."

"Can I assume that your answer is no? He didn't leave you anything?"

"That is correct. He did not leave me anything."

"Did you consider contesting the will?"

"Certainly not."

"He left you destitute?"

"Hardly that. I'm not a fool, Max. I've always worked. I still have a select, very high-paying clientele. Hugo was occasionally extremely generous. And I have always saved my money. But—"

"Of course. But. And you did have the car."

Marguerite looked up sharply. "You know about the car?"

"The weekend that I met you, you went to an auto auction with Hugo. He bought the Duesenberg for himself and the Packard for you."

"That's right. A Packard Darrin."

"Nineteen forty-one?"

"No. Nineteen forty. A beautiful car, Max. All of the Darrins were custom-made."

"And after the funeral, Freddie Eckeles drove it to your house. So at least you had that."

Marguerite said nothing. So I went on, "Freddie also told me that you were the only good thing that ever happened to Hugo. Other than Astrid and his car collection."

Marguerite's face softened with a sad smile. "Freddie always liked me."

I got to my feet.

She looked up. "Are you leaving?"

"Not quite. There are three more questions I have to ask you before I go. First, did Hugo own a handgun?"

"Why do you want to know that?"

"I don't want to know. I already told you that my client doesn't care who killed Stanfield Standish. Wylie Nolan wants to know."

"Mr. Nolan is the gentleman you introduced me to. He is your fire investigator?"

"Correct."

"Why was he staring at me like that?"

"Because his manners aren't as good as mine. I've been having a hard time not staring at you myself. You are a very beautiful woman."

Marguerite shrugged off the compliment and stood up. "I don't know if Hugo had any guns in the house in Stilton-on-Hudson. I never went back there after we became lovers, and prior to that, I never saw one. As to the condominium. Absolutely not. What was your second question?"

"Where were you on the night that Stanfield Standish was killed?"

Marguerite looked at me archly.

"I see," she said. "This is something in the nature of a police investigation."

This time I shrugged.

"It was the Scheidler name with which I had an association. Not Standish. I have no particular memory of when Stanfield Standish died, and therefore, I can't tell you where I was. When did Stanfield die?"

"Valentine's Day. Five years ago."

Marguerite at first said nothing. Then she asked, "And what was your third question?"

"It's not exactly a question. I wanted your son's address. If you have no objection, I'd like to talk to him."

"I have no objection."

Marguerite walked across the room to the same table from which she had previously gotten the cigarettes. She had incredible posture. Shoulder blades back. Head held as though she were balancing a flute of champagne. She returned with a small card bearing her son's address.

"I think he's still there. Why do you want to talk to him?"

"It's not my idea."

"No. I suspect not. It's the idea of your friend again. The fire investigator. The one who stares."

CHAPTER
27

Wylie Nolan was waiting for me in his car outside the door to Marguerite's apartment building. I got in and asked, "What was that all about?"

"I thought she'd be more talkative if I weren't there."

I filled Wylie in on what he'd missed, and added, "No gun. No current contact with any of the Standish heirs. And no contact with her own son. But I got his address. He lives in SoHo."

"Trendy. What does he do for a living?"

"Hugo got him a job years ago at Stanfield Standish News. Marguerite gave me the impression that he stayed with the company after Astrid sold off SSN."

"Interesting. Complicated. Messy. Did you ever drop a bunch of wire clothes hangers, Max?"

"Whenever I hold them I drop them. It's a law of nature. Like bread falling butter-side down and standing in the wrong line at the bank."

"And when you try to pull them apart," Wylie continued, "the hooks of the hangers that were facing in the same direction a second ago are all jangled up now. You try to put them straight and sort them out, but they have a will of their own. That's what it's like with the people in this case. All we want from Marguerite is her thoughts on who might have taken Hugo Scheidler's ring. But what does she tell us? That Hugo put her son through private school. That Hugo was part of his life. That Hugo got Dennis his first job in television. That Dennis probably worked for Stanfield Standish on the night that he died. That he still works for a Standish concern. We didn't ask for that. We didn't want it. We didn't expect it, and it's a complication."

Wylie pulled up to a traffic light and removed his pipe from the dashboard ashtray. As he was filling it with tobacco, I said, "And don't forget Freddie Eckeles."

Wylie struck a match and sucked in the flames. Loose bits of tobacco pulsated orange hot. I stared at them, making silent bets with myself about when they would land in his lap.

"Freddie Eckeles," Wylie puffed. "Freddie worked for Hugo Scheidler for—how long?"

"Twenty-five years."

A glowing cinder jumped out of Wylie's pipe bowl and did a swan dive onto the pocket of his sports jacket.

"Wylie," I said. "Your coat is on fire."

He looked down. A bright red ember was eating a small hole into his tweed jacket. He casually brushed it away.

"Wylie," I began calmly, contemplating the irony of my fire expert being a moving fire violation. But he either didn't hear me or was ignoring me.

"After Freddie gives Hugo Scheidler twenty-five years of loyalty," Wylie continued, "Hugo dies. His son, the ever-popular Stanley Scheidler, A.K.A. Stanfield Standish, takes over. But before Standish can fire Freddie, he quits. So, now we have Freddie Eckeles added to our mixed-up pile of hangers. Does Freddie qualify as a disgruntled former employee? Or is he just a nice guy who loved his old boss and has no use for his boss's son? And speaking of disgruntled employees, we have to consider Mark Greenberg. When Standish fired him, Greenberg was already a pretty influential journalist in his own right, and maybe he didn't exactly cotton to the idea of being fired."

"Wylie, doesn't it even bother you that you're always setting yourself on fire?"

He looked down again at the hole in his jacket, and then over at me. He rolled down his window, turned his pipe upside down, and slammed it several times against the steel casing on his rear-view mirror. A glowing trail of orange cinders flew out behind us like a comet tail, probably starting fifteen fires along the way. Then he rolled up the window and put his pipe in his jacket pocket.

"Sorry," he said. "I didn't realize that it bothered you."

I swear, I saw smoke begin to rise out of his pocket.

"When you were upstairs talking to Marguerite," Wylie went on, "I called my office for messages. Do you remember my friend Vincent? The lawyer down the hall?"

"Who could forget a guy who tap-dances on weekends with two daughters named Ginger and Judy."

"Vincent was in my office when I called, and—"

"Wylie, *why* was he there? I know it has nothing to do with this case, but the dynamics of your office fascinate me."

"His photocopy machine broke down."

"Don't any of the people in your building lock their doors?"

"He has my key. Do you want to know what Vincent said or don't you?"

"Fire away."

"He showed the videotape to his friends. The one of the people in front of Standish's gate. You wanted to know who the old guy carrying the poster was."

"I keep thinking he's somebody I should know."

"It was Emil Bergman."

"Emil Bergman. Emil Bergman," I muttered, rehashing mentally a list of old movie names. Then I said, "Emil Bergman worked for

Cinema Select Artists for over twenty years. The good years. He wrote the movie scores for *A Poor Man's Paradise*, *The Man Who Laughed*, *Central City*, and *Idlewild*. A year or two ago, he was given a life-achievement award from the American Academy of something or another. I watched the ceremony on TV. That must be why I half-remembered his face. At the ceremony, he said that his favorite score was the one he wrote for *Idlewild*, because all he'd had to do was close his eyes and think of Louise Eastman's face. Miss Eastman was in the audience at the time. He held the award out to her from the podium and said something like, 'To your eternal beauty, my dear Louise. It is still such that you could inspire even a mediocre artist to write great music.' When he finished talking, there wasn't a dry eye in the place."

"Bingo." Wylie said. "*Idlewild*."

"Right. The Image Transformer. The IT Machine. That's why Bergman was in front of Standish's gate. Proprietary interest. He wrote the music for the movie. Louise Eastman inspired the music. And like the others, he didn't want to see it or her changed."

Wylie turned his eyes away from the traffic and said, "That would be a powerful motive to kill."

"What do you mean?"

"The night Standish announces he's going to get rid of Louise Eastman's face, the face you just said inspired Bergman to write his favorite piece of music, Standish is found dead."

"Let me think about this for a second." I reassembled a few facts in my head.

We were going downtown on Second Avenue, and traffic had slowed a few blocks north of the 59th Street Bridge.

I stared out the window. Wylie asked, "Do you mind if I smoke?"

I didn't answer. Then I said, "But if Emil Bergman had a motive to kill Stanfield Standish, so did everyone else, because Standish was planning on transforming the images of all the old stars. Arlene de Grasse, Howard Ingram, Louise Eastman, Roy Douglass, Kirby Clark. And after he'd finished transforming their images, who knows where this new technology would have led to next?" I shook my head. "Stanfield Standish wasn't the only one to have access to historical imagery. First movies. Then photographs. Then newscasts. Then old newsreels. Turning a seventy-year-old actor into a rock star isn't a big technological jump to altering the images in old documentaries to accommodate the prejudices of this or that group of revisionists. And once that got started, if it isn't already underway, it wouldn't be long before, instead of seeing old black-and-white newsreels of Auschwitz being liberated by American soldiers, we'd be seeing suntanned guys on vacation marching under the colorized sign of a concentration camp whose lettering has been Image Transformed to spell out the words SHANGRI LA.

"Scary, Wylie. It's scary what lies, ulterior motives, and manipultion can do to history. Movies are *part* of our history, and what Stanfield Standish almost succeeded in doing to them could break a man like Emil Bergman's heart."

The pipe was back in Wylie's mouth.

"Motives," he puffed gently against the stem, as though he hadn't heard a word I'd just said. "We have arson for profit. Arson for revenge. Boy-girl arson. Arson set by a pyromaniac. Arson set by a Vanity Fire Setter. Arson to conceal evidence of another crime. And a new one, according to you. Arson to prevent someone from altering images on film. Arson for art. Eenie Meenie Minie Mo, throw a match and let it go. Everybody hated Stanfield Standish for one reason or another. And more than one person wanted him dead."

"What about Dennis Cataliz?" I fell in with Wylie's train of thought. "If he killed Standish, what would his motive have been?"

"Ask me again tomorrow."

"Why tomorrow?"

"Because before he leaves for work in the morning, he's getting a surprise visit."

"What do you expect him to tell you?"

"Not much. But I'll get a chance to look him over. Gauge how he reacts to me. See if I can provoke him. And while I'm doing that, you'll be talking to Mark Greenberg."

"I will?"

Wylie grinned.

"I guess I will. What am I supposed to talk to Mark Greenberg about?"

"I'll give you a clue. Greenberg was at Standish's party on the night that Standish died."

"Him and just about everybody else in the world."

"But everyone else wasn't a former employee of Standish, and everyone else wasn't fired by Standish after broadcasting a story contrary to Stanfield Standish's point of view."

"True."

"And everybody else didn't write a best-selling biography of Emil Bergman."

"Right."

"And everybody else isn't Emil Bergman's nephew."

"Ouch," I said."

"Ouch what?"

"I think that one of your wire hangars just jumped out of the pile and poked me in the eye."

CHAPTER
28

As far as an intelligent, funny, good-natured suspect goes, you just couldn't beat Mark Greenberg. He's such an entertaining, affable guy that if he picked your pocket, you'd probably want to shake his hand and thank him for doing it in such a nice way. By which I don't mean to imply that Mark is or was dishonest. Only that he's one of the most downright likeable people I've ever had the good fortune to suspect of setting a fire.

I liked him so much that when he opened the door to his apartment, I shook his hand with the enthusiasm of greeting a long-lost brother. I'd already watched him three or four times on television, so I felt that we were friends. It didn't occur to me until his mouth twisted into an ironic smile that *he'd* never seen or heard of me. I suppose celebrities go through that all the time.

Mark lived in a converted factory about two blocks from the Brooklyn Bridge. I'd called him at the television station earlier in the day to ask for an interview. I explained who I was and who I represented, and that I wanted to ask him a few question about the night that Stanfield Standish died.

"What's the big deal?" Mark Greenberg said. "He died as a result of an accidental fire in his car."

"No, he didn't."

"What are you getting at?"

"I believe that Standish was murdered, and that his car was intentionally set on fire."

The phone went silent for a few seconds, and then Mark Greenberg asked, "Can you prove what you just said?"

"I can prove that Standish was murdered. I can't tell you yet by whom."

"This is all very interesting, Mr. Bramble. But what does it have to do with me?"

"You were on Standish's property the night that he died. You may have noticed something."

"You mean I may have noticed something, or I may have killed somebody."

I thought Greenberg was as likely to have killed Standish as anyone else, but I didn't want him to know that, so I lied, "No. Not really."

Mark laughed. "I'm resourceful. I could probably be devious. I certainly disliked the man. I like to play with matches, and I have strong teeth. I could have killed Standish just as easily as anybody else."

I couldn't figure out how to respond to this, so I didn't say anything.

He laughed again. "Sure. Come on over. But be careful what you drink at my house. There's always the possibility I might slip some arsenic in your tea."

•

Mark Greenberg was wearing a flannel work shirt, jeans, and moccasins. He had big, round brown eyes and short, curly brown hair. There was a crooked, off-beat alignment to his features that gave them an impish expression, and he looked exactly like a guy you'd expect to be spattered with motor oil, his head buried in the engine compartment of your car, saying, "Spark plugs are dirty, but your oil doesn't have to be changed." He was an intellectual with the smile of a good-hearted grease monkey.

Mark led me to a sofa. He sat down in an armchair opposite me, and said, "Okay. Blast away."

So I did.

I asked him what he knew about the movie people who'd been demonstrating outside Stanfield Standish's estate. How had they gotten to Stilton-on-Hudson? How long had they stayed in town afterwards? How, with whom, and when had they departed? And who did he consider the best candidate for murdering the man who'd been about to transform most, if not all, of their images in Cinema Select Artists films?

Instead of responding after I finished my oratory of questions, Mark got up and went into his kitchen. He came back a few minutes later with a coffee tray and a large platter of cookies.

"Food for thought," he said. "I'm going to need a great deal of energy to come up with answers for all that."

He popped a cookie in his mouth and winked at me. One of those aside-to-the-audience comedy winks.

Mark Greenberg was a self-educated journalist and a successful author. His approach to politics was provocative and iconoclastic. He deliberately put himself on the unpopular side of populist issues. He openly opposed all pressure groups and declared that he believed only in *human* rights, and not ethnic, racial, religious, sexual, or national rights. He was a TV talk-show commentator and a political analyst, a refugee, and the son of refugees killed by communists in Cuba. He was a man with every reason to be cynical, every excuse to look bitter, hostile, and reclusive. Except that he wasn't any of those things. Instead, he had the look of a guy eating potato chips, sharing a beer with a friend, and discussing the relative merits of the thong bikini bathing suit.

We weren't drinking beer, though, we were drinking coffee; and we weren't talking about girls, we were talking about murder.

"Have another cookie," Mark said.

I did. Then I had another. "These are really very good."

"I know. They're also a serviceable psychological weapon. You will notice that it's difficult for an adversary such as yourself to conduct an effective interrogation when his taste buds are knee-deep in chocolate chips. My girlfriend makes them. She does everything well. Except agree with people. She isn't very good at that. And behaving sedately or being passive. Those aren't her strong points, either. But when I get her to marry me, it will be different. I was thinking maybe of a small, attractive leg iron for her ankle. Nothing showy, of course, and not too thick. Just enough to keep her within ten or twelve feet of the kitchen. She'll be home in ten minutes, give or take, so let's get going on these cookies. She's a cookie fiend and would as likely look at you as snatch one of these babies out of your teeth."

He popped another cookie in his mouth and said, "What was it they called themselves? I think it was The Curators for the Preservation of . . . of American Films. I suppose you figured out who organized their protest by now."

I shook my head. "No, I haven't. That's what I wanted to ask you. There must have been a lot of money involved."

"There was. All very hush-hush. But that was five years ago. There's no reason not to tell you what I know now if it will help your client, because it couldn't possibly hurt her. Not now. Incredible woman, anyway. Pleasure to talk about her. Proud. Nerves like bridge cables. Tough. Beautiful. I had a caveman crush on her before Rebecca sank her talons into me. Rebecca is my cookie maven. But the other one. Very rich. Very smart. And not the least bit interested in me. Fortunately, Rebecca is. Which is just as well, because Rebecca has absolutely no sense of humor. Consequently, she keeps me laughing all the time."

I poured myself another cup of coffee and then stared blankly at my host.

"Mr. Greenberg," I said. "I don't have the foggiest idea what you're talking about."

"Of course, I'm making no sense. Who could make sense when he's talking about Astrid Scheidler."

I wasn't sure I was hearing him right.

"Are you telling me it was Astrid Scheidler who subsidized the demonstration against her brother, right outside the gates to his estate?"

Mark nodded his head vigorously. "Ballsy of her, wasn't it?"

I couldn't believe it. That on the very night Stanfield Standish was killed, a highly visible, emotion-charged protest had been covertly organized by the woman with the serene eyes and pale blond hair that I'd met for lunch only the other day.

"What a chance she was taking!" I said. "Think of what would have happened if the press had found out."

"I was the press, and I knew all along. A lot of us did. We didn't tell anyone, because we liked what she was doing. We were rooting for Astrid Scheidler. I was hoping her little protest in Stilton-on-Hudson would mushroom into a nationwide anti-Standish campaign."

I shook my head, amazed. "Jesus, why did she take the risk?"

"You don't know?"

"I don't know much of anything about Astrid Scheidler. I only met her once."

"Once is all it takes. For starters, she organized the demonstration. She bought tickets for all of the old stars, including my uncle Emil, to fly into the Stilton-on-Hudson airport. She rented as many limousines as it took to carry them, and she put them up ten miles south of Stilton-on-Hudson at the Chicoutimi Resort Hotel. She hired Salvatore Ponte to recreate the outfits they wore in the original Cinema Select photograph. She brought in makeup artists, hairdressers, manicurists, and secretaries to pamper the old people and make them feel like they were still stars. She hired a graphic artist and had the posters made. She had press releases prepared and ready to go. Start to finish, it was her idea. She met them at the airport with bouquets of flowers, gave them pep talks at the hotel, told them where to stand, how to stand, and what to do with their hands. They were professionals, used to taking direction. And she gave that direction very well."

I stared at Mark Greenberg, trying to take in all the ramifications of what he'd said. Astrid Scheidler, Stanfield Standish's sister, had been just a few miles away from him on the night that he was killed.

"Did Astrid have—" I started to ask. But before I could finish my question, we heard a key jiggle in the door. Mark went to the door and jerked it open.

The minute she walked in, I recognized her as the long-legged brunette who pulled Mark Greenberg off-camera in the videotape I'd seen. She was wearing a blazer over a turtleneck and a short suede skirt. Her hair was shorter, softer, and curlier now than it had been five years ago. But she still had those go-on-forever chorus-girl legs.

She darted a kiss at Mark Greenberg's lips.

He turned to me and said, "Excuse me for a moment, will you, Max?" Then he spun the woman around, threw her body back against his arm, leaned over her, and gave her a pretty good Rudolph Valentino kiss. She was laughing even before he let her go. When she started to smooth out her sweater, she jutted her head in my direction.

"Who's the guy?"

Mark took her hand and led her to the sofa.

"Be a nice girl, Rebecca. Try to behave. This is Max Bramble. He's an attorney and he's my guest."

"I hate lawyers," Rebecca said. She plopped down opposite me and leaned towards Mark. "Are we being sued?"

"No, flower of my heart, but Mr. Bramble's client is being sued."

"Good," Rebecca took a cookie, nibbled at one edge and glared. "He probably deserves it. Who is your sinister client, Mr. Bramble?"

"Call me Max."

Mark shook his head and put a finger to his lips. "No. No. No, Max. You don't want to encourage familiarity. This is an extremely dangerous woman."

Rebecca crossed her long, long, long legs. She was wearing those slim, spiky high heels that should be highlighted as erotic artifacts in back issues of *National Geographic* for adolescent boys to learn about real, primitive, primordial sex.

"My full name is Rebecca Katz," the pair of legs across from me said. "But I'd rather like it if you called me Rebecca. Why is your client being sued, Max? Who did he kill?"

I took a deep breath and raised my eyes to her face. She had perfect, hard-edged features. When she'd introduced herself, I had recognized the name. Rebecca Katz. She was a journalist, and she was smart and sassy and had the look of the 1940 actresses who could outdrink, outsmoke, and outwisecrack any guy in the scene. With her face and figure, if anyone ever wanted to make a new movie of her life story, they'd have to cast her to play the lead.

I thought the time had come for me to start being a little more assertive, though, or soon I'd have indentation marks from her spike heels on my ego.

"First of all, Miss Katz," I said. "My client did not kill anybody. And secondly, my client isn't a 'he,' it's an 'it.' I represent Courtland Motors, and the lawsuit against them involves a 1930 Duesenberg touring car, of which only a small number were originally made, and none of which in the intervening sixty years since they were manufactured has ever intentionally or unintentionally killed anybody or started a fire."

"I know, I know," Rebecca Katz said sarcastically. "Cars don't kill people. People kill people. So, what do you want from Mark? And what are you doing here in my house eating my cookies?"

Touchy. Touchy.

I mentioned The Curators, and I told her I wanted to find out more about their anti-Standish demonstration so that I could decide who had the motive, the opportunity, and enough anger to kill him and then set fire to his car.

Rebecca Katz glared at me. "You're sitting here in our living room, eating *my* cookies, and calmly telling me that you're going to hunt down frail little old men and little old ladies for no other reason than that they may have killed that asshole with the laminated hair?"

Mark patted Rebecca on the hand and smiled at me. "Volatile lit-tle darling, isn't she?"

Rebecca leaned forward. "Do you know who I am?"

I looked over to Mark Greenberg for help. How was I supposed to answer that one? He just shrugged and mouthed the words, "Have another cookie."

"I'm a reporter."

What was that supposed to mean? That she wanted me to put her in jail so that she could recite the Fifth Amendment?

She went on, her voice hard, curt. Her words fast, clipped. "You read Stanfield Standish's last words in the papers, didn't you? I assume that even lawyers can read. Well, I'm the one who got them. I went behind his house, and I caught him before he could sneak off in that mausoleum he was driving, in your *client's* mausoleum. And I got it all on tape. The ass-brained son-of-a-bitch. By the time my story was printed, everybody was glad he was dead."

I nodded, "I remember. You're talking about what Standish said to justify what he planned to do to the old films: 'Bottom line, they're mine.' Those four words have been following around Stan-dish's reputation like an albatross since the day he died. Congratu-lations. It was a good story."

Rebecca was now playing with her cookie. First she tapped it against her clenched teeth. Then she started to nibble around its edge. Then she popped it into her mouth and began to chew. There was a solemn expression on her face. She looked over to Mark Greenberg and said, "Kick him out."

Mark sat down again opposite me. He responded amiably, "I love it when she gets testy."

Rebecca demanded, "Why won't you kick him out?"

"Because my dearest and most delightful darling, I like him."

"If you're not going to kick him out, then tell me what you two talked about before I got here. At least I can do damage control."

"In all fairness, Rebecca," Mark answered. "I think you could say that we pretty much talked about everything."

I broke in. "I still have a few more questions about—"

"No." Rebecca pounded a fist against the table. "No. No. No. No.

No." She glared at Mark. "And please, please don't tell me that you told him who organized the protest."

"All right. I won't tell you."

"You told him? Oh, Mark. How could you!"

"The question isn't how could I, but why shouldn't I. Five years have gone by, nothing ever came of it, and a good time was had by all. No one is going to get hurt if I tell this very nice man here something that may help his client but isn't going to affect anybody else. It's not as if Astrid killed her brother and we have to shield her from detection."

At first, Rebecca Katz did not reply. She stared down at her long, thin, fashion-model fingers with nails painted fire-engine red, and then she looked up at me and I could see fury on her face.

"A big, hotshot lawyer like you, picking on talented actors and actresses who have more than paid their dues and earned the right to be left alone. And more contemptible than that, hounding a woman who's nothing short of a hero." She pointed a finger at me and jabbed at the air. "Astrid Scheidler is a hero, Mr. Bramble." Oh. Now I was *Mister* Bramble. "Are you aware of that?"

I hadn't been, but I nodded my head anyway. Her fingernails were longer than mine.

Mark was now standing behind the sofa where Rebecca Katz was seated. Again he was forming silent words with his lips. I think what he said was, "She's crazy, but she has great legs."

I didn't know if I should defend myself against Rebecca or laugh at her along with Mark Greenberg. But she wasn't finished with me yet.

"Just because your client's stupid car was set on fire isn't any reason to persecute durable personalities—great, great stars. And that's what you're here for, isn't it, you Judas. For god's sake, what do you really think happened that night, anyway? That Arlene and Louise tucked switchblades into their bras, sneaked up on Standish, and stabbed him? Or that Astrid Scheidler—my *friend* Astrid Scheidler—masterminded some psychotic plot employing octogenarians to tiptoe in tennis shoes to a murder scene and then set fire to your client's stupid car?"

And on. And on. Rebecca wore me out.

Mark finally sat down again. I guess he was getting tired, too.

Then, after about five more minutes of this, Rebecca turned on him.

"I hated Stanfield Standish," she said. "And I don't trust your friend—your *lawyer* friend over here. Next thing you know, he's going to accuse *you* of killing Standish. Or me. Both of us were there that night."

He just shook his head, and rolled his eyes at me.

"I saw that. You don't believe me, but I'm right. He wants to crucify Astrid. And I won't have it! I adore Astrid Scheidler. She's clear-sighted and smart. She's passionate about old movies and she loves art. She is wonderful, and if she killed her brother, she should receive the Congressional Medal of Honor. So I won't, won't, won't have this traitor in our house. Mark Greenberg, you get up this minute and take him out of here."

To hell with her. As Shakespeare once said, "the better part of valor is discretion." So I got up myself.

"Miss Katz," I said not too gently. "The only reason I'm here is to investigate false claims that my client's work was the cause of a fire in a vehicle in which Stanfield Standish was found dead. Courtland Motors is being sued for in excess of fifty million dollars. If they lose the case, the family of the man you hate will be awarded that sum by the court. If I win they will not. I am not your enemy but your friend. I am not a traitor. I am not out to terrorize old ladies or to persecute Astrid Scheidler. You, on the other hand, are quick to come to conclusions, overly emotional, and exhausting." I walked to the door. "But you make very good chocolate-chip cookies and you *do* have great legs."

Mark Greenberg followed me out into the hall. "I don't know," he said thoughtfully.

"Don't know what?" I almost barked.

"If that leg iron I was planning on getting her will be strong enough. What do you think?"

"A muzzle," I said.

Mark smiled at me. I smiled back. We shook hands. Then he pressed the button at the elevator bank and whispered, "That was the downside. The up is that it's never dull when Rebecca is around the house."

CHAPTER
29

Dennis Cataliz lived in a nicely maintained building in SoHo, just south of Houston on West Broadway. There was a system of buzzers and a telephone receiver wired into a video camera in the lobby, with a TV monitor in the tenant's apartment.

Wylie picked up the receiver, stood in front of the camera, held up his New York State Private Investigator's license so that Cataliz could see it, and pressed the buzzer.

Almost immediately, an annoyed voice came through the speaker. "Yeah. What do you want?"

"My name is Wylie Nolan. I represent Courtland Motors Corporation, and I'd like to talk to you about the fire that occurred five years ago in Stanfield Standish's Duesenberg."

"What about it?"

"I'm doing background research on Mr. Standish."

"What's that got to do with me?"

"In the course of my investigation," Wylie lied, "I've come upon certain facts that lead me to believe Mr. Standish didn't die of injuries sustained in an accidental fire, but that he committed suicide. Since you used to work for him, I hoped you could help confirm that."

"Suicide!" Cataliz's voice crackled. Either from static or righteous indignation. "Where'd you get a stupid idea like that? He never would have—"

"I spoke to six witnesses who told me that right before his death, Mr. Standish was severely depressed, and that both in his professional and personal lives, he couldn't—"

"Which six witnesses?"

"I'm sorry to have to be the bearer of bad news, Mr. Cataliz. And I know that Mr. Standish was your employer, but—"

"Employer *and* friend."

"Exactly. Which is why I'm here. Before we go public with our theories, we wanted to make sure we've got all our facts straight. Which is where you come in."

"I'm not going to help you. I think your theory stinks."

"No problem," Wylie responded. "What I'm after are facts. If the facts put Courtland Motors in the bag, then so be it. If they prove that Standish committed suicide, amen to that, too. My thinking, though, is that if you want to know what a guy was like, you talk to his friends first. And from what I hear, you were one of Mr. Standish's best friends."

Flattery. Flattery. Oh, Wylie Nolan. Have you no shame?

Dennis Cataliz resisted for about fifteen seconds before he gave in.

"Fourth floor rear," he said. "Turn right when you get off the elevator. And make it fast. I don't want to be late for work."

When Wylie Nolan was a New York City Fire Marshal, he had a ninety-eight percent conviction rate. His explanation for this is that people like to talk to him. Why do they like to talk to him? Because

Wylie's eyes tear up with crocodile compassion. Because his voice re-assures. Because his smile and manner are sympathetic. What they convey to a suspect is: I'll understand. You can trust me. You can tell me. And that's exactly what they do. The criminals he interrogates are like cobras hypnotized by their own images in the mirror. And Wylie Nolan is the mirror. And after their defenses are down, and they aren't quite sure what the rules are or what should be happening next, Wylie touches them. It may be nothing more than the pressure of three fingers against a jacket cuff, or just a pat on the back. But it's physical contact. A touch. And it creates a bond.

Once, I saw Wylie do it to a guy who was suspected of setting fire to a milk pump in a barn. By the time he was through, the arsonist thought that Wylie was his best friend.

He's the most manipulative, cold-blooded, effective, lying son-of-a-bitch on the planet. But he catches bad guys. And it works.

Dennis Cataliz was waiting at the door to his apartment. Wylie held out his P.I. license, but Cataliz waved it away. "For Christ's sake, I'm not paranoid. You want to talk to me, come on in. Get the lead out, I don't have all day."

Dennis Cataliz was wearing the latest in pleated, baggy trousers with an oversized tweed sports jacket that had stupid looking rolled-up sleeves. He had manicured fingernails, Italian loafers, a thick gold chain under the open collar of a black silk shirt, and a diamond pinky ring.

Wylie described Dennis's overall appearance as "early Hollywood on Lex." Lex, as in Lexington Avenue.

Cataliz led him through a small living room to an even smaller kitchen.

"I got some coffee left over," he said. "You want some?"

Wylie said, "I know that you're in a hurry, but I never turn down a cup of coffee. I'll get right to the point. My client's defense of the fire that occurred in the Duesenberg is going to be arson-suicide. We believe that at the time of his death, Mr. Standish was despondent, and that while temporarily insane, he set fire to himself in the front seat of his car."

Wylie told me that until a few seconds before his conversation with Cataliz, there had never been a category of fire formally called "arson-suicide," but that he thought it sounded sufficiently sinister to loosen Cataliz's tongue.

"No way," Dennis said. "There's absolutely no way that Mr. Standish would have killed himself. It didn't happen like that. What you're saying is just a bunch of rot."

"I'm not insensitive to your feelings, Mr. Cataliz," Wylie oozed. "Suicide is a painful subject and I hate to even bring it up. But after analyzing the burn patterns, both in the car and on Standish's body itself, it doesn't seem that any other explanation is possible. Of course—"

"Bottom line." The words came out of Dennis Cataliz's mouth in an angry hiss reminiscent of his former boss. "Bottom line is—what did you say your name was?"

"Nolan. Wylie Nolan."

"Okay, Nolan. The bottom line is this. You want something from me. If it's to trump up a suicide motive for Stanfield Standish, you came to the wrong guy. I knew the man personally."

Dennis held up his right hand and stuck out his first two fingers like a blessing from a pissed-off pope. "We were like this. Me and Stanfield Standish. Him and me. We shared what we felt. We went way back. We were like family. He was more to me than a boss. He was like a father. He said dozens of times that I was his protégé. Suicide." Cataliz sneered. "You're playing with yourself."

"So young to die," Wylie nodded his head sympathetically. "So much talent. And such a tragic waste."

"I really miss him, man. I couldn't miss him more if he'd really been my old man."

"But he wasn't, Mr. Cataliz, was he? In fact, he was the son of the man your mother—"

"My mother!" Dennis spit out the words as if the syllables were singeing his tongue. "What does my mother have to do with any of this?"

"It's my understanding that at one time Stanfield Standish's father and your mother were—how can I say this—that they had known each other in the biblical sense."

Cataliz violently pushed aside his coffee cup. Wylie caught it just before it crashed into the sink.

"Hugo Scheidler, that old fart. Talk about losing touch with reality. He even wanted me to call him 'Dad.' That's a laugh. Yeah, sure. He was my father and I'm Robin Hood. Losers, that's what Hugo and Marguerite were. The both of them. And if you screw around with losers, you're going to get lost. Stan taught me that."

A second ago it was "Mr. Standish." Now it was "Stan?"

Wylie pretended not to notice. He leaned against the refrigerator and said, "It must have torn you apart the night he committed suicide."

"Cut it out, Nolan. Or get out. I already told you it didn't happen like that. Who's been saying it did? My mother, right? She's always—"

"Not your mother. I talked to a few of the people at the party he gave on the night he died. You weren't there, but—"

"Bullshit, I wasn't there. I told you, me and Stan. We were like that." Another double-fingered blessing. "I was his right-hand man. He wanted something, I got it done. That's how it was between us. Ever since I was a little kid. He gave me my first job when I was still in college. I was a gofer for SSN. Now I'm associate producer. But I work for The Scheidler now. Everything's different with Stan gone."

"How different?"

"It stinks. That's how. And I'll tell you something else, too. Stan didn't kill himself and he sure as hell didn't die in an accident. She killed him, that's what I think."

"Who is 'she,' Mr. Cataliz? Who do you think killed Stanfield Standish?"

"The Scheidler. That's who."

"I take it you mean Astrid Scheidler?"

"Damn right I do. Hey, you know, maybe it's a good thing you came here to talk, because I never said this to anyone before. But it's been bugging me ever since Stan died. I just didn't know what I should do. It's not like I'm in the field. Not like I'm a private detective. But you are. You're a professional. So maybe you can find the proof."

"Proof? Proof of what?"

"That she killed him."

"Why would Astrid Scheidler kill her brother? Motive, Mr. Cataliz. There has to be a motive before there can be a crime."

"Motive," Dennis snorted. "I'll give you a motive. Power, for starters. He had it and she wanted it. You want another motive. How about hostility? Hostility was The Scheidler's middle name. She hated Stan. Hated everything about him. It wasn't like she just wanted him dead. It was like she wanted him never to be. Like as if he should go back to the Land of Never Was."

"I don't follow."

"Christ, it's obvious. Or, I should say, capital 'I,' capital 'T' is obvious. Get it? I.T. as in IT Machine, as in Image Transformer."

"What did the Image Transformer have to do with the relationship between Astrid Scheidler and her brother?"

"That's all they ever talked about. From the minute he bought it until the night he died, she never got off his back."

"Why not?"

"Because she hated it. That's why. She accused him of ruining all of the great old movies. Ruin the movies! He didn't ruin them, he saved them. Ungrateful bitch. If it weren't for Stan, where would all those 'great old movies' be? In the shit can. That's where. Nobody wanted them. Not until Mr. Standish put up the money. They were printed on silver nitrate film, and all of the old film stock would have disintegrated. It cost Stan a fortune to save them. Then, all of a sudden, they were 'cinema masterpieces' and everybody wanted them. But if Stan hadn't come along and plunked down the cold cash, there wouldn't have been anything left to save.

"Hell, Stan loved movies. He told me that maybe a million times, and he loved the old ones best. He revered them; that was how he explained it to his sister. And that if he didn't transform the images of the old movie stars so that younger generations could relate to them, then all the great stories, all the great production values, all of the great direction—it would all be lost. He said he had to make art accessible to the people. That's how he explained it to The Scheidler. Those are the words he used. But she wouldn't let it go. Always picking on him. Always making him feel like shit. She even tried to buy the movies right out from under his nose. Offered him twice as much as he paid. But he just laughed in her face. That's why she killed him. Look into it. See if I'm not—"

The telephone rang.

Dennis Cataliz reached for it and barked into the receiver, "Yeah. Yeah." Then he hung up and snapped at Wylie, "I'm late. We're out of here."

They rode down in the elevator together without saying another word. And they walked through the lobby, out the apartment door. When they hit the sidewalk, Wylie stopped Dennis by putting a hand on the younger man's arm. Maybe he did it to delay Dennis for a few extra seconds. And maybe he was trying to suggest, by touching him, that he understood, felt compassion, and could be trusted.

"Just one more thing." Wylie's voice was low. Ingratiating.

Cataliz stopped. "Make it fast."

"All right. Short and sweet. A question."

"What about?"

"Your mother."

"Yeah. Go on."

"It's obvious to me why an intelligent young man like you would grow up hating his mother's boyfriend. But damned if I can figure out why you hate Marguerite."

"Hate Marguerite?" Dennis Cataliz repeated as though her name was a message transmitted from an alien galaxy. And then he said it again, as though transfixed. "Hate Marguerite?" His voice lost all of its anger and all of its defensiveness and suddenly sounded like that of a fourteen-year-old boy. "Hate Marguerite? How can you even *say* such a terrible thing. I don't hate my mother. I love my mother, and my mother loves me."

CHAPTER
30

The Friday before the trial, Wylie Nolan and I flew to Detroit. Oscar Courtland arranged for us to tour Courtland Classics and also to visit a private owner of a J series Duesenberg car. This individual was described to us as being a real car lover, because instead of having bought his restored Duesenberg for investment purposes, he kept it in his personal garage (temperature controlled) and drove the car around himself.

I can't reveal the Duesenberg owner's name here, because he's adamant about his privacy; but I can tell you that after having been driven around for forty-five minutes in this crown prince of all cars, I'm ruined. I am now a spiritually bereft man.

It's like this. Let's say that by a stroke of dumb luck, you married the perfect woman. You lived happily together for a few dozen years. Then she died. How could you think about getting married again? I mean, after perfection, then what? Sure, you could do it. But in the back of your mind, a dissatisfied voice would always be saying: More. More. I used to have it and I still want it. More. More.

That's what driving in a normal car was like after having driven the J series Duesenberg sedan.

Let's start with the interior.

One way it's easy to know you're in a vintage automobile before you even get inside is that the doors open up the wrong way. Another is that you can't just slide into it. You have to climb in. It's that big. And even then, you have to take another half-step or two to get to the seat. It's as if you're entering a small, luxurious salon.

Underfoot, you'll notice a carpet. Reach down and touch it. It's thick, soft, woolly, and dove gray. The upholstery of the car seats are also dove gray and are made from a material that feels like a cross between cashmere and felt. It's soft and pliant. When I was growing up, all of the cars my father drove had that same kind of fabric covering their inside roofs. As a kid, I used to pat and poke it. I asked Wylie Nolan if he'd done the same thing in his dad's old cars, and he had. Why did kids used to poke the roofs of their father's cars? Who knows?

There was mahogany woodwork on the dashboard. The window ornaments in the front and back of the car were Art Deco. So were the opera lights on either side of the passenger compartment. There was also a secondary mahogany instrument panel for the passengers in the back seat that displayed a stop clock and a speedometer, so that they wouldn't have to ask Jeeves what time it was or how fast the car was going.

Before Wylie and I climbed into the Duesenberg, Oscar Courtland asked its owner, who was going to be our driver, to open one side of the center-hinged hood so that we could look at the engine compartment inside. We leaned between the raised fender and side-mounted spare tire to admire the Duesenberg's polished aluminum cam covers, nickel-plated shafts, and the spotless cylinder block and crankcase. Then, with our heads still bent over the engine, the owner started the car. The engine purred. Oscar Courtland motioned us backward and closed the hood. We weren't standing more than a foot away, and we could barely hear the engine idling. Wylie put his hand on the hood to feel for vibrations. I pressed my ear against it. Barely a ripple. Barely a hum.

Then Oscar told us to get inside.

Being chauffeured through a small suburban town in a 1930 Duesenberg by an anonymous millionaire was the high point of what had, so far, been a grueling, down-and-dirty case. It was the flip side of groveling through fire-blackened debris in a cold and drafty garage and, for a lawyer working in product liability, was just about as close to heaven as lawyering can be.

We drove through three more small towns before we turned west. In less than twenty minutes we were on an empty stretch of highway with farmland on both sides. I looked at the back-seat speedometer. It read an easy sixty miles per hour. The car rode smoothly and felt massive. The wheat fields waved like a poet's ocean, and for a second I could have been on a mighty land-locked QEII. I looked outside. Barns, tractors, and silos streamed by. I looked down at the speedometer. We were now going one hundred and two miles per hour.

"And we're still in second gear," Oscar Courtland informed me quietly from the front seat. In the Duesenberg, it was possible to hear Oscar Courtland's diminutive voice without straining.

"Shall we put it into high gear?" the chairman of the board of Courtland Motors asked softly.

Wylie Nolan said, "Let her rip, sir." And when I looked at the speedometer again, we were cruising at one hundred and twenty-seven miles per hour.

What did it feel like? It felt like wealth. It felt like the happy forward momentum of power. It felt like riding in a work of art—all due respect given to the perspicacity of Freddie Eckeles. It felt sexy. It felt great.

The feeling lasted longer than road did, though, and right after we hit what I thought was our top speed, we ran out of highway. The Duesey's owner said, "It could go faster, you know." Then, he applied the brakes gently, and without a jolt, he eased us out of the godlike state that the comfort and speed of the Duesenberg had put us in and returned us to the status of being merely human beings.

•

Oscar Courtland's chauffeur drove us back to Courtland Classics in the company's newest luxury car. Aptly named The Pegasus, it was sleek, beautifully appointed, and powerful. And it seemed to fly. On any other day in our lives, we would have been impressed.

Back at the plant, Wylie and I went to the engineering department to go over key aspects of his testimony with Halburton Kramer, who was going to be testifying about the work that had been done by Courtland Classics on Stanfield Standish's car. Halburton came with us to the Graphics Department, where Wylie gave some last-minute instructions to the artists about the exhibits that were being prepared. Wylie asked for more modified shading on the overlays and smaller flames on the hood so that they didn't detract from the burn patterns on the car.

Then we took a tour of the plant. This was my second go-round. Still, it was impossible to come away from that place without being impressed. The beauty of the individual parts going into the cars awakened the latent mechanic in me. Only one of the cars being restored was a Duesenberg, but everything that went into it was either chromium-plated or finished in polished aluminum. And the parts that were lying around for later assembly—fenders, doors, hoods, and trunks—had been painted, layer upon layer, until their surfaces gleamed, as if each were illuminated by its own separate sun. The work space was spotless. The entire factory smelled of craftsmanship, competence, expensive equipment, and whatever you want to call that intangible that fills an area when professionals perform labors of love.

Earlier, I told you a few things about Oscar Courtland. You know that he was over eighty-five, still active in the corporation, and chairman of the board. Behind his back, it was said that he ruled the company with a porcelain fist. He was so frail, you'd think he couldn't lift a teacup, let alone manage the oldest and most successful family-owned car manufacturer in America. He was very small and very,

very thin, and he came up to my chin. He looked as though he should be fed flower petals and birdseed just to keep him alive. He wore a fashionable business suit with a conventional tie. No jewelry, but the shine on his shoes would have made a diamond look murky.

His face was also small, almost delicate, with a tiny nose, small, sunken cheeks, and a buttonhole mouth with thin, slightly purple lips. His skin had the dusky look you see on the pages of old books of poetry. Very white. Almost transparent. His eyes were light blue, intelligent, and fierce.

He followed us everywhere we went in the plant. He had lunch with us in the factory cafeteria. He listened to the conversations I had with Halburton Kramer, the graphic artists, and the mechanics on how best to handle Halburton's direct testimony and how we should deal with Clyde Prouty's bullying tactics on cross. Very rarely, he interrupted to ask a question or to make a suggestion. Two or three times, when we walked from one place in the plant to another, he pointed out Duesenberg engineering feats of which he was particularly proud—like the aluminum intake manifolds with double-flow feeding cylinders or the hydraulic braking system with only one piston per wheel cylinder in order to reduce leakage.

After listening to Oscar Courtland and talking to Halburton Kramer, I was tempted—really tempted—to defend our fire case using engineering data alone. Because the Duesenberg was such a beautifully designed and perfectly constructed machine. Elements of heat and ignition had been so well insulated and so carefully isolated from anything of a combustible nature that there was no way a Duesenberg automobile could internally and spontaneously burst into flames. There would have to have been the application of an external ignition source.

But juries don't always understand pistons, carburetors, exhaust systems, and timing mechanisms. So I couldn't just qualify Dr. Halburton Kramer as an expert engineer, put him on the witness stand, and have him tell them that unlike lesser machines, the Duesenberg has *two* intake and *two* exhaust valves per cylinder. Twice as many as almost any other car. And that it was designed this way because four smaller valves per cylinder can be cooled much more effectively than two larger ones. Much as I would wish that the jury's heart would beat faster if Halburton told them that the valve seats are fully surrounded by water passages, and that the valve stem guides are water-cooled for almost their entire length, I didn't want to bet my client's entire case on it.

Now, I'll grant you that talk like that excites the Courtland brothers and makes their little hearts go pitter-pat. But it puts juries to sleep. On top of which, and despite any and all claims of engineering excellence, a plaintiff's attorney can always counter by saying, "Yeah. Great. Sure. On paper the car's a miracle, but that doesn't mean the parts manufactured weren't defective, or that the mechanic who installed them wasn't a man-slaughtering klutz."

Which meant just one thing. That instead of defending our product based on engineering excellence, our defense had to be based on the fire.

Only then would our nonculpability (or "innocence," as Wylie calls it) be made fully and visually comprehensible in a court of law. In doing so, we could hold up our graphic exhibits of the exhaust manifold and, by adding or removing the overlays, demonstrate to the jury that there was no burn pattern leading to or from any of its component parts. And we wouldn't have to ask the jury to take what we were saying on faith. We could actually *show* them the burn patterns, explain what we meant, and appeal to their basic intellect and common sense.

Item by item, we would follow this same procedure with every other source of heat or ignition in the car. Item by item, we would eliminate them as points of origin of the fire.

Wylie and I had finished our work with the graphic artists, told Halburton Kramer where to meet us on Monday, and were on our way out the door to catch a plane back to New York when Oscar Courtland literally apprehended us in the hall. He grabbed Wylie by one arm and me by the other. He turned us around and led us in the direction of the aircraft-hangar-size area where Courtland Classics does restoration work on its cars.

As he walked, Oscar Courtland said in a small, articulate, and barely audible voice, "There's somebody I want you to meet. You, Max. And you, Wylie Nolan." He always referred to Wylie by both names. He walked very, very slowly, his small, metronomic steps moving in opposition to the wide range and rapid pace of his mind.

"Around this great country of ours, a new philosophy has arisen." Wylie and I both had to lean towards Oscar's mouth to hear what he was saying. "And this new philosophy has six words as its keystone. And these six words are: 'Somebody's going to pay for this.' And implied in those six words, Max and Wylie Nolan, is the intention that somebody *else* is going to pay for it. Not me. Even and specifically if it can be proven beyond the shadow of a doubt that the damage that arose to me is and was my own fault."

A secretary rushed across the floor, stopped in front of Mr. Courtland, and pushed a letter on a clipboard into his hands. His eyes scanned the paper. She handed him a pen. He signed the letter and curtly motioned her away. Then he grabbed onto our arms again and continued talking and shuffling across the room.

"This is an ugly, ugly philosophy, I say to you, Max Bramble, my attorney, and to you, Wylie Nolan, my authority on all matters relating to fire. It is a philosophy that rewards those who will not take responsibility for their own actions. It is a philosophy that punishes the inventors, the manufacturers, the innovators, and the heroes."

We shuffled past a bright red Ruxton five-passenger sedan. I wondered how it had run when it was new. If the engine had been smooth or choppy. If the seats had smelled of new leather and fresh paint.

"I do not understand, gentlemen, from where this destructive philosophy has come, but I do know that there is an atmosphere of evil about it more potent than any I have ever previously encountered."

He shook his head sadly, and went on in his small yet commanding voice, "In our restoration work at Courtland Classics, we produce the majority of the parts for the automobiles ourselves. Occasionally, we rely on an outside source. However, we engage in this activity only after we have ascertained that the part will be made to exact specifications, that there will be no compromise in quality, and that what we order will be delivered in perfect condition and on time. Do you see the man standing in front of the shop foreman's office?"

We looked about forty feet to the right. The man Mr. Courtland had indicated looked strong enough to lift a horse onto the back of a flatbed truck. He was wearing old workshoes, worn jeans, a faded plaid shirt, and a scuffed leather bomber jacket. He had the weathered complexion of a man who works outside, with deep-set, honest eyes and a heavy jaw. At first, I thought that his face was expressionless. But on closer examination, I decided that it might have too much expression.

Oscar Courtland said, "His name is Sherman Decker. He lives about forty minutes from here. He has a ninety-acre farm that he bought twenty years ago, because he wanted his family to get fresh air and exercise on weekends. Until then, they all lived in Detroit.

"Right after he made his down payment on the farm, his machine shop in Detroit was burglarized. The burglars took every press, metal cutter, die-cut mold, lathe, and calibrator that Sherman Decker owned. Every dollar he had was tied up in that shop, and in one night he lost it all.

"The mortgage on his house in Detroit was five hundred dollars a month. The mortgage on the farmhouse was only two hundred. So he sold the house in the city and moved his family to the farm. He went to work for the Welton Tool and Die Company as a salesman. He saved his money. He worked nights and weekends. And about sixteen years ago, he reopened his machine shop in the barn behind his house. It's a family business. His wife is his bookkeeper, and the machine operators are each of his five children.

"Everyone who ever met Sherman Decker likes him. He's honest. Hard working. Good-natured. He machines parts for Welton Tool and Die, where he used to be an employee. And I've been doing business with Sherman for fourteen years. He supplies me with a good number of parts, but for the Duesenberg Arlington that we restored for Hugo Scheidler, he supplied only one thing. And that was a rear main-bearing, oil-drain block screw."

Oscar Courtland removed his hand from my arm and reached into his pocket. He took out a small steel screw.

"Although it is a matter of both public record and fact that Courtland Motors Corporation is being sued, it is less well known but far more reprehensible that we are not standing alone with regard to this liability. As you know, Max, but as perhaps, Wylie Nolan, you do not know, the Sherman Decker Tool Company has also been named by the Standish heirs in their lawsuit."

He held up the screw that he'd taken out of his pocket.

"Look at this perfectly manufactured piece of metal and tell me that the machinist who made it is a murderer, and that he should be in jeopardy of losing all of his life's work."

Oscar took a minuscule step forward and dropped the tiny screw into my hand.

"Remember that Sherman Decker made this, Max. Keep it with you throughout the trial as a reminder that the law isn't a game, and a lawsuit isn't just a matter of insurance companies exchanging assets. This is serious, deadly business. Now come with me. I want you to meet him."

Mr. Courtland resumed his old man's shuffle away from us. I stared for a few seconds at the screw. Then I held it out toward Wylie Nolan. There was a tight, hard glint in his eyes.

I put the screw in my pocket and we followed Oscar Courtland.

"Hello, Sherman," he was saying. "I want you to meet these gentlemen, since they will be representing our interests on Monday at the trial."

Sherman Decker didn't budge. He didn't say a word, and his jaw was shut so tightly it gave his face the look of a clenched fist.

I took a step backward.

Wylie stepped forward and asked, "Will you be in New York for the trial, Sherman?"

Decker looked at Wylie. "I'll be there."

His eyes were cold and dead, like his voice, and at that moment, I realized that desperation isn't the same thing as defeat or despair. It has mileage left in it. And it's dangerous, because those who feel it have nothing left to lose.

"Which one of you is the lawyer?" Sherman Decker's eyes landed hard, first on me and then on Wylie Nolan.

"I am," I said.

His eyes swung back to me.

"What's your name?"

"Max Bramble."

"All right, Max. Then hear this and hear it good, because I don't have it in me to say it more than once. If I lose this case, I lose everything I ever worked for. Everything me and my family own. And if you let those lying sons-of-bitches take me down, I swear to you on everything I hold sacred that I'm going to take every blasted one of them down with me."

•

Arthur H. Harris wrote, *"In the conduct of your case, you will see falsehood and deceit gaining over your just cause, the opposing counsel will maliciously pervert the facts and distort the law, he may even turn upon you personally with vile insult or bitter sneer; but I hope and pray that your temper may not betray you into descending to similar methods in reply."*

My hand closed around the screw in my pocket. My eyes went to Sherman Decker's tormented face. Monday morning would be the beginning. And to keep my temper from betraying me in the defense of this falsely maligned and honest man, it was going to be an uphill battle all the way.

CHAPTER
31

Just before I passed the bar, my father started sending me long, handwritten letters that expressed his philosophy of law. These letters were written with a fountain pen which, being an old-fashioned implement, added mood, character, and depth to the ideas that were being conveyed.

Other than giving me a much-needed sense of support during my last year at school, the letters also carried me away from the dry drudgery of the law and introduced me to the concept of LAW per se. Pure, Sacred, and Golden.

In one letter, my father wrote that "the courtroom is where you can do your laboratory work, where you can see the practical application of the principles you have gleaned from the books." In another, he expressed his hopes that one day I would "be reading the old decisions and the old texts" when "a sudden realization" would come upon me "of the wonder, the magnitude, the glory, the mystery, and the grandeur of English law." And in a third, he said he wouldn't insist that I "become a legal philosopher," but would be satisfied if I just became "an honest and upright lawyer who has an old-fashioned regard for the worth of his word."

The gift that my father gave me through his letters was his love of law. I came to understand that the law was his mistress, and that to him, her beauty was boundless.

Over the years—how many sons have said this about their fathers?—I have come to agree with him.

I almost never express any of these sentiments in private, and I never do in public. Wylie Nolan knows how I feel about the law. And I know how he feels about fire investigation. He's the guy at a fire whose mind becomes a rivet of focus and whose whole body goes on red alert. And I'm the one who, as my father said in one letter, "cannot enter a courtroom without a peculiar feeling that the great sovereign state itself is present in the room."

This is, I admit, a feeling that often puts me at odds with other attorneys in an era where I've heard plaintiff's lawyers brag at dinner parties about moving locations of accidents or incidents blocks away from where they actually occurred in order to involve a non-culpable corporation as a defendant in a lawsuit.

Canon Fifteen of the Professional Code of Ethics of the American Bar Association stated: "The office of attorney does not permit, much less does it demand of him for any client, violation of law or any manner of fraud or chicanery. He must obey his own conscience and not that of his client."

The first time I read that excerpt was in one of those letters my father wrote me in college a long time ago.

Since then, most of the rules, to say nothing of the Code of Ethics themselves, have changed.

"Stirring up strife and litigation is not only unprofessional, but it is indictable at common law."

That's Canon 28 of the American Bar Association's Code of Professional Ethics. Reassuring, isn't it? The problem is I'm quoting from the 1933 Code. In a 1977 decision, the Supreme Court found that a lawyer's right to advertise is "free speech," and as such is protected by the Constitution. It was from that point on that we started to see and hear all of those "sue your neighbor" ads on the radio, in the newspapers, and on television.

When my father first went into law, it would have been considered a violation of the Code to seek out "those with claims for personal injuries or those having any other grounds of action in order to secure them as clients, or to employ agents or runners for like purposes, or to pay or reward, directly or indirectly, those who bring or influence the bringing of such cases to his office."

Today, lawyers are not only permitted to stir up strife and litigation, they're encouraged to do so.

Which doesn't mean that we have to, though. Or, to quote Canon 30 as it relates to Justifiable and Unjustifiable Litigations, an attorney's "appearance in court should be deemed equivalent to an assertion *on his honor* that in his opinion his client's case is one proper for judicial determination."

I happen to believe that America is still the professional roosting place for thousands of decent, honorable lawyers who prefer the more stringent ethical code, but that, like the malefactors in days of old, they prefer to do their good deeds under cover of darkness.

I first read the Code of Ethics that dates back to August 1933 in one of those letters my father wrote me, which brings this story around again to my last year of law school. I was home on spring break. My father and I were smoking contraband Havana cigars in his den, and, as usual, discussing The Law. My mother called out from the kitchen that she needed my father's help, so when he went out of the room, I was temporarily left to my own devices. After a few minutes, I got bored and started to poke around on his desk.

At the bottom of a stack of depositions, I noticed the corner of an old paperbound book. I pulled it out and studied it. Parts of the binding were ragged, and all four corners of the cover had started to curl.

The title and author of the book were italicized inside a large, ornate oval, beneath which were the words "West Publishing Co."

Letters
to a
Young Attorney
by
Arthur M. Harris

I thumbed through the book.

LETTER III on page thirty-five said, *"When you remember that hundreds of other law schools all over the country will disgorge as many as your school, if not more, you can see that there is not going to be a dearth of legal advice in this country."*

My father had written me those exact words in a letter just a week before.

On page one hundred and two, I read, *"Nothing so coarsens a man as politics. There is something about the unholy swelter that takes the fine edge off a man's sensibilities."* He had written that to me so recently there was still smoke coming off the tire treads behind the words.

I kept flipping through the book.

On every page, I recognized a thought or idea that my father had communicated with bold, inky strokes of his fountain pen. I was literally flabbergasted. I didn't know if I should laugh, or accuse him of moral turpitude, or take him to task for blatant plagiarism.

Before I could do anything, though, I heard a noise at the door and looked up. My father had two cups of coffee in his hands, and a proud-of-himself expression on his face. He didn't look guilty at all.

"If I'd given you the book earlier," he said. "Or sent it to you, or told you that you had to read it, it would just have seemed a dry legal tome to you. Another assignment. Another obligation. You would have read it as a labor of labor instead of as a labor of love, and possibly even missed the import of what Arthur M. Harris had to say."

He put the cups down on his desk. "In the cause of wisdom, however, paternal subterfuge is not only a good thing, it is often a necessary one. You may have the book if you want it, Max. It's yours to do with as you will."

I took it.

I grabbed it off the desk and held onto it, and wouldn't give it back to him if he'd begged. And I'm still holding onto it to this day.

•

In Europe, rich people sometimes keep a modest apartment in a poor or marginal area of their city. They call it their pied-à-terre. Translated literally, this means "foot on the ground." It's said that their purpose in maintaining these small apartments is to remind them of their roots and to keep them in touch with reality.

And that's exactly why I always keep my tattered copy of *Letters to a Young Lawyer* in my briefcase. The words within, the philosophy, Harris's love of simplicity and reverence for the law—this is my psychological pied-à-terre.

•

I spent the night before the trial began at my desk. My experts were as ready as they were ever going to be. The graphics had been delivered to my office. I had outlined my opening statement and given Sarah instructions on how to handle my other cases during the grueling time ahead. Trial preparation was over. I expected that the trial itself would last two weeks.

I reached for my Arthur M. Harris.

"How solemn a place the courtroom becomes, where all men, regardless of creed or race, may resort for the amelioration of their wrongs and the enforcement of their rights!"

I was ready.

CHAPTER
32

Big court cases in many ways resemble the opening night of a theatrical play. The tension, the excitement, and the electricity of a trial, in spite of the exhaustion that results after a daisy-chain of eighteen-hour days, starts with jury selection and doesn't let up until the bailiff leads the jurors back into the courtroom, and everybody leans forward to hear the verdict, as anxiously as any audience ever waited for the denouement of a suspenseful play.

"What a noble and worthy duty is the jury's!"

Jury selection is the casting call in the theater of the law. And, as with all open auditions, there are usually so many farcical, frightening, or unqualified people who have to be examined that the worst symptoms of pretrial jitters disappear in the course of wading through the requirements of the day.

Jury selection can also be looked at as the first chance an attorney gets to study his opposition. Will the lawyer who's trying the case be the same as the one who attended the depositions? Is a junior partner handling jury selection, or does the firm think it's important enough for a senior partner to appear? Is plaintiff's attorney wearing a three hundred dollar suit, or is he doing his rumpled man-of-the-people routine? Is he carrying a Bible in his hand to show the jury that he is a devout Christian? Is he wearing a lapel pin of an American flag? And who are his assistants? Who will be sitting second chair? How does he use his hands to indicate strength, resolve, or deception? Does he walk right up to the witness during direct examination, or does he keep his distance? Does he raise his voice when he's angry? Is he a cajoler or an attacker? Does he use fact or resort to flair? Is his technique hammer and fist? Or carrot and stick?

Not only is jury selection the first chance plaintiff's attorney and I get to look each other over, it's also the first chance the jurors have to look at the lawyers from both sides.

During *voir dire*, when counsel asks jurors specific questions to flush out those he thinks will be prejudicial to his case, the potential juror is making mental notes about the attorneys, too. He's noting the lawyer's style, the image he projects, if he has dandruff on his collar, if his eyeglasses are held together with a safety pin, the way he stares or blinks or parts his hair. The attorney thinks he is just there to try a case, but from the minute he enters the courtroom, he is on trial himself.

Arthur M. Harris described his own father (also an attorney) this way, *"Your grandfather's carriage in the courtroom was perfect. I have seen bailiffs reading newspapers; lawyers lolling over two or three chairs, yawning and gaping; even the judge tilted back, half dozing in his chair; yet your grandfather always entered the room and took his seat with quiet dignity and an attitude that spoke eloquently of his respect for the profession and for the court."*

Like Arthur M. Harris's father, I believe that first impressions count.

The reason I'm so alert to how an attorney presents himself and is perceived in court stems from an experience I had my first summer out of graduate school, when I was called for jury duty on a civil case.

The defendants were the owners and managers of a large Manhattan commercial occupancy. The plaintiff was a Puerto Rican living in New York who worked for a messenger service. His allegation was that while in a passenger car in their building, the elevator went into an abrupt free-fall of short duration, and that as a result he experienced a soft-tissue, whiplash type of injury.

Right off, I am prejudiced in favor of the defense, because I think soft-tissue injuries are about as credible as table rattling at a seance. In essence, a soft-tissue injury is an alleged injury for which there is no physical evidence. "Soft-tissue injury" is a medical term that was probably invented by plaintiffs' attorneys to explain why their clients limp without a broken leg, buckle over in "pain" without ever having bled, and are unable to hold down a job because of "injuries" that have no external or objective evidence in muscles, tendons, skin, and/or bone.

In any event, the case seemed bogus to me from the start. The attorney who represented the messenger was about six feet tall. She was wearing a lint-covered skirt and a blouse with a button missing. Her hair was dirty. Her voice was coarse. I didn't like her, and I didn't like her case.

But when she looked at the jurors, she looked us right in the eye; and when she talked to us, she spoke as though her case had merit and we were capable of an intelligent response. She told us both her client's position and that of the defendant, without any apparent prejudice toward either side. And she projected not only concern for her client, but also that the time she would be spending in jury selection was valid, valuable, and worthy of her respect.

On the other hand, the attorneys for the building owners looked like three snot-nosed Ivy League law school graduates who hated every minute they were spending in that dingy, uncomfortable room and considered both the jury and the entire jury selection procedures to be professionally and socially beneath them.

It was obvious that they didn't care about their case. They gave plaintiff's attorney a wide advantage when they let *her* describe the issues. They looked annoyed and bored; and because of their arrogance, the messages conveyed to us, the potential jurors, by the *defense* were these:

One. We need three lawyers to come up against your one lawyer because we have a lousy case;

Two. We sent three junior lawyers right out of law school because we don't think jury selection is important enough to waste a senior partner's time; and,

Three. The three lawyers we sent aren't really interested in the proceedings because this is a bullshit case.

If I'd been a partner in the firm representing the building owners, and I had seen the demeanor of those three lawyers, I would have fired them on the spot.

Over the years, I've seen many, many nonculpable defendants hire arrogant, aloof attorneys like those three stooges in pin-striped suits. Watching them in action, I have often muttered to myself, "No wonder you're going to lose the case."

The reality of the situation is this. A jury can be prejudiced for or against a lawyer long before his opening statements by something as simple as remembering or forgetting to thank them for their time and attention after he has described the incidents involved in the case.

•

Jury selection for *Standish* versus *Courtland Motors Corporation* began promptly at nine o'clock on Monday morning and was over by five o'clock on Tuesday afternoon.

Wednesday, first thing in the morning, Clyde Prouty, the plaintiff's attorney, gave his opening statements; and, to paraphrase the Seventh Amendment to the Constitution of the United States of America, "the right to trial by jury" was under way.

CHAPTER
33

The trial involving the matter of *Standish* versus *Courtland Motors* took two weeks, and I told our corporate counsel at Courtland that I wanted Wylie Nolan there with me the whole time, because fire touched every aspect of the case. Legal. Medical. Mechanical. Photographic. I wanted Wylie to help me wade through the rhetoric and keep us focused on fire.

Since that's what this was. A fire case. And our defense had to rely, not on circumstantial evidence, but on burn patterns and on our ability to convince the jury that burn patterns are *facts*.

Every day, Wylie and I, and Halburton Kramer, Courtland's engineer, met for breakfast, talked about what the plaintiff would do or try to do that day, attended trial, reviewed our progress at lunch, spent the afternoon at court, and over dinner, planned our strategy for the next day. After dinner, we worked until midnight, making up lists of questions for me to ask plaintiff's witnesses on cross-examination and rehearsing what my own experts were going to say.

Over a six-day period, plaintiff presented twenty-two witnesses. First, there were the relatives: eagerly bereaved mother, Eva Scheidler, and the two sisters, Felicia and Victoria Scheidler.

Over coffee and a muffin, our excuse for breakfast the day of their testimony, Wylie said to me, "You realize, of course, that they're going to cry."

"I don't think so," I told Wylie. I knew the Scheidlers hadn't been a close family, which was one reason to preclude tears. Another was basic human dignity. I didn't think that Hugo Scheidler's ex-wife—Stanfield Standish's mother—would stoop to histrionics in public.

"Wrong," Wylie said. "She's going to have the mandatory cry for the newspapers. If she finishes early, she'll have another cry for the jury. She's good for at least two. The sisters will pull out all of the stops."

"Wylie," I said. "You're a cynic. People can't just cry on cue."

But I was wrong. Mrs. Scheidler cried when and how Wylie said she would. And both sisters wailed with so much abandon that Victoria started to hyperventilate and had to be excused from the stand.

Prouty's other witnesses included members of the Stilton-on-Hudson Fire Department, the fire experts from the State Police, Prouty's own fire expert, plaintiff's videotape photographer, their mechanical engineer, the fire explosions expert, their medical expert (who testified on how much pain and suffering Standish experienced before he died), miscellaneous Standish Enterprises executives, and so on.

The gist of all their testimony was basically the same as their complaint. Stanfield Standish had been a corporate genius, a benefactor of mankind, a healer of dissident political factions, a loving brother and son. The big, bad Duesenberg restored with malice aforethought by Courtland Motors Corporation, had *somehow* (unspecified as to how) incinerated him.

Prouty's experts talked gobbledygook, and it wasn't hard for me to poke holes in their testimony. They may have known something about modern vehicles, but they had absolutely no idea about how a luxury car was built sixty years ago.

Dr. Paiamee, their mechanical engineer, didn't even know that the Duesenberg had an aluminum chassis; Prouty's fire expert didn't realize that the flow of hot gases to the intake manifold and return was controlled by a thermostat located on the right side of the cylinder block. And so on.

Everything Prouty's experts thought was a source of ignition had at least two backup systems that prevented spontaneous combustion; everything they said was flammable turned out to have been surrounded by water-cooled ducts or to have been divided into small chambers that rapidly and efficiently dissipated heat.

While Clyde Prouty was presenting his case, which wasn't all that interesting, the courtroom started to fill up with people who were. Mark Greenberg was there from day one. Mark told Wylie—they met in the Men's Room—that he was covering the trial for his television show. Rebecca Katz sometimes showed up, too. Every few days she would stride in, whisper vehemently at Mark, glare at me, and raise my spirits with a stiletto flash of leg.

For whatever reason, Wylie latched on to Mark Greenberg. He told me he even watched *Point of View* one night on television. I thought they were an unlikely duo and couldn't decide if Wylie actually enjoyed talking to Mark or if—which I find more plausible—he and Mark were each cultivating the other for ulterior motives of their own.

As far as the others in the courtroom went, the only people I found conspicuously absent were the old-timers from Cinema Select. Not even Mark's uncle Emil Bergman showed up for the trial. I had a few theories about why they hadn't come, some of which I thought were pretty good. But Wylie, with characteristic sensitivity, said it was simpler than that, and that the only reason they weren't there was because they'd all checked into a nursing home to die.

Chief Lon Bandy stuck in his head every day or so. Since he was a defense witness, he didn't have to appear until the second week. Speaking of Bandy, I could never understand why Clyde Prouty didn't call him as a plaintiff's witness. All I can figure was that he must have thought Bandy's testimony wouldn't carry the weight of a state trooper's or state fire marshal's, since the chief was just a part-time law officer who worked for the Highway Department five days a week.

Prouty's loss. Our gain.

Clyde, by the way, is said to be unbeatable. Corporate defense attorneys pronounce his name in the hushed tones usually reserved for hospital rooms where someone is expected to die. Personally, I don't see him as a black-robed skeleton with a scythe. Take away his phony indignation and exaggerated posturing, and all that's left is a guy who hasn't adequately prepared his case.

He did present plaintiff's case smoothly, though. I helped that along by treating his experts with the respect I thought their integrity was due. Instead of going after them with a meat cleaver, I dissected them delicately, using only precision surgical instruments and kid gloves.

This worked to our advantage, because it got the jury thinking. Mrs. Scheidler and Standish's sisters overdid the crying routine, and Stanfield Standish's character witnesses became so hackneyed after the fourth hour that jurors started to look at their watches and squirm on their rock-hard seats. That was all nice, but not enough to pin any hope of a defense verdict on.

I knew, though, that at some point, Prouty had to respond to our allegations about arson, which meant getting to the actual facts of the case, and that's almost never a strength for a plaintiff's attorney. And from that point on, I felt I had him.

But, as the wise old jurist once said: You can never tell what a jury is going to do.

Prouty called his last witness on the Monday afternoon of the second week of the trial.

We followed with the witnesses we had promised the jury during our opening statements. And we were planning to call only seven of them: Ralph Arkus, the handyman who worked at the Cliff Overlook Restaurant and who discovered the Duesenberg at three o'clock in the morning on Snake Hill Road; Chief Lon Bandy of the Stilton-on-Hudson Police Department, who responded first to the scene;

Dr. Eli Timmerman, our photogrammetrist; Dr. Alexander Urda, former Chief Medical Examiner of New York City and our expert in forensic pathology; Dr. Halburton Kramer, our expert engineer from Courtland Motors Corporation; Freddie Eckeles, Hugo Scheidler's former chauffeur and the man who took care of the Duesenberg for fourteen years; and Wylie Nolan.

Wylie strongly suggested (translated, that means Wylie told me) that he should testify last. "I go after everybody else because you want to leave the jury thinking about the fire."

Made sense to me.

My opening statement had been brief. A week earlier, I'd told the jury that our defense would be based upon evidence that demonstrated the fire in Stanfield Standish's Duesenberg was the result of arson; that we could unequivocally prove that the car had not been operational at the time of the fire; that a second person had been present; and that this second person had introduced a flammable liquid to the vehicle, the ignition of which was a factor in the condition of Stanfield Standish's body after his death.

I called Ralph Arkus as my first witness.

With Arkus, I established what the Duesenberg looked like when he'd first come upon the scene. Our forensic weather check told us the temperature that night had been about thirty degrees; it had been windless and cloudless, and there had been a full moon. This was important to our case, because Ralph Arkus told the police he'd seen black smoke coming out of the smoldering car.

"Thin black smoke?" I asked him.

"No. It wasn't thin."

"Then, would you say it was thick?"

"It was black, thick, heavy smoke. Like what comes out of a chimney when the oil furnace is burning dirty fuel."

"And where was this thick, black smoke coming from, Mr. Arkus?"

"Hell, you mean where *wasn't* it coming from!"

"I take it then that there was a lot of this thick, black smoke coming from the Duesenberg?"

"Yes, sir. It was coming from everywhere."

Clyde Prouty didn't know what I was getting at but figured that if I wanted there to be thick, black smoke, then he *didn't* want there to be thick, black smoke. He tried to challenge Ralph Arkus's memory, not realizing that when you're dealing with a man who possesses only about seven functioning brain cells, the facts that brain has chosen to retain become precious to their owner. Clyde Prouty couldn't budge Ralph on anything he had said.

My second witness was Chief Lon Bandy.

When Bandy and I met briefly the day before he testified, he told me that his son, Patton Bandy, would be in the courtroom to watch his dad.

I had forgotten all about it until Chief Bandy moved past another man on his way to the witness stand. The second man was wearing the uniform of a lieutenant in the New York State Police and looked so much like the old cop, he had to be Bandy's son.

Patton Bandy is a broad-shouldered, big-boned redhead. He has an old-fashioned handlebar moustache, a square-jawed, good-natured face, and slow-moving, intelligent eyes. When his father sat down on the witness stand, I saw Pat Bandy wink at him and give him a covert thumbs-up.

From that point on, he could do no wrong as far as I was concerned.

Chief Lon Bandy was my time bomb, so I kept him up on the witness stand as long as I could and took my own sweet time in setting him off. I started his testimony with Ralph Arkus's call, Bandy's radioed response, and his arrival at the location of the still-smoldering Duesenberg on Snake Hill Road. Then I led him through what he saw and heard from the time he pulled over his patrol car until he eventually left the scene.

I questioned Chief Bandy slowly and made sure the jury heard and understood everything he said. I spent a lot of time, as I had done with Ralph Arkus, on the heavy, black smoke he'd seen when he first got there. I let Bandy go into detail on his examination of the vehicle. I made sure he related his observations about Standish's body to the jury. In response to my questions, he described the position it was in when he found it in the driver's seat, what he smelled when he stuck his head through the car window—"like an Exxon fuel spill at the morgue"—and his suspicions that the origin of that odor might have been part petroleum product and part burned flesh.

I had Chief Bandy explain his philosophy of forensic investigation—that he treated every police incident as though it were a crime scene—because I wanted the jury to understand why he always had a camera in his car and why he always had extra batteries and extra film.

Then I showed Bandy the four-by-six pictures he had given me and asked him to identify them as the ones he'd taken that night. Using enlargements of those same photographs, I asked Chief Bandy to tell the jury where he had been when he'd taken each picture and what he'd thought was relevant about the subject matter of each at the time.

I took Bandy through the events preceding, during, and after the arrival of the State Police, fire department, and other official and nonofficial visitors to the scene.

Bandy described how the fire department had flooded the vehicle, even though the fire was already out; he told the jurors that the police cars had driven right into the scene, destroying any evidence of the presence of another car. He described the removal of the body from the Duesenberg without official photographs first having been taken to substantiate its position and condition in the car; the virtual absence of any methodical vehicular examination; the absence of a forensic photographer to photodocument other aspects of the fire scene; and then the arrival of Standish's people and what he described as their "hijacking" of the body of the deceased.

During cross-examination, Clyde Prouty tried to discredit Chief Bandy, making sarcastic asides about the size of the Stilton-on-Hudson Police Department (one part-time employee), and Bandy's apparent lack of professional expertise. Bandy sat patiently through this ridicule, seeming not to resent anything that was being said, just chomping his teeth down comfortably on his imaginary cigar.

Until Prouty said to Chief Bandy, "Isn't that true?"

Which was a mistake.

Bandy then began to quote New York law as it applies to the proper treatment of a dead body when the deceased is discovered in a location other than a hospital and not under the supervision of a physician. Among these statutes is one directing that the scene of the unattended death be preserved for a police investigation, and that the body be transported to a facility where an autopsy can be performed.

Prouty said snidely and vehemently that there was no reason to treat what was obviously an accidental fire as though it had been a crime scene. And *I* objected that plaintiff's attorney was testifying instead of cross-examining my witness.

The judge sustained my objection. Prouty barked, "No further questions." And Chief Bandy was dismissed.

As he was leaving the witness box, I saw the chief look toward the back of the room and do almost a comic-strip double take, followed by a big grin. I turned to see what he was looking at, and just before she slipped into the last bench at the back of the courtroom, I caught a glimpse of Astrid Scheidler.

Interesting.

Dr. Eli Timmerman hunkered up to the witness stand next. Wylie and I had spent half an hour the night before going over his testimony with him, and the other three hours trying to teach him how to react like a living, breathing, normal human being. We weren't altogether successful. Employing an expert witness who looks like what primitive peoples worshipped at Stonehenge is a challenge. We told him to try to make sounds when he walked. Juries don't like to be sneaked up on. We tried to teach him how to smile. He smiled. We changed our minds and told him not to smile.

By the time he'd taken his oath, I wasn't completely unhappy with his appearance. A blue suit with a conservative shirt and tie hid his monolithic form. Granted, we hadn't been able to do much about his monosyllabic answers to my questions, but in a technical witness that isn't altogether bad.

After he'd qualified as an expert in photogrammetry, which took about forty-five minutes, since his resume is six single-spaced pages long, Eli Timmerman's direct testimony was like a thirty-second station break.

I deliberately kept my questions short and sweet. And Eli explained to the jury in language even I could understand exactly what photogrammetry was, how photo-enhancement works, and how it doesn't distort or in any other way alter the original image recorded on the film.

I brought out the photographs Eli had enhanced and enlarged, asked him to identify them, and entered them into evidence.

The reason I introduced Dr. Timmerman to the jury first was to establish the scientific validity for his procedures, because almost everything my next witness said was going to be based on his work.

My next witness was Dr. Alexander Urda.

Urda's testimony was almost as important to my defense as Wylie Nolan's. As I watched his pudding-bowl body move toward the witness stand, I thought that he was more knowledgeable than any of the other medical examiners I know—but that the biggest difference between him and his peers was his attitude towards the spotlight. He seemed to enjoy the occasional headline or celebrity case, but unlike many of his colleagues, he didn't *need* to be the focus of media attention. He's the only forensic pathologist I know of who served over a year as Chief Medical Examiner of a major city without having gotten into any trouble.

As Urda was passing me, my eye caught another bit of drama at the back of the room. The door swung open, and a dark-haired man darted inside. He was wearing a blazer over a white T-shirt, which I know is the "in" style for young executives, but which I think looks dumb. He had the same thick black hair, large, soulful black eyes, narrow face, and high cheekbones I'd seen in his photograph on his mother's piano. It was Dennis Cataliz. He was moving toward the last bench on the left side of the courtroom when he noticed that Astrid Scheidler was already sitting there. For a second, he stopped and just stared at her. Or should I say, glared at her. Then he changed directions and went instead to the right side of the aisle.

During that brief few seconds, I also noticed that Pat Bandy had moved. He wasn't on the bench next to his father anymore, he was leaning against the back wall of the courtroom. His arms were crossed over his chest, and he was staring at Astrid Scheidler. His wasn't a hard stare, and it wasn't a spider-and-fly stare. If I were a bad guy, I wouldn't want those eyes on me. But if Astrid knew about them, she just might like them being right where they were. I think Astrid felt his eyes on her. She sat very still, as if the slightest movement would break a spell or scare a butterfly off a blade of grass.

Then I turned. Dr. Urda was being sworn in.

Before I brought him to the specific circumstances of the Duesenberg fire, I asked Urda to tell the jury what were the proper procedures for handling a D.O.A. at a fire scene, apropos of what had
or had not been done to the body of Stanfield Standish at the scene
of the crime.

Of course, as soon as I said "crime," Clyde Prouty leaped to his
feet and objected.

Objection was sustained. But by then, it was too late. The jury had
already heard me, and they were thinking. Thinking.

Dr. Alexander Urda is a colorful, extremely interesting witness.
He can talk about a dead body with enough respect to almost, but
not quite, make you believe he isn't enjoying himself. When he
speaks, he never seems to be testifying; instead, it's as if he's telling
the jury a story. Gather around, children, and I'll relate how the victim of a sudden death *should* have been handled by the police.

Urda confirmed Chief Lon Bandy's contention that at an unattended death, the deceased should be photographed, evidence
should be preserved, and a state-law-mandated autopsy should be
performed.

Again, Clyde Prouty objected. This time he complained that my
line of questioning implied to the jury that the cause of Stanfield
Standish's death was not known, whereas everybody knew that Standish died as a result of the accidental fire that started in the Duesenberg.

The judge not only overruled Prouty's objection, he angrily reminded plaintiff's attorney that *he* and not Prouty was sitting on the
bench, and that the reason we were all in court was to determine why
and how Stanfield Standish died, which, despite Prouty's objections,
everybody did *not* know.

That accomplished, I eased Urda into a question-and-answer
type of testimony. I put Chief Bandy's photo-enhanced pictures on
an easel facing the jury, and I asked the former chief medical examiner what each photograph told him about the manner in which
Standish had met his death, and if he would use his pointer to explain his answers to the jury.

He did. He gave them the same answers he had given me and
Wylie Nolan in the Old Budapest Restaurant over three bowls of

goulash. Dr. Urda told the jury that there were five ways in which a body could burn, and that this body had been burned by flame impingement.

Each photograph he analyzed showed a different part of Stanfield Standish's corpse. Dr. Urda pointed out areas of deep burning on Standish's legs and thighs, surrounded by areas that had barely been touched by fire; he explained that hopscotch burning like this was characteristic of a fire where a flammable liquid had been introduced.

When Urda got to the photograph of the shinbone sticking out through the charred tissue on Standish's leg, the good doctor lectured us on chemistry. We were told that given the high water content of the human body, this bone could not have burned through the tissue unless the temperature inside the car got as high as 1800 to 2000 degrees Fahrenheit.

And when I showed Dr. Urda the photographs of the small, round hole on the right side of Standish's forehead, he was unequivocal.

"That is a bullet wound from a small caliber pistol."

Clyde Prouty shot to his feet.

"Your honor, I object."

The judge gazed down at him. "To what?"

"To . . . to . . ." Then he slumped back in his seat.

I went over a few more photographs with Dr. Urda and reiterated a few of the more incriminating facts just to make sure that the jury wouldn't forget. But it was tough to top the bullet wound as the high point of his testimony.

Prouty huffed and puffed and tried to blow Urda's credibility down on cross-examination; but the more vitriolic he got, the more he alienated the jury. And it didn't exactly endear him to me, either.

By the third day of the defense's case, the drama taking place at the back of the room was getting as interesting as the one up front. Mark Greenberg and Rebecca Katz were now in court all the time. He usually looked bemused by the proceedings; but the way she looked reminded me of something my father used to say to anyone who called himself "mad": Dogs get mad; people get angry. Notwithstanding, Rebecca Katz looked mad.

Lieutenant Pat Bandy of the New York State Police had moved

away from the wall he'd been holding up, and seemed to have achieved his preliminary objective. He was sitting next to Astrid Scheidler on a bench. Dennis Cataliz was still sitting by himself; occasionally, I caught a glimpse of him glaring at Astrid. Rebecca Katz's eyes seemed to be drawn in that direction, too. But Astrid didn't look to her left, and she didn't look to her right. Even when her lips moved, and I assumed she was talking to Pat Bandy, she did so with no movement whatsoever of her head.

Thursday was our engineering day in court. Not very dramatic, but informative. Much to my surprise, the jury stayed awake. My first witness was Halburton Kramer, our Courtland Motors engineer. He testified to specifications of the J series Duesenberg vehicle, specifically the 1930 Arlington sedan.

Halburton showed a videotape about Duesenbergs. The judge previewed the video and let us show it because it explained to the jury how these vehicles are so different in concept and construction from the assembly-line automobiles of today. One difficult concept to get across is the custom-designed coach-built body.

In the 1920s and 1930s, the prospective owner of a Duesenberg would first buy the chassis, and then order a custom-designed coach and interior in much the same way a home builder would sit down with an architect to discuss the design of a house. Rollston of New York City custom-designed the body on the Duesenberg Arlington sedan in which Stanfield Standish was found dead. I'm sure Rollston had never planned it to be the crematorium for Standish's last remains.

Clyde Prouty tried to keep out the second video Dr. Kramer brought. He claimed that it made our client look so good, it was advertising, not evidence. The judge admitted it, though, because it showed where and how the cars were restored and gave the jury some insights into Courtland Classics' standards of workmanship and so on. Things I'd discovered during my tours of the plant.

Halburton went on to tell the jury about the Duesenberg's mechanical parts; and although they can't really have been all that interested, none of the jurors nodded off.

He told them how Duesenberg had minimized the distance the flame front would have to travel in the engine's combustion chamber, because the spark plug had been put in the center of that chamber; he described the rapid cooling of the four valves in the cylinder head and the efficient introduction and expulsion of gases with very little friction loss. Dr. Kramer also showed the jury how Duesenberg had stabilized the engine by installing it on rubber blocks; he described the three-filter engine oil lubrication system, the duplex carburetor with a single float chamber and single auxiliary air valve, the seven-gallon-capacity water-cooling system, and the rugged cast-aluminum dash with a wooden toe-board.

I asked Halburton to show a diagram of this dashboard to the jury, since it would become relevant when Wylie Nolan testified. And I prodded him to give them a detailed overview of Courtland's methodology in restoring cars so that by the time each left the plant, it was as near its original condition as a vintage car could possibly be.

Halburton showed samples of the paint that was used and gave us its flammability rating; he told us that the car seats had been reupholstered with only natural fabrics or leathers. He then went on to describe how the car drove: How fast it went. How it felt on the road. How smoothly it came to a stop when a slight pressure was applied to the brakes. After four hours of this sort of testimony, it was obvious to me—as it must have been to the jury—that Halburton Kramer was a man in love.

With a car.

During cross-examination, Clyde Prouty made the mistake of asking Halburton to tell him how many car fires there had been in Duesenbergs over the years.

Dr. Kramer answered, "There hasn't been a single one."

Prouty attacked that statement from about five different angles and was just about as successful as a bee trying to get at honey through a sealed glass jar.

I didn't bother with redirect, and called my next witness, Freddie Eckeles.

Freddie was as out of place in a business suit as a scarecrow in a tuxedo. When he walked to the witness box, he looked behind himself after each step, as though to make sure he wasn't being followed. This made me worry about the impression he was making on the jury. I knew he was scared to death about testifying, and years of experience have shown me that fear often looks like guilt.

I brought Freddie up to speed gradually, establishing the relationship he'd had as Hugo Scheidler's chauffeur, first with Hugo himself and then with Hugo's cars, more specifically with the Duesenberg.

I wanted the jury to know how well the cars had been taken care of, in what setting they were kept (I had Freddie describe the temperature-controlled barn and the Gershwin music), and in what condition the Duesenberg Arlington sedan was at the time Standish inherited Hugo's estate and Freddie lost contact with the cars.

Freddie's direct testimony was perfect. The more he spoke, the less guilty he looked; and if the jury was left with any impression at all, it was that it was an odd thing for two apparently sane and very different men—Halburton Kramer and Freddie Eckeles—to both be in love with the same car.

On cross-examination, Clyde Prouty got brownie points because Freddie was unable to testify to the mechanical condition of the Duesenberg during the year after Standish inherited it and before it was found on Snake Hill Road. But if we lost points on that, we gained them back again when Freddie inadvertently set himself up as a suspect for Standish's murder.

"There were never any problems with the Duesey while Mr. Hugo owned her, sir." Freddie said on the stand. "But there's no saying how Mr. Standish may have mistreated that beautiful automobile after I left his service and opened up my own garage."

"I take it then that you were not one of Mr. Standish's fans," Clyde Prouty said.

"Well, sir. It's like this. If a boulder were rolling downhill towards Stanfield Standish and the Duesenberg, and I only had the time to save one of them, at the end of that day, I'd be driving the Duesenberg."

"Are you telling me and the jury that you valued a machine more than you did a human life?"

"I sure as heck valued *that* machine more than I did *that* human life."

"If you would not make an effort to save Mr. Standish, can we assume, then, that the reverse is also true. You would not hesitate also to—"

I thought and hoped that Prouty was going to continue with this line of questioning. But he stopped himself just in time. He must have realized that to set Freddie up as a suspect would be to distract from the product-liability aspect of the case.

Clyde Prouty didn't want the jury to think that Freddie had killed Stanfield Standish.

So Freddie Eckeles was excused.

Court adjourned for the day.

The next day would be Friday. And at long last, I could call Wylie Nolan to the stand.

CHAPTER
34

I found that with Wylie Nolan direct testimony is a breeze. I took him slowly and methodically through the procedures for investigating a fire scene. Using enhanced photos and blowups of the Duesenberg, Wylie pointed to unusual burn patterns on the engine block, hood, seats, floor, and tires, which had been caused by someone splashing, pouring, or squirting a flammable liquid onto the car.

Wylie explained to the jury that to get the kind of burning there had been in the Duesenberg—fire adhering to a vertical surface and burning at the same time—the accelerant used probably combined a flaky laundry soap and a petroleum-based product such as kerosene.

He used his pointer and overlay graphics to illustrate each of the separate, distinct, and unconnected fires he had found in the car. An enlarged photograph of each area of the car under discussion formed the base of each graphic. A plastic sheet flopped down over the picture, and to show the jury where the fire had started, how far it had spread, and at what point it had gone out, little bits of flame had been painted on the overlays.

There were nine separate and distinct points of origin throughout the car, as well as disassociated low burning on each of the four tires.

Wylie showed the jury the flammable liquid pour-and-spatter marks he'd found on the exterior right side of the hood, on the interior engine block, on the underside of the hood, on top of the trunk compartment, on the passenger-side running board, against the upright cushion of the back seat, in the carpet on the floor of the passenger compartment, on the floor of the front seat, on Standish's body, and on each of the four tires.

We've gone over all of this before, so I won't go into detail on the rest of Wylie's direct testimony. I will mention, though, the few points I really pushed, because I didn't think we could win our case unless the jury grasped their importance.

The first was the thick, black smoke Ralph Arkus saw when he arrived at the fire scene.

To convey the significance of this smoke to the jury, Wylie explained in a relaxed, conversational manner, "When I first became a fire marshal, all our instruction manuals were outdated. Not because the chemistry of fire had changed. Oxygen still interacts with fuel and an ignition source in the same way. What had changed were the materials that compose the products we use in our everyday life. Fibers, fabrics, fluids, and solids that are commonplace now had not been invented when fire investigation first became a science.

"For example, the old manuals told us that if you saw thick, black smoke coming out of its interior when you responded to a car fire, this was a pretty accurate indication that a flammable liquid had been introduced to the vehicle and that the cause of the fire was arson.

"Over the years, though, car companies began to incorporate synthetics into their automobiles. It wasn't long until when you looked at a car, instead of seeing sheet metal, steel, wood, wool, leather, nickel, chrome, and rubber, most of what you saw was made out of products with a petroleum base.

"Modern cars have plastic dashboards, fiberglass bodies, nylon or rayon seat cushions, Orlon carpets, nylon seat-belt straps, and so on. When they are burned, all of these oil-based synthetic products release hydrocarbons into the atmosphere, and the fires that result produce black smoke.

"And that's one reason why we had to stop using the old fire-instruction manuals. Fifty years ago, black smoke meant arson. Today, all it means is that the car is on fire."

I looked at the jury to see if they were following. Their eyes were open. That was a good start. Two of them were taking notes, and the jury foreman was leaning forward on the bench as though he didn't want to miss a single word.

I turned back to Wylie Nolan and asked him why the chemical makeup of the materials used to build a car was relevant to the fire that had taken place in Stanfield Standish's Duesenberg.

"Because the Duesenberg was built in 1930, before petroleum-based synthetic products were made; and it was restored with only the kinds of materials that were available when Mr. Standish's car was first built."

"Thank you, Mr. Nolan. Now, would you please tell us what that means in terms of the color of the smoke that was coming out of the car when Ralph Arkus and Chief Lon Bandy arrived at the fire scene?"

Wylie spoke directly to the jury, "Thick, black smoke is always an indication that hydrocarbons are present in the material that is being burned. Since there were no hydrocarbons naturally present in the Duesenberg because it contained no synthetic products, the thick, black smoke told us that a flammable liquid had been introduced to the vehicle."

"Was there anything else in the car that could have produced that color smoke?"

"No."

"How about gasoline having ignited in the engine compartment, a fire starting, and black smoke coming from the flames that extended throughout the car?"

Wylie didn't answer right away. He went to the evidence table, searched through the stacks of photographs, and found the two graphics he wanted. The first gave an overview of the engine compartment. He used his pointer.

"As you can see here, there's only surface burning where a flammable liquid had been spattered along the top of the engine block." Wylie pointed. "The fire self-extinguished before it even spread to the engine mounts."

He lifted the second graphic onto the easel.

"This picture shows the Duesenberg's firewall. It's a solid piece of aluminum that separates and seals off the engine compartment from the passenger compartment." Again, Wylie used the pointer. "This aluminum barrier goes all the way down to a narrow area called the toe-board, which is made out of solid oak.

"You can see here that the toe-board has been discolored by smoke, and there's some charring from drop-down fire. But at no point did the fire ever burn through the firewall, from the engine compartment *to* the passenger compartment.

"In fact, the fire in the engine compartment barely burned down at all. Here are the fuel pump, the timing box, the intake manifolds, the carburetor, the ignition distributor, and the generator. Except for smoke discoloration, they exhibit no burning. No melting. No fire impingement. Essentially, they are all clean."

I asked Wylie more questions. He put up different sets of graphics and told the jury why there were rivulet-like burn patterns in the leather cushions of the back seat; how fires had been set at ground level and burned halfway up the tires to the wire rims; why there was only minor burning on top of the trunk, and so on.

He spent a lot of time on the Duesenberg's distended metal roof. As he had explained to me earlier, he told the jury that there is so much plastic in the interior of a modern vehicle, it takes almost no time for furnace-like temperatures to be reached. But in the 1930 Duesenberg, the roof would not have distended unless excessively hot temperatures had been reached, which could have been achieved only if a flammable substance with a petroleum base had been introduced.

Which led us to the subject of temperatures in general and Stanfield Standish's body in particular.

Flame impingement on human beings is a subject that crosses over between the disciplines of forensic pathology and that of fire investigation. Although some of the information Wylie conveyed echoed what Dr. Urda had already said, I thought it was worth repeating.

"In some places on Standish's body," Wylie said, "the tissue burned right down to white bone, consuming flesh and muscle more readily than other, more combustible, materials surrounding Mr. Standish in the car. Since no materials naturally present in the interior of the Duesenberg would have burned long enough or hot enough to have this effect, we can consider this another indication of the presence of a flammable liquid in the car."

The jury liked Wylie Nolan, and I could see that he was keeping their attention; but it wasn't until he told them about the keys that they all—not just the jury foreman—leaned forward in their seats and nodded their heads openly to let him know that they understood.

I put an enlarged photograph up on the easel.

"Can you tell the jury what this is, Mr. Nolan?"

"This is a piece of burned floor mat in the passenger compartment of the Duesenberg. It's directly beneath the ignition switch." He used the pointer. "You can see a pour pattern here that suggests the use of flammable liquid; and over to the right, imbedded in the rubber, are two keys."

"Please tell the jury the circumstances under which you found these keys."

Wylie gave an abbreviated account of the day we examined the Duesenberg in Clyde Prouty's cold barn. He alternated between graphics and photographs to dramatize digging through the debris, discovering the keys in the floor mat, and photodocumenting what he'd found. He described how he'd carefully removed the keys from the mat, found the right one for the starter switch, inserted it and turned it to the "ON" position to prove that the keys he'd found on the floor really had been the keys to the car.

And so that they understood exactly what all of this meant, Wylie told the jury that if there had been no key in the ignition switch, then the motor was off at the time of the fire; and therefore, it was impossible that the fire had been caused by an accidental source of ignition.

Clyde Prouty had apoplexy.

"I object, your honor. If the key had been on the floor at the time of the fire, why didn't we find it?"

The judge peered complacently down at plaintiff's attorney over the tops of his eyeglasses and said, "Perhaps, Mr. Prouty, that's a question you should be asking your own experts, instead of the gentleman testifying here."

Prouty slammed back down in his seat.

But we weren't done yet. I riffled through the rest of our photos and put another one up on the easel.

"Mr. Nolan, can you tell me what this is?"

"Yes, sir. It's a photograph of the area surrounding the gas pedal on the Duesenberg."

I changed photographs.

"And please describe this."

"I took this picture when I was cleaning out the floor area under the gas pedal." He used the pointer. "You can see a little bit of gold showing right over here."

"Mr. Nolan, may I ask what you were looking for when you took this shot?"

"Yes, sir. But as a matter of fact, I didn't know what I was looking for. A fire scene is a lot like an archeological dig. You don't always know what you're going to find under all of those layers of debris. You just know what the appropriate procedures are for digging out the scene, and you know that whether you find something interesting or not, you still have to look."

I put up a third enlargement.

"What *did* you find, Mr. Nolan?"

"I found a man's gold ring, inscribed on the inside and mounted with four small diamonds."

"Did you make an effort to determine if this ring had belonged to the deceased?"

"Yes. I did."

"What did you discover?"

Wylie found a picture of Stanfield Standish standing on the running board of the Duesenberg. Both of his hands were raised over his head in a championship pose.

"This was taken on Valentine's Day, at Mr. Standish's party, approximately five hours before his body was discovered in the car. You can see here and here," he pointed to Standish's fingers, "there are no rings on either of Mr. Standish's hands."

Wylie put up two smaller pictures. They were closeups of Standish's hands.

"I also researched videotapes and photographs of the deceased dating as far back as twenty years. He wasn't wearing a ring in any of that photodocumentation, either."

I heard a rustle of movement coming from the back of the courtroom and looked around, but before my eyes could isolate out where the noise had come from, it stopped. I turned back to my witness.

"Then, Mr. Nolan, given your experience not only as a fire expert, but also as a fire marshal empowered by New York State to investigate the crime of arson, what did you conclude about the ring you found under the gas pedal in Stanfield Standish's car?"

"I concluded that the ring had been brought to the car by an individual other than Mr. Standish."

"And . . ."

"And that this individual may also have been present with Mr. Standish at the time of the fire."

"And . . ."

"And that he may have been the arsonist."

•

On cross-examination, Clyde Prouty tried to lessen the impact of what Wylie had said by picking away at the ring. How did Wylie know that the ring hadn't been left there by the chauffeur? Or by the car's mechanic? Or by Stanfield Standish himself?

But by then, the jury didn't care.

Even though I knew who the ring had belonged to, I decided not to introduce evidence of its ownership for two reasons. First, I didn't want Clyde to suggest the possibility that Hugo Scheidler had dropped the ring in the Duesenberg eight, ten, fifteen years ago and that nobody had found it since; and second, I wanted to give the jury a nice, complicated mystery to solve, all wrapped up with a pretty pink bow.

The trial was going very well for Courtland Classics. Now, the subject of conversation buzzing around the courtroom was no longer *how* Stanfield Standish had accidentally died in a car fire, but *who had deliberately killed him*.

My product-liability case had become an arson-homicide.

Lead had been turned into gold.

Clyde Prouty said, "I have no further questions, your honor."

I presented my closing arguments, and I rested my case.

CHAPTER
35

Frankly, I was baffled by the events of later on that morning. So were Wylie Nolan, Alexander Urda, and Eli Timmerman. We'd been so sure that we had won. I thought the jury would adjourn, talk about the case for no more than ten minutes, take a vote, and come right back in with a verdict for the defense.

One. Two. Three.

But I've said it before and I'll probably be saying it for the rest of my life: You can never tell about juries.

The judge gave them his charge at about noon. They filed out of the courtroom and disappeared behind a closed door.

Wylie and I waited.

And we waited.

Dots of perspiration were beginning to form on my ego.

I got a message from Sarah to call Courtland Motors. I found a phone.

Oscar Courtland was anxious about the verdict. He told me that the board of directors had unanimously voted that if we lost the case, they were going to close down Courtland Classics and go out of the business of restoring cars.

Pressure. Pressure.

I said I'd call as soon as the jury came back.

Right after I hung up the receiver, a bailiff came over to me.

"The judge wants to see you in his chambers," he said. "Now."

Clyde Prouty had gotten there ahead of me. He was standing by the window. When I came in, he turned and cleared his throat.

But the judge spoke first.

"Mr. Bramble. I have just been informed by Mr. Prouty that his client has agreed to settle this lawsuit for one million dollars."

I didn't say anything.

I hadn't expected this.

But I hadn't not expected it, either.

I turned to look at Clyde Prouty, and for some reason, I wanted to smile.

Not a nice smile.

"Be careful, Mr. Bramble," the judge said. "If you lose this case, the court could award the plaintiff over fifty million dollars of your client's money. If you settle right now, they stand to lose a significant amount less."

This time Clyde Prouty smiled.

He had done this so many times. He was so sure of himself. He knew plaintiffs and he knew defendants. He knew that when a potential loss of fifty million dollars is looming, a settlement offer of one million could seem like a win to both sides.

What he didn't know, though, was my client.

And he didn't know me.

"Thank you for your concern, your honor. But if we win, my client will not have to pay anything at all. Furthermore, we would intend to sue Mr. Prouty's client for all of the court costs that we incurred in the course of presenting our case."

The judge did not look happy.

Clyde looked distinctly unhappy.

I said whatever else I had to say to get out of there, and went back to the courtroom, thinking the jury would have to be back by now.

They were still out.

What was wrong with them? What was there left to deliberate about? It was an open-and-shut case. We'd gone way beyond proving that the Duesenberg hadn't caused the fire. (I know that technically, the burden of proof is on the plaintiff, but in actual fact, the manufacturer is always expected to prove that his product *wasn't* defective). Not only had we given the jury *one* alternate cause for Standish's death, we gave them *two*. A smoking gun (literally). *And* an arsonist.

I started to pace.

Maybe *that's* it. I argued with myself. Maybe our defense had been *too* good. Maybe we'd created a backlash of sympathy for Stanfield Standish's heirs. Maybe . . .

Wylie walked over. His pipe was in his mouth.

"So, Max. What do you think?"

I relied on the old standby. "You never can tell with a—"

"Screw the jury. I'll buy you a cup of coffee."

We walked down a flight of stairs to an open area with four or five vending machines. I popped a few coins in EXTRA-LIGHT EXTRA-SUGAR. A paper cup shot out of a tube, and black coffee and milk started to stream into it from two sides.

"Mr. Bramble?"

I turned around. The kid who worked for Clyde Prouty had sneaked up behind me. Last time I saw him, Wylie was digging through the debris in the Duesenberg, and I'd been freezing to death in that old barn.

"Lindsey," I said.

"Right."

"You work for Clyde Prouty."

"Well . . . I do. I did. But . . . what I mean is . . . I don't want to anymore."

"Why not?"

"Because I'd rather work for you, Mr. Bramble. I like your style."

"I haven't won this case yet."

"I know. That's why I wanted to talk to you now. So that you know my motives are pure."

I grinned.

Lindsey laughed self-consciously and added, "Well. Sort of pure."

I asked, "Are you serious about a job?"

"I'm serious."

"Why me? Why not just another plaintiff attorney like Clyde Prouty? That's where the big money is."

"Well, sir, it's like this. No matter how often you keep telling yourself you're just doing it for love, if you work in a whorehouse long enough, everybody knows what you really are, and after a while, you can even figure it out for yourself."

I looked at Wylie. He looked at me. He shrugged.

"How do I know if you're any good?"

"I'm good."

"All right. Call my office. Talk to Sarah. Send her your résumé. I'll look it over and I'll think about it. Now get out of here. You still work for Clyde Prouty, and you're making me nervous."

I took my coffee out of the vending machine, and was about to take a gulp when Wylie said, "Well, will you take a look at that."

I lowered my cup.

"What?"

"Across the room."

I looked across the room. Astrid Scheidler was leaning against the wall between the Ladies' Room and the Fire Door. There was a large rectangular sign over her head. In big, bold red letters, it said:

NO SMOKING

She dug into her purse, pulled out her gold cigarette case, and put a cigarette to her lips. Lieutenant Patton Bandy, looking very correct and official in his State Trooper's uniform, walked over to her. He stopped. He reached for the area of his belt near his gun.

She looked up at him.

He looked down at her.

He pulled out a disposable lighter. He flicked it once and held it toward the tip of her cigarette.

She leaned forward into the flame.

Their eyes locked.

Wylie said, "Love conquers Law."

We went back upstairs.

A few minutes went by. I started pacing again. Wylie asked the bailiff if there had been any word yet from the jury.

Nothing.

Eli Timmerman offered to go across the street and bring back sandwiches. I let him go. His footsteps didn't make any noise when he walked down the hall.

It was going to be a long, long lunch.

•

At exactly 1:30 P.M., we were called into the courtroom. The jury had reached a verdict.

I walked back to the defense table and sat down. For a moment, I had one of those flashes of ego-terror every lawyer gets when he realizes that maybe he didn't win his case.

What if this was one of those juries that don't care what caused a fire or an accident and maintain the position that no matter what happened, the defendant should always be made to pay? I hoped I hadn't gotten a plaintiff's jury. Because there was more at stake here than fifty million dollars and the fate of Courtland Classics.

My hand slipped into my pocket.

Oscar Courtland had told me that a trial is not a game.

My fingers closed around a small steel screw.

I thought of Sherman Decker.

The jury filed back into the courtroom.

I can remember very clearly what the jury foreman looked like. He was small. He had thick, black-rimmed eyeglasses and a bald spot surrounded by a Friar Tuck fringe of hair; he had a big nose and a small mouth. He was wearing a brown suit, and in the right pocket of his shirt he had a white plastic pencil shield with six ballpoint pens. I counted them. He was an optometrist, and he had shy eyes.

As he rose to his feet, the courtroom fell completely silent.

The judge asked. "Have you reached a verdict?"

"Yes, your honor."

"Have you found in favor of the plaintiff or in favor of the defense?"

The jury foreman looked down at a small piece of folded white paper. He unfolded it and read, "Your honor, we find in favor of the defense."

And that was that.

Somebody in the back of the courtroom let out a loud whoop. People all around me offered congratulations. Shook my hand. The room became a caldron of noise. People stood. People sat.

The judge slammed down his gavel.

He demanded order in the court.

Again, all conversation stopped.

I sat down.

The judge peered over his eyeglasses, first at plaintiff's attorney. Then at me.

"I want it to go into the record," he said, "that I am recommending that this case be forwarded to the Office of the District Attorney for a criminal investigation into the arson-homicide death of Stanfield Standish."

CHAPTER

36

Some lawyers, and I'm one of them, like to poll the jury to find out what the individual jurors were thinking and how they arrived at their verdict. This helps us to see how we're perceived by others in a court of law. Did they like Halburton Kramer? Did they understand what Dr. Timmerman had to say? How did they respond to Wylie Nolan? Had one of the jurors been a holdout? Had the others tried to pressure him or her into agreeing with the majority?

That sort of thing.

After the suspense this particular jury had put us through, there was no way you could keep me from polling them. Why had it taken them almost two hours to decide on a verdict? What had we done so wrong to prolong what should have been an open-and-shut case?

The jury foreman provided me with the answer. He looked shyer than he had in the jury stand and even a little embarrassed when he said, "Well, Mr. Bramble. You see, we'd been serving on this jury for over two weeks, and frankly, we were all a little bit sick of it. As soon as we retired to the jury room, we took a vote; and, actually, it only took us two minutes to agree that your client wasn't guilty."

I looked at my watch and shook my head. "But the bailiff didn't call us back into the courtroom until 1:30. That's an hour and a half after you left. If you came up with a verdict in two minutes, what took you so long to tell it to the judge?"

"Well, you see," continued the little optometrist, looking more shy and embarrassed than ever, "it was lunchtime, and all of us were hungry. So we ordered a pizza first. Before we told the bailiff that we'd taken the vote. That way, the court had to pay for it. If we'd come right back as soon as we'd voted, though, then we all would have had to pay for our own lunch."

Juries.

Trust me.

You can never, never figure out what they're going to do.

CHAPTER
37

I called Wylie Nolan at six o'clock on Monday morning.

"Did you see today's newspapers?"

A groggy voice answered, "No. I'm still asleep."

"The district attorney is exhuming Stanfield Standish's body. They're reopening our case."

The phone went silent for a few seconds. Then I heard a match strike and a long intake of breath.

"Okay. I'm awake now. Where are you? Right this minute?"

"Why?"

"Because we did the trial your way and you won the case. They're digging out Standish, so it's my party from now on. I'm taking you for a ride."

"Why? Where? I'm not at my office."

"I'll pick you up in half an hour."

"You'll never find me. You'll get lost."

"Ah, ye of little faith."

Wylie went west off the Saw Mill River Parkway instead of east. Then he drove around in figure eights for another twenty minutes before he pulled up in front of my house. It had taken him two hours to get to me after I'd hung up the phone.

Wylie Nolan *likes* to get lost. He flashed me a big grin.

I got into the passenger seat.

"Where are we going?"

"We're going for a ride," was all I could get out of him.

We returned to the Saw Mill River Parkway and went north to the Tappan Zee Bridge. We crossed it and went west. Twenty minutes later, I knew we were on our way to Stilton-on-Hudson.

In another forty minutes, we were driving through Belton-on-Hudson on Walter Link Road.

Again, I asked Wylie where we were going.

This time, he got around not answering by telling me a long-winded story about Moishe. Moishe had been born on New York's Lower East Side. When he was twenty years old, he moved to Philadelphia. In Philadelphia, he married Bella and raised two beautiful daughters, Sarala and Berela. When he was sixty years old, Moishe and Bella retired to Florida. He lived in Miami Beach for the next twenty years. Then he got sick, and the doctor told Sarala and Berela that their father didn't have long to live.

Not knowing where Moishe would want to be buried, his oldest daughter, Sarala, said to him, "Papa, you were born in Manhattan, you raised a family in Philadelphia, and you spent your golden years in Miami Beach. Everywhere you lived, you made friends. Everywhere, you have memories. Everywhere, you were happy. So, when the time comes, God forbid, for the good angel to call you to heaven, where do you want to be buried?"

Moishe raised his tired old head off the pillow, looked at Sarala, smiled at Berela, and said, "Surprise me."

The meaning of the story, I took it, was that Wylie wasn't going to tell me where he intended to go.

And as he said, this was his party.

But I thought I knew where we were going.

The trial was over. Before and during case preparation, I had insisted that our job wasn't to solve a crime, but just to prove that one had occurred. My client doesn't care, I had assured the people we'd interviewed, *who* killed Stanfield Standish, but only that *someone* did. And neither did I.

But Wylie Nolan had never made such assurances.

My list of witnesses, I now realized fully, was *his* list of suspects. And even though I didn't believe that I'd been put on this earth to solve arson homicides, it was becoming increasingly obvious that Wylie Nolan believed that he had.

Mentally, I went through the list.

I started with Chief Bandy.

How good did he look as a suspect in Standish's death?

Stupid question.

If it hadn't been for Bandy's photographs, we'd never have found the bullet hole in Standish's head. But if Bandy had shot Standish himself, why draw attention to the physical evidence of the crime?

Scratch Bandy off the list.

But blood isn't thicker than evidence, and Chief Bandy has a son. Son number one, then, becomes suspect number two. Patton Bandy.

How did Pat fit as a suspect in my mind? He was still in love with Astrid Scheidler. That was obvious from his behavior at the trial. And she'd gained the most as a result of Standish's murder. She inherited a lot of money. A lot of power. An estate. A collection of valuable cars. And what had probably meant the most to her, she'd gotten rid of the dreaded "IT Machine." A dramatic list of possibilities.

Yet all of them pointed only to Astrid Scheidler; none of them said anything about Pat Bandy. What about Pat, though? What reason would this lieutenant in the New York State Police have for killing Stanfield Standish?

A lot of reasons, I decided. Starting with what could have been a well-nurtured, fifteen-year grudge.

I drew up a mental image of the tall, red-headed state trooper with his handlebar mustache and easy-going grin. He had what I call "territorial eyes." When he looked at things he looked at them hard and close. Inside and out. Some of what he saw he retained. Some of it he discarded. All was processed by some private agenda in his brain.

I tried to imagine Pat Bandy plotting a murder. If he had killed anyone, I didn't think that it would be spontaneous. It would have to have been planned long in advance of the event. It would be neat. Efficient. No loose ends.

Fire was too unpredictable a weapon for Pat Bandy. A bullet to the side of the head of an unsuspecting victim, not manly enough. Too sneaky. Too covert. No. If Pat Bandy had killed Stanfield Standish, it would have been out in the open. A duel at Sunset in the middle of town. A showdown on Main Street in front of the Rendezvous Bar and Grill.

I eliminated Pat Bandy and went on to the next name on my list. What was it he had said at the trial?

That if a boulder were rolling downhill at Stanfield Standish and the Duesenberg, and he could only save one of them, he would have let Standish die. Something like that.

I pictured Freddie Eckeles in the office of his spotless garage, with his snappy waxed floors and a telephone so clean you could see your own reflection.

Damn, I *liked* Freddie Eckeles. I liked his loose, long-jointed, amiable way. But how amiable would Freddie be with someone he hated? Someone like Stanfield Standish? Someone he perceived as threatening to Hugo Scheidler's valuable collection of classic cars?

In my mind, I put Freddie behind the steering wheel of a beat-up truck. I parked him and the truck at the end of Standish's driveway with the headlights turned out. I had him sit there and wait. And when Standish pulled out of the driveway in his Duesenberg, I had Freddie silently track him. First south. Then west. Then north along the reservoir. It would be bleak, barren, and abandoned on Snake Hill Road.

Why was Standish driving there and how did Freddie get him to stop? I didn't know, but I could *see* Freddie Eckeles pulling Stanfield

Standish to the side of the road. I could see him motioning to Standish to roll down the window of the Duesenberg. I could—

I heard a loud bang. A gunshot, I thought. Then, I heard another. The second one brought me back to the real world. A car going in the opposite direction had backfired. I was sitting in the passenger seat. Wylie Nolan was driving. We were still on Walter Link Road. I turned to my right, looked out the window, and saw Freddie's Service Station glide past us.

"Aren't we going to stop?" I asked Wylie.

"Hell, no."

Cross another suspect off my list. Which was just as well, because a minute after I'd snapped out of my reverie, I realized two things. First, that I'd had Freddie shoot Stanfield Standish on the wrong side of his head; and second that even though he might have happily murdered Hugo Scheidler's son, he never would have done anything to hurt Hugo Scheidler's car.

We drove by the C & J Bake Shop. Chief Bandy was sitting at a table in the window, smoking a cigar. He was hunched over a dish that probably held a custard bun. Maybe the same dish that had once served Wylie Nolan as a facsimile for the engine compartment of a car.

Walter Link Road dead-ended at the Reservoir. But instead of going to the left, where Standish's body had been found, we took the fork to the right. We turned right again on Locust Drive and went up the hill towards the estate that Standish had inherited from his father and Astrid Scheidler had inherited from him.

Astrid Scheidler. Always back to Astrid Scheidler. If I had ever wanted to find out who killed Stanfield Standish, and it looked as though Wylie was forcing me to, Astrid would be the last person I'd choose as a suspect. But if she hadn't killed Standish, what were we doing here the day after the district attorney had reopened the case?

We turned into the driveway. Wylie braked the car, and we continued very slowly up the long, circular drive.

Off in the distance I could see the outbuildings of the estate. Up ahead was the big white house with its wide porches and tall, impressive columns. And parked at the end of the driveway, blocking the porch steps, was a car with the blue-and-yellow markings of the New York State police.

Wylie pulled to a stop and honked his horn twice. I looked at his face. The son-of-a-bitch was smiling. I heard noises on the porch. Astrid Scheidler opened the door. She was wearing a thin white summer dress. She stood for a few seconds silhouetted in the sunlight, and gave the impression of pale insubstantiality. Like a displaced aristocrat on her way to the guillotine. A second later, a door slammed and the illusion went with it. Pat Bandy strode out on the porch. What was he doing in Astrid Scheidler's doorway? Why in uniform? Why driving his patrol car? And why today of all days?

Again, it came back to Astrid. It always did. Like in the courtroom. So much happening at the front of the room, but so many people absorbed by Astrid Scheidler in the back. Pat Bandy. Had I misinterpreted what it meant when he'd stared at her? Was it possible that he believed Astrid was guilty of arson homicide? And Rebecca Katz—lest we forget the beautiful, long-legged Rebecca—did Rebecca think that Astrid had murdered Stanfield Standish? Or had Rebecca killed Standish herself? Either way, if Astrid was Suspect Number Four, then Rebecca had to be Suspect Number Five. Or was it six? Rebecca Katz. A volatile, passionate, very competent personality. One who resented Standish as an artistic impediment and a political slob. So much so that Rebecca might—just might—have considered herself justified in putting a bullet into him herself.

Which left Dennis Cataliz. Son of the woman Stanfield Standish's father had taken as a lover. Friend and employee of the mother's lover's son. A complex mix. One that could easily explain hostile feelings toward Hugo Scheidler or Stanfield Standish, but not toward Astrid Scheidler. Yet it was against Astrid that his hostility was directed. Always Astrid Scheidler. Was Dennis hostile because he really believed Astrid had killed Standish? Or was there a more sinister, subtle, and selfish motive behind his hatred? Had he perhaps—

"Max?" I heard a voice call out.

The voice rang out again and snapped me out of my reverie, drawing my eyes to the woman standing on the porch. She looked confident. Friendly. Glowing. Not at all like an aristocrat on her way to the guillotine. And not the least bit guilty.

"Hello there, Max Bramble," Astrid said as she waved a hand at me.

I waved back.

Pat Bandy loomed over her for what I thought was a tense moment. Then he ruffled her hair and strode down the porch steps to his police car.

So much for Suspect Number Four.

He got behind the wheel, stuck his head out the window, and said to Wylie Nolan, "Follow me."

We did. Back down the driveway to the fork in the road. This time we turned north and continued along the reservoir up Snake Hill Road.

The road veered sharply to the left. Pat Bandy slowed down. We continued at twenty miles an hour for a mile or two. Bandy was driving with his window open. He dropped his speed to fifteen miles an hour. And then we crept along at ten. He was obviously looking for something. When he stopped his car in the middle of the road, I guessed he had found it. Wylie pulled up behind him and got out of the car.

"Right over by that bush," Pat Bandy pointed. "That's where they found the Duesenberg. You fellows need anything else before I go?"

Wylie shook his head and stuck out his hand. "Not a thing, Buddy. Thanks for the escort."

Pat Bandy winked, gave him a quick handshake, spun his car expertly around in the narrow roadway, and disappeared south on Snake Hill Road.

"Wylie, what's going on here?" I asked.

Wylie looked to his left and then to his right.

"Based on the look of the place, not a single, goddamn solitary thing."

•

We stayed there for about an hour. Spring was still weeks away, and it was a cold day. South of us, toward the city, there were buds on the trees. Up here, though, nothing. No buds. No grass. Nothing green. Snake Hill Road was just about the bleakest place any human being would ever not want to be. North of us was a tortuously winding, single-laned road with a wide dirt shoulder on either side. West was what looked like a dried-out riverbed. No shrubs. No rocks. No vegetation. Just a few spindly, barren trees.

To our east, off the shoulder, was the solitary bush pointed out to us by Pat Bandy as being near where the Duesenberg had burned. And beyond that, the reservoir itself. None of it would inspire great poetry. The water in the reservoir was below us, down a long ripple of pebbly gray sand. And way, way down at around the level of the water was a derelict rowboat stranded on an outjutting of ice.

Nobody to the north of us. Nobody to the south. No one to our east. No one to our west. Nothing anywhere except cold air and desolation. Any residue of the crime that had been committed five years earlier had long since disappeared, except for a feeling that this was a place where a crime should have been committed.

Stanfield Standish had died in a lonely, terrible place.

I shivered involuntarily.

Wylie and I stood. Not talking. Not thinking. Waiting.

But for what?

A little over an hour went by. The sounds of a car sputtered north towards us. At first, I saw nothing and concentrated on the slowly approaching sounds. The vehicle chugged and wheezed up the sloping road like a fat woman making her way up a long flight of stairs. When the sound was about a thousand feet away, the car made a curve into our line of vision. It was an old Zephyr. I knew the car. I remembered it from my notes. Zephyr. Zephyr. Where had I—?

The driver stopped, rolled down his window, and stuck his head out.

"Hello, there, fellas. I ain't seen you folks since the trial."

Well, what do you know. Ralph Arkus. Not only had Ralph been my first witness, he'd also been the first person to come upon Standish's body on the night that Standish was killed. And now, here he was, not six feet away from me on that same desolate, bleak, abandoned stretch of reservoir road. Spikes of gray hair jutted out from under his dirty checked hunter's cap. There was a bovine expression on his thick-featured, brutish face.

What if, I asked myself as I stared dumbly at what looked like the wood stock of a shotgun on the seat beside him, instead of finding Standish dead in the Duesenberg at three o'clock in the morning, Arkus had killed him himself? And what if, instead of being my first witness, Ralph should have been my first suspect? And what if that glimpse of wood stock I was looking at on the seat beside him really was a shotgun, and what if—?

"You fellas lost?" Arkus's gravelly voice finally rasped through the silence.

Wylie leaned up against the window of Ralph's car. His eyes took in the object next to Ralph on the front seat.

"Howdy," Wylie said. Friendly enough, but not too friendly. "Not lost. Just tying up some loose ends. You?"

"On my way to work." Ralph put his car in gear, and Wylie stepped away from the window. "Shrimp tonight," he said. "All you can eat."

He drove away.

Wylie looked at me. "It was a shovel handle, not a shotgun," he said, reading my mind. Then he looked at his watch.

"It's Monday. The weather is good. Cold but clear. The nearest town is four miles south. Ralph's restaurant is seven miles north. Bandy says that other than Ralph, the locals don't use this road. Only someone who takes a wrong turn and gets lost. But I wanted to check it out myself. Now it's a little before noon. If it's this dead in the middle of the day, think what it must have been like at three o'clock in the morning the night Standish was killed."

We got back in the car.

"Take notes," Wylie said.

I'd heard that song before. I pulled out a pad and pen.

"The odometer says 11010.3 miles. Write that down."

I wrote that down.

We drove north.

After a short distance, we saw an old sign on the left side of the road.

**UNINCORPORATED VILLAGE OF PADDY LAKES,
POPULATION 200**

The odometer read 11012.1.

Twenty feet north of that, a narrow road twisted to the left. At that intersection, someone had hand-painted a sign with the words VES-PER DRIVE. Wylie eased to the left. We followed the winding road another three-tenths of a mile. Then he stopped the car.

"Write down 11012.4 miles."

I did.

"All right. Now subtract the first mileage I gave you from the number you just wrote down.

I did that, too.

"What was the difference?"

It was exactly two and one-tenth miles from where we'd stopped the car on Vesper Drive to the place on Snake Hill Road where Stanfield Standish had been killed.

We got out of the car. There was a weathered country mailbox at the beginning of a gravel driveway that disappeared into underbrush. The writing on the side of the mailbox had faded, and the only letters left were a "C" and an "I" separated by rust.

"What are we doing here, Wylie?"

He jerked his head in the direction of the gravel driveway and said, "Solving your case."

We walked about four hundred feet. The driveway curved to the right. Then to the left. Then it took a sharp right turn again so that when the clearing broke through the trees in front of us, it was something of a surprise.

The house that sat in the middle of the clearing was small. Like a cottage in a fairy tale. It had probably been built in the 1930s by someone with enough money to indulge a whim. It was made out of white stucco; dark beams of wood did a gingerbread crisscross along the facade, and the roof curved over the eaves the way they do in books that begin "Once upon a time."

Off to our right was a smaller version of the same thing. It took me a few seconds to realize that the second cottage was a garage. The garage door was open, and inside I could see the front grill of a late-model American car.

We continued up the drive to a slate path that crossed the lawn. The closer we got, the shabbier the cottage looked. The stucco needed painting. The putty around the window panes had cracked.

Large chunks of cement were missing from the steps that went up to the front door.

The door itself was recessed in an archway. It had a small leaded-glass window and a heavy iron knocker.

Wylie slammed the knocker twice.

We waited, but nobody came.

He knocked again.

Another few minutes went by. Then we heard footsteps inside the house and the loud click of a deadbolt lock.

The knob turned.

Marguerite Cataliz opened the door.

CHAPTER
38

I can't say that I expected it, because I didn't. But when I saw her framed in her doorway, I wasn't really surprised. Again, as she had done that first time, she looked briefly at me, and then past me to Wylie Nolan. Her eyes flashed and held steady at the same time.

Wylie held her gaze.

They were doing it again. That same provocative dance of the eyes they'd done the first time they met. But who was the provoker and who was the responder? What was the nature of the challenge, if that's what it was, and where was it coming from?

Then I saw something in Marguerite's eyes pull back and go cold. She blinked and turned away.

Wylie Nolan. Marguerite Cataliz.

Odd.

She stood to one side as we walked past her through a cluttered hallway into a small, sad room. There were scratches and dents in the wood of the cheap pine furniture, and cigarette burns on the arms of old tweed sofas and chairs. There were no framed pictures on the walls or on tables. No plants. No magazines. The air was dead. The window panes were dusty. It looked as though a long, long time ago, Snow White and the Seven Dwarfs had moved out.

Marguerite indicated to Wylie that he should sit in a chair next to a low coffee table. She sat stiffly on the edge of the matching chair opposite him. She pointed me to a tatty sofa in between.

Without makeup, Marguerite's face was severe and gaunt, her beauty almost ascetic. She was wearing a black, low-cut leotard that revealed her sculpted collarbones. Her skirt was made of the same clinging material as the leotard. She had colorless hose on her legs and ballet-like slippers on her feet.

Despite the stagnant air, the room we were in was chilly. There was no wood in the log rack beside the empty fireplace. The pendulum clock over the mantelpiece was still. The only signs of life were those of impending departure. Cabinet doors flung open. Drawers pulled out. Clothes tossed in corners or discarded in heaps. And in between a bookshelf and a closet in the hall, there was a disorderly stack of cartons, address labels, marker pens, and string.

Wylie Nolan's eyes briefly met mine before they moved across the narrow space that separated him from Marguerite Cataliz.

"Would it be fair to assume that you were planning on going somewhere?" Wylie asked softly.

Marguerite didn't answer.

He took his pipe out of his jacket pocket and slowly unfolded his tobacco pouch. He filled the bowl with loose tobacco, struck a match, and inhaled. Then he carefully balanced the pipe on the scarred table so that none of the cinders would fall out.

"You love your son, Mrs. Cataliz," Wylie said evenly, his voice modulated to soothe instead of intrude. "In spite of long periods of absence, you love him. In spite of his harsh words, you love him. In spite of his angry and unjustified recriminations, you love him. And

Dennis also loves you. Loves you and loved you enough to go to the trial at your request. Loves you and loved you enough to rush out of the courtroom and telephone you immediately after Max introduced the photographs of Hugo Scheidler's ring. Loves you and loved you enough to warn you that he had seen that ring before. That he had seen it and that he remembered *where* he had seen it. That he knew who it had belonged to. That he had *seen* it, Mrs. Cataliz." Wylie emphasized the words. "And that now he knew who Stanfield Standish's killer had to be."

Wylie picked up his pipe and unconsciously tapped the forefinger of his right hand against the bowl.

The expression on Marguerite's face didn't change. She didn't move. She said nothing.

I looked at Marguerite. I looked at Wylie.

"This was Dennis's home, too, wasn't it, Mrs. Cataliz?" He went on. "Dennis grew up here. He went to school here. He visited dentists here. He learned how to play baseball here.

"And here is where he found the ring that you stole from Hugo Scheidler more than seven years ago. Maybe your son had come to Paddy Lakes to pick up an article of clothing or to drop something off. Maybe he was out for a few days in the country. Maybe he just came upon Hugo's ring coincidentally, when he was rummaging through a drawer or a box. Probably, though, when he found it, he hadn't been looking for it. He hadn't expected to find it, or anything else, and it didn't mean anything to him."

Wylie flicked his eyes toward me to see if I was following him. He returned them to Marguerite.

"The ring didn't mean anything to Dennis *then*, when he found it. Only when Max introduced the enlarged photographs of the ring in court did he make the connection. It was a subtle connection. But your son, Dennis, is an intelligent man. Hugo's ring. Standish's car. How did it get from one place to the other? In whose possession had it been last? In whose house had he last seen it? And who had put it there? The answers to all of those questions is the same. Because you had the ring last. And you had put it there. Didn't you, Mrs. Cataliz."

Marguerite got out of her chair and crossed the room to a jacket hanging on a hook in the hall. She probed the pockets for a pack of cigarettes and a book of matches, and then silently returned to her seat. When she lit her cigarette, she barely inhaled and barely exhaled the smoke, like a statue pretending that it knew how to breathe.

Wylie reached over for the matches, struck one, and reignited the tobacco in his pipe. Then he threw the matchbook back down on the table.

"Fact." Wylie said the word as though it were a chapter heading in a book. "When Hugo Scheidler died six years ago, you were living with him in his apartment in the city. At the same time, you retained possession of this house. This is the house you bought with your husband when you married Dennis's father. This is where you lived as a widow and where you raised your son. It was here that you were called by the nurses' registry, and from here that you were sent to Hugo Scheidler's house to work.

"Fact. You could no longer afford to live in New York, because Hugo Scheidler left you nothing in his will and you had to move out of his condominium in Manhattan.

"Fact. You did not want to return to Paddy Lakes, to a house that you felt you'd outgrown."

Marguerite raised her cigarette to her lips. The motion was stiff and artificial. She looked like a wooden marionette.

"The other facts were harder to come by, but they flesh out and provide depth to the same sad story. A story about a man and a woman. A woman and a man's son. A woman and a couple of cars.

"Cars, Mrs. Cataliz, never meant very much to me, vintage, classic, or otherwise. I wouldn't be able to tell a Pierce-Arrow from a Cord from a Stutz-Bearcat. Once Max here asked me what I thought about a Duesenberg that had just passed us in the road, and I told him that unless he set fire to it, my opinion wasn't worth a damn.

"But I know people who know about expensive automobiles, and so I found out one or two things. Like that car collectors are plugged into a tight communications network; and when a valuable car comes on the market, everyone who is interested knows when and where it will be auctioned, what the reserve price is, if the car sold, who it sold to, and often at what price the car was sold."

Again Marguerite lifted her hand to her mouth. She took a shallow draw on her cigarette and then lowered her hand. The ash on the end of the cigarette got longer. She didn't remove her eyes from Wylie Nolan. There was still no expression on her face.

"After Hugo died, Mrs. Cataliz, you were under the impression that you possessed that one valuable asset given to you by Hugo Scheidler during a love affair that lasted fifteen years. You thought the 1940 Packard Victoria convertible belonged to you. And if you'd been right, if it had belonged to you, if you'd been able to sell the car six years ago, when Hugo died, it would have been worth almost a quarter of a million dollars. You'd have had the means to continue to live in New York City. But you couldn't sell the car then, could you, Mrs. Cataliz?"

The ash at the end of Marguerite's cigarette had grown so long, I wanted to say something. To draw her attention to it. But I also didn't want to interrupt Wylie's spell.

The ash fell.

I reached over and brushed the ashes off her skirt. She didn't notice. She didn't move. Then, I took the cigarette out from between her fingers and crushed it in an ashtray.

Marguerite's ashtrays were all filled with dead cigarettes that had become long cylinders of ash. She hadn't crushed out any of them. All had self-extinguished.

"It wasn't until I found out that you'd lived here alone for over a year after Hugo died, that I realized Max and I had completely misunderstood something Freddie Eckeles told us."

I leaned forward.

"What was that, Wylie?"

"Do you remember the first time we talked to Freddie?"

"Yes."

"We were in the stable where Hugo Scheidler had kept his cars. Freddie was telling us that Standish had inherited Hugo's collection."

"I remember."

"He spoke of Hugo Scheidler dying."

"Go on."

"And he spoke of Stanfield Standish dying."

"That's right. Standish died about a year later."

"And then, Freddie told us that he had driven the Victoria Packard convertible to her house." Wylie turned to Marguerite. "To *your* house, Mrs. Cataliz. Because the car belonged to you. I asked Freddie when he drove the car over here, and Freddie answered 'immediately after the funeral.'"

Wylie looked at me. I turned to Marguerite.

I asked, "Did Freddie Eckeles really drive your car over immediately after Hugo's funeral?"

Marguerite met my eyes briefly. I saw a flicker of fear.

The words Wylie said next came out slowly, and they almost seemed to be tinged with regret. "I know what happened, Marguerite."

He used her first name. For the first time. It wasn't unintentional. I knew Wylie Nolan. I knew his interrogation technique. Excessive politeness. Complete courtesy. Establish the illusion of a personal, intimate bond. Gain trust.

Marguerite shuddered. So would I.

"That was what threw me at first," Wylie went on, "The funeral. Freddie said he'd driven the Packard over after the funeral. But what I didn't realize at the time was that he hadn't told us *which* funeral. He didn't mean he drove it over after Hugo Scheidler's funeral; he meant he'd driven it over after Stanfield Standish's funeral.

"It took me a little bit of time and a lot of thinking to figure out what happened. But as soon as I did, I knew why Stanfield Standish had died. And I knew who had killed him. From then on, it was just a matter of checking records. I needed a name, a date of birth, an address, and access to the Department of Motor Vehicles. The rest was easy.

"Twenty years ago, on the same day that Hugo Scheidler bought a 1930 Duesenberg, he also purchased a 1940 Packard Darrin Victoria convertible. He told you that he'd bought the Packard for you, and he had. But he never transferred the car's ownership to your name.

"I think it would be fair to assume that his failure to make the transfer was motivated by generosity instead of greed. He probably didn't want you to be hassled with any of the paperwork or expenses involved in owning a vintage car. So the insurance policies, gas station credit cards, owner's registration—all were in Hugo Scheidler's name. And this created a situation where when Hugo died, you had absolutely no tangible proof that the Packard Darrin had ever really been yours."

I interjected, "But would that really matter in the long run, Wylie? As long as she got the car."

"She didn't get the car, though, Max. That was the problem."

He turned to Marguerite.

"At the time you sold it, the Packard Darrin Victoria automobile was worth—" Wylie pulled a small square of paper out of his jacket pocket and read, "Two hundred and fifty-two thousand dollars and sixty-seven cents." He tossed the paper on the coffee table. "Your condominium cost one hundred and eighty-five thousand dollars. You bought the condominium two weeks after you sold the car. You paid cash."

Marguerite had stopped smoking. She also stopped staring at Wylie. Her skin was so pale she seemed almost transparent. She sat on the edge of her chair without moving. She barely seemed to breathe.

I looked at Wylie with concern, and then looked back at Marguerite.

He got up and went to the kitchen. He opened some cabinet doors, rattled some bottles, and came back a few minutes later with a whiskey glass. He put it on the table in front of Marguerite.

Instead of returning to the chair opposite her, though, Wylie sat down on the sofa, leaned forward and put his right hand on Marguerite's chair, almost touching her left forearm. I thought she was going to jump out of her skin or move away; she didn't. But I saw goose bumps suddenly appear on her arm. Wylie was giving me goose bumps, too.

His voice went on, smooth. Hypnotic. Confidential.

"Six years ago, Marguerite, you were with Hugo in the apartment you had shared together on the night that he died. That's what you told Max. But you didn't tell him everything, did you, Marguerite? You didn't tell Max what happened to you after Hugo died." Wylie's voice lulled, became even more mesmerizing, more seductive. "Tell us, Marguerite. You were alone with Hugo. Hugo died. And then . . ."

Her hand moved forward slowly and closed around the glass. She lifted it to her lips as though she were sleepwalking, sleepdrinking, sleeptalking, and in a voice as soft and passive as the smoke that she barely exhaled, she said, "Hugo was dead, and neither he nor I had prepared for it. We are born and we die. I'm a nurse. I should have known. I should have accepted it. I should have expected it. I should have been ready, but I wasn't. I responded like a bereaved child.

"I telephoned Hugo's doctor. The same doctor who had hired me all of those years ago. He was a kind man. He was also a diplomatic man. He told me to wait for him in the apartment while he drove in from Stilton-on-Hudson. It only took him an hour and a half. When he arrived, he said to me, 'I think perhaps that we ought to avoid any unnecessary awkwardness, my dear.' I was in shock, so it took me many, many minutes to understand what he meant. He kept trying to spare me what he knew was about to happen. He did everything he could to get me out of Hugo's apartment, short of packing me up himself and putting me into a cab. But I didn't hear him. I wouldn't hear him. And so, I was still there with my dead lover when they arrived."

Marguerite looked at Wylie Nolan. Then she looked at me. She continued, "First, Mrs. Scheidler arrived. The wife. Hugo's wife. His legitimate life partner. Then his two daughters, Victoria and Felicia. I had never met Astrid. She was in Europe at the time of her father's death. Perhaps if she had been there, some kindnesses might have been shown. One can only surmise. Astrid had always been the gentle one. The one who never showed any contempt. The one who loved her father. But she didn't come. Stanfield came. And after he had arrived, it was fast. Brutal. Bewildering. 'Get her out of here,' Mrs. Scheidler said to her son. Stanfield looked at me. He had curious eyes. Did you ever look at his eyes, Max?"

I nodded my head without saying anything. I didn't want to interrupt her flow of speech.

"Stanfield walked up to me, to about six inches away from me, and he said two words. 'Out,' and 'Now.' For fifteen years I had lived for Hugo Scheidler at Hugo Scheidler's convenience. I saved his life. I made him happy. And it had all been reduced to those two words. 'Out,' and 'Now.' Hugo's physician walked me to the door. He whispered kind things to me. He told me that he would have my possessions sent to my house in Paddy Lakes. He told me to be gentle to myself and to get away from those people as soon as I could. He took me down to the lobby. He put me in a cab. I was in a daze. I was stripped of my mourning. I was the mistress. I had no status. I didn't belong."

She stopped talking for a moment. I watched her slender chest rise once, and fall.

"What happened to you then, Marguerite? After you left. Did they ever send your things?"

"Oh, yes. The doctor saw to it that they were shipped. My clothing. My books. A few photographs. Only those of me. None of Hugo. It was as though they had cleaned out the maid's room."

Again, Marguerite fell silent.

Wylie prodded her gently, "How soon was it before you found out about the car?"

"My car? My Packard?"

"Yes."

"Stanfield Standish is a very efficient man."

"He took it?"

"He *stole* it."

"From your house? From the apartment? Or from the stall in Hugo's stable?"

"From here. Outside. From my garage in Paddy Lakes. When I left to spend the week with Hugo in Manhattan, the car had been locked in my garage. When I got back, it was gone."

Wylie turned to me.

"After Standish took the Packard," Wylie said, "he installed it on the estate along with the rest of Hugo's car collection. Marguerite didn't get the car back until a year later, when Freddie Eckeles drove it here right after Standish's funeral. Marguerite kept the Packard only long enough to sell it."

I nodded.

Wylie turned back to Marguerite.

"Tell us about the ring."

286

She looked down at her long, slender fingers. She seemed lost. Confused. Barely able to focus. "I don't have any rings."

"I'm talking about Hugo's ring, Marguerite."

"Hugo's ring?"

"Yes."

She turned her head to the left. To the right. A tentative, sad motion of negation. "I never liked Hugo's ring."

"Did you take it?"

Marguerite did not answer.

"Why did you take it, Marguerite?"

Still no answer.

"You took the ring because you knew—Hugo had told you—that his children had given it to him for Father's Day. You took the ring because Hugo had never seen fit to introduce you to his daughters. You took the ring because to you, it symbolized his *children*. His children's peace of mind. His *children's* happiness. You took the ring because it was a constant reminder to you of everything that came first in Hugo's life—everything you had come to hate."

Again, Marguerite's chest began to rise and fall perceptibly, but there was no change of expression on her face.

Wylie leaned away from her chair, and his tone became almost conversational. "I don't know what you said or how you did it, Marguerite, but somehow you used the ring as bait to get Standish here the night that he died. You waved it in front of him, and he grabbed for it. He bit.

"Maybe you telephoned him at his office, told him you'd just found his father's ring, and promised that if he came here, you would give it to him. Maybe your call to him was friendly, and Standish's response was friendly, too. And maybe Stanfield Standish came here to see you simply because coming here was exactly what he'd wanted to do. Max told me that he always tried to emulate his father. That he had to look like Hugo looked. Act like Hugo acted. Have what Hugo had. And Hugo had always had you."

Marguerite again reached for the whiskey glass. Her eyes were steady on Wylie Nolan. She sipped. I couldn't tell if she was terrified, or relieved, or maybe even too numb with feeling to feel.

"Stanfield Standish left his party a little before midnight on February fourteenth. He followed your directions to get to your house by Snake Hill Road, taking the back road along the reservoir, where nobody would see and remember such a conspicuous car.

"When he got here, Marguerite, did you let him come into your house? Somehow, I doubt it. I think you met him at the end of your driveway and that just as he was getting out of the car, you gave him the ring. The same ring that you had stolen from his father. And he put it in his pocket. Later, during the fire, when Standish's clothes burned off, it would fall out of his pocket and roll under the gas pedal on the floor, where I eventually found it.

"But that was later. After he'd pulled his Duesenberg into your driveway but didn't get out, because you gave him a reason why you should get into the car with him. Maybe you asked him for a ride down the driveway to the mailbox. Maybe you told him you needed a lift to town. Maybe you promised to run away with him. But once you stepped into the passenger seat of that Duesenberg, Stanfield Standish was just a guy who didn't know yet that he was already dead.

"Bang!" Wylie said suddenly, shocking me out of the role of the listener.

"I know about the gun, Marguerite," he said, and then turned to me.

"When you were in her apartment, you asked Marguerite if Hugo had ever owned a gun, and she answered, truthfully, that he had not. At the time, neither of us considered that the gun we were looking for might have belonged to her. But it was hers." Wylie turned back to Marguerite. "I know all about it. I know which firearm you used. I know when you got it. I know when you reported it lost. I know everything, Marguerite.

"A friend of mine in the fire marshal's office spent a day at the License Division of the New York City Police Department tracking down your registration. It's all there in the records room. Gun application, reference material, bill of sale."

Wylie paused for a few seconds, and then leaned very close to Marguerite's left ear. He said in a low, low voice, "You shot Stanfield Standish with an Iver Johnson .22 automatic."

As soon as he said that, Marguerite's head literally reeled backward. The face I was looking at wasn't expressionless any longer. She looked terrified.

"I'm not sure exactly how you did it, Marguerite, but the easiest way would have been just to walk into the precinct where Hugo had his condominium and report that your gun had been stolen. Hugo bought it for you when the two of you first met, because he was worried about your driving home alone on the reservoir road.

"Getting a carry permit wasn't difficult. Rich people always know somebody who knows somebody at City Hall. But reporting the theft of the gun *before* you used it to kill Standish—that was a stroke of genius."

As Wylie talked, I continued to look at Marguerite. The fear had not left her eyes. But the look of confusion was gone. And I sensed by her posture that she was still proud in an alien, haughty, dangerous way. She sat stiffly on the edge of her chair. Her head was up. Her shoulders were back. And she was erect again. Like a dancer. Like a dancer waiting to be shot by a firing squad. But passive. Not resisting or fighting against Wylie's accusatory words.

Wylie's voice again became lulling and seductive. His tone was intimate in an odd contrast to his words.

"When did you shoot him, Marguerite? Before he'd taken his car out of the driveway? Or did you have him drive you first the two and one-tenth miles to the reservoir and tell him to stop the car? That would have been easier, Marguerite, and I think that's how you did it.

"It was past midnight. Nobody ever travels that late along Snake Hill Road. You had Standish stop the car opposite the bush where earlier you had hidden the few items that you would need. A small bag would have held them all. You'd prepared your flammable liquid mix beforehand. It had been easy enough to add soap flakes and kerosene to an empty gallon-size plastic container. Just that and a box of kitchen matches were all that you needed.

"After you got Standish to drive you to the spot that you had selected, you shot him. One small-caliber bullet to the side of his head. It wouldn't have been difficult, because Standish had no suspicions. He may not have liked you. Or he may have liked you too much. Maybe he resented you. Maybe he lusted after you. Maybe he hated you. But he wasn't afraid of you.

"So you shot him. You shot him because on the night that his father died, he'd humiliated you and brutalized you; you shot him because over the years his father had allowed him to treat you with contempt; you shot him because his Valentine's Day party presented you with the perfect opportunity to shoot him. But most of all—most of all, Marguerite, you shot him because he had stolen your car, and because that car was your ticket out of Paddy Lakes and back to Manhattan where you felt that you belonged.

"So you shot Stanfield Standish. One bullet. Bang. He died instantly and slumped against the driver's door. You took the keys out of the dashboard to unlock the engine compartment hood. After you unlocked it, you tossed the keys back into the front seat of the car. You uncapped your plastic bottle and splashed around the accelerant. You were careful not to get any of it on you. You threw some on the engine. Some over the trunk. You poured some at the base of each of the four tires. You opened the car doors and splashed some around on the interior. And then you took what was left, and poured all of it over the body of Stanfield Standish.

"For fifteen years, you had lived with a car buff, a millionaire who'd earned his fortune as a mechanic. You knew about cars. You learned about fire. How to burn a car. How to ignite a body. You read that it isn't the flammable liquid itself that's dangerous. The danger and combustibility come from the fumes. So you stood back as far as you could, struck a match, and threw it. Maybe the fumes ignited on your first attempt. But kerosene isn't as volatile as gasoline, so it may have taken you three matches or four. Or possibly even five or ten. But it wasn't long before one of your matches stayed lighted long enough to set the whole car on fire in a giant, terrifying whoosh.

"Did you get burned when you were committing arson-homicide, Marguerite? You may have. A lot of arsonists do. But you'd be too smart to check into any of the local hospitals. And, of course, if you had been burned, you would know how to take care of yourself because you're a nurse.

"After the fire had started, you gathered up your matches and your empty gallon container. You walked the two and one-tenth miles along the road back to your storybook cottage in Paddy Lakes.

"You put the matches back into your kitchen cabinet. You washed out the plastic bottle and threw it in with the rest of your recyclable containers. And the fire in which Stanfield Standish died was declared to be accidental, and everybody believed that Standish had died as a result of a defect in an improperly restored car. Or, that is, everybody except Max here. And Chief Bandy of what's probably the smallest police department in the world. And, of course—me."

Wylie got up from the sofa. He began to prowl methodically around the room. He pushed aside clothes, opened drawers, and looked into closets. Then he stopped and pulled something out of a cardboard box in the hall. He brought it back to the sofa and sat down. It was a folded newspaper. Today's paper. He unfolded it and read aloud, "Northland County District Attorney to Reopen Standish Case."

He threw the paper down.

I turned to Marguerite.

She wouldn't look at me.

I said to her, "*Say* something."

Still, she refused to react or respond.

"Do you want me to call the district attorney?" I asked. "Do you want to scream and yell and deny Wylie's accusations? Do you want to confess? Do you want me to recommend a good lawyer?"

Nothing.

"Marguerite," I pleaded with her. "You have to do something. You can't just pretend that none of this is happening. That none of it exists."

Very abruptly, she got up. Briefly, her eyes flashed on mine. Her face held a look of grim purpose. She walked to the center of the room and spun around. Her shoulders were drawn back, her body was tense, immobile; that haughty expression was back on her face.

I looked at her. Beautiful. Passionate. Proud. Two decades earlier, I'd perceived her as passive, enduring, accepting. She had been such a meek and resigned creature. And now she was the woman she had turned into, an object lesson that there is only so much even the most tolerant of us can take.

Hugo had been a fool to treat her as he had.

But she'd been a fool to permit it.

Suddenly, Marguerite came to life. Her eyes went past Wylie Nolan's to mine. This time, they stayed with me.

"Max," she said, her voice low, intimate, that single syllable hovering for a moment in the air like a musky perfume.

"I want *you* to represent me."

I didn't respond. I *couldn't* respond immediately to what she'd said, because I don't practice criminal law. I'm a product-liability lawyer. I'm not supposed to care about the guilt or innocence of people. That's what Wylie Nolan does. All I'm supposed to care about is exculpating my client's product if it isn't involved in an accident or a fire.

I was trying to come up with a tactful way to explain this to Marguerite when I remembered my good friend Arthur M. Harris. Toward the end of his correspondence with his son, he had written, **"You will almost of necessity have to practice some criminal law."**

He had anticipated my dilemma.

"Whenever possible, you should willingly accept such cases, and give your client the benefit of your best advice."

That's easy to *say*. But what if she's guilty?

"You need not feel that you are helping the guilty to defeat the ends of justice."

I'll feel like that, anyway.

"You will find at the trial that the police officers will very ably look after the interests of the state."

That may be true, but—

"And you are doing no less than your sworn duty when you see that in points of evidence and law, a man, however guilty, does not suffer injustice."

For a second, I shifted my eyes away from Marguerite and looked at Wylie Nolan. Wylie had loved being a fireman. Every time I'd been with him during the past month, Wylie would stop what he was doing when a fire engine screamed by and get a glazed look of pride in his eyes. Then he'd murmur, "There go the good guys."

Every time.

Wylie was one of the good guys. He was my fire expert. He was arguably the best arson investigator in the world. But it was Wylie who cared about stopping fires, solving crimes, and closing cases. Not me. Even though the boy I'd been had wanted to be a cop, the man I'd become was a lawyer.

Wylie caught me staring at him. I think he knew what *I* was thinking, because he winked.

Inwardly, I laughed.

Outwardly, I turned to where Marguerite Cataliz was waiting for my answer; and slowly, repeatedly, I nodded yes to the question in her eyes.